W9-DDN-151

LPB   Lacy, Al.
F   A time to love
Lacy
c.1

WITHDRAWN

NO   '99

MOUNT LAUREL LIBRARY
100 Walt Whitman Avenue
Mount Laurel, NJ 08054
856/234-7319

DEMCO

A TIME
TO LOVE

Also by Al Lacy
in Large Print:

Mail Order Bride series
(coauthored with JoAnna Lacy):

Secrets of the Heart (Book One)

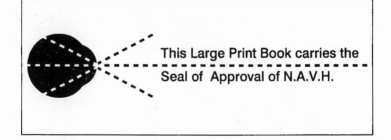

This Large Print Book carries the
Seal of Approval of N.A.V.H.

A TIME TO LOVE

MAIL ORDER 2

Al & JoAnna Lacy

Mount Laurel Library
100 Walt Whitman Avenue
Mt. Laurel, NJ 08054-9539
(856) 234-7319

Thorndike Press • Thorndike, Maine

Copyright © 1998 by Lew A. and JoAnna Lacy

All rights reserved.

Scripture quotations are from:
The Holy Bible, King James Version

This is a work of fiction. The characters, incidents, and dialogues are products of the author's imagination and are not to be construed as real. Any resemblance to actual events or persons, living or dead, is entirely coincidental.

Published in 1999 by arrangement with Multnomah Publishers, Inc.

Thorndike Large Print ® Christian Fiction Series.

The tree indicium is a trademark of Thorndike Press.

The text of this Large Print edition is unabridged. Other aspects of the book may vary from the original edition.

Set in 16 pt. Plantin by Rick Gundberg.

Printed in the United States on permanent paper.

Library of Congress Cataloging-in-Publication Data

Lacy, Al.
    A time to love : mail order 2 / Al & Joanna Lacy.
        p.   cm.
    Originally published in the series: Mail order bride series ; no. 2.
    ISBN 0-7862-2052-X (lg. print : hc : alk. paper)
    1. Frontier and pioneer life — Nevada Fiction. 2. Mail order brides — Nevada Fiction. 3. Women pioneers — Nevada Fiction. 4. Nevada Fiction. I. Lacy, Joanna. II. Title. III. Series: Lacy, Al. Mail order bride series ; no. 2.
    [PS3562.A256T56   1999]
    813'.54—dc21   99-33152

To our dear friends Jerry and Linda Weddle
who have been with us through
thick and thin,
laughter and tears,
sorrows and joys.
Thank you for always being there.
We love you.
Al and JoAnna
PROVERBS 27:17

*To every thing there is a season,
and a time to every purpose under the heaven:
A time to be born, and a time to die . . .
A time to love . . .*
ECCLESIASTES 3:1–2, 8

Prologue

The *Encyclopedia Britannica* reports that the mail order business, also called direct mail marketing, "is a method of merchandising in which the seller's offer is made through mass mailing of a circular or catalog, or advertisement placed in a newspaper or magazine, and in which the buyer places his order by mail."

Britannica goes on to say that "mail order operations have been known in the United States in one form or another since Colonial days, but not until the latter half of the nineteenth century did they assume a significant role in domestic trade."

Thus the mail order market was known when the big gold rush took place in this country in the 1840s and 1850s. At that time prospectors, merchants, and adventurers raced from the East to the newly discovered gold fields in the West. One of the most famous was the California Gold Rush in 1848–49, when discovery of gold at Sutter's Mill, near Sacramento, brought more than 40,000 men to California. Though few struck it rich, their presence stimulated economic growth, the lure of which brought even more men to the West.

At this time, the married men who had come sent for their wives and children, desiring to stay and make their home in the West. Most of the gold rush men were single and also desired to stay in the West, but there were about two hundred men for every woman. Being familiar with the mail order concept, they began advertising in eastern newspapers for women to come west and marry them. Thus was born the "mail order bride."

Women by the hundreds began answering the ads, wanting to be married and to make the move west. Often when men and their prospective brides corresponded, they agreed to send no photographs. They would accept each other by the spirit of the letters rather than on a physical basis. Others, of course, exchanged photographs.

The mail order bride movement accelerated after the Civil War ended in April 1865, when men went west by the thousands to make their fortunes on the frontier. Many of the marriages turned out well, while others were disappointing and ended in desertion by one or the other of the mates, or by divorce.

As we embark on this fiction series, we'll

tell stories that will grip the heart of the reader, bring some smiles, and maybe wring out some tears. As always, we will weave in the gospel of Jesus Christ and run threads of Bible truth in the stories that apply to our lives today.

1

It was a clear, warm night with twinkling stars the Friday of June 8, 1877. A full moon shone over Boston Harbor, its reflection dancing on the rippling waters.

At the church on the corner of Fulton Street and Paul Revere Avenue, organist Letha Myers played in low tones as the wedding rehearsal got under way.

Linda Forrest, the bride to be, stood in the vestibule with her father, Nolan, whose face showed a gamut of emotions. He'd attended a lot of weddings in his forty-four years, but that was different from being the father of the bride.

Doris Stanford, the director of the wedding rehearsal and the pastor's wife, hastily lined up the three bridesmaids. Among them was Linda's best friend, Joline Jensen, who would have her own wedding soon.

When Doris was satisfied the bridesmaids were positioned correctly, she placed the maid of honor just behind them and then began to patiently instruct the little boy and girl who were ring bearer and flower girl.

Joline looked back at her dearest friend and said, "Just think, Lin . . . when Frank and I get married in a couple of weeks, you'll be an old married woman by then."

Linda Forrest giggled.

Her father put on a sad face and said, "It's hard enough to think of my little girl as a bride, Joline, but to realize she will be the *matron* of honor in your wedding is almost too much to bear."

"Oh, Daddy," Linda said, "you're glad to get me grown up, married, and out of the house, and you know it!"

Nolan glanced at his other daughter, Janet, who was Linda's maid of honor. "It was difficult enough when you moved out of the house into your own apartment, Janet, and I have hopes that you'll come back and live at home. But it's even more difficult with your little sister. Marriage to Lewis will take her away permanently."

Janet was two years older than Linda. Although the sisters were about the same size, the similarity ended there. Janet's hair was blond; Linda's was a deep auburn. Janet could be considered pretty, but Linda was beautiful. And there were strong differences in personality and their approach to life.

Even as Nolan Forrest finished speaking, a sour look came over Janet's face that told her father she would never live under his roof again.

The low tones of the pump organ barely seeped through the closed double doors leading to the auditorium.

Linda slipped her hand into the crook of her father's arm and gave it a comforting squeeze. Janet's father and mother had been deeply hurt when their elder daughter, at twenty years of age, had moved out of the Forrest house. She had been gone for two years, and had come by the house maybe four or five times since moving out.

The Forrests knew that one of the reasons Janet had moved out was to get away from what she termed "the boring life of church people." Her life choices were so at odds with the way she had been raised that she no longer had anything in common with her family. All they knew about her life was that she worked a job in downtown Boston and spent her free time in drinking establishments and other places of ill repute.

Linda had chosen Janet as her maid of honor strictly to please her parents. Yet her heart was heavy for her only sister, whom she wanted to be saved.

Doris Stanford nodded at the two ushers waiting in the vestibule, indicating they should open the double doors. Immediately the pump organ's volume increased, moving into "The Wedding March."

"All right, girls," Doris whispered to the bridesmaids, "go."

Linda caught the miserable look on Janet's face as she turned to face forward and started down the aisle.

As Linda brought up the rear with her father, her eyes went to her mother standing at the second pew on the left-hand side. Next to her was Aunt Beth Chalmers, who had lovingly made Linda's wedding dress.

Her gaze shifted to the platform where Pastor Lloyd Stanford stood, holding his small black-covered wedding manual. Then her eyes focused on Lewis Carter.

He is so handsome! she thought. *And he's all mine! Oh, we're going to be so happy together!*

The groomsmen met the bridesmaids and the maid of honor one by one and escorted them up the steps to the platform. They spread out, facing the preacher at an angle.

Lewis Carter gave one nervous glance at Linda's father, then set his gaze on Linda, who warmed him with a loving smile.

Just as Nolan and his daughter came to a halt, the organ's volume lowered.

"All right," said the pastor, "you've all done real well, just as Mrs. Stanford instructed you. Linda, at this point you will let go of your daddy's arm and let him take hold of your right hand. I will then say, 'Who gives this woman to be married to this man?' Nolan, you will speak loud enough for everyone in the church to hear you and say, 'Her mother and I do,' then place Linda's hand into Lewis's."

"Then I'll kiss your cheek through the veil, Daddy," Linda said.

Nolan nodded, and Doris Stanford — who had come down the aisle behind them — continued her instructions. "At this point, Nolan, you will turn and take your place beside Adrienne, there in the second pew."

The pastor spoke up. "Linda and Lewis, when Nolan is in place, I will nod to you, and you will come up the steps together. And Linda . . . let me caution you, tomorrow night you will be in your long wedding dress. You'll have to lift the front of the dress a bit as you mount the platform steps to avoid tripping on it."

"I'll remember," Linda assured him.

"Come on up," said the pastor.

As the bridal couple moved up the steps, the pastor said, "Of course, tomorrow night there will be a white lattice arch here, and you two will stand directly under it during the ceremony."

As Linda and Lewis stood attentively before him, the pastor said, "First, I will make some opening remarks about marriage being instituted by God in the Garden of Eden. You will recall that in our last counseling session, we agreed I would quote from Ecclesiastes chapter three, verses one, two, and eight: 'To every thing there is a season, and a time to every purpose under the heaven: A time to be born, and a time to die . . . A time to love . . .'"

Stanford ran his gaze over the faces of the wedding party and said, "I will then point out that God has loved the human race from the time He created Adam and Eve, but His special 'time to love' was when He gave His precious Son on the cross of Calvary so that sinners could be saved. After I give a clear presentation of the gospel, I will turn the attention of the audience to the love that Linda and Lewis have for each other. As they become husband and wife, their special 'time to love' has come."

Standing nearby were the deacon chairman, Ed Diamond, and his wife, Frances. The Diamonds were close friends of Nolan and Adrienne Forrest, and were having the rehearsal dinner for the wedding party at their house.

"That's beautiful, Pastor," Diamond said. "I've never heard you use that particular

15

Scripture passage in a wedding ceremony before."

Stanford smiled. "I thought it fit Linda and
Lewis so perfectly. It's certainly evident
they're head over heels in love."

Lewis let a slight smile curve his lips as
Linda looked into his eyes and squeezed his
arm.

When the pastor had concluded his instructions about the ceremony, Ed Diamond
spoke up again. "Okay, everybody, let's all go
to my house. Grandma's got the fancy dinner
just about ready, I'm sure."

Adrienne Forrest noticed her oldest daughter push past Linda and head toward a side
door. "Janet!" she called. "Where are you
going? Aren't you going to ride to the Diamonds' house with Daddy and me?"

Janet paused. "I'm not going to the dinner,
Mother. My apartment's not very far. I'm
going home."

Everyone in the group fell silent.

Nolan moved quickly to his daughter's
side. "Honey, this isn't polite. The Diamonds
have gone to a lot of trouble to provide this
dinner. Since you're part of the wedding
party, it's only right that you attend."

Janet's features darkened. "Look, Dad, I
just want to go home, all right?"

Nolan's lips pressed together tightly as he

16

said, "I don't like this, Janet. But at least you should go over there and excuse yourself to Ed and Frances."

A wing of Janet's yellow hair had come loose and was hanging over one eye. She gave her head a toss and said, "If you insist."

She walked toward the Diamonds, her body rigid, and said, "I really need to be going home. Thank you for the invitation." With that, she pivoted, gave her parents and sister a cold look, and walked out the side door.

Nolan Forrest looked nonplussed as he turned to his friends and said, "Ed . . . Frances . . . I'm sorry for Janet's rudeness. I hope you —"

"Don't worry about it," Ed replied. "It's evident she's uncomfortable with all of us. C'mon, everyone. Let's go eat!"

Grandma Esther Diamond had prepared a sumptuous meal for the wedding party. She was a small, frail woman of seventy-five, with deep lines in her face and a thick head of snow white hair done up in a bun on top of her head. Her bright eyes sparkled as she looked the group over and said, "Soup's on, folks! Take your places!"

She moved up to Lewis and Linda. "How'd the practice go, children?"

"It went fine, Grandma," Linda said with a smile.

"Sure wish I could be there tomorrow night to see it, but I have to catch my train about an hour before weddin' time."

"We wish you could be there, too, ma'am," said Lewis.

As the guests were taking their places, Grandma noticed there was a vacant place at the main table. "Oh-oh. Did I count wrong?"

"No, Mom," Frances said. "Linda's sister, Janet, had to get home after wedding practice."

"Oh. Okay."

The pall Janet's behavior had put on the evening was soon dispelled as Pastor Stanford told funny stories about strange things that had happened at weddings he'd performed over the years. Soon he had everyone laughing.

After the meal was over and the women had begun to clean up the tables, the men went to the parlor.

The pastor edged up to Nolan Forrest, and he said in a low tone, "Is there anything I can do to help Janet?"

"I think you've done all you could, Pastor. You must have talked to her three or four times while she was still under our roof. She's just got to get saved if there's going to be a change in her."

"I know. She's really turned away from anything to do with the Lord, the Bible, or God's people. If you'd like, Doris and I will go to her apartment and try to talk to her again."

"Well, it sure can't hurt anything, Pastor. Our hearts are heavy for her. Adrienne and I put a little pressure on Linda to ask Janet to be her maid of honor. We thought maybe just being back in the church and at the wedding might light a spark inside her . . ."

"We'll see how it goes with her after tomorrow night," said the preacher. "If being in the wedding should cause her to come on Sunday, that will at least be a step in the right direction. But Doris and I will pull a little surprise visit on her this coming week, no matter what."

"Thank you, Pastor. I'll tell Adrienne. That'll encourage her."

When the women had finished clearing the dining room table, Frances and Grandma told them to go on home, the two of them would tackle the dishes. Adrienne and Nolan Forrest remained to help their friends while the others said their thanks and good-byes.

Linda and Lewis, who had planned a moonlight drive along the shore of Boston

Harbor, thanked Grandma and the Diamonds for the sumptuous dinner, then left.

When Adrienne and Nolan were finally preparing to leave, Grandma said, "If I'd known about this here weddin' when I left home five weeks ago, I'd have planned to stay another day or two so I could attend it. But I've got to catch that train tomorrow and head back to Philadelphia."

"When will you be back again, dear?" Adrienne asked.

"Prob'ly in about six months. I'll come back and pester Ed and Frances again for another five weeks."

"Pester?" Frances said, laughing. "Mom, it's always a blessing to have you here! Besides . . . Ed won't say it, but he still likes your cooking better than mine!"

"He'd better!" Grandma said with a grin.

Lewis gave Linda his hand as they stepped up to the buggy. The moon was a silver disk in the sky, spraying them with soft light.

"I love you, my darling," Linda said.

"And I love you, sweetheart," Lewis replied, looking into her eyes.

Their kiss was sweet and tender, then Lewis helped Linda into the buggy, rounded the rear of the vehicle, and climbed in beside her. "Where would you like to go?" he asked.

"To the harbor. I love the reflection of the moon on those deep, dark waters."

Lewis guided the horse through the dimly lit streets of Boston. They met a few carriages and buggies along the way as they headed east toward the harbor. Linda tucked her hand under Lewis's arm and said, "Mr. Higgins said he'll have our apartment all freshly painted and ready when we get back from our honeymoon."

"When did you see him?" Lewis asked as he watched a drunken man staggering along the street.

"This morning. Mother and I drove over to see how it was coming along. Are you as excited about the honeymoon as I am?" she asked.

Lewis didn't answer immediately.

"Darling?"

"Hmm?"

"I said, are you as excited about the honeymoon as I am?"

"Oh. Sure. I've always wanted to see Vermont in the summertime."

"Me, too," Linda said, taking a deep breath. "Oh, Lewis, I'm so happy! Just think of it! By this time tomorrow night, we will be Mr. and Mrs. Lewis Carter on the train heading north for Vermont!"

There was a moment of dead silence, then

Lewis said, "Yeah! Just think of it!"

Linda leaned forward to look at Lewis's eyes by the glow of the street lanterns. "Darling, is something wrong?"

"No. Why?"

"You seem so pensive. Like your mind is a million miles away."

Lewis chuckled hollowly. "Oh. I'm sorry. Of course there's nothing wrong. I'm just a little nervous, that's all."

"About what?"

"About what!" he said incredulously. "In case you didn't know it, girl, yours truly has never gotten married before! I'm a groom for the first time in my life! So I'm nervous!"

Linda laughed. "Well, I've never been a bride before, either! I'm pretty nervous myself."

The harbor came into view, and Linda's attention shifted.

"Oh, look, darling!" she said. "The moon's reflection is magnificent on the water's surface."

Suddenly they heard pounding hooves and iron wheels grating on the cobblestone street. A police wagon whipped past them, accompanied by an officer on horseback. He glanced back at them as he rode by. The police wagon and horseman sped toward the edge of the harbor, then made a right turn up the shoreline.

"I wonder what that's all about," said Lewis.

Linda craned her neck to follow the movement of wagon and rider, but they soon passed from view.

Lewis guided the buggy up to the rim of the dark water and pulled rein. "Would you like to get out for a few minutes?" he asked.

"Oh, yes. I love to stand right at the edge and watch the moonlight flicker on the surface. It's very romantic."

Lewis set the brake and jumped out of the buggy. He hurried around to Linda's side and helped her down, keeping hold of her hand as they stepped to where the water lapped the shore.

They could hear excited voices from the direction where the police had gone.

"Trouble of some kind," Lewis said, looking in the direction of the sounds.

After a moment of silence, Linda said, "Lewis, I hope Janet doesn't embarrass us some way tomorrow night."

Lewis nodded. "Yeah. Me, too."

"I think Mother and Daddy are sorry they pushed me into asking her to be my maid of honor. She certainly embarrassed them tonight."

"That she did."

"I'm really not sure why Janet agreed to be

my maid of honor. She actually surprised me."

Lewis shrugged.

"Well," Linda continued, "she sure made it clear tonight that she'd rather have been just about anywhere else."

There was silence again, then Linda said, "Lewis, I just thought of something."

"What's that?"

"As cantankerous as Janet was tonight, I wouldn't put it past her to just not show up tomorrow night."

Lewis's eyes widened. "You mean not be there for the wedding?"

"Yes. Especially after Daddy made her excuse herself to the Diamonds before she left tonight."

Again they heard the sound of pounding hooves. Soon the police wagon and galloping team materialized out of the darkness and rumbled by within a few feet of where they had parked the buggy.

When Lewis saw the policeman on horseback coming, he led Linda to the street. The policeman saw them and drew rein.

"Sorry we about ran you over when we came by earlier, folks," said the officer, his Irish brogue strong.

"What happened?" Lewis asked.

"A young woman tried to commit suicide

24

over there by those warehouses. She jumped in the 'arbor and a couple of night workers saw 'er go in. One of 'em dived in to save 'er while the other one went for help. I was on me beat at the time near there. By the time I got to the spot, the fella had pulled 'er out, but she'd almost drowned 'im, fightin' him off, screamin' that she wanted to die. While he pumped water from her lungs, I rode fast for the paddy wagon so's we could get 'er to the hospital."

"Will she be all right?" Linda asked.

"I think so, missy. She was breathin' a bit shallow an' coughin' when we put 'er in the wagon, but at least she was breathin'." He shook his head. "Ever' once in a while, we have somebody wants to end it all an' takes a jump into the 'arbor. We usually don't know about it till the body washes up on shore. This girl was plenty fortunate somebody saw 'er go in an' cared enough about savin' 'er to jump in after 'er."

"And the man who went in after her?" said Lewis. "How is he?"

"He'll be all right. Took in some water and got himself some scratches on the face, too." The officer pulled out his pocket watch, angled it toward the nearest street lamp, and said, "Ain't you two out a little late?"

"We're getting married tomorrow night,"

25

said Lewis. "We were just spending some time in one of Linda's favorite spots."

"Gettin' married tomorra night, are ya? Well, congratulations. I hope ye have a happy life together. My Maureen and I 'ave been married now for forty-two years."

Linda smiled. "Well, congratulations on that, Officer —"

"Shanahan, missy. Patrick Shanahan."

"I hope you and your wife have many more happy years, Officer Shanahan."

"Thank ye, missy," the officer said and grinned. "Well, I've got to stay on me beat. You two don't stay 'ere too much longer, okay?"

Lewis pulled the buggy up in front of the Forrest house, hopped out, and helped Linda down. When she felt his arms encircle her waist, she raised up on tiptoe and kissed him.

He led her up onto the front porch, kissed her soundly, and said, "Good night, Linda."

She sighed. "Well, darling, the next time I see you will be through my veil when Daddy and I start down the aisle."

"And I'm sure you will look beautiful," he said, and kissed her again. He watched her go inside, then climbed into the buggy and drove away.

As Linda stepped inside the house, she

could hear her parents talking in the parlor.

Adrienne cut off in the middle of a sentence when she saw Linda come in. "Have a nice drive?" she asked.

"Yes. The next time I see Lewis, he will be standing in the church, waiting to make me his blushing bride."

"Sure you don't want to call it off till you turn forty, honey?" Nolan asked. "It's hard to let go of Daddy's little girl."

Linda leaned over his chair and kissed his cheek. "Now, Daddy, you wouldn't want your little girl to be an old maid, would you?"

"Sounds all right to me," he said with a chuckle. "At least till you're forty."

"Maybe your sister will be the old maid," said Adrienne. "The rate she's going."

"I heard what you were saying about Janet when I came in, Mother, and I agree that her attitude was bad tonight. She made no pretense of the way she feels to be a part of the wedding."

Nolan glanced at Adrienne and said, "I wish now that we hadn't pressured Linda to make Janet her maid of honor just because she's her sister."

Adrienne's face took on a pinched look. "I . . . I was so hoping that by her being with Christians in the wedding party, she might decide to get her heart right with God."

"I'm afraid it's going to take more than that to get Janet interested in turning to the Lord," Nolan said.

Linda sighed. "You're right, Daddy. I wish Joline was my maid of honor. But all we can do now is proceed as planned."

2

The Boston Railroad Station was bustling with summer travelers as Ed and Frances Diamond escorted Ed's mother toward the terminal building.

"What time is it, son?" Grandma Esther asked.

"It's 5:20, Mom. We're doing fine. Your train doesn't leave for another twenty-five minutes."

"Well, I want you to put me on the train and leave right away. I don't want you two being late to the wedding."

"You worry too much, dear," Frances said. "We'll stay till you pull out, then head for the church. The wedding isn't till seven o'clock."

They passed through the doors to the terminal and into a milling crowd.

As they threaded their way through the press, they saw trains marked for New York City; Washington, D.C.; Portland, Maine; Atlanta, Chicago, Kansas City, and New Orleans. Just beyond the latter was the train to Philadelphia.

"See, Mom," Ed said, pointing to Grandma's train. "We made it in plenty of time."

Ed and Frances helped Grandma into her coach and sat her down next to an elderly woman about her age. Before Ed had finished putting the luggage in the overhead rack, the two ladies were chatting. Ed and Frances hugged and kissed Grandma good-bye, then stepped off the train just as the conductor was giving his last call to board. They moved up close to the coach and waved at Esther through the window. The engine bell rang and steam hissed from the sides of the train as the whistle blew and the big steel wheels began to turn.

The deacon chairman and his wife watched until they could no longer see Grandma's window, then weaved their way through the crowd, heading toward the parking lot. They were approaching the spot where the train to New York City was taking on passengers when Ed grabbed Frances's arm and stopped cold. "Look at that!" he said.

Frances's gaze focused on the boarding passengers, and her eyes widened in shock.

Nolan and Adrienne Forrest drove through the streets of Boston with their youngest daughter sitting between them. The parents were already in their wedding clothes, but Linda wore a simple day dress and everyday shoes. Her wedding dress, shoes, and other paraphernalia were carefully boxed and lying in the back of the carriage.

Linda was thrilled about establishing a new home with Lewis, but pulling up roots long buried in Forrest "soil" wasn't easy. It was a little frightening to be leaving the security of her childhood home. She had grown up in a warm and caring Christian love, one she had vowed to duplicate in her own home with her own family.

The carriage was drawing near the church, and the sight of it caused Linda's heart to pick up pace. It was almost six o'clock, and there were other vehicles already in the church parking lot, two of which belonged to Todd Oliver and Earl Watson, two of the grooms-men. The third groomsman, Harold Smith, had planned to ride to the church with Earl Watson.

Linda looked around for Lewis's buggy and thought that best man Frank Simons had no doubt "borrowed" it to decorate with banners and a sign saying Just Married. It was proba-bly hidden somewhere around the church at the moment. Lewis might very well have rid-den here with Todd Oliver or Earl Watson.

"Daddy," Linda said as her father climbed out of the carriage, "would you go inside and see if Lewis is anywhere he might see me? You know the groom isn't supposed to see his bride on their wedding day until she comes down the aisle on her father's arm."

"Sure, honey. Be right back."

As Nolan hastened inside the building, Linda gripped her mother's arm. "I'm nervous, Mom," she said. "Were you this way when you married Daddy?"

Adrienne pursed her lips and nodded. "Uh-huh. I sure was. When I started down the aisle on your grandfather's arm, my knees felt like they had turned to water, and I thought they were going to give way and embarrass me right there on the spot."

"Good. Then I don't feel so bad. I guess this is just normal, right?"

"*Very* normal, honey," said Adrienne, patting her daughter's hand. "And we females handle this kind of thing better than men do. I imagine right now Lewis's stomach is churning and the palms of his hands are sweating. When he stands at the altar and sees you start down the aisle with Daddy, he'll feel like his nerves are going to jump right through his skin. And talk about knees turning watery . . . his will for sure."

Nolan emerged from the church and headed their way. Smiling, he called, "Lewis hasn't shown up yet. His groomsmen say he's coming on his own. He should be here any minute. Let's get you inside quick."

Various Sunday school rooms had been set up by Doris Stanford for participants of the wedding party to prepare and wait for their time to put in an appearance. The largest room had been set aside for the bride.

Aunt Beth was already in the room when Linda and her mother stepped inside. She had brought all the things she might possibly need to fix Linda's hair and to put the final touches on the dress and train.

Doris advised Linda and Adrienne that the bridesmaids were preparing themselves with the help of their mothers and sisters in a room down the hall and told them where she had placed the little flower girl and ring bearer, who were in separate rooms being coached by their parents.

With the help of Aunt Beth, Adrienne, and Doris, Linda slipped out of her day dress and shoes and into her white wedding shoes, then stood ready as her aunt carefully lowered the lovely white organza dress over her neatly coiffed, shining auburn hair.

The dress glided smoothly over her slender form. Not one curl was disturbed, but Beth had spotted a couple of curls that might need a little attention.

Linda's mother moved behind her and began buttoning up the pearl buttons on the back of the dress that ran from the neck to Linda's tiny waist. Aunt Beth took care of the wayward curls, then fussed with the lace at the neck of the dress and the delicate ruffles that cascaded down the back into a short train.

When Beth was satisfied that every flounce and fold were proper, she took the filmy veil and placed it among the curls on Linda's head.

Adrienne smiled with pride. "You're the most beautiful bride I've ever seen, honey."

"You might be just a mite prejudiced, Mom," Linda said, smiling sweetly.

Doris Stanford laughed. "Well, if you are a little prejudiced, Adrienne, you have good reason to be. She's stunning."

Adrienne smiled with pride.

As Aunt Beth fluffed out the veil then pulled a short length of it over Linda's glowing face, there was a light tap on the door.

"I'll get it," Doris said.

Organist Letha Myers and soloist Peggy Wilson stood outside. "Could we see Linda for a moment?" Letha asked.

"Sure. Come in."

Peggy, who was barely nineteen, said, "Wow, Linda! Lewis is going to drool all over himself when he sees you!"

The other women laughed, then middle-aged Letha, who was short and rotund, said, "When I get to heaven, I'm going to ask the Lord why He made Linda so slender and gorgeous, and made me stumpy and barely able to trap a husband!"

"Oh, Letha," Linda said, "you're one of the most beautiful people I know!"

"Thanks, honey," Letha said with a chuckle. "Well, it's almost time to start playing the organ. See you out there."

"You're going to stun the whole crowd, Linda," Peggy said, and followed Letha to the door.

Linda hugged both women, thanking them for what they were doing to make the wedding so perfect, and Doris shooed them out.

A long mirror on a stand had been placed in the room so that Linda could see herself front and back. She viewed herself from every angle, then turned and hugged her mother with one arm and her aunt with the other. "Thank you, Mom, for making my hair look so good . . . and thank you, Aunt Beth, for making this beautiful dress."

Tears threatened to spill down Linda's cheeks, and she quickly steeled herself to keep them back. Then she turned to embrace Doris and said, "Thank you for working so hard to make this wedding all that it should be."

"It's my pleasure and joy, honey," Doris

said, kissing her cheek.

Linda took a deep breath. "Well, I guess I'm ready."

As sounds of the arriving guests came through the door, Linda swallowed hard. "Oh, Mom, I've got a million butterflies in my stomach!"

"I know the feeling, honey."

"So do I," Doris said.

"Me, too," spoke up Beth, who had been widowed almost a year previously.

There was another tap on the door. Doris swung it open to see Joline Jensen with a worried look on her face. She looked past Doris and said, "Oh, my! Linda, you look ravishing!"

Doris stepped back and allowed Joline entrance into the room, then quickly closed the door.

"Thank you," Linda said a bit uncertainly, taking in the worried look on her best friend's face. "Is something wrong?"

Joline looked the room over. "Well, maybe. Janet's not around here, is she?"

"You mean she's not getting ready in the bridesmaids' room?" Doris asked.

"No. We thought she would be with us, but we got to wondering if maybe she decided to get ready down here with Linda."

Linda's face lost color as she looked at her

mom and said, "Where could she be?"

"Honey, I don't know, but you know your sister has always been the tardy one. Certainly she'll be here any minute."

Doris lifted the decorative pin watch on her dress and checked the time. "It's 6:35. If she doesn't get here pretty soon, she isn't going to be ready to march down the aisle."

At that very moment, they heard Letha Myers start up the pump organ.

"That's my cue," Doris said. "I need to check on the flower girl and ring bearer, then I'll look in on the other bridesmaids." To Joline she said, "Everybody else in your room ready?"

"Yes."

"Okay. I'll be back shortly."

Deep lines formed on Linda's flawless brow. "Oh, Mom, what'll we do if Janet doesn't get here in time?"

"Now, honey, don't let this upset you. Maybe by now she's already down in the room with the other girls."

"I'll go see," Joline said.

In the pastor's office — where the groom and his groomsmen were to meet with the pastor before entering the auditorium for the ceremony — best man Frank Simons was pacing nervously. "Where could he be, Pastor?" he asked.

"It's not like Lewis to be late to *anything*," Todd Oliver said, "but especially not to his own wedding."

The door burst open, and groomsmen Harold Smith and Earl Watson came in.

"Nobody's seen him," said Watson.

As the minutes ticked by, traffic in the hall outside the bride's dressing room was heavy.

"Sounds like we're going to have a crowd, honey," Adrienne said.

Linda nodded, biting her lip.

There was another tap on the door, and Joline entered without waiting for someone to open the door. "She's not there, Linda. Nobody's seen her."

Adrienne noted the time and said, "It's seven minutes to seven. In two minutes, it'll be time for me to be escorted down the aisle."

Agonizing minutes passed in Pastor Lloyd Stanford's office.

"This is strange," he said. "I've had some bizarre things happen in some of my weddings, but I've never had a groom late for the ceremony." As he spoke, he went to the door that led into the sanctuary and opened it a couple of inches, peering into the beautifully decorated church. Adrienne Forrest was just being seated by an usher in the second pew.

Stanford thought of Lewis's parents, who had been members of the church until their deaths. He wished they could be there to see their son marry lovely Linda.

But where was Lewis?

From the side of his mouth, Stanford said to the other men as he swept his gaze over the guests, "The place is almost full. Just a few stragglers being seated by the ushers."

After another minute or so, the pastor closed the door, glanced at the clock on his office wall, and said, "Two minutes to starting time. You gentlemen stay put. I'm going to do some checking of my own."

At seven o'clock on the dot, Peggy Wilson left her chair behind the organ, stepped up beside Letha Myers, and said in a low voice, "Time for the first song, Letha."

Adrienne Forrest turned slightly to look toward the back of the church. She smiled at the couple who sat directly behind her, then caught the eye of one of the ushers and gave him a hand signal.

Jack Morgan came immediately, bent close to her, and said, "What can I do for you, Mrs. Forrest?"

"Jack, would you go and see if Janet is in the room with Linda? Or if she might be with the bridesmaids?"

Morgan's eyebrows raised. "I don't understand, ma'am. Are you saying you want to talk to her?"

"No, no. It's just that she hadn't yet arrived when I was escorted here to my seat."

"Oh, my!"

"I need to know if she's shown up."

"I'll check, ma'am, and be right back."

Peggy was nearly halfway through her song and was a bit distracted by Jack Morgan's return down the aisle, but kept her concentration.

Jack bent over Adrienne and whispered, "She isn't here, Mrs. Forrest. I checked with Mrs. Stanford. Janet hasn't shown up."

"All right. Thank you."

Adrienne's imagination went wild. Had Janet been injured in some way? Was she in the hospital? Or had she decided to just not show up to the wedding? Her attitude at the rehearsal last night made Adrienne think she might be pulling this stunt to spite her family. "Too wrapped up in church," Janet had said on more than one occasion. "Not getting any fun out of life. I don't want any of my friends to know what utter religious fanatics my parents and sister are."

There was nothing Adrienne could do. She dare not get up and walk to the back of the church. There was going to be enough of a

40

stir in a few moments. No sense in causing one now.

With Peggy's sweet voice and the sound of the organ seeping through her dressing room door, Linda was on the verge of tears. She turned to Aunt Beth and said, "Do you suppose something has happened to Janet? You know, an accident of some kind? Maybe she's lying hurt somewhere."

Beth took hold of Linda's shoulders and looked her in the eye. "I don't mean to be ugly about this, honey, but after her performance last night at the rehearsal, I think Janet has decided to be her old self. She's torn your heart out before. It's my opinion that she's tearing your heart out again — this time by not showing up for the wedding."

Linda bit down hard on her lower lip, and her voice was close to a wail as she said, "What am I going to do, Aunt Beth? Frank won't have anyone to escort up the platform steps. It will mess up everything!"

"Linda," Beth said in a soothing tone, "we'll get through this even if Janet doesn't show up."

Peggy Wilson was singing the last verse of her song when there was a tap on the door. Linda's heart leaped in her chest as she gasped, "Oh! Here she is!"

41

Her countenance fell when she saw it was not Janet, but Doris Stanford, with the ring bearer, the flower girl, the bridesmaids, and Linda's father standing behind her. "It's time to line up in the vestibule, Linda," Doris said. "We'll have to go on without Janet."

Even as she spoke, Peggy finished her song, and the organ played the last few bars.

"Someone needs to let Frank know," Linda said, her voice tight with frustration. "He'll have to walk down the aisle and mount the platform alone."

Nolan stepped closer to the door and said, "I'll go tell Frank, Linda. But we need to get to Letha and let her know what's going on. This will take a little time. She's probably already wondering why we aren't in the vestibule."

"I'll do that," said Doris, lifting her skirts and hurrying away. Nolan followed right behind her.

Beth turned to her niece and saw that her hands were trembling and she was about to cry. Grasping both of Linda's hands, she said, "Don't break down now, honey. It's going to be all right. You and Lewis will be just as married, even though your no-good sister wasn't in the wedding."

Linda drew a shuddering breath and said, "Oh, Aunt Beth, how could Janet do this to me? How could she be so cruel? I'm already so embarrassed. How am I ever going to get through the ceremony?"

"You'll do fine, honey. You won't even think about what Janet has done once you start down the aisle toward Lewis."

Several times Letha had scanned the vestibule doors, watching for Doris's nod to start the wedding march. So far, no one from the wedding party had appeared in the vestibule, so she continued to fill in with music. Something was definitely wrong.

Suddenly, Doris slipped through the unobtrusive door into the sanctuary beside the organ and moved up behind Letha. Peggy was seated behind the organ waiting to do her next song, and she looked at her, wide-eyed.

Bending close to Letha's ear, Doris said, "Janet hasn't shown up. We've got to get the message to Frank, which Nolan is doing right now. Just keep playing whatever you want till I give you the signal from the vestibule."

Letha nodded. "Will do."

Nolan hurried across the back of the church and entered the hall leading to the pastor's office. He stopped short when he saw the pastor talking to deacon chairman Ed Diamond just outside the office door.

Pastor Stanford's face was sheet white. He looked ill as he turned and noticed Nolan. He said something to Ed that Nolan couldn't hear, then Ed hurried past Nolan, looking sick himself.

"I've got terrible news, Nolan," the pastor said.

3

Doris Stanford paused at the door behind the organ and looked at the wedding guests. There was an air of restless movement and the sound of whispering all over the church.

She closed the door and hastened down the hall to the room where Linda waited. She entered to find Beth Chalmers holding her weeping niece in her arms.

Doris moved close and laid a hand on Linda's shoulder. "Please don't cry, honey. You'll have your eyes all swollen. I talked to Letha, and she's going to keep playing until I give her the signal from the vestibule to start the wedding march. As soon as your daddy gets back here, we'll get started."

Linda blinked against her tears and said, "I'm sorry. It's just that I thought this was going to be such a happy day, but my sister has chosen to put a damper on it."

Beth used a hankie to dab at Linda's tears. "Like I told you, honey, you and Lewis will be just as married without Janet in the wedding party."

There was a soft tap at the door, and Doris

opened it to find her husband and Nolan Forrest standing there with serious expressions on their pale faces.

"May we come in?" the pastor asked.

Beth studied Nolan's features as he took his daughter in his arms. "Honey, I'm sorry," he said.

"Daddy, what is it?" Linda asked, pulling her head back to look into his eyes.

Doris and Beth turned to the pastor, who looked ill. He licked his lips, but said nothing.

"Linda, I —" Nolan began.

"Something bad has happened!" Linda gasped. "What's happened to Janet? Daddy, is she hurt . . . sick . . . worse?"

Nolan looked helplessly at the preacher, and Stanford moved closer under the watchful eyes of Doris and Beth. "It's . . . ah . . . it's not just Janet, Linda," he said. "It's Lewis, too. He isn't here, either."

Linda's heart started to race. Her mind went in every direction, searching for an answer to what she had just heard. "Well, th-then, there's been some sort of dreadful accident. What in the world — Wait a minute. What am I saying? It was silly of me to say that. Lewis and Janet wouldn't be coming to the church together. If something bad has happened, it couldn't be to both of them.

46

Why . . . why are neither one of them here? I
. . . I—"

"Linda," said the pastor, "this is very difficult to say."

"Well, tell me, Pastor! Please! What's happened?"

"Lewis and Janet are together. But they're
not on their way to the church."

Nolan held his daughter tightly, knowing
what was coming. He gave Beth a helpless
look.

"They've run away together, Linda," Stanford said weakly. "They're on their way to
New York."

Beth sucked in a sharp breath. "Pastor,
what are you saying?"

Nolan felt his daughter's body stiffen. Her
breathing grew laborious, and her voice came
out as if she were choking. "H-how do you
kn-know this, Pastor?"

Stanford rubbed the back of his neck,
shifted on his feet, and said, "Ed and Frances
Diamond told us they were taking Grandma
to the railroad station late this afternoon to
put her on a train for Philadelphia . . ."

"Yes?"

"Well, the Diamonds arrived here just a few
minutes ago. I had just come out of my office
to search for Lewis myself, when I saw Ed. He
. . . he told me that he and Frances were on

47

their way out of the depot after putting Grandma on her train, and they saw Lewis and Janet board a train for New York City together."

Linda became like a statue behind her veil, her eyes staring blankly.

The pastor went on. "Ed said they were holding hands and laughing as they boarded. He and Frances watched them enter the coach and sit down, then they kissed."

Linda's head went light. Her first thought was that her tired mind was playing tricks on her. The pastor couldn't have said what she just thought she heard. Looking at her father for confirmation that it wasn't so, she said, "D-Daddy . . . he . . . he didn't really say Lewis and Janet are together on a train to New York . . . did he?"

"Yes, honey. He did."

As her knees gave way, Nolan kept her from falling. "No . . . no," she moaned. "Lewis loves me. He wouldn't do that." Her eyes took on the blank look again, and her eyelids drooped. "No. This can't be happening. It just can't be hap—"

Her eyes rolled back, and she passed out. Nolan held her close, feeling a great need to sit down himself.

"I'll get some water," Doris said. "It's best, Nolan, if you lay her down on the floor."

As he eased Linda to the floor, he said, "Beth, would you go get Adrienne, please?"

"Of course," Beth said, and hurried out the door on Doris's heels.

Doris met the bridesmaids and other attendants in the hallway.

"Mrs. Stanford, what's wrong?" Joline Jensen asked. "Why is the wedding delayed?"

"Look, girls," Doris said, "take the children and go back into the room across the hall. Sit down and wait. All I can tell you at this moment is that the wedding is off. Just go into the room and sit down. I'll get back to you later."

"The wedding is off?" echoed one of the bridesmaids. "What on earth has happened?"

"I can't tell you right now, Shirley. Please, just do as I've asked you." With that, Doris hurried toward the kitchen at the rear of the building.

Adrienne felt a sense of foreboding as she listened to Letha Myers playing hymns. There had to be more to this delay than Janet's absence. It was nearly twenty minutes after seven.

She turned to catch the eye of an usher again and felt a hand touch her shoulder. Nearly everyone in the place was looking on as Adrienne turned to see the face of her sister.

"Come with me," Beth whispered.

As Adrienne got up and followed Beth to the back of the sanctuary, the low rumble of voices grew louder.

Nolan held Linda's head in his lap and caressed her face. "Oh, Pastor, this is horrible. My poor little girl."

"Bless her heart," said Stanford. "I just don't know what to make of Lewis."

"Me, neither. Janet, with that attitude of hers and the way she's been living, I can understand. But Adrienne and I have had absolute confidence in Lewis. We thought he was such a fine Christian man and would provide for Linda and make her happy. Pastor, this is beyond anything I could have imagined. I'm at a total loss to explain it."

"I can't explain it, either," Stanford said. "Of course, the devil's got his hand in it."

"Of course. But God allowed it."

"That's right. He knew all along that Lewis was playing the hypocrite, and by allowing him to run off with Janet, it's not hard to see that the Lord was saving Linda from marrying him. If she had married him, and then Lewis had run off with Janet, it would have been that much worse."

Nolan nodded in agreement. "I just hope we can make Linda see that."

Pastor Stanford started to comment but stopped as Linda began to moan and toss her head back and forth. At the same time, Doris came in carrying a cup of water.

"She's starting to come around," Nolan said as Doris knelt down beside them.

Linda's eyes fluttered open. They were glassy with shock.

"Here, honey," Doris said. "I brought some water. Let me give you some."

The pastor turned his ear toward the door. The organist was still playing hymns. "Apparently Mrs. Myers knows to keep playing until further notice," he said.

"Yes, dear," Doris said. "I told her to stay with it until she saw me give the signal to start the wedding march."

"Well, she won't have to keep it up much longer. As much as I hate to do it, I've got to go out there and tell that crowd there isn't going to be a wedding."

Doris gave Linda small sips of water. "They *are* getting restless, dear. They know something's awry."

Adrienne stopped and tugged at her sister's arm. "All right, Beth. Tell me what's happened."

Without breaking stride, Beth said, "Sister, dear, your Janet and Linda's Lewis Carter have run off together."

"Run off? What are you talking about?"

"Lewis hasn't shown up either, Adrienne. He and Janet are on a train to New York City right now."

"What? You're not serious!"

"I've never been more serious."

"How did you find this out?"

"Ed and Frances took Grandma Diamond to the depot and put her on a train to Philadelphia."

"Yes, I know."

"They saw Janet and Lewis boarding the train to New York . . . even saw them kissing after they got on and sat down together."

Adrienne put a hand to her mouth and stopped a few steps from the door where her daughter waited. The raw, surging emotion that swept over her made her feel nauseated. Cold sweat formed on her brow. "Beth, I . . . I don't feel so good."

Beth gripped her sister's hand. "Sweetie, you've got to hold up for Linda's sake. She passed out when Pastor Stanford —"

"*Passed out!* She passed out?"

"Yes. Nolan and the pastor are with her. Doris was on her way to get water for her when I came after you."

"Oh, Beth! How terrible!"

"I'm sure Doris is in there with the water by

now. Linda will be all right."

Adrienne pressed fingertips to her temples and said, "You were saying that Linda passed out when Pastor *something* . . ."

"She passed out when Pastor told her what Ed Diamond said about seeing Lewis and Janet board that train. When she comes around and the cold, hard fact hits her, she's going to need you. You've got to get a grip on yourself for her sake."

Adrienne nodded and took a few deep breaths. "I'll be all right in a moment. I *have* to. You're right. My little girl needs me." She blinked in confusion. "Beth, how could Lewis and Janet do such a wicked thing? I know Janet is willful, but I never dreamed she was *this* bad. And Lewis . . . who would ever think — Oh, well. I'm ready now. Let's go in."

Adrienne rushed ahead of her sister and found Nolan sitting on a chair, holding Linda on his lap. Her veil lay on another chair. She had nestled her head against his chest, but there was a vacant look in her eyes.

The pastor and Doris stood on either side of them, looking as if someone had died.

"Oh, my baby!" Adrienne gasped as she bent over Linda and cupped her face in her hands. "Sweetheart, are you all right? Aunt Beth told me what happened."

Linda's eyes lost their vacant look as she focused on her mother's face and then reached for her.

"Oh, honey, I'm so sorry for what Lewis and Janet have done to you," Adrienne said as she put her arms around her daughter.

Linda's whole body was shaking. She sniffled, and tears began streaming down her cheeks. She made an effort to say something, but it wouldn't come out. Finally she broke into heavy sobs.

"Go ahead, honey, cry. Let it out."

Linda sobbed loudly for a minute or so, then grew quiet and wept softly.

The preacher looked pale as he said, "I've got to go out there and make the necessary announcement, but before I go, I want to pray for Linda."

Stanford laid one hand on Linda's shoulder and the other on Adrienne's, and called on the Lord to give comfort to Linda. He asked for God's loving hand to touch her heart, give her peace, and help her remember that Jesus said, "I will never leave thee, nor forsake thee."

"And, Lord, please give strength to Nolan and Adrienne. They're hurting in one way for what their oldest daughter has done to Linda, and in another way because of what Janet has turned out to be. We pray for Janet's salvation, Lord, and that you will quickly show her how much she needs you in her life. In Jesus' name I pray, amen."

To his wife, Stanford said, "Doris, would you see that the bridesmaids and the rest of the bridal party come into the sanctuary, please? I want everyone to hear me make the announcement."

The Stanfords moved to the door together, then the preacher turned and said, "Linda, the Lord loves you. Doris and I love you. Your parents and Aunt Beth love you. The people of this church love you."

The bereaved girl looked at him through a wall of tears and nodded silently.

When the Stanfords stepped out of the room, Doris headed for the door across the hall, and Lloyd made a beeline for his office.

The groomsmen and best man jumped to their feet when the pastor came in, and waited for him to speak.

"Gentlemen," Stanford said, "the wedding is off."

"What's happened to Lewis, Pastor?" asked Frank Simons.

"All of you come out onto the platform with me. You can hear it at the same time I tell it to the people out there."

The crowd in the sanctuary was buzzing above the sound of the pump organ as Stanford emerged from his office onto the platform with four dismal-looking young men behind him. They halted a few feet behind the flowered white lattice arch as the preacher stepped in front of it.

In the Sunday school room, Linda Forrest found her voice and said, "Mom, Daddy . . . would you take me home now, please? I don't want to be here when the people come out of the sanctuary. I don't want anyone to see me."

"Sure, honey," Nolan said. "Let's go, Adrienne."

"I'll stay here," Beth said. "It's best that the three of you have some private time together."

The buzzing trailed off in the sanctuary when Pastor Stanford appeared and moved to the center of the platform. He gave a hand signal for Letha to stop playing the organ. The music stopped abruptly. Stanford waited a few seconds for Doris and the bride's attendants to enter the sanctuary from the vestibule, noting that Beth Chalmers came in behind them and stood by the open doors. He then ran his solemn gaze over the faces of the crowd.

"Ladies and gentlemen," he said, the words coming with difficulty past the lump in his throat, "I am sorry to have to make this announcement, but there will be no wedding here today."

There were gasps, moans, and groans as the people looked around at each other. Then there was a low rumble as everyone began talking at once.

An obviously upset Stanford held up his hand and went on. "I am not at liberty to give you any more information at this time, but I ask the people of this church to hold up Linda Forrest and her parents in prayer. Thank you."

Having said this much, Stanford pivoted and went to his office, plopping down in his chair. "Lord, help that dear girl," he said in a low voice.

There was a tap on the door.

"Come in."

The groomsmen and best man entered. "Pastor," Frank Simons said, "shouldn't we, as members of the wedding party, be told what has happened?"

"Oh . . . of course," said the preacher. "I'm sorry. You certainly have a right to know. To put it as plain and simple as I can, Lewis and Janet ran away together. They were seen about an hour before the wedding, boarding a train for New York City. Ed and Frances Diamond saw them."

At the Forrest home, Nolan paced the floor outside Linda's bedroom.

She was in a state of shock and only stared into space while Adrienne worked at removing the wedding dress from her rigid body.

When the dress was finally off, the heavy-hearted mother said, "Here, honey, sit down on the bed. I'll be right back."

Adrienne picked up the veil from the dresser and took it with the dress to the door. When she opened it, her pacing husband stopped and looked at her expectantly. "Not yet," she told him. Extending the dress and veil, she said, "Would you hang these up in our closet, please? If I put them in her closet, they'll be there for a reminder. She doesn't need that."

"All right," Nolan said.

"I'll put a robe on her and then you can come in."

He nodded and started down the hall.

Adrienne closed the bedroom door and headed for the closet. Linda watched her mother's movements with languid eyes.

Returning from the closet with a soft white robe, Adrienne said, "Here you go, honey. Let's get this on you. Your daddy wants to be in here with us."

When the robe was on and buttoned up,

Adrienne said, "Lie down on the bed, sweetheart."

A strange expression flitted across Linda's face. She sucked in a shallow breath, let it out raggedly, and said, "I want to die."

Adrienne's eyes widened. "Linda, I know you're terribly upset, but you don't want to die! Jesus loves you. He's going to see you through this horror you're facing right now."

"If . . . if I died, I would go to heaven and be with Jesus. Then I wouldn't have all this hurt inside me. He would hold me in His arms and I would never feel like this again."

Adrienne bit her lower lip. "Linda, Jesus can take away your hurt while you're still here on earth. Come on. Lie down."

When Linda lay in the center of her bed, Adrienne said, "I'm going to bring Daddy in. Please, honey. No more of this talk about wanting to die."

Moments later the parents eased down on either side of the bed, and each took one of Linda's hands in their own.

The horrible trauma brought on by Lewis and Janet's betrayal filled Linda's mind. In the brief time since it happened, it had become part of her — like her pulse, like the steady beat of her heart. The agony showed on her mottled face and in her puffy eyes.

Nolan and Adrienne's hearts ached for

their sweet Christian daughter. Compared to the emotional pain they had suffered because of Janet's rebellion, this was far worse. Linda had shown only love to Janet, and had trusted Lewis, promising to be his wife. To see her suffer like this was overwhelming. Linda didn't deserve to have her heart crushed.

"I love you, sweetheart," Nolan said, looking into his daughter's listless eyes.

She met his gaze weakly and nodded.

Adrienne looked across the bed to her husband. "Oh, Nolan, how could Janet cause this pain to her own sister? What kind of child did we raise, who could have such a callous, evil streak in her?"

"It's a mystery to me," he said, shaking his head. "We raised them both exactly the same way. Janet was exposed to as much gospel and Bible truth as Linda was."

"I know. I just don't understand it. Janet made a profession of faith in the Lord when she was seven."

"Yes, and you remember how we talked with Janet when she claimed to be saved but had no desire for spiritual things."

Adrienne nodded. "And she swore she was saved. What else could we do? We couldn't ram salvation down her throat."

"And she's quite obviously been running from God ever since she left this house to live on her own. And then there's Lewis," Nolan said with a note of disgust in his voice. "How —"

His words were interrupted by a knock at the front door.

"I'll get it," he said, letting go of Linda's limp hand. "You stay with her, dear."

While Nolan was gone, Linda looked up at Adrienne and said, "Mom, I want to die."

"Linda, please don't talk this way. You've still got your whole life ahead of you. The Lord has someone else for you to marry."

"No. My life is nothing now."

"Honey, listen. Right now, the full impact of this terrible thing is on you. This is the worst part. It's totally understandable why you feel like you do. But believe me, it will get better as time passes."

"I'd rather be in heaven, Mom. I don't like this wicked old world, with all its heartache and pain."

Voices came from the hallway, punctuated by footsteps.

"Please, Linda," Adrienne said, "don't talk about wanting to die. Everything will work out. The Lord has a plan for your life."

Pastor and Mrs. Lloyd Stanford and Beth Chalmers followed Nolan into Linda's room. She watched them impassively.

Beth forged ahead of Nolan and touched

Linda's hand. "Hello, sweetheart. Are you doing any better?"

Linda's eyes softened. She loved her Aunt Beth. "I . . . I don't think so."

Beth forced a smile. "Well, it'll all work out for the best. God's Word says so."

Linda held her gaze but said nothing more.

The Stanfords drew up beside Adrienne. Doris leaned down and said, "I know you're hurting something terrible, Linda. I can't say I know *how* you feel, because I've never been through what you're experiencing. But I know you're hurting more than you ever have in your life. Pastor and I have come to tell you we love you, and to see if there's anything we can do to help."

The preacher leaned close and said, "Linda, Jesus knows you're hurting. He loves you more than anyone else in this room does. He is God, and God is love. His capacity to love is greater than ours. Let Him speak to your heart and comfort you through His sweet Holy Spirit."

Linda nodded but didn't respond.

"Honey," Nolan said, "Pastor and I were talking at the church. He said something that made good sense in the face of all this, and I'd like for him to tell it to you."

Stanford looked at Nolan. "You mean

about if the Lord had let her marry Lewis?"

"Yes."

The preacher leaned close to Linda again. "God knew all along that Lewis was playing the hypocrite, and that by allowing Lewis to run off with Janet, the Lord was keeping you from marrying him. If you had married Lewis, and *then* he had run off with Janet, your devastation would have been that much worse. A marriage would have been broken."

"That's a good way to look at it, Pastor," Adrienne said. "It would have been even worse if they had brought children into the world, then Lewis had run off."

Beth squeezed Linda's hand. "So you see, honey, it could have been much worse if the Lord hadn't let this thing happen when He did. Can you understand that?"

Linda closed her eyes and set her jaw. She strained every muscle in her body until she was as stiff as granite. Then she said calmly, "I want to die."

4

Pastor Stanford blinked at Linda's words and then glanced at her parents.

Nolan looked stunned.

Adrienne gripped her daughter's hand and said to the others, "She already said this to me twice when we were alone."

Nolan dropped to one knee beside the bed and laid a hand on Linda's shoulder. "Honey, you mustn't talk like that. I know everything looks bleak right now, but it'll get better."

Linda held her gaze on her father's face for a few seconds, then ran her eyes to each person. Looking back at Nolan, she said, "I am so utterly shattered and embarrassed by this. I've heard people joke about a bride being 'left at the altar,' but I can't believe it has really happened to me. I'll never be able to face anybody who was at the wedding. I could never look them in the eye."

Doris said, "Linda, with prayer and the passing of time, you will get over it. Besides, none of this is your fault. Lewis and Janet are the ones to blame. You must look at it this way and go on with your life."

Linda shook her head. "I appreciate what you're trying to do, Mrs. Stanford. And all of you, for that matter. But something inside me —" She teared up and her lips quivered. "Something inside me went dead when I heard what Lewis and Janet had done. I won't get over it. Ever. I never want to see anybody in the church again. I don't want to face our neighbors or anybody else who —" She choked on her tears and cleared her throat. "I don't want to face anybody who knows about this. I . . . I want to die."

She broke into uncontrollable sobs.

Linda's parents held her and talked in low tones, trying to make her see the bright side, as Pastor Stanford had pointed out. She only sobbed all the more, wailing that there was no bright side. Her life had been destroyed by the man she had loved and trusted . . . and by her wicked, heartless sister.

After a while, the emotional upheaval in Linda subsided, and she quieted down to sniffling and shuddering breaths.

Beth spoke up. "Linda, dear, I'm afraid your Aunt Beth owes you an apology."

All eyes turned to Beth.

Linda squinted, shook her head, and said, "Why do you owe me an apology, sweet aunt?"

Beth cleared her throat. "Well, I guess I

65

should have said something to you before now."

"About what?"

"Lewis and Janet."

Linda frowned, and the others fixed Beth with inquisitive eyes.

Beth cleared her throat again. "Twice recently, within the past month or so, I saw Lewis and Janet together downtown. They didn't see me either time, so they didn't know I had observed them. Once they were in McIntosh's Department Store, looking at women's clothing. The other time . . . about a week later, they were standing together at the corner of First and Main. They were laughing about something."

Linda's lips began to quiver.

"Honey, I couldn't believe there was anything to it. I wondered why Lewis would even keep company with Janet, but I still thought he was a fine Christian man and gave him the benefit of the doubt. Rather than upset you, I kept it to myself. Now I see I was wrong not to realize what was going on. I'm sorry. Please forgive me."

Linda pressed fingertips to her lips, closed her eyes, and said in a dead tone, "There's nothing to forgive you for, Aunt Beth. I was as trusting of Lewis as you were. For all you knew, they had simply run into each other those two times you saw them downtown."

Turning her eyes to her parents, Linda said in the same lifeless voice, "Mom . . . Daddy . . . how could Lewis want Janet instead of me?"

Nolan and Adrienne shook their heads but didn't know what to say.

"Lewis gave me such a convincing line, with all the talk about wanting a Christian home like his had been, and like ours is. It was all a lie. Why? Why did he deceive me?" Her voice grew louder. "Why all the lies . . . lies . . . lies?" Again she started sobbing and wailed, "Oh, I wish I could die! I wish I could die!"

After a few minutes, she gained control of herself and said, "I appreciate your trying to help me, Mom and Dad. And Aunt Beth, too. And Pastor and Doris. Thank all of you for caring. But I need to be alone for a while."

"All right, honey," Adrienne said. "We understand. But Daddy and I want just a few more minutes with you first. Okay?"

Linda nodded.

"We'll let ourselves out," said the pastor. "Doris and I will come by tomorrow to see how she's doing."

"I need to get home," said Beth. "I'll come by tomorrow, too."

When Nolan and Adrienne were alone with Linda, Adrienne said, "Honey, your daddy and I are very concerned that you keep saying you want to die. You mustn't feel that way. You have plenty to live for. Please don't even think like that."

Linda was weeping silently, her hands covering her eyes.

Nolan looked at his wife and said meaningfully, "Adrienne, I think I should go get Dr. Kurtz. He can give her a sedative to calm her and help her to sleep."

"No! Please, Daddy. I don't want our family doctor to know about this. I'll be all right. Please."

Adrienne laid a hand on her husband's arm. "It might do her more harm than good if she has to face Dr. Kurtz in her present state of mind."

Nolan studied on it a moment. "All right. You may be right, dear."

To Linda, Adrienne said, "Daddy and I will give you a little time alone, honey. We haven't had anything to eat in several hours. I'll go fix something for the three of us."

"I'm not hungry, Mom."

"Well, maybe you will be by the time I get it ready. You just lie there and talk to Jesus. He can help you better than any of us."

When her parents had gone, Linda shut her eyes and said, "Lord Jesus, why did this have to happen? Why was Lewis such a hypocrite

68

and a liar? Why would my own sister do this to me? Why?"

Linda was unaware of how long it had been since her parents had left the room, but it seemed like only a few minutes had passed when the door opened again and her mother came in, carrying a tray.

"I've made some of your favorite tea, honey," Adrienne said. "And here's some toast for you. Come on. Sit up. You feel any hunger now?"

"No."

"Well, you need nourishment anyhow. Let's see what you can do with this."

Linda rose to a sitting position and leaned back against the head of the bed. She eyed the steaming cup of tea and the buttered toast. "I'll try, Mom, but right now my stomach is in knots."

"Well, let's see what you can get down."

Linda took a few sips of the tea and nibbled at a corner of the toast as Adrienne looked on. Finally she said, "That's all I want, Mom. Thank you."

Worry etched itself on Adrienne's face. "A little more tea would help you to sleep."

"Okay. I'll drink some more."

"That's a good girl," Adrienne said, taking the tray from Linda's lap. "I'll go see to your father now."

Adrienne returned to the kitchen and laid the tray on the cupboard. Nolan was seated at the table, drinking his own cup of hot tea.

"She only ate a little toast, Nolan, but she downed most of the tea."

"You know what I'm afraid of?" he said. "I'm afraid Linda will pull into a shell and withdraw from her friends, the way she's talking."

"Me, too. And if she does, it may be that she'll even withdraw from you and me . . ."

Nolan's features were drawn and pale as he reached for Adrienne's hand. "Come sit down, honey. Let's take this to the Lord in prayer right now."

Linda moved like a sleepwalker to the washstand. She tipped the water pitcher and poured some of its contents into the basin, then splashed her face with cool water, holding it to her swollen eyes.

When she had put on a nightgown, she blew out the lantern and crawled beneath the sheets. She knew she wouldn't sleep, but maybe if her parents saw no light under her door, they would go to bed and get some rest themselves. She was sorry her parents had to be hurt so deeply, and she didn't want to worry them, but right now all she could focus on was her own pain.

In spite of the fact that Linda had put out the light, her parents came in to check on her. When they found her awake, they prayed with her for a few minutes, then went to their room.

After her parents left, Linda lay in the dark, thinking about Lewis and Janet, trying not to hate them. She wondered how long they'd been seeing each other on the sly. The thing that puzzled her the most was why they went so far as to attend the wedding practice last night.

That was when the urge to hate them rose the strongest in her breast. If they had run off together even last night before the rehearsal, it wouldn't have been the embarrassment it was with a church full of wedding guests. They must have planned it this way to hurt her as much as possible.

She gritted her teeth. Why would they want to hurt her so? She wondered how it got started between her sister and Lewis, and then her thoughts went back to a Saturday about a year ago. Yes. It was the third Saturday in June last year. Janet had made one of her infrequent visits to the Forrest home on Friday evening, and her parents had asked her to go along with them and Linda the next day for a picnic on the shore of Boston Harbor. . . .

71

★ ★ ★

The family was sitting around the kitchen table, drinking coffee. Janet brushed her blond curls back from her forehead, and said, "I'm sorry, but I can't do the picnic with you. I have plans all set to go somewhere with a bunch of my friends. Maybe some other time."

As Linda watched her sister, she noted what a hardness had overtaken her. It showed in her eyes especially.

Linda knew Janet didn't mean it when she said "some other time." She'd made it quite apparent that she detested being with her family. But they continued to invite her because they loved her and hoped to see a change in her life. They couldn't influence her in the right direction if they didn't spend time with her.

With a heavy heart, Adrienne said, "You know we want you with us as much as possible, Janet."

"Sure, Mom. I know."

The next day, as the Forrests drove away from the house in the family carriage, Linda sat between her parents. It was a beautiful day with a clear sky. Perfect for a picnic on the harbor shore.

"I sure wish Lewis had been able to come," said Nolan, guiding the carriage around a corner.

"Me, too," Linda said. "He seldom has to work on Saturdays, but he said his boss really needed him today. Some big shipment coming in from England. He said he'll be thinking about us enjoying all this food, and him having to carry a lunch bucket so he can grab a few bites while unloading the ship. He'll be right there on the docks all day."

They had gone a few blocks when Nolan said, "Oh! I almost forgot. I've got to swing downtown and make a stop at the hardware store. I can't fix that leaky water pipe in the cellar without the proper wrench."

Adrienne laughed. "Well, let's not forget the wrench, husband dear. I'm afraid the bucket that's catching the water from the pipe is about to spring a leak, too!"

Soon they were downtown, pulling up in front of Kruger's Hardware. The women stayed in the carriage while Nolan went into the store to make his purchase.

Mother and daughter sat silently for a few minutes, just watching the people pass by on the street. Adrienne broke the silence by saying, "Well, honey, a year from now, you and Lewis will be husband and wife."

"Mm-hm-m-m-m!" Linda said, smiling happily.

"One of the many things your daddy and I appreciate about Lewis is that he wanted to get some money put aside before he took you as his bride. That shows he has character."

"Oh, he's so wonderful, Mom! We're going to be so happy together!"

"That's what Daddy and I want for you, sweetheart. And we couldn't have picked a better young man for you to marry if we'd gone on a hunt ourselves!"

Nolan returned with a paper bag and tossed it on the floor in front of the backseat. "Okay! Now, the pipe can get fixed . . . but before that happens, we're going to have us an enjoyable day."

The carriage swung out on the busy street, and Nolan aimed it eastward toward the harbor. They were passing an intersection when Adrienne suddenly pointed to a group of people standing on the corner. "Look! There's Janet!"

When Linda's gaze flicked that way, her eyes widened. She saw her sister in the middle of a group of people. The women had the same hard look Janet had taken on. Everyone in the group was about Janet's age. But Linda's attention was drawn to a man standing next to Janet with his back toward the street. Her glimpse of the man was brief, but his size and shape were very familiar.

Linda swallowed hard. The man standing next to Janet strongly resembled Lewis. She couldn't be sure. She had barely gotten a look at him.

As the carriage moved on toward Boston Harbor, Linda said nothing to her parents. She closed her eyes and tried to picture the man in her mind. He certainly was built like Lewis, and he looked to be exactly the same height. And the hat he wore was very much like one of Lewis's.

After a few minutes, Linda dismissed it from her mind. Of course it wasn't Lewis. For one thing, he was at work on the docks. And for another, Lewis was a Christian. He wouldn't run with the ungodly crowd Janet hobnobbed with.

And another thing. Why would Lewis be with Janet? It was simply a man who resembled Lewis. . . .

Lying there in the darkness, Linda clenched her teeth and said in a hissing whisper, "It *was* you, wasn't it, Lewis! So your little affair has been going on for at least a year!"

She trembled with anger as she said a bit louder, "Why didn't I see what was going on? Sure, I had to dismiss the scene on the street corner because I didn't get a good enough look at you, Lewis. But there must have been some other hint of some kind . . . something I was too love-blind to see — Wait a minute! The locket! Yes, the locket!"

Her mind flashed back to one day in early March, a little over four months ago. . . .

Linda and Lewis were leisurely strolling along one of Boston's downtown streets on a Saturday afternoon. They had been window shopping when they came upon Laster's jewelry store. A display of gold and silver lockets and necklaces lay on black velvet in the window.

The sun was at just the right angle to strike the display with its bright rays, and it caught Linda's eye.

"Oh, Lewis!" she said, stopping to look in the window. "Look at this! Do you see those beautiful lockets?"

"Mm-hmm. They really are nice."

"I know we're putting away money for when we get married," she said, "but someday when we're well off, I'd like to have a locket to put your picture in. You know, so I can have your likeness with me when I wear it."

Lewis smiled. "And if you could pick one of these lockets, which one would it be? I realize all of these will be sold by the time I can afford to buy you one, but if I have some idea what you like best, I'll be able to come close, maybe."

Linda's eyes danced as she ran her gaze

over the display of lockets, pausing at those that most caught her attention. "I see it!"

"Which one?"

Pressing the tip of her forefinger against the glass, she said, "Third row from the left, fourth one down."

The gold heart-shaped locket hung on a delicate gold chain. It had an intricate design of dainty flowers etched into it.

"Oh, yes," said Lewis. "That's a pretty one. I'll have to keep it in mind so I can come as close as possible."

Linda's thoughts shifted to March 22. The last time Janet had come by to see the family — on Christmas, so she could pick up her presents — Adrienne had told her she would prepare a special dinner on her birthday. Since Linda and Lewis were engaged, Adrienne had invited Lewis to the meal and to Janet's little party afterward.

The aroma of baked chicken and hot bread filled the Forrest house when Janet arrived that evening for the dinner in her honor.

Linda ran to her, saying, "Happy birthday, big sis!" and hugged her.

Janet reacted coolly and didn't return the hug. Nolan and Adrienne came into the parlor and wished their oldest daughter happy birthday.

"Take your coat off, dear," Adrienne said.

"Dinner's about fifteen minutes from being ready. Lewis should be arriving any minute."

When Janet had removed her scarf and coat, light from the lamps in the parlor glistened off a gold locket that hung on a delicate gold chain around her neck. Linda was surprised to see that it was exactly like the locket she had pointed out to Lewis in the window display at Laster's.

Curious, Linda said, "What a beautiful locket! Where'd you get it?"

Janet hung her coat and scarf on a nearby clothes tree, lifted the locket with her fingers, and said, "One of my boyfriends gave it to me this morning for my birthday."

"Oh? Who was that?" Adrienne asked.

"Hmm?"

"What's the fella's name who gave you the locket?"

"Ah . . . George Kendall."

Nolan laughed. "He must be a pretty good boyfriend. A locket like that doesn't come cheap."

"Yes," said Janet. "He's pretty stuck on me."

There was a knock at the front door.

"That'll be Lewis!" Linda said, rushing to open it.

Lewis came into the parlor beside Linda, smiled at her parents, then said, "Happy birthday, Janet."

"Thank you," she said warmly. "And how have you been, Lewis?"

"Just fine."

Linda touched shoulders with Lewis to get his attention and said, "Did you notice Janet's locket, Lewis?"

"What's that?"

"Janet's locket."

Lewis's line of sight went to the locket. "Oh. Mm-hmm. It's really nice. Birthday present, Janet?"

"Yes. From one of my boyfriends."

"Look closer at it, Lewis," Linda said.

He gave her a quizzical look but did as she said.

"Do you recognize it?" Linda asked.

It took him a few seconds to say, "Oh, sure! It's like that one you showed me at Laster's when we were downtown a couple weeks ago. It really is pretty, isn't it?"

"It was the prettiest one in the window."

Lewis chuckled. "Well, I guess when your birthday comes, I'll have to get you another kind, so you and Janet don't have identical lockets."

The memory of the incident burned in Linda's mind as she lay in the darkness. "You bought that very necklace for Janet, Lewis!" she said aloud. "But you covered your underhanded deed quite cleverly, didn't you?"

Her mind went to her wedding rehearsal and the drive to the harbor afterwards. Lewis had seemed so preoccupied, and when she'd asked him if anything was wrong, all he'd said was that he was nervous about tomorrow.

Linda sat up in the bed and gasped with a sudden intake of breath, then pounded the covers and said loudly, "Nervous! You were nervous, all right, you snake-in-the-grass hypocrite! Not because you were marrying me but because you and Janet were scheming to run away together on the very day of our wedding! I hate you, Lewis Carter! I hate you! I hate you! I h—"

The door burst open, and Nolan plunged into the room, carrying a lighted candle. Adrienne was right behind him.

"Honey, what is it?"

Linda was on her knees in the middle of the bed, the breath sawing in and out of her throat. "I hate him, Daddy!" she said through her teeth. "I hate him!"

Adrienne moved to the bed and laid a hand on her daughter's arm. When Linda turned her face toward her, hot tears fell swiftly and silently down her cheeks and off her chin. "Mom," she squeaked, "why didn't I see what was happening? Lewis and Janet were carrying on behind my back and I didn't have a clue. Now I've been remembering things that should have told me something was wrong. Why didn't I see it?"

"Sweetheart, they say love is blind. You loved Lewis so deeply that it blinded you to what was going on."

"Well, I don't love him anymore! I hate him, Mom! I hate him!"

Nolan kept his voice level as he said, "Linda, you can certainly hate what Lewis did to you, but you mustn't hate him."

Her eyes grew wild. "I *do* hate that vile beast of a man, Daddy! I hate him as much as I used to love him! And I hate my wicked sister, too!"

Nolan started to speak again, but Adrienne laid a hand on his shoulder. "Nolan, she's too upset for us to reason with her. We must understand how deeply she's been hurt. It's best that we save the admonitions for later."

Linda set her jaw. "I feel so ashamed and mortified by the predicament those two have put me in. Oh, how could I have been so blind?"

"Honey," Adrienne said, "get back in bed now. You need to rest."

Linda looked at her with pain-filled eyes. "All right, Mom. I'm sorry I woke you two up." As she spoke, she slipped back under the covers.

"It's all right," Nolan said, bending over to caress her cheek. "Mom and I love you, Linda. You're our daughter, and when you hurt, we hurt. You try to get some sleep."

Both parents kissed her, told her they loved her, and quietly left the room.

Once again Linda said in a bitter tone, "Never again will I love with such total trust. Never. That's a promise to *you*, Linda Lee Forrest."

Hot tears spilled down her cheeks, soaking her pillow.

"And here's another promise, Linda Lee Forrest. I will never again face those people at church, nor anyone else in Boston who knows me. Never. I couldn't stand the awful embarrassment."

She lay in the dismal gloom around her, trying to harden her heart against the pain within.

5

Linda tossed and turned through the long night hours, but sleep refused to come. Her emotions were like the maelstrom of a storm-tossed sea, and her nerves were strung tight. She kept picturing Lewis and Janet together, having a good laugh on her.

Sometime in the night, she left her bed and walked to the window and looked at the shimmering white stars in the black sky above. They were cold, brilliant, aloof.

Under those same stars, she thought, *the two traitors are about to arrive in New York City.* What then? Were they going to stay there, or would they come back to Boston after they had their fling?

Linda stood quivering with wrath. *They wouldn't dare show their faces around here again!*

Slowly she turned and went back to the bed. Soon there was a slight hint of gray on the eastern horizon, and it touched the window of her room. Little by little, a drowsiness began to come over her, and when the fan of dawn's orange light filled the eastern sky, Linda fell asleep.

★ ★ ★

Nolan paused behind Adrienne at Linda's door and peeked over her shoulder as she turned the knob and inched the door open. They could see that their daughter was sleeping.

Adrienne closed the door and motioned for Nolan to come back with her to their room. Once inside, she said, "I'll stay home with her, Nolan. You go on to church."

"You sure? Maybe it's best I stay here, too. One or both of you might need me."

"We'll be fine. People at church will want to know how Linda's doing. The way word gets around, I'm sure by now that many of them know every detail of the wedding that didn't happen."

"All right. I guess one of us needs to be there."

As the morning passed, Adrienne looked in on Linda every half hour and was pleased that she was still sleeping.

It was almost 11:30 when Adrienne tiptoed to Linda's bedroom door and quietly turned the knob. As she pushed it open to get a glimpse of the bed, she saw her daughter sitting on the room's padded chair, fully dressed, groomed, and looking out the window.

Linda turned and set bleary eyes on her

84

mother. Her features were pallid and drawn.

"Good morning!" Adrienne said brightly. "I'm glad you got some sleep."

Linda released a faint smile. "Mm-hmm. Me, too. I was awake most of the night."

"I was afraid you would be."

"Daddy go to church?"

"Yes."

"You didn't have to stay here with me, Mom."

Moving close to her, Adrienne said, "I couldn't leave you alone. I wanted to be here if you needed me."

Linda's second smile of the day was a little wider. She rose from the chair, opened her arms to embrace her mother, and said, "You're the best mom in the whole world."

Adrienne kissed her cheek. "I don't know about that, but you're the best daughter in the whole world."

Linda turned and looked out the window. "Sure. The best daughter. You mean the one who couldn't keep her fiancé and make him her groom?"

"Honey, don't blame yourself. It wasn't your fault."

"How did my sister do it, Mom? What does Lewis see in her? Why did he dump me for her?"

"Linda, all I can say is that if Lewis was the

Christian he led us to believe he was, he would never have chosen your sister over you. Now, how about some breakfast, honey? Or, I guess maybe it would be lunch now."

"Maybe I'm a little hungry. How about just some toast and tea like last night?"

Adrienne sat across the table from her haggard-looking daughter and watched her eat all of her toast. When she had finished her first cup of tea, Adrienne quickly said, "How about a second cup?"

"All right."

Just as she rose from the table to pick up the teakettle from the stove, the family carriage passed by the window. Nolan was at the reins, and Aunt Beth was beside him.

Linda jumped up. "I don't want to see anybody today except you and Daddy," she said, hurrying from the kitchen.

"Honey, it's only Aunt Beth!" Adrienne called after her.

There was no reply. Seconds later, the sound of Linda's bedroom door slamming echoed through the house.

Nolan and Beth entered the kitchen from the back porch, and as Beth preceded her brother-in-law, she said, "Hello, Adrienne. How's our girl doing?"

"She got up about eleven. When I checked on her at eleven-thirty, she was dressed, had her hair brushed, and was sitting in her chair. I was able to get some tea and toast down her. She's in her room now."

"May I see her?"

Adrienne's brow furrowed. "I'm not sure she wants to see anyone right now, but let me go ask her."

Beth and Nolan waited in the kitchen.

In less than three minutes, Adrienne returned and said, "Beth, Linda's in a low state of mind, as you know."

"Of course."

"She said to thank you for coming, and to tell you she loves you, but she really needs some privacy right now."

"Is she in a lower state of mind than last night?"

"I think so. When she was having the tea and toast, she kept talking about Lewis and Janet, saying she hates them because they've destroyed her life and taken away her reason to want to go on."

Beth's features paled. "Adrienne, Linda said yesterday that she wants to die. You don't think —"

"No. She isn't going to take her own life. She's still in a state of shock, and hurting miserably, but she's not suicidal."

"Are you sure?"

"Of course. I know my own daughter." To

her husband Adrienne said, "Nolan, you don't have any concern along that line, do you?"

"No, honey. Linda is suffering like she's never suffered in her life, but she's not going to do anything like that. It would be totally out of character."

"But that is the very thing that shocks people when someone commits suicide," Beth said. "Most of the time it's done by a person nobody thought would do it. I wouldn't worry so much, except that she's stated that she wants to die."

"That's just the hurt talking, Beth," Nolan said. "Like Adrienne said, she knows her daughter. And so do I. Linda's not going to do a drastic thing like that."

Beth's face puckered with sympathy. "Bless her precious little heart. I wish I could take the hurt for her."

"We'd do that, too, if we could," Adrienne said.

"Well, I'd better get on home. Maybe my sweet niece will let me see her tomorrow."

Linda could smell Sunday dinner cooking as she sat in her chair, looking out the window. She thought about the honeymoon she and Lewis had planned. Ten days in Vermont.

Never to happen.

She thought about the apartment they had rented on the second floor of Carl Higgins's house. They couldn't move anything into the apartment until they returned from their honeymoon. The previous renters had to go out of town to attend a funeral, and this had delayed their moving plans by some five days. Once they were out, Mr. Higgins wanted to do some painting in the apartment before his new renters moved in. He'd promised to have it all done so they could move in immediately upon arriving home from Vermont.

It had upset her that they would have to wait to take their clothes and other belongings to the apartment until after they returned from their honeymoon, but as Linda pondered it now, she felt a strange sense of relief. She couldn't imagine having to go there now and bring her things back home.

"Thank You, Lord," she whispered softly. "I can see Your guiding hand in the timing of that. You knew all of this was going to happen and at least spared me that heartache. I . . . I just don't know why You ever let me fall in love with that despicable man in the first place."

She broke down and wept once more, saying, "Lord, I don't want to go on. I can't ever face anyone who knows me here. Why don't

You just let me die? Take me to Your home, where I won't hurt like I'm hurting now."

There was a tap on the door, accompanied by her father's voice. "Sweetheart, can I come in?"

"Yes, Daddy."

Nolan stepped inside, smiled, and said, "Mom wants to know if you'd like to eat with us."

"I'm not hungry, Daddy."

"I was glad to hear that you ate some toast and drank some tea," he said, moving toward her. "Mom thought maybe you'd feel like eating something more substantial now." He bent down and kissed her forehead. "You won't forget that I love you, will you?"

She looked up through weary eyes. "No, Daddy. I won't forget."

"Aunt Beth said she'd come back tomorrow."

Linda nodded.

"Well, I'll see you a little later. Mom's about got dinner ready."

"Daddy . . ."

Nolan stopped and turned. "Mm-hmm?"

"I suppose everybody at church knows that Lewis dumped me for Janet."

He scratched his head. "Well, some of them do. There were several who said to give you their love and to tell you they're praying for you. Joline was crying when she asked about you."

This made tears well up in Linda's eyes. "She's the best friend I have in the world, Daddy."

"She loves you a lot, I know that. See you later. Mom and I know you want some privacy, so we won't bother you for a while. But you know we're right here for you if you need us."

"Yes. I know that."

When her father was gone, Linda stared out the window for several minutes, then rose from the chair and went to the cedar chest at the foot of her bed. It had been her hope chest for nearly two years. She lifted the lid and took out a scrapbook, which lay on top of the linens and things that almost filled the chest.

She carried the scrapbook to the small desk in a corner of the room and sat down. Her fingers trembled as she touched the cover. She knew what she was about to look at was going to cause more pain, but somehow she felt compelled to do it.

She flipped past the pages that held photographs of family, then paused at the first page that had photographs of Lewis and herself.

She looked at the two of them — at church, at the harbor shore, at church picnics, in Lewis's buggy, and together in the yard of the

Forrest home. There were even photographs at the Forrest home with Janet in the background.

A mixture of pain and anger swirled within her as she thought of all the hopes and dreams she'd built on Lewis.

She quickly wiped the tears from her cheeks when she heard a light tap on the door.

"Honey," her mother said, "Pastor Stanford and Doris are here to see you. They had dinner with one of the church families and came by because they're concerned about you."

"I really appreciate them coming by, but right now I just don't want to see *anyone*. Please tell them I love them, but I need to be alone."

The door opened, and Adrienne took a step inside. Her line of sight swerved from the chair where she had expected to find Linda, to where she sat at the desk. "You need help, honey," she said. "And the best people to help you are your pastor and his wife."

"I'm all right, Mom. Please, I just need to be left alone."

"I'm trying to understand, honey, and so is your daddy."

"Thank you."

"Well, I'll look in on you later."

When her mother's footsteps died out

down the hall, Linda turned back to the scrapbook. There were little love notes that Lewis had often handed her at the end of a date, or at church. She had loved him for being such a romantic.

She closed the scrapbook, rested her head against it, and wept.

After a while she dried her tears and carried the scrapbook across the room, then laid it on the floor beside her hope chest. She knelt in front of the chest and began pulling out linens and other items that she'd started putting away ever since she and Lewis had admitted they were serious about each other.

Memories rushed through her mind as she looked over her handiwork and recalled every loving stitch she had sewn. With each towel, washcloth, pillowcase, sheet, and crocheted doily there had been a sweet dream of a happy life with the man she loved. She had dreamed of the new home they would establish on their wedding day . . . of her joy of cooking, washing, ironing, sewing, and all the things a wife does for her husband. And of course there were the dreams of children . . . happy laughter and the patter of little feet around the house.

Ashes, now. Only ashes.

Once again her tears began to flow. She put the scrapbook at the very bottom of the chest, then placed the linens and other things on top of it and closed the lid.

She must let Mr. Higgins know they wouldn't be needing the apartment. She would have her father go by and tell him. She gave a sigh of relief that she wouldn't have to pick up her clothes and other personal belongings and bring them back from the apartment.

Her clothes.

Linda's eyes swung to the closet where the door stood partly open. She hadn't seen the wedding dress in her closet when she dressed that morning.

She went to the closet and fumbled through the dresses. Not there. *Mom must have put it in her own closet, thinking that it would upset me to see it.*

Sweet, caring Mom.

For some unexplainable reason, Linda needed to see the dress.

She went to her door, opened it slightly, and listened. The Stanfords were still in the house. She could hear a murmur of conversation between them and her parents.

She hurried down the hall to her parents' bedroom. It took only a few seconds to find the wedding dress and take it back to her room. Her whole body trembled as she carried the beautiful white dress to the bed, sat down, and held it before her eyes.

"Why do you torture yourself, Linda?" she said in a whisper. "This was the dress you were wearing last night when you went through the worst nightmare of your life — being left at the church by the treacherous man you loved and trusted."

She held the dress to her face, staining it with her tears. When another tap came at the door, she forced her voice to remain steady and said, "Yes?"

Adrienne's eyes widened when she saw the dress in Linda's hands. "Honey, what are you doing?"

Linda held the delicate dress in clenched fists and said, "I just had to look at it."

"Why? I put it in my closet so you wouldn't have to see it."

"I don't know why, Mom. I just had to."

Adrienne sat down beside her and put an arm around her shoulder. "An upheaval of our emotions can do strange things to our minds, Linda. I know that. Has it helped you any to look at it?"

Linda held up the wrinkled dress and said, "It's helped me to feel more hatred for Lewis Carter. He should have been named *Judas!*"

Adrienne thought of giving her a good lecture on what hatred would do inside her if she held it there but decided this wasn't the time. "Honey, Joline's here to see you. Frank drove her here. He's waiting with your father in the parlor. Joline is just down the hall."

"Are the pastor and Doris still here?"

"No. They left a few minutes before Frank and Joline arrived. Will you let her come in and see you? I told her you weren't seeing anyone today, but she said for me to ask if you would give a few minutes to your best friend."

Linda swallowed hard and thought on it a moment. Then looking up, she said, "All right. I would like to see her. Send her in."

Adrienne stepped into the hall and motioned to Joline.

The young woman rushed through the door and then stopped abruptly when she saw Linda holding the wedding dress. "Oh, Linda!" she gasped, and dashed to her side.

Adrienne watched for a few seconds as Joline folded Linda into her arms with the dress between them and just let Linda sob out her grief.

Adrienne smiled to herself. Joline would indeed be able to help her daughter. She stepped into the hall and closed the door.

Joline held her weeping friend and said, "Thank you for seeing me. I came for one reason. Not to lecture you on how to react to your devastation, nor to preach to you and tell you you're weak spiritually if you let what's happened get you down. You're a human being made out of the same kind of flesh I am. I know you're hurting. I just came to cry with you."

Her words caused Linda to sob all the harder. She let go of the dress and wrapped her arms around her best friend, and hung on. The sobs seemed to come from deep within — wordless wails of inexpressible anguish.

As Joline felt Linda's inward pain, her own tears streamed freely down her cheeks.

When Linda could form words again, she clung to her friend and cried, "Oh, Joline, I wish I could die! I can't ever face the people who know me! I want to die!"

Joline patted her friend on the back of the head and said, "Sh-h-h! Now, you don't mean that."

"Yes, I do! Yes, I do! I want to die!"

"But, honey, there are still many people who love you. Your parents love you. *I* love you. Pastor and Mrs. Stanford love you. The people at church do, too. Betty and Shirley love you. They're waiting for me to tell them at church tonight how my visit went. They want to come and see you, too."

These were Linda's other bridesmaids — Betty Madison and Shirley Wells.

"No, Joline! No! I can't face them! I can't!"

"All right, honey," Joline said, this time patting her upper back. "I understand. I'll explain it to Betty and Shirley." She eased back to look Linda in the eye. "I have to go now. Frank and I need to be heading for church."

Linda's eyes were swollen and red, and she spoke jerkily as she said, "Thank you for coming to cry with me."

"Of course," Joline said as she dabbed at her wet cheeks with a hanky. "But, honey, before I go . . ."

"Yes?"

"No more of this talk about wanting to die, okay?"

Linda bit down on her lower lip and gave a tiny nod, but her heart wasn't in it.

Joline knew the nod was all she was going to get. She hugged Linda again, kissed her cheek, and said, "May I come back soon and see you?"

"Yes."

Joline walked to the door, pulled it open, then looked back and said, "I love you, Linda."

"I love you, too. Thank you for being my very best friend."

Joline smiled and closed the door softly.

When she entered the parlor, Frank said, "How did it go?"

"Pretty well, except —"

"Except what?"

The Forrests had their eyes fixed on Joline.

"Well . . . she's saying she wants to die.

That worries me. What if she decided to take her life?"

"Linda's not going to take her life," Adrienne said. "It's not in her to do a thing like that. She was talking that way last night. Beth was worried about the same thing, but as Nolan told her, that isn't Linda talking. It's the hurt inside her talking. With prayer and lots of love, she'll come out of this state of despondency, and she'll be our happy, cheerful Linda again."

Lewis Carter and Janet Forrest left Manhattan's Grand Central Station early on Sunday morning.

As Lewis carried their overnight bags, Janet held his elbow with one hand and pointed at the surreys that stood in line for passengers all along the street on the depot side. "There's one of the Hudson Transportation Company surreys, darling. See it? Remember, Max said in his letter to hire one of them because they're the best in New York."

"Oh. Sure."

Lewis focused on the waiting vehicle and the large sign on its side:

Hudson Transportation Company
We Cover All Five Boroughs
Reasonable Rates

99

As they walked toward the surrey, Janet squeezed Lewis's arm and said, "Oh, darling, I'm so happy!"

"Me, too," he breathed.

"It sure was great of Max to work out your transfer down here," she said, a lilt in her voice.

"Yeah. And it was plenty nice of him to get the apartment rented for us, and ready to move into."

"I'll say."

"Max was a good friend when he was my foreman in Boston, and he's even a better friend now."

"He didn't know anything about you and Linda when he left Boston and came to Brooklyn, did he?"

"No. When he transferred here, Linda and I were just starting to see each other on a steady basis."

"Good. No questions to answer then."

"That's right."

The driver smiled as he slid off the seat. " 'Mornin', folks," he said in a friendly tone. "Needin' a surrey?" He was a short, chubby man with rosy cheeks and a heavy handlebar mustache.

"We sure do," Lewis said. "We need to go to Brooklyn. My fiancée will be staying at the Kensington Arms Hotel. Know where that is?"

"Sure. On Church Avenue, right by Prospect Park."

"Okay. And I'll be staying at a friend's house on Flatbush Avenue six blocks south of Linden Boulevard. He lives at 3119. It's a two-story house."

"Got it. The fee will be four dollars, plus the fifty cents to take the ferry across and back."

Soon the surrey was heading south toward the ferry dock, where they would cross the East River to Brooklyn. Lewis and Janet sat behind the driver, who told them his name was Bob Long and joked that they'd named Long Island after him.

Long proved to be quite talkative. He pointed out places of interest and told little stories about incidents that had happened on particular streets.

The couple held hands, more interested in each other than in what Long was saying. He went quiet a moment, then said, "So where you folks from?"

"Boston," Lewis replied.

"Yeah? Boston's a nice place, but I like New York better. So when you gettin' married?"

"Tomorrow."

"Oh, really? Church weddin'?"

"No. My friend Max Burton — the one whose house you'll be taking me to — has us

101

lined up to take our vows before a judge in his chambers in the morning."

"I see. So you're gonna be livin' in Brooklyn?"

"Yes."

"What business you in?"

"Shipping. I work for the Dunbar Shipping Company. We have docks both in Boston and South Brooklyn. We're at the big pier on Gravesend Bay."

"Oh, yeah. I've seen the sign, now that you mention it. So the company transferred you down here, eh?"

"Yes. Max was my foreman in Boston until they transferred him here a couple years ago. He put in to have me come down and be his number-one assistant."

As they drew near the ferry dock, Long pointed ahead to a massive bridge under construction, spanning the East River to Brooklyn. "Take a look at that!" he said. "That's the Brooklyn Bridge! Won't be completed for another three years or so. When it's finished, it'll be the longest bridge in the whole world. Sixteen hundred feet!"

"It's a big one, all right," Lewis said, eyeing the massive superstructure with awe.

Janet was bored with Long's commentary.

"Masterwork of a fella named John Augustus Roebling," Long said. "It's the first bridge in the world to use steel for cable wire. The deck is supported by four of those huge cables. There's a walkway for pedestrians, too. Well, here we are. The ferrys leave on the half hour, so we're just in time to catch the next one."

Lewis and Janet were married the next morning. They would not be able to take a honeymoon; Lewis was due to report in for work on Tuesday morning at seven o'clock.

On Monday evening after they had eaten supper at a local café, they entered their apartment, and Janet threw her arms around Lewis, saying, "I'm so happy! Just think of it — I'm now Mrs. Lewis Carter!" She paused, then laughed. "My baby sister wanted to be Mrs. Lewis Carter, but I outfoxed her. I got her man! Ha! I wish I could have seen her little dollface when she finally realized we weren't going to show up for the wedding! I wonder how long it took till she and everyone else knew there wasn't going to be a wedding."

Lewis had gone quiet.

"Hey, what's the matter, honey?" Janet said. "Something bothering you?"

"Oh . . . ah . . . no." He hugged her close. "Nothing's bothering me."

Janet pushed herself out of his arms, took a

step back, and said, "Don't lie to me, Lewis. Something's eating at you. Here we are, just married, with everything working out exactly as we planned, and you're down about something. C'mon. What is it?"

"It's nothing, Janet. Nothing."

"Well, you sure don't seem very happy! I'm your wife now. That's what you wanted, wasn't it? You and me together . . . forever?"

"Yes. Of course."

"Then can't you smile?"

"Sure." Lewis forced his lips into a curve.

Janet narrowed her eyelids to thin slits and said with sand in her voice, "You're not wishing you'd gone ahead and married little dollface, are you?"

"Uh . . . no, honey. No. It's just —"

"Just what?"

"Well, you said a moment ago that you'd like to have seen her face when she finally realized we weren't going to show up for the wedding."

Janet raised her thinly plucked eyebrows. "So what?"

"I just wish you and I had been honest with Linda. Simply told her a year ago that we were in love, and I was breaking off the engagement. It wouldn't have been such a jolt to her. This going through the wedding rehearsal, then taking off on Saturday afternoon was *your* idea, you know. I shouldn't have listened to you."

Janet's eyes widened in disbelief and her face turned crimson. "Sure, it was my idea! I wanted to show that little pasty-faced, goody-goody sister of mine just what kind of contempt I have for her! She knows now, I can guarantee you. I hope it hurts all the way from the top of her head to the bottom of her feet."

Lewis's features paled. "There's no need to be so unfeeling about it, Janet. Like I said, I shouldn't have listened to you."

Janet moved up close to him, trying to subdue her anger. "Look, honey. It's done now. Linda will get over it. We have each other. Let's be happy. Okay? Give me a smile, now, and tell me it's okay."

With effort Lewis said, "Sure, honey. It's okay."

In spite of her parents' optimism, Linda became more despondent as the days passed. She stayed in her room except to eat, and though well-wishers came by to see her, she holed up in her room and refused to see them. She prayed and tried to read her Bible, but the dead feeling inside kept her from getting hold of God and allowing the Word to penetrate her heart.

On Friday evening — a week beyond the wedding rehearsal — the Forrests were invited to go out to dinner with Ed and Frances Diamond. Linda was given a special written invitation from Frances.

Nolan and Adrienne stood in their daughter's room, dressed to go out, and Adrienne said, "You have to start sometime, Linda. You can't be a recluse for the rest of your life."

"I can if I want. I'm not going out there where the public is, Mom. We might run into other people we know. Besides, I'm not hungry."

Adrienne looked at her husband. "I don't think we should go away and leave her."

"I don't either," Nolan said. "When Ed and Frances arrive, we'll tell them we've changed our minds."

"No, Daddy," Linda said. "You two go on. I'll be fine. I like being alone."

Nolan and Adrienne discussed it for a minute while Linda insisted they go. Finally they gave in, kissed her good-bye, and said they would be home about ten o'clock.

When Linda heard the front door close behind her parents and the Diamonds, she sat down in her chair by the window. Would this dead feeling never go away? Would she never have peace? Was she destined to live the rest of her life grieving over what her sister and fiancé had done to her?

Suddenly she bolted for the door and ran down the hall toward the stairs, weeping. She dashed through the kitchen and out the back door, leaving it open.

As she walked at a fast pace toward the harbor, a still, small voice kept saying inside her head, "My grace is sufficient for thee. My grace is sufficient for thee."

When she reached the harbor, she went to the very spot where she and Lewis had gone the night of the wedding rehearsal. She stood at the edge, and the wind plucked at her long auburn hair as she looked down into the deep black water some thirty feet below.

Behind Linda, some distance away, a man in a blue uniform slid from his saddle and slowly made his way toward her. He was glad the slapping of the waves at the base of the ledge helped to cover the sound of his footsteps. His heart thudded against his rib cage when he drew close and reached out to grasp her shoulders.

At the touch of his hands she let out a startled shriek.

"Little lady," he said, spinning her around so she could see his cap, uniform, and badge, "I'm just trying to keep you from jumping!"

When Linda saw who it was, her heart

pounded like a trip-hammer. "Oh! Officer Shanahan!"

The graying policeman blinked, squinted, and said, "Hey, I know you! You and that young fella you were gonna marry were here just a few nights ago. Linda! Yes, that's your name. He called you Linda. What are you doing here by yourself?"

"The wedding didn't happen, Officer Shanahan," she said flatly.

"Oh? Can you tell me about it?"

While the wind blew and the waves washed against the shore, Linda told the officer her story. When she finished, he said, "So you were gonna jump in and end it all, weren't you?"

She looked at him in surprise. "Oh! No, sir! I . . . I've felt like I wanted to die and even said so several times, but I would never take my own life, sir. I'm a born-again Christian. I wouldn't do that. I just came out here to get away from the house . . . and to pray. On my way here, I got real peace from the Lord. I kept thinking of that Scripture where the Lord told Paul: 'My grace is sufficient for thee,' and just about the time I reached the edge here, I broke down and cried, thanking the Lord for His sufficient grace. I'm all right, Officer. I'll go home now."

"That ye will, lassy," said Shanahan, "but

my horse and I will escort you."

It was almost nine-thirty when Officer Patrick Shanahan and Linda Forrest turned the corner on her street. The horse carried Linda while Shanahan led him by the reins.

Suddenly they heard a woman's voice crying out hysterically as a buggy came bounding from the back of the Forrest house and hit the street.

"Those are my parents!" Linda said. "They're home early. They found me gone, and Mom's terribly upset. Come on, we've got to stop them!"

The buggy, however, turned their way. Immediately, Shanahan let go of the reins and dashed up under the nearest street lamp, waving his arms.

Nolan Forrest drew the buggy to a halt, and Adrienne jumped out of the buggy and ran to her daughter, crying, "Linda-a-a-a! Where have you been?"

While both parents held on to their daughter, the officer said, "I found her standin' at the edge of the 'arbor, folks. We have people jump in quite often. I thought —"

"Oh, Linda!" Adrienne gasped. "You were going to jump in! You've been saying you wished you could die! Oh-h-h-h!"

"No, Mom. I wasn't going to jump in. Yes,

I was very upset. I left the house in that condition, but not to kill myself. I just wanted to go out to the harbor and look at the water in the dark. I'll explain it better when we go into the house, but the Lord just showed me tonight that His grace is sufficient for my suffering, just as it was for a suffering apostle Paul."

Linda's parents wept for joy, thanking God for answered prayer. Belatedly they turned to Officer Shanahan and thanked him for bringing their daughter home, then took her inside.

Everybody in the Forrest household slept well that night.

The next day was Saturday. Joline Jensen came by to see her best friend and was overjoyed to learn of the victory Linda had experienced the night before.

The two young women went to Linda's room to talk. Joline sat on the bed, and Linda sat in her padded chair. As the conversation progressed, Joline said, "Now that you've got peace in all of this, Linda, let me say something. God could have prevented what Lewis and Janet did to you. Right?"

"Right."

"But He let it happen."

"Yes."

"The Lord let it happen, honey, because he

has somebody better picked out for you. Certainly you want the husband *God* has chosen for you."

"Of course. But now I'm wondering if I can ever trust another man."

Joline smiled. "Remember the passage of Scripture Pastor Stanford was going to use in the wedding ceremony? From Ecclesiastes?"

"Yes. *'A time to love . . . '*"

"Sweet Linda, believe me, you will have your time to love. The Lord has the man, the time, and the place. Let Him work it out."

After Joline left, Linda gazed out the window at her mother's flower garden in full glorious bloom. The sun was shining down out of a clear azure sky.

There was deep peace in her heart now, and even though the ache was still there, it didn't hurt as before. It had been cushioned by the love and care of her heavenly Father. With her gaze on the sun-kissed flowers, she prayed for guidance in her life, and a sense of sweet comfort flowed within her soul.

She went to the closet and took her wedding dress and veil from their hanger, then went to the cedar chest and opened the lid. She carefully folded the dress and placed the veil inside it, then gently placed the folded dress on top of everything else in the chest and looked at it lovingly one last time.

Then she firmly closed the lid on her past, and just as firmly tried to close the sad memories in her heart.

When she returned to the window, Joline's words came back to her mind: *"Sweet Linda, believe me, you will have your time to love. The Lord has the man, the time, and the place. Let Him work it out."*

6

The sky over Sacramento, California, was flat and gray. Outside the city to the west a large crowd had gathered on a hillside around an open grave. The wind whipped through the cemetery, rustling the full-leafed branches of the trees and toying with the sand-colored hair of handsome Blake Barrett.

Next to Barrett stood Haman Warner, vice president of Sacramento's Pacific Bank and Trust Company. Six pallbearers, one of whom was Haman Warner, had placed the expensive coffin on a small wooden platform next to the grave. A large bouquet of bright-colored flowers adorned the top of the coffin.

Blake Barrett's pastor, Duane Clarke, had just read a passage of Scripture and was commenting on it, making his gospel message quite clear, which he had also done in the service at the funeral chapel.

The deceased was fifty-five-year-old Bradley Barrett, Blake's father. Bradley had founded the Pacific Bank and Trust Company some twenty years previously, and it had grown into a solid, profitable institution.

Blake's heart was heavy with the knowledge that he would not see his father in heaven. He wiped a hand across his face as if he could pull off and cast away the unease he felt. Bradley Barrett had been a stubborn man and early in life had set his mind on the belief that the Bible was only a book written by fools and fanatics. He had died a blatant infidel.

Blake thought of his darling mother, who had come to know the Lord Jesus Christ a few years after she married Bradley Barrett. It was Clara Barrett who had led Blake to the Lord when he was nine years old. Blake took comfort as he stood on the bleak, windy hillside that his mother was waiting for him in heaven, as was his younger brother, Brett, who had died in infancy.

Pastor Duane Clarke closed the graveside service in prayer, then stepped up to Blake, put an arm around his shoulder, and said, "I hope you feel I handled it all right, Blake."

Haman Warner looked on solemnly as Blake said, "You sure did, Pastor. There was no way you could say Dad was in heaven, though a lot of preachers would have said so just to comfort his friends. I appreciate the way you handled it with kindness and compassion, yet didn't compromise Bible truth. And you certainly made salvation clear enough. No one can walk away from here and say they've never heard how to be saved. Thank you for being so faithful to the Word of God."

The pastor nodded and made way for the mourners to offer their condolences to Blake. Haman Warner stayed by Blake's side.

A few members of the church waited until the bank employees, businessmen, merchants, and other people of the town and surrounding area had passed by before speaking to Blake.

Blake smiled at Bill and Evelyn Borah as they drew up with their two daughters, Susan and Lucy, along with Susan's husband, Ralph Duncan, and Lucy's fiancé, Cliff Winters. When each had conveyed their love and sympathy, Blake said to Bill, "Dad's death has slowed us up a couple of days on your loan application. But I can tell you right now, there won't be any problem. I've got to meet with our attorneys about Dad's estate early this afternoon, but I should be able to complete the loan work before quitting time. I'll eat supper at the café this evening. I can give you the details then."

Borah shook his head. "Blake, you can work on my loan tomorrow. I mean . . . after all, you're burying your dad today."

"It's all right, Bill. Business still has to go on, and you need to know about the loan so you can hire a contractor to put the addition on the café. I'll see you this evening."

The last to approach Blake was Nora Clarke, the pastor's wife. Her husband stood behind her. Nora embraced Blake in sisterly fashion and said, "God bless you, Blake. You've held up well."

Blake managed a slight smile. "The Lord has given me peace, Nora. Sure, it hurts to know Dad died lost, but the Comforter, who lives in my heart, has eased the pain."

The Clarkes spent a few more minutes with Blake, then walked away. Haman Warner, who had stood silently beside the grieving Barrett all this time, laid a hand on his arm and said, "I'd better get back to the bank."

Blake nodded. "Thanks for the support here. I appreciate it."

Haman, who was exactly Blake's height at just under six feet, said, "Hey, Blake. What are friends for?"

The clouds were breaking up, and warm shafts of sunshine touched the earth as Blake Barrett approached the law offices of Laymon, Studdard, and Griswold. His mind was on Haman Warner. Haman was not a Christian, though Blake had witnessed to him for the past four years.

As Blake stepped into the outer office of the

116

law firm, he was greeted with a smile by secretary Veronica Naylor. Veronica was a widow in her late fifties, and Blake was aware that she was about to leave her job and go south to Los Angeles to live with her sister, who was also widowed.

Seated at the desk next to Veronica was a lovely young woman whom Blake had yet to meet.

"Hello, Mr. Barrett," Veronica said. "Please know that you have my condolences."

"Thank you."

"I'd like you to meet Linnie Chapman, Mr. Barrett," Veronica said, nodding at the pretty lady, whom Blake guessed would be about twenty-five. "*Miss* Linnie Chapman."

Blake did a half bow and said, "My pleasure, Miss Chapman. Am I to assume you're going to take Veronica's place?"

"Yes, sir," replied Linnie, overwhelmed by Blake's good looks and rugged masculinity. "I just came to work yesterday."

"I'll be training her for two weeks," Veronica said, "then I'll be heading to Los Angeles."

"Well, we sure will miss you around here."

"Thank you." Veronica smiled, then rose from her chair and headed down the hall, saying, "Mr. Laymon and Mr. Studdard are ready for you."

As Blake followed her toward the conference room, Linnie said, "Nice to meet you, Mr. Barrett."

"You, too," he said over his shoulder.

Veronica tapped on the door and opened it. "Mr. Barrett is here," she told the two middle-aged men who sat at a long table.

The attorneys rose to their feet as Blake moved inside.

Veronica closed the door and returned to the desk. As she sat down, Linnie said, "What a handsome man! Who is he?"

"Blake Barrett is now the owner of the biggest and most prosperous bank in Sacramento. His father founded the Pacific Bank and Trust Company some twenty years ago. You heard me give him my condolences?"

"Yes."

"His father's funeral was this morning. Blake inherited the bank in total. There are no other heirs. He graduated from college in 1871, at twenty-one years of age, and came to work immediately for his father at the bank. He has served as executive vice president since being promoted to that position four years ago. And believe me, he had to earn the promotion. His father was a hardhead."

Linnie counted on her fingers. "Let's see. That makes him twenty-seven now, right?"

"Yes."

"I assume he's married."

"No, he's not."

Linnie's eyebrows arched. "Engaged? Promised?"

"Not that I know of."

Linnie's eyes lit up. "Twenty-seven years old. He's not married or engaged, and he owns a big successful bank all by himself! I think I'll get to know him better!"

Veronica laughed. "It'll take more than getting to know him to get him to the altar, honey. There are lots of women in this town who'd make their play. But there's a catch as to whom he will even date, much less marry."

"A catch?"

"Uh-huh."

Veronica looked hard at Linnie and said, "Do you know what a born-again Christian is?"

"Well, sort of."

"That's what Mr. Blake Barrett is. And believe me, honey, his standards for a wife are sky high. They start with the fact that the lady has to be a born-again Christian or he won't even consider her."

"Oh. My minister back home has always said that born-again talk bordered on foolish fanaticism."

Veronica shrugged. "To each his own. Well, let's get back to work here."

★ ★ ★

When Veronica Naylor closed the door behind Blake Barrett, attorneys Dan Laymon and Myron Studdard rose to their feet to shake his hand. They both commented on the excellent job Pastor Duane Clarke had done at the funeral service and at the graveside service.

"I appreciate you gentlemen attending," Blake said.

"We were glad to do it, Blake," said Laymon. "And Jack Griswold would have done so, too, if he weren't in Los Angeles. As you know, we've had an excellent business relationship with your father ever since he started the bank."

"Yes, and you've always done him well."

"Please, sit down," said Studdard, who was tall, thin, and bald.

Laymon was stocky and much shorter than Studdard, and he had a full head of salt-and-pepper hair.

Both men had file folders and papers on the table before them.

Studdard looked across at Barrett. "Blake, you knew your father had us prepare a new will for him just two weeks ago."

"Yes. He's known for three months that he was terminally ill, and about a month ago he told me he was going to make some changes in the will. He said he wanted to leave something for Haman Warner, and asked if I objected. I told him I had no reason to object. Haman has served Dad and the bank well for over seven years. If Dad wanted to honor that faithfulness by putting Haman in the will, it's all right with me."

Studdard nodded. "So he never told you what he did for Mr. Warner?"

"No. I hope he treated him well."

"Let me explain it, Blake," said Laymon, "since I did the wording on it."

"Sure."

"Since you're the only heir up until this change, you were to inherit the bank and your father's house and belongings."

Blake nodded.

"Now your father has it in the will that as long as Mr. Warner is employed at the bank, he is to receive a bonus at the end of each calendar year equal to 5 percent of the bank's annual net income."

Blake smiled. "Haman deserves it. Maybe one of these days he'll find the right woman and get married. That annual bonus would build a comfortable nest egg for them."

Myron Studdard chuckled. "What is it with you bankers? You like being bachelors? Warner's older than you, isn't he?"

"Mmm-hmm. A little better than two

years. He'll turn thirty before I turn twenty-eight. Neither of us is a confirmed bachelor. We just haven't had the right women walk into our lives yet."

"Well . . . maybe one of these days."

Dan Laymon went on. "Blake, your dad put a stipulation in the will about Haman."

"Oh? Something more?"

"Yes. While you're alive, if circumstances of any kind render you incapable of directing the bank properly . . . so as to keep it from operating as it has in its twenty-year history, it will become the property of Haman Warner."

"Circumstances of any kind . . ." Blake said.

"Yes. Your father had the utmost confidence in Warner and felt that he would take the bank on to greater success as Sacramento grows."

"Not that he didn't have the same confidence in *you*, Blake," interjected Studdard. "You certainly have proven your capability to run the bank ever since he made you executive vice president and began acting only in an advisory capacity to you. He was simply making provision should something happen to you. You know, some sickness or accident that would render you unable to function as owner and president of the bank."

"Are you talking about something that

could cause my *mental* capacity to render me incapable of directing the bank properly? For instance, if I had to be put in an asylum for the rest of my life — is that it?"

"Yes," said Studdard. "And when you read the will, you'll see that even then there is to be five hundred thousand dollars provided from the estate to care for you the rest of your life."

"I'd say a half-million would pay an asylum quite well, even if I lived to be a hundred and twenty," Blake said with a chuckle.

Both attorneys laughed. Then Studdard said, "So you see, Blake, the only way the bank would go to Warner is if something happened to you mentally that would keep you from properly directing the bank. Even if you came down with some dread disease that made you bedridden, but you could direct the bank as stipulated, the bank would remain your property."

Laymon's mouth curved in a teasing grin. "That is . . . unless you were sent to prison, where you would absolutely be out of it! Then it would go to Warner.

"Seriously," Laymon continued, "your father made your death an exception as far as Warner is concerned as secondary heir. If you should die while properly running the bank, your entire estate, including the bank, would go to the beneficiaries you have named in your own will — at this point, your pastor and his wife."

"Right," Blake said. "If I die, the Clarkes will simply sell the bank, and the money that it brings will be theirs. Of course, should I find the right little gal one of these days and get married, she'll become my sole beneficiary."

"If I remember correctly," Studdard said, "you didn't even tell the Clarkes about being your beneficiaries at the time you set up the will. Do they know it now?"

"No. Be a nice surprise for them if I die. But if I get married, they won't have to feel a letdown when my wife becomes sole heir."

"Just like your dad," said Laymon. "Always thinking ahead."

"Blake," said Studdard, "we feel that Haman Warner should be given a copy of the will. It would prepare him to step into your shoes should some unfortunate incident occur. If you should die as things stand now, we would simply notify the Clarkes of their windfall, and they could go to Warner and say, 'Put the bank up for sale.' But for such an unexpected event to drop on Warner, who would no doubt want to keep the bank for himself, calls for preparedness. Would you mind if I give him a copy?"

"Of course not. I don't object in the least.

Haman has proven himself valuable to the bank, a faithful employee to Dad, and a loyal friend to me."

"Good. I'll have Veronica make a copy for you and one for Warner. As you know, we'll keep the original here in the safe. One of us will deliver Warner's copy to him tomorrow at the bank."

That evening, Bill and Evelyn Borah were behind the counter at the Blue Pacific Café when they saw Blake Barrett come in. The place was a beehive of activity.

"Hello, Blake," Evelyn called.

"Hi, Blake," said Bill.

"Howdy," Blake said, glancing around. "Business is good, eh?"

"Sure is, praise the Lord," Evelyn replied.

"That's why you need to build on, so you can add more tables, isn't it?"

Bill grinned. "You've got that right."

Blake patted the pocket of his suit coat. "I have your loan figures right here, Bill. When you get a little break, come on over. I see an empty table back in the corner. You'll find me there."

As Blake weaved his way among the tables, several people spoke to him, offering their condolences.

The Borahs' two daughters were the café's

waitresses. Blake picked up a menu and watched Susan and Lucy hurrying to deliver food on trays and take more food orders. Both girls were pretty. Blake had once begun to develop an interest in Susan, but before he could properly make a move, he learned she was engaged to Ralph Duncan, who was a member of the church.

Shortly thereafter, he found an interest sparked within him toward Lucy. He had decided to ask her for a date while at church one Sunday, but noticed her sitting with Cliff Winters and learned from one of Lucy's friends that very day that she and Cliff were going steady.

"Always a little late, aren't you, Blake?" he whispered to himself. "Now Susan's married and Lucy's engaged."

Just at that moment, Blake saw Lucy heading toward him, carrying a coffeepot in one hand and a cup in the other. She smiled warmly as she drew up. "Hello, Blake."

"Hi, Lucy."

She set the cup down and started pouring the steaming black liquid. "I only got to speak to you briefly at the funeral, Blake. I know you must feel additional sorrow that your father died without the Lord. I want you to know that Cliff and I took time to pray for you before we left the cemetery."

"I appreciate that. Yes, it's a burden about my dad, but praise the Lord, He's cushioned the pain with His own love. And I know it's because people like you and Cliff have prayed for me."

Susan came by, carrying a tray to a nearby table. "Hi, Blake."

"Hi, yourself," he responded with a smile.

"Okay," Lucy said, "what can I get you?"

"Chicken and dumplings, ma'am. Tell the cook not to heap it too high. My appetite isn't quite up to normal right now."

"You want two hot rolls or one?"

"One will do."

"All right. Chicken and dumplings with one hot roll coming up."

Susan had emptied the tray at the other table and stepped up to Blake's table. "You doing all right, Blake?"

"I'm fine."

"Ralph and I have been praying for you."

"Thank you. I appreciate that."

"Oh, hi, Pops," Susan said as her father appeared.

"Get to work, girl!" Bill said in a mock tone of anger. "There isn't time to stand around and chat with the good-looking male customers!"

"Why not?" she giggled. "Mother does!"

"You git!"

Susan laughed and threaded her way among the tables to the kitchen.

Bill pulled out a chair and sat down.

"Some girls you have there, Bill," Blake said, chuckling.

"That's for sure. Wouldn't trade 'em for a million worlds. How are you holding up?"

"I won't say it hasn't been rough, but the Lord has answered the prayers of my many precious friends and given me a great measure of strength and peace."

"That's wonderful. Evelyn and I have been praying for you ever since we learned your father had died."

Blake reached into his coat pocket and drew out an envelope. Handing it to Bill, he said, "See how those figures look."

As Bill pulled out the papers to look them over, Lucy arrived with Blake's order. She placed a heaping plate of chicken and dumplings in front of him, set a small plate with two large rolls next to it, and gave him a broad smile.

Blake frowned. "You were supposed to bring *one* roll and a small plate of chicken and dumplings."

"I know, but the cook figured your appetite might be better by now."

Blake chuckled. "Okay, Lucy. I'll eat as much as I can."

"Hope you like it. I'll be back with more coffee in a few minutes."

When Lucy was gone, Bill looked up from the papers and said, "That's a pretty good interest rate, Blake. And the terms are more than fair."

"We try to treat our customers right."

"Well, you sure are treating me right, I'll say that."

"Come by the bank tomorrow, and we'll put the money in your account."

"Will do," said Bill, stuffing the papers back in the envelope and handing it to Blake.

Blake looked at the food before him, and his appetite seemed to grow stronger as the aroma of hot rolls and chicken and dumplings teased his nostrils. Smiling at Bill, he said, "This looks pretty good."

"Better be," said his friend. "I'll let you pray, then we can talk a little."

Blake thanked the Lord for the food, then said, "You talk, Bill. I'm going to eat."

Bill Borah talked about the new building project and his plans for expansion. He would have to add to the kitchen, hire another cook, and hire a couple more waitresses.

Lucy returned and filled Blake's cup with fragrant coffee, and as he ate, Blake was surprised at how hungry he had suddenly become.

When Bill was in the middle of describing how he would rearrange the entire café, a young couple from the church stopped at the table. Mike and Rosie Brannan had moved to Sacramento from Placerville, California, about four months ago. They had been at the funeral that morning and now shared their sympathy with Blake once more. He thanked them, and they left.

In the next few minutes, more people stopped at Blake's table to offer their condolences.

Bill Borah smiled. "All of us in the church think the world of you, Blake. And the rest of the town does, too, including the women. I'm surprised that some fortunate female hasn't latched onto you and married you."

Blake laughed hollowly. "Tell you what, Bill. Like with your daughters, all the single Christian young women in Sacramento are either married, engaged to be married, or are dating some man steadily. There aren't any young women available."

"Well, my boy, the Lord's got just the right girl picked out for you. She'll come along one of these days."

"I'm patiently waiting for her to show up, Bill. I'm less than three years from thirty. It's time I got married, all right. I've prayed a lot about it, but I just have to wait on the Lord."

Bill stood up suddenly and said, "Evelyn's giving me the evil eye. I'm keeping you talking, and your food's getting cold. I'd better get back to the counter."

Blake went back to work on his meal. A few minutes later, he saw Pastor and Mrs. Clarke come in. Lucy greeted them and explained that all the tables were full; they would have to wait till one opened up.

Blake stood up and called, "Pastor! Come on over here. I'll share my table with you and Nora."

Pastor Clarke gave a little wave and allowed Nora to go ahead of him as they worked their way toward Blake's table.

Being the perfect gentleman, the sandy-headed man rose to his feet in honor of Nora Clarke. As the preacher seated his wife, Lucy came with coffee and cups. After pouring the coffee, she took their orders and headed for the kitchen.

"Go ahead and eat, Blake," Clarke said. "Your food will get cold if you wait for ours to come."

While Blake continued to eat his meal, the pastor said, "I want to thank you for what you did in the offering last Sunday."

Blake grinned. "I was glad to do it."

"I can't tell you what a blessing it is. Your gift will completely pay for the new Sunday school wing we've been needing so badly."

"The glory goes to God, Pastor," Blake said humbly. "If He hadn't blessed me financially, I wouldn't be able to do things like that. It makes me really happy to be able to help the church."

"Well, you know what the Bible says . . . when you sow bountifully, you reap bountifully. Nobody ever outgives the Lord."

"That's for sure. We use a teaspoon when we give. He comes back with a scoop shovel!"

Blake entered his apartment, lit a couple of lamps, and looked around, knowing he would soon leave it and move into his father's house, which he had inherited.

The apartment took up the complete second floor of a lovely Victorian home. He had filled it with rich mahogany furniture upholstered in jewel-toned fabrics. The same fabric was used for the window coverings. The glowing lamps illuminated the patina of the ornately carved woodwork.

Blake had collected several pieces of beautiful artwork. Delightful paintings were displayed on the walls, and exquisite sculptures adorned tables and shelves.

His housekeeper kept everything in mint condition, and Blake always enjoyed coming home to this peaceful setting at the end of a long day. Before he moved into his father's house, he would have it done over to resemble his apartment.

Weary from the strain of the day, he decided to go to bed early. As soon as he slipped between the sheets, he began praying.

"Lord, please help me to be an effective witness at the bank. Let me use Dad's death as an infidel to help the employees see they need to be ready to die. I'm concerned especially for Haman. Please work in his heart. Help me to be a shining light for You to the community, too, Lord.

"And, Lord . . . I . . . I sure am lonely. You provided Adam a wife because You said, 'It is not good that the man should be alone; I will make him an helpmeet for him.' Well, it isn't good for *this* man to be alone, either. I only want the woman You've chosen for me. You haven't seen fit to bring her into my life yet, but I'm asking You to do so soon.

"Lord, I thank You for the way You've guided my life ever since I was saved as a boy. And I'm thanking You in advance that You will answer my prayer for a wife."

7

By midmorning the next day, Blake Barrett had moved his personal items into his father's office at the bank. Bradley Barrett's office was large and well furnished. He had also kept a desk just outside the office in an area where Blake and Haman had their desks, plus desks for a secretary and a secretary-receptionist. The area was surrounded by a waist-high railing and was entered by three separate gates.

Once Blake had arranged things in the inner office to suit himself, he did the same with the desk in the enclosed area. While he was moving the last of his things, he saw Bill Borah enter the lobby and he reentered the large office to pick up Borah's loan papers, which he'd left on the desk there.

Borah spoke to a couple of customers who were waiting in line at the tellers' cages, then approached the receptionist, Sandy Benton.

"Good morning, Sandy. Mr. Barrett is expecting me to come in today and close on my loan."

"Yes, Mr. Borah, he mentioned that to me

earlier." Sandy looked over her shoulder. "He was at his outer desk just a moment ago. Come on through the gate. I'll tell him you're here."

Sandy had just risen from her chair when Blake came out of his office carrying a folder. "I saw him coming, Sandy. Hi, Bill. Come on over here and sit down."

As Borah passed secretary Hortense Reed's desk, she looked up from a stack of papers and smiled shyly. "Hello, Mr. Borah. Nice day."

"Sure is," he said.

Haman Warner had a customer at his desk and only nodded at Bill, then put his attention back on the customer.

Within twenty minutes, Borah was shaking hands with Blake, thanking him for the loan.

As he was leaving, he held open the gate for a well-dressed young couple who had just been invited by Sandy to come in and sit down in front of her desk.

Blake was placing papers back in Bill Borah's file folder when he heard the man say, "I'm Ben Roper, ma'am. This is my wife, Minnie. We just got married, and we want to open a checking account."

"I'll be happy to take care of that for you, folks," Sandy said.

Blake slid some papers to the center of his desk and began going over them while picking up bits and pieces from Sandy's conversation with the young couple.

Roper pulled out a wad of currency. "I've been working the gold mines in the Sierras, ma'am. I didn't have a checking account. Did everything by cash. But now that I've married Minnie and am going to settle here in Sacramento, I figured it was time to put my money in the bank."

"Smart move," Sandy said. "Did you two meet in the mountains?"

"Well, not exactly," Minnie said. "We met by mail first, then after a few months of corresponding, I came out here from Baltimore, Maryland, to be Ben's mail order bride."

Blake's head came up with a start.

"Oh! I think that's wonderful!" Sandy said. "How romantic!"

Sandy asked all the necessary questions to process the Ropers' account and then placed signature cards before them and held out pen and ink. The Ropers signed the cards and Sandy blotted them, then picked up the thick wad of currency and said, "How much do we have here, Mr. Roper?"

"Eight thousand dollars, ma'am."

Sandy nodded, filled out a deposit slip, then rose from her desk and said, "I'll take this to one of the tellers and be back with your receipt."

Blake left his desk and approached the young couple. "Hello," he said, extending his hand to Ben. "My name is Blake Barrett. I'm president of the bank."

The Ropers looked a little shocked to see such a young man bear the title of president. Ben Roper stood up and shook hands with him. Minnie offered her hand, and Blake gave it a gentle shake, then said, "I couldn't help overhearing what you told Mrs. Benton, ma'am. You came from Baltimore as this gentleman's mail order bride?"

Minnie looked up at Ben and smiled. "Yes," she said, sighing with contentment. "And I'm sure glad I did."

"Not half as glad as I am," Ben said, reaching for her hand.

"I've heard, of course, of young women coming from eastern cities to become mail order brides," Blake said, "but I've never met one."

Minnie smiled. "Well, Mr. Barrett, you'll never be able to say that again, will you?"

Blake chuckled. "You're right about that!"

"Isn't she something?" Ben said, his gaze roaming over Minnie's features.

Blake grinned, but didn't reply. "So how did you find her, Mr. Roper? Newspaper ad?"

"That's right. *Baltimore Globe.*"

"Did you put ads in several newspapers?"

"I guess about a dozen of them. All in newspapers in large cities."

"I hope you don't mind my asking these questions."

"We don't mind at all," Ben replied.

Blake grinned again. "So did you get a lot of responses?"

"Sure did. Must've had some fifteen or sixteen women write me."

"How did you happen to pick this young lady?"

"Process of elimination. I only wrote back to four women. The others didn't interest me."

"But how did you eliminate the other three and finally narrow it down to Mrs. Roper?"

"Well, the four women and I exchanged photographs and wrote about our likes and dislikes . . . that kind of thing. One of them didn't write me back. Maybe she decided I was too ugly."

"Oh, Ben," Minnie said, giving his hand a squeeze. "That couldn't have been it! Not as good-looking as you are!"

Roper put a hand under her graceful chin. "You just keep thinking that, honey." Then to Barrett: "The three women and I corresponded for about two months, and soon I knew it was Minnie."

"You see, Mr. Barrett," Minnie said, "at the same time I was writing to Ben, I was also corresponding with two other men whose ads I had answered. How do I put it . . . there was something about Ben's personality that pulled me toward him. You can tell a lot about a man when you're getting long letters from him two or three times a week."

Ben's eyes held an expression of pure adoration as he reluctantly turned from looking at Minnie and said to Blake, "So by the time we'd been writing about three months, we both knew we had the same interests and goals in life. We dropped the others and seriously pursued each other. We —"

Sandy Benton came through the gate near her desk. "Oh, sorry," she said. "I didn't mean to interrupt."

"It's all right, ma'am," Ben Roper said. "As I was about to say, Mr. Barrett, Minnie and I corresponded another month or so and decided it was time to get together. I sent her the money, and a few days after she received it, I met her at the Sacramento depot. She lived in a boardinghouse in Placerville while I continued my gold mining. After about six weeks of getting acquainted in person, we tied the knot. And boy, am I glad we did!"

Minnie giggled.

Sandy raised an eyebrow at Barrett and said, "Thinking of getting yourself a mail order bride, boss?"

The surprise on both the Ropers' faces was comical.

"I figured you were married, Mr. Barrett," Ben said.

"Me, too," said Minnie. "Fine-looking man like you."

Blake blushed.

Sandy said in a joking tone, "Mr. Barrett has the ideal young lady pictured in his mind, folks, but I'm afraid she doesn't really exist."

"Oh, yes, she does," Blake responded. "She's somewhere in this world, and one of these days she'll come walking into my life. And I'll know her when I see her."

Sandy handed Ben Roper his receipt and said, "Hope you folks enjoy banking here. Oh!" She opened a desk drawer. "And here are your checks."

Ben Roper thanked her. As he and Minnie were about to leave, he said, "Mr. Barrett, maybe your ideal young lady is in the East somewhere, just waiting for an ad from a bank president who needs a wife. You ought to give it a try."

Blake grinned. "Maybe I will."

"Let us know if you do . . . and how it turns out."

Blake laughed. "Sure!"

When they had gone out the door, Sandy wiggled her eyebrows and said, "Mail order bride for Mr. Blake Barrett, eh?"

Blake gave her a mock scowl. "Mind your own business, woman!"

Sandy giggled as he walked back to his desk and picked up Bill Borah's file, then carried it to Hortense. "Put this away, please, would you?"

Hortense nodded with a smile.

Haman's customer had left before the Ropers, and Haman had heard the last part of Blake's conversation. He smiled at Blake and said, "Maybe that's what you and I both should do, B— Oops! I'm not supposed to call you by your first name anymore, now that you're the man in the big office."

Blake put his hands on top of Haman's desk, leaned down, and whispered, "You can still call me Blake, except in the presence of customers. The employees are so used to hearing us call each other by our first names, they'd think we were at odds if we did anything else."

"You're right about that," said Haman, also keeping his voice low. "We certainly wouldn't want the employees to think we weren't getting along, would we? Not when we've been such good friends ever since you graduated from college and came to work here."

"That's for sure. Mr. Hayworth was at your desk for quite a while. Did you get the information we need?"

"Sure did. His corporation wants to build a new office building right here in downtown Sacramento. They're trying to buy the two vacant lots between the other bank and Martin's Clothing Store."

Blake pursed his lips. "That would be a good spot for them. He say how the purchase of the lots looks?"

"Yes. Says it's looking pretty good. And —"

"Mr. Barrett . . ." came Sandy Benton's voice.

Blake turned and saw attorney Dan Laymon standing by her desk, a briefcase in his hand.

"Mr. Laymon is here to see Mr. Warner," she said. "He says you know what it's about."

"Yes, Sandy. Come on over, Dan."

Haman's brow furrowed. "He wants to see me?"

"That's right," Laymon said as he passed through the gate.

"I hope somebody's not suing me, or something like that," Warner said with a chuckle.

"Ah . . . no. What I have is good news. Very good news."

"Oh. Well, I'm always happy to hear good news!"

To Blake, the lawyer said, "Could we use your father's office? I mean, *your* office, now, I imagine."

"Yes," Blake said. "It's my office now, but since I know what this is about, and I understand the privacy you need, you're welcome to use it."

Haman looked at Blake quizzically. "You know what this is about?"

"Mm-hmm."

Haman shrugged, looked at the attorney, and said, "Well, if the boss knows about it, and he's still willing to let us use his new office, it really must be good."

"You gentlemen have a nice time," Blake said. "I've got paperwork up to my ears on the desk right here. Haman, we'll get together later on John Hayworth and the Ridgely Corporation."

"All right."

Laymon and Warner entered the large office and closed the door.

When Haman had taken his seat, he looked expectantly at Dan Laymon and waited for him to speak.

Laymon set his briefcase on the edge of the desk and took out a file folder. From it he produced two official-looking sets of papers. He handed Warner one set of the papers and said, "This is a copy of Mr. Bradley Barrett's last will and testament."

Warner stared at the lawyer blankly. "Yes?"

"Mr. Barrett had our firm make some changes in his will shortly before he died. There was something he wanted to do for you, and I'm here to show it to you."

Haman's blood started to race.

"Mr. Warner, Bradley Barrett thought a lot of you, and he's done something that is quite rare for a man to do for an employee."

Haman blinked. "Oh?"

"Would you please turn to the second page . . ."

Some seven or eight minutes later, attorney Dan Laymon emerged from the inner office and came to Blake's desk.

Blake looked up. "Was he surprised?"

"Very much so. He would like for you to come into the office."

"Sure," Blake said, rising from his chair.

Laymon had his briefcase in hand. "My part is done; I'll see you later."

"All right. And thanks."

Haman Warner was on his feet, standing in the center of the office, when Blake entered and closed the door. He was dabbing his cheeks with a handkerchief as he said, "Blake,

I never dreamed your dad would do a thing like this for me. He was always good to me, of course, and paid me well, as you know, but this —" He choked up, then drew in a deep breath and said, "This is wonderful. The 5 percent bonus is terribly generous. I don't deserve such magnanimous consideration."

"Dad figured you do. And I'm in total agreement."

"That means more to me than I can ever tell you, Blake. But 5 percent of the net annual income is that much less you will get."

Blake cuffed him playfully. "Hey, my friend, you are a great part of what makes this bank successful. I'm glad to see you get the bonus."

"Rest assured I will always *try* to earn it."

Blake laid a hand on his shoulder. "Dad saw you work hard the seven plus years you've been here. He knew your heart was in it, and he wanted you to be rewarded for your faithful service. And I certainly do, too."

Haman's lips quivered. "Thank you."

"Now what you have to do, my good friend, is find yourself a wife so she can enjoy your financial gain with you."

Haman chuckled. "Yeah. One of those mail order brides, huh?"

"That Ben Roper sure did all right for himself by mail."

A grin spread over Haman's not-so-handsome face. "Mm-hm-m-m-m! If I could get one that pretty, I'd be one happy ex-bachelor, I'm telling you!"

Blake chuckled. "There's only one thing in this life that would make you happier."

Haman's grin faded. "Yeah. I know. Get saved."

"Right."

"You know I don't want to offend you, Blake. But as I've told you probably fifty times, I'm like your dad when it comes to this religious stuff. I just don't need it."

"And as I've told you probably fifty times, opening your heart to the Lord Jesus and letting Him save your hell-bound soul is not religion. It's *salvation*. Dad died without Jesus, Haman. I don't want to see you do the same thing."

"Well, I'm just a few years younger than your dad. In fact I'm only two years older than you, Blake. I've got plenty of time to think about dying."

"The only problem with that kind of thinking is that lots of people who believe they've got till midnight to live, die at eleven-thirty. The greatest need you have is Jesus Christ. You die without Him, and you lose everything . . . even your own soul."

Haman changed the subject. "Blake, I

know you're having a headstone made for your dad's grave."

"Yes . . ."

"Could I at least show my respect for him, and my appreciation, by paying for half of the stone?"

Blake peered into Haman's eyes. "You really want to do this?"

"Yes, I do."

"Well, because Dad thought so much of you, I'll let you share half the cost as you ask."

A smile curved Warner's thick lips. "Thanks. Please let me know when you need the money."

"All right."

A serious look came over Haman's features.

"Yes?" said Blake.

"I just want to say that I appreciate your friendship."

"And I yours."

"I . . . I hope you and I can develop the same kind of friendship I had with Bradley Barrett."

"Me, too," said Blake.

That evening, when Haman Warner entered his apartment, he sat down at his small kitchen table to look over Bradley Barrett's will. At the office Dan Laymon had only discussed the 5 percent bonus with him, then told him to read the rest of the will for himself, since there was more in there that concerned him.

Haman had eaten a rich meal at the Blue Pacific Café, and he belched as he took the will out of the envelope Laymon had provided. Before he started reading, he chuckled, saying out loud, "I've got that stupid Blake Barrett eating right out of my hand! He's as muddle-brained as his old man. If Blake only knew . . . if the old man had only known of the money I've stolen from the bank in the past seven years!" He laughed heartily.

"Yes, sir! Good ol' Haman Warner bilked Brad Barrett of thousands! And not even once was he suspected when the losses were discovered! Clever man, Haman! Too smart for the old boy and the rest of the stupid people at the Pacific Bank and Trust Company!"

He threw back his head and snorted. "Yes, sir, Brad ol' boy! All that money I took from you is sitting safely in a San Francisco bank under my assumed name, and nobody's the wiser! And now —" He laughed, belching again. "And now, clever Haman Warner is getting 5 percent of the profits! Not bad! Not bad at all! And just for being so loyal to you, Brad!"

He laughed so hard he cried, this time wiping genuine tears unlike those he'd shed in Blake's office.

When he gained control of his mirth, he gleefully muttered, "Everybody at the bank thinks Haman Warner is such a nice guy! Well, they'll never know any different, either! I'm too smart to get caught! Blake, ol' pal, I'm gonna steal money right from under your nose, just like I did with your old man!"

He picked up the will and began scanning the document. When he came to the stipulation that the bank would become his property should Blake become incapable of directing the bank properly, his mouth dropped open. He read it again. And again.

A wicked smirk worked its way across his lips. "Well, whattaya know! If Blake dies, whoever he's left his estate to will get it all. But! If he's rendered incapable of directing the bank properly . . . well, now, this calls for a drink!"

He went to his liquor cabinet, poured himself a big shot of whiskey, and downed half of it in a gulp. "Except death, eh? All right. What if Papa Barrett's little 'born-again Christian' boy was behind bars for a good long stretch? Like . . . ah . . . *ten to fifteen years* for stealing depositors' money? There's no way he could properly direct the bank from a prison cell!"

It would take some time to work out a foolproof plan, but before long he was going to own the Pacific Bank and Trust Company and have the riches he'd always dreamed about.

For the next several days, Blake Barrett thought about Ben and Minnie Roper and how they had found each other. Ben's words came back over and over again: *"Maybe your ideal young lady is back East somewhere, just waiting for an ad from a bank president who needs a wife."*

Blake wrestled with the decision for a few days, finally deciding it wasn't for him. Certainly the Lord wouldn't have him put advertisements in eastern newspapers in order to find a wife. He tried to dismiss the idea from his mind, but it kept coming back. Maybe the Lord was trying to tell him something after all.

Pastor Duane Clarke was in his office at the church preparing a sermon when he heard a light knock on the door.

"Well, Blake! What brings you here this time of day? Aren't you supposed to be at the bank loaning money and that kind of thing? Come in."

"You're right, Pastor. That's what I'm usually doing, five days a week. But since I'm the boss now, I can take off whenever I want. I need to talk to you. Do you have time now?"

"Of course. A pastor's time is for caring for his sheep." He closed the door behind Blake and motioned to one of the two chairs that stood in front of his desk.

When both were seated, Clarke said, "Now, what can I do for you?"

"I need some guidance about something."

"All right."

"It's about the fact that I'm going on twenty-eight years of age, and I'm not even engaged, much less married. I'm lonely as a bachelor, and since the Lord said it wasn't good that Adam be alone, and He made Eve for him, I feel that it's not good for me to be alone, either."

"Makes sense. I sure wouldn't want to be without my sweet Nora."

"My problem is, I wouldn't want to marry someone who isn't genuinely saved and living to please the Lord."

"No, you shouldn't be unequally yoked. God makes it clear in His Word that He wouldn't want you to."

"I know that, and I only want to please Him. It's just that —"

"There are no available young women in this town who meet the qualifications?"

"Yes, sir."

"Blake, the Lord has already chosen the right young woman for you. In Psalm 37:23, He tells us the steps of a good man are ordered by *Him*. If you'll let Him order your steps, He will guide you to the woman He's chosen for you."

Blake nodded. "All right. Then this chosen lady must also be looking for the mate the Lord would have for her."

"No doubt."

"So, would the Lord put it on my heart to make a move in what seems to be the right direction — a direction that would result in bringing the two of us together?"

"He might do that very thing." Clarke's brow furrowed. "Have you got some move in mind?"

Blake scratched his head. "Well-l-l —"

"Something you're not sure you should do?"

"Right. That's why I'm here. I need you to tell me what you think of what I've got in mind."

The pastor smiled and eased back in his chair. "I'm listening."

Blake cleared his throat. "How about if I put ads in eastern newspapers for a mail order bride? Of course, I would specify that the lady must be a born-again Christian and ask her to tell me how she got born again. If I was satisfied with her answer, I would then lay down some other specifications, such as basic doctrinal beliefs, and living all out for the Lord."

Without hesitation, Clarke said, "If you do it like that and pray hard while you're doing your corresponding, the Lord may very well bring the two of you together in that way. May I ask what made you think of going the mail order bride route?"

Blake told him about the Ropers and that they seemed so happy. Ever since that day, he had not been able to get the mail order bride idea out of his mind.

"Pastor, I sort of figured you'd tell me right away not to pursue this course. But you seem to look at it favorably."

"Number one, I look at it favorably because of the specifications you already plan to put in your ads. Number two, I've seen it work."

"You know some Christians who were brought together through the mail order bride system?" Blake said, eyes wide.

"Yes, and so do you. They're members of our church."

"Who?"

"You know Mike and Rosie Brannan, don't you?"

"Sure."

"Well, when they came to talk to me about joining the church, they told me they'd found

153

each other — as Christians — through an ad."

Blake smiled broadly. "Whattaya know about that! Mike and Rosie. Since the Lord gave Mike a wife that way, He sure can do it for me!"

"I don't know why not," said the preacher. "Just be sure to keep those strict specifications in your ads, and pray a lot. You want this kept confidential, don't you?"

"Ah . . . yes, sir."

"Okay. I'll be praying for the Lord's perfect guidance for you."

After they prayed together, Blake left the office and walked back to the bank.

Two days later, he sent advertisements to six eastern newspapers, stating his firm requirements. In the ads he said that he was a banker, without revealing that he was the owner and president of Pacific Bank and Trust Company. Wealth, he told himself, should not be a factor in something as important as this.

8

At the Forrest home in Boston, Linda got up early and dressed each morning and kept herself occupied. She helped her mother with the many chores around the house, and when her mother went shopping she even did jobs that were ordinarily Adrienne's.

The peace God had given Linda was real, and her parents were delighted that she no longer spoke of hating her sister or Lewis Carter. In fact, she seldom even mentioned their names. At the same time, she still could not bring herself to go out among people, which resulted in a dismal existence for her.

Although she was helpful around the house, she did her work almost by rote, as if she were in a daze. She ate little, and her dresses were beginning to hang loosely on her. No prompting from her parents could give her a better appetite.

Once her chores were done, she either went to her room or into the shaded backyard. Only recently had she ventured out the door. In either place, she sat in quiet solitude, thinking and praying for hours on end.

Nolan and Adrienne were deeply concerned about Linda's obvious lack of interest in life, and they continually asked God for an end to this difficult time for her, and that He would give her total victory to be the girl she had once been.

Pastor and Mrs. Stanford came to the house at least twice a week to counsel Linda. Joline Jensen Simons was the only person Linda would allow to come any time she wished. Hence, Joline came almost daily. As time passed, Linda also allowed her two good friends Betty Madison and Shirley Wells to visit her. Betty and Shirley began coming to the house two and three times a week. Shirley was now engaged to a young man in the church.

One Saturday evening, the Stanfords showed up on the Forrests' doorstep just after supper. Nolan led them to the parlor. "We saw you coming," he said. "Adrienne has gone to Linda's room to get her."

"How's she doing?" Pastor Stanford asked.

"About the same. She reads her Bible two or three times a day and spends a lot of time in prayer. She's staying close to the Lord. It's just . . . we can't get her to go outside that front door."

"The Lord has the answer for this, Nolan," Doris said. "We've simply got to keep praying, and make sure she knows we love her and are here for her when she needs us."

Adrienne appeared, saying that Linda would be along in a moment.

When Linda appeared in the doorway, Doris went to her and wrapped her arms around the girl, saying, "I sure do love you."

Linda squeezed her tight. "I sure do love you, too." Then she looked over Doris's shoulder, and said, "That goes for you, too, Pastor."

The preacher smiled. "Your pastor loves Miss Linda, too."

When everyone was seated, Lloyd Stanford said, "Linda, Doris and I came by this evening especially because tomorrow's Sunday. We'd sure love to see you come back to church. How about tomorrow?"

Linda's face lost color as she replied, "Pastor, I . . . I wish I could do as you ask. But I just can't. Please try to understand. I just can't. The shame and embarrassment of being stood up at the church is still very much with me. I really appreciate your caring enough to come and give me a special invitation. But when I think of facing people who know what happened, I turn cold all over."

"It's only recently that she's gone outside," Adrienne hastened to add.

"And only to the backyard," Linda said.

"And even then, when I've seen the neighbors walk down the alley, they give me that stare."

" 'That stare,' dear?" Doris said.

"Yes, as if they're thinking, There's Linda Forrest. You've heard about her, I'm sure! Got herself all gussied up to get married, and her groom ran off with her sister! Left her standing right there at the church, wondering where the groom and the maid of honor had gone!"

Adrienne swung her gaze to the pastor and his wife. "I've told her this is just her imagination, but she insists I'm wrong."

Linda's face twisted. "Mom, by now everybody in Boston has heard about the girl who got left at the altar. Certainly our neighbors know about it. And you haven't seen their eyes. I'm telling you, they stare at me as if I was a freak or something."

"Linda," said the pastor, "I know this awful thing has gone deep into your mind. But the Lord can give you victory over it like He's given you victory over the hatred you first felt toward Janet and Lewis. If you would just come to church and be among those who love you, and hear some Bible preaching and teaching, it would get you over it more quickly."

"But Pastor, I can't make myself go out among people who know about me. Please believe me. I'm not trying to be difficult. This is something the Lord alone can change. At this point, He hasn't seen fit to do it."

Doris looked at Linda with compassion. "Your parents are sticking with you on this, honey, and so are Pastor and I. It's good that you also have Joline, Betty, and Shirley. We'll keep praying, and we'll keep coming to see you. The Lord will do His work in your heart and mind when it's His time. Don't forget . . . we love you."

A few days later, Linda was sitting in a rocking chair on the back porch, reading her Bible. She heard voices in the alley, and presently two elderly women appeared, walking along slowly.

Linda recognized them. They were widows who lived together in the same block, at the other end of the street. They were speaking in low tones, and Linda couldn't make out what they were saying. When they glanced her direction, she closed her eyes and whispered, "Please, Lord, help me."

When she opened her eyes, they were out of sight.

"There you are!" a cheerful feminine voice greeted her.

Linda turned, and a smile broke across her face. "Hi, Joline."

159

"Hi, yourself." Joline sat down in another rocker beside Linda. "How you doing?"

"Okay, I guess." Linda closed her Bible and held it on her lap.

"One of these days you'll go out in the front yard, sweetie," Joline said with assurance. She began talking about the church services over the last few weeks, the good preaching the pastor was doing, and what was going on in some people's lives at church. She named at least a dozen people who had mentioned Linda of late, saying they really missed her.

"You're so sweet to tell me, Joline," Linda said. "I'm glad they miss me at church."

"The door is always open," Joline said softly.

"I know. I just can't go through it."

"Honey, the Lord gave you the grace to get over the hatred toward Lewis and Janet you were harboring, didn't He?"

"Yes."

"Don't you think that same grace can take you through the church door to see all the people who love you?"

Linda thought on it a few seconds. "Yes. But He hasn't given it to me yet."

"He will."

"I'm waiting."

Joline nodded, then closed her eyes.

Linda squinted at her. "Is something wrong, Joline?"

"I can't really call it wrong, honey. But right now I'm facing something quite difficult."

"What do you mean?"

"Well . . . I've got something to tell you that isn't pleasant."

Linda straightened in the rocker. "What is it?"

Tears misted Joline's eyes. "Frank has been offered an excellent job in Pittsburgh. We've prayed about it for almost two weeks now. Frank asked me not to say anything to anybody until we made our decision about it. We both got real peace yesterday, and we feel the Lord is in it. It's a tremendous opportunity for him. He wired them this morning that he would take the job."

Linda's face looked desolate. "H-how soon will you be leaving?"

"They want him there day after tomorrow. So we're leaving on the first train in the morning. Six o'clock."

Tears flooded Linda's eyes as she rose from the chair and laid her Bible on the seat. Joline stood up and wrapped her arms around her friend, and they wept.

When their crying had diminished to sniffling, Linda said, "Honey, I'm glad for Frank

— the job and all — but I'm going to miss my best friend something terrible!"

"I'm going to miss my best friend something terrible, too! That's why I said I had to do something unpleasant. I didn't want to upset you!"

Adrienne came out the back door with a worried look on her face.

"Joline and Frank are moving to Pittsburgh, Mom," Linda said. "They're leaving tomorrow morning."

"Pittsburgh! Why are you going to Pittsburgh?"

Joline told Linda's mother about the job and that she and Frank could see God's hand in it. After telling Joline she would miss her, Adrienne said, "I'll let you two best friends have your time together. Come and let me hug you good-bye on your way out, won't you, Joline?"

"I sure will."

When Adrienne had gone back inside the house, Joline said, "I have to go in a few minutes, but I want to repeat to you what I've said before. The Lord has a special man all picked out for you. Right now, it seems like nothing's happening. But honey, God's hand is working even though you can't see it. He loves you, and He's going to give you that special man at just the right time."

Once again, Linda and Joline hugged each other tightly.

"Now, you write to me, Linda, especially when that man walks into your life, all right?"

"Yes."

"Promise?"

"I promise."

For the next two days Linda cried a lot over Joline's move to Pittsburgh. But finally she adjusted to the fact that life was full of change, and this was just one of those changes. She was happy that Frank had landed such a good job.

Joline had been gone a little over a week when Adrienne went shopping with Frances Diamond and Betty Madison appeared at the Forrests' front door.

This was the first time Betty had visited without Shirley Wells. Linda looked past her and said, "Where's Shirley?"

"Oh, she and her fiancé are out buying things for their wedding. I've been wanting to see you alone, so I took advantage of this moment to come by."

"Well, trot your little self in here. I could use some company."

"You miss Joline, I'm sure."

"Yes. But I'm so glad I still have you."

Betty looked down for a moment and then

said, "Where would you like to talk?"

"How about the parlor?"

When they were seated facing each other, Linda studied her friend's face and waited for her to speak.

"Linda," Betty began, putting her hands together and interlacing her fingers, "there've been some pretty big things happening in my life that I haven't told you about on these visits."

"Oh?"

"It isn't that I wanted to keep something from you, I just wanted to be sure that what was appearing to be God's will for my life was really so before I told you about it. It's the biggest thing that's happened to me, other than being saved."

"Makes sense," Linda said, giving her a slight smile. "Better to have something that important settled before telling your friends about it. So, now that you know it's the Lord's will, let's hear it."

Betty bounced on the couch to adjust her position. "Well . . . have you ever heard about the mail order brides who are going west?"

"Why, yes. I've heard about the mail order bride concept. Started back in the gold rush days, didn't it? About 1848 or 1849?"

"Yes."

"I really don't know much about it."

"Well, I read recently that out west there are about two hundred single men for every single woman. And for the most part, the only women who go out there are those who go with their husbands. So, in order for those single men who are already out there to come up with a wife, they have to get them from here in the East. And that's what they're doing."

Linda nodded. "Mm-hmm. Advertising in eastern newspapers for women to come out there and marry them. I remember reading something about it not too long ago. Must have been in a magazine. I hardly ever read a newspaper. We don't have them around the house."

Betty nodded. "Linda, let me tell you what I did. You know the Lord hasn't yet brought the right man into my life for marrying."

"Not up till now, at least."

"Well . . . I answered an ad in the *Boston Herald* several weeks ago."

Linda's jaw dropped. "You what? You answered an ad about being a mail order bride?"

Betty giggled. "Yes! The ad was written by a born-again man in New Mexico who was looking for a born-again woman to come and be his wife."

"Betty! You didn't! You're kidding me!"

"No kidding about it, honey. I did. And

165

yours truly is going to New Mexico!"

"Betty! You're going to marry a man you've never met? Just because he says he's a Christian?"

"It's not exactly like that, Linda. Let me explain it. His name's Clint Jackson. He's twenty-six . . . four years older than me."

"Go on."

"His letter came real soon after mine had gotten to him. I anticipated that he would want to hear my Christian testimony and what church I go to. So I put it in the letter, telling him I've been praying for the Lord to send the man of His choice into my life. I asked for his testimony of salvation and what kind of church he attends."

"And what did he say?" Linda asked, suddenly intrigued.

"In his letter, he told me how glad he was that I asked him for his testimony. He attends a Bible-believing church just like ours. The testimony of how he got saved rings as true as can be. His father was an officer, and he was raised in army forts. A chaplain at one of the forts led him to the Lord."

"So what does he do out there in New Mexico?"

"He's foreman on a huge cattle ranch. Being raised around horses in the forts, he grew to love them. He worked on a cattle ranch in

Texas for a couple of years, he said, before going to this one in New Mexico."

"I see."

"Linda, we've exchanged exactly ten letters now, and I'm satisfied that Clint is a genuine, dedicated Christian, and a hardworking man. He told me about several cowhands on the ranch he has led to the Lord."

"That sounds good, Betty. Just where in New Mexico is this ranch?"

"Near Santa Fe. Oh, Linda, up until now the Lord hasn't seen fit to bring the right man into my life, but after much prayer, I'm convinced it's God's will that I marry Clint."

Linda frowned. "But Betty, what if you should get out there and find you've made a mistake? I mean, you're human. And we can sometimes misjudge what we think is the Lord's will. In a case like that, you could seriously mess up your life. You can't really get to know a man by writing letters. You have to meet him in person."

Betty smiled as she nodded her head in agreement. "Clint and I discussed this in our letters. We've agreed to have a reasonable amount of time for a courtship. We've left it open that if during that time either of us doesn't have peace in our hearts about the marriage, we won't go through with it."

"Oh. Well, I'm glad to hear that. From

what little I've known about this mail order bride business, if a lady tells a man she's coming and he sends the money to get her there, the deal is on, no matter what."

"That's the way it is with lots of them, but Christians wouldn't do it that way."

"Do you have a photograph of Clint?"

"I thought you'd never ask." Betty reached for her purse and took out a small photograph of Clint Jackson from an inside pocket and handed it to Linda. "Here. Take a look."

Linda saw a tall, slender man in a ten-gallon hat, standing beside his horse. She could tell by the look in his eyes and the smile on his face that he was an amiable person. "Nice-looking man," she commented, handing the picture back to Betty. "He has a warm smile."

"I think he's got a warm heart, too," Betty said, looking at the picture wistfully, then placing it back in her purse. "Well, Linda, I must be going."

"How soon are you leaving for New Mexico?"

"Day after tomorrow. I received the train fare from Clint yesterday. I don't think I'll have time to come back and see you again. So this will have to be good-bye."

A spark of interest had been kindled in

Linda's mind about Betty's mail order bride story. She said nothing to her parents that evening about Betty's departure to New Mexico. It would keep for a day or two till she could think about it.

That night, as Linda lay in bed with silver moonlight coming through the windows, she pondered Betty's situation. She seemed so happy. Linda hoped it would work out as planned.

As she pondered it further, Linda told herself that if the same thing could happen to her, it would be the way to get out of Boston and escape the shame, embarrassment, and stares of the people who knew about her wedding fiasco. Though she doubted she could ever fall in love with a man the way she had with Lewis, still she could feel affection for him and be a good wife. Her "time to love" might never really come. Still, it would be better than staying in Boston as a recluse.

But how many genuine Christian men would use the mail order bride system?

Linda thought about it long into the night. Finally she came to a decision and fell into the first dreamless sleep she had experienced since that heartwrenching day on the ninth of June.

Linda was up early the next morning and

took renewed interest in her personal appearance. She spent more time on her hair than usual. After trying on and laying aside several dresses that no longer fit, she found one that would do.

There was a spring in her step as she made her way to the kitchen to start breakfast. She built a fire in the cookstove and had bacon and eggs frying when Adrienne entered the kitchen to find her stirring pancake batter in a bowl.

Linda looked up with a bright smile on her face and said, "Good morning, most wonderful mother in all the world! Sleep well?"

Adrienne saw the gleam in her daughter's eyes and took note of the work she had put into her hair. "Why . . . yes. Yes, I slept well, honey. I didn't expect you to start breakfast ahead of me. We always do that together."

"Well, I thought it would be nice today if I got up a few minutes earlier than usual and saved you a little work."

Adrienne was delighted to see the change in Linda. She hadn't smiled like that or had a lilt in her voice since —

"Looks like breakfast is on a bit early this morning," Nolan said as he entered the kitchen.

"Good morning, most wonderful daddy in

all the world!" Linda said, flashing him a pearly white smile. "Did you sleep well?"

Nolan noticed the change in Linda's appearance and looked at Adrienne, who raised her eyebrows as if to say, *I don't know what brought this on, but I sure like it!*

Nolan hugged his daughter. "Yes, honey, I slept like a log."

Linda surprised her parents again by giggling as she said, "And just how does a log sleep, O Father of mine?"

Nolan chuckled. "Well, it doesn't. That's just a figure of speech."

Linda poked a playful finger at his nose and said, "Well, that figure of speech doesn't tell me a thing, then, does it? Maybe if a log could sleep, it still wouldn't sleep very well."

Nolan flicked a glance at Adrienne and winked, then wrapped Linda in a tight hug. "You know what I do to smart-aleck, mouthy females?" he said.

Linda giggled. "No. What?"

"I hug 'em till they can't breathe!" As he spoke, he squeezed her until she ejected a little grunt and squeaked, "Okay! Okay! I give up! I'll be good!"

As the three of them sat down to the table and joined hands, they bowed their heads and closed their eyes. Nolan thanked the Lord for His blessings on them, for Calvary, and for the food they were about to eat. Before he closed, he said, "And Father, it's so good to see our little girl with a smile and a happy glint in her eyes. Thank You! We praise You in Jesus' name, amen."

Adrienne was brushing tears away as Linda and Nolan raised their heads. She squeezed her daughter's hand and said, "Has the Lord done something special, honey? Something to cheer you up and put the old smile back on your lips?"

Linda glanced at her father, then back at her mother, and said, "I can't really describe it, Mom. Let's just say that He's given me uplift of heart and soul. Maybe I can tell you more as time passes."

"Well, He's answering prayer," Adrienne said, a glow on her face.

While they were eating, Linda said, "Daddy . . ."

"Yes, honey?"

"Would you do me a favor?"

Nolan grinned. "Name it."

"On your way home from work this afternoon, will you buy me a copy of the *Boston Herald*? I know that newsstand is just outside the main door of your office building."

Nolan gave her a quizzical look. "I'll be glad to, but why do you want a paper?"

"There's something I've heard about in the

classified advertisement section that I want to check out."

"Oh. Sure. I'll bring you a copy."

When the head of the Forrest household arrived home from work late that afternoon, Linda was waiting for him at the door. He had the newspaper rolled up in his hand.

"Oh, Daddy!" she said, smiling. "You remembered!"

He put the paper behind his back, grinned impishly, and said, "How bad do you want it?"

"What does that mean?" she asked, giggling.

It was a joy for Nolan to hear Linda giggle again. "It means, do you want it bad enough to give your old father a big kiss to get it?"

"Well, of course!"

Linda raised up on tiptoe and planted a loving kiss on her father's cheek.

He touched the spot and said, "I'll never wash that side of my face again!"

The paper was still behind his back.

Linda laughed and held out her hand. "All right, Father dear . . . the paper, please!"

Nolan laid the rolled-up afternoon edition of the *Boston Herald* across her palm.

"Thank you!" she chirped, then dashed toward her room with a private smile on her lips.

When the sound of her door closing echoed through the house, Adrienne stood at the open door of her nearby sewing room and said, "Can you believe the change in her?"

"It's almost like I'm dreaming," Nolan replied, shaking his head. "I had to pinch myself every time I thought of her today." He moved to Adrienne and took her in his arms, kissing her sweetly.

"Did she tell you what she's expecting to find in the classified section of the paper?" he asked.

"No, dear. I figure she'll let us in on it sooner or later."

Nolan nodded. "I'm sure she will. Do you suppose whatever she's looking for in the *Herald* has anything to do with this wonderful change in her?"

"I have a feeling it does, but I didn't want to pry."

"Of course not, but it sure stirs up one's imagination, doesn't it?"

"Does it ever!" Adrienne said with a sigh. "I haven't the slightest idea what it could be, but whatever it is, if it helped bring her out of that shell, it has to be good!"

Linda closed the door behind her as she entered her room and hurried to the desk. She opened the paper and flipped pages to find the classified advertisement section, then laid the paper open on the desk and took a deep breath. "Dear Lord," she said with a tremor in her voice, "You did a wonderful thing for Betty by letting her find Clint right here in the *Boston Herald*. I'm not saying You have to do the same thing for me, but I sure don't want to be an old maid. Especially one who's a recluse. I want to get back among people — especially Christian people, but I just can't do it here in Boston. I sure would appreciate it if You would do for me like You did Betty."

The classified ads filled two complete pages. She ran her eyes up, down, and across both pages, but there were no columns labeled "Mail Order Brides," or anything akin to it.

There was a tap at her door. "Linda," came Adrienne's voice as she opened the door a few inches, "it's time to start supper."

Suddenly Linda spotted a black-bordered box in the lower right-hand corner of the page that said: Mail Order Bride section on next page.

Her pulse quickened. She wanted to turn the page immediately, but she closed the paper and said, "Okay, Mom. The assistant cook of the Forrest household is now on duty!"

In her heart, Adrienne praised the Lord for the sudden change in Linda as they walked toward the kitchen together.

9

As the Forrest family ate supper together, Nolan looked across the table at his daughter and said, "Linda, did you find what you were looking for in the *Herald*?"

"I'm not sure, Daddy," she replied after swallowing a mouthful of mashed potatoes. "I might have. I have to do some more reading before I'll know."

Adrienne looked puzzled. "Linda . . ."

"Mm-hmm?" came the response as Linda chewed fried chicken.

"Honey, I really don't mean to pry. I told your daddy that you'd let us in on this sooner or later. But you've got my curiosity screaming wildly inside me. How about sooner?"

Linda swallowed the mouthful of food. "I really have to do some more reading, Mom, before I can tell you."

Adrienne studied her. "Are you looking for a job?"

Linda smiled. "Well, yes, in a manner of speaking. As soon as I have something definite to go on, I'll talk to both of you."

"May I ask you this, then?"

"What, Mom?"

"This mysterious something you're looking for in the *Herald*, which is a job in a manner of speaking . . ."

"Mm-hmm?"

"Has it got anything to do with the fact that you're at least partially back to your old self?"

Linda grinned. "Yes'm."

Adrienne and Nolan exchanged glances.

"Okay," Adrienne said. "That's good enough for now. Whatever the mystery is, I'm going to like it because it's bringing my baby girl back to her old cheerful self."

After supper, Linda helped her mother clean up the kitchen, but her mind was on the newspaper waiting in her room. She had high hopes that a mail order bride ad like the one that had brought Clint Jackson into Betty's life would bring God's chosen man into her life, too. A move west to start a new life away from where her horrendous devastation took place would be the answer to her dilemma. As she helped her mother with the dishes, she silently asked the Lord to let her go west and start a new life.

When Linda returned to her room, she rushed to the desk, picked up the *Herald*, and found the Mail Order Bride section.

178

She began reading slowly, starting at the top and working her way down. The ads took up more than half a page and were from almost every state and territory west of the Missouri River.

Linda had to laugh at some of the ads. Others gripped her heart as she thought of the lonely men who had written them. As she read on, there was nothing that mentioned being a Christian, or anything near it. She was about to despair when the words "born-again Christian" caught her eye.

She held her breath as she read the ad. It had been placed by a twenty-seven-year-old banker in Sacramento, California, whose name was Blake Barrett. He had never been married, and stated that he was looking for a young woman near his age who was also a born-again Christian. This information was followed by a list of strict qualifications that an interested young woman would have to meet. He had added the words, "Please do not reply if you don't meet the qualifications listed above."

Linda read through the ad two more times and felt a thrill of excitement.

She could now tell her parents what was on her mind. But what if they were against it? She wouldn't want to displease them.

Linda decided to talk to them right away

lest she lose her nerve. She paused to ask the Lord to work in her parents' minds so they would be in agreement with it if it was His will that she become a mail order bride. Then she picked up the section of paper that contained the classified ads and went to the library, where her parents were spending a quiet evening of reading.

When she reached the door, she paused and took a deep breath in an attempt to calm her thumping heart. "Help me, Lord," she said softly, and then moved inside.

Nolan and Adrienne sat in identical overstuffed chairs, sharing a glowing lamp on a table between them. They faced the fireplace, which of course, had no fire in mid-August. Both parents looked up from their books when Linda planted herself in front of them, holding the newspaper.

She knew that if this Blake Barrett should want her to come to Sacramento in view of becoming his mail order bride, it would be a difficult thing for her parents to handle. She could go without their consent, but she wouldn't do that. She wouldn't hurt them the way Janet had.

Janet had gone off to New York and had not so much as sent word that she was all right. Unless God intervened and Janet got saved, Nolan and Adrienne Forrest would probably never see their oldest daughter again.

If Linda went to California and married Blake Barrett, they would see very little of her in the future. So, unless they were in agreement that she should go, she would not do it.

Her parents had taught her to have a measure of independence and to rely on the Lord in her decisions, and she took courage in that as she stood before them with her news. Her heart was filled with love for these two people who meant the world to her.

"I'd say our little girl is about to reveal the mystery to us," Adrienne said to her husband.

Nolan set kind eyes on Linda. "Well, sweet baby girl, we're waiting."

"Mom . . . Daddy . . . let me begin by telling you about Betty."

"Betty?" said Adrienne. "What about Betty?"

"She's leaving for New Mexico right away to get married."

"What?" gasped Adrienne.

"Are you serious?" Nolan asked.

"Very serious. Betty came by to tell me good-bye yesterday. You were shopping with Frances, Mom."

"You didn't tell me she'd been here when I came home."

"No, because her new life in the West is

part of why I wanted to look at the classified ads. I wanted to tell you about the whole thing at one time if I found what I was looking for."

"And did you?" Nolan said.

"Yes."

"Wait a minute," Adrienne said. "Before we get into that, who is Betty marrying? I've never heard her talk about a fiancé. How did she come up with one in New Mexico?"

"What I'm about to tell you is exactly how she found the man she's going to marry, even though she's never been to New Mexico, and up until a few weeks ago didn't know the name of one person out there."

A light came on in Nolan's eyes. "Now, hold on," he said, looking at the newspaper in his daughter's hand. "You're not talking about Betty becoming a mail order bride, are you? Tell me that's not what this is all about."

"That's exactly what it's about, Daddy. Betty answered an ad in the *Herald* from a foreman on a cattle ranch near Santa Fe, New Mexico. He's a born-again Christian, and he laid out some strict qualifications for the woman he would bring from the East in prospect of marrying. Betty told me she's prayed about it and feels that the Lord is in it. Even then, both she and Clint — his name's Clint Jackson — both of them have agreed that once she gets there, he'll court her, but if either one does not feel they should go through with the marriage, it's off. No strings attached."

Adrienne turned pale. "Linda," she said, choking on the word. "Y-you aren't going to tell us that you're considering answering an ad and becoming some man's mail order bride. . . ."

"I am, Mom. But let me explain some things, then I want to show you an ad."

Linda's parents listened intently as she told them how Betty had described the mail order bride system operated. Linda figured that if the Lord had led Betty in this way, He just might have a Christian man out west for her, too. And if God led her to go, it would get her away from Boston. She wouldn't be a recluse anymore.

Nolan blinked in shock as he said, "Honey, your mother and I have been deeply concerned that you were going to become a permanent recluse. We've prayed about it a lot. We've asked the Lord to give you victory in it, but we never meant that we wanted you to leave here."

"But Daddy, can't you see that might be exactly what the Lord has in mind? He may know that the only way I can live a normal life is to relocate. Go where nobody knows me — where nobody knows what Lewis and Janet did to me. If I can live somewhere else, I can go on with my life and not have to carry the shame and embarrassment of June 9, 1877."

Adrienne rubbed her temples with her fingertips. "Are you about to tell us you found an ad you want to answer?"

"Yes, Mom. Let me show it to both of you."

Linda placed the paper in her father's hand. "It's near the bottom of the page in the third column. I marked it with a pencil. See it?"

Nolan's eyes trailed down the page. "Yes." He leaned toward Adrienne and held it so both of them could read.

While they were doing so, Linda prayed silently, *Lord, I only want Your will. Please, if You have a plan for Blake Barrett and me, help Mom and Daddy to know it and give me their blessing.*

When they finished reading Barrett's ad, Adrienne said, "Nolan, what do you think?"

"I have to say he sure sounds like a fine man. His Bible principles come through quite clear."

"That's what I thought," Adrienne said. "I never dreamed our prayers for Linda would be answered from a direction like this. But maybe God has reserved Blake Barrett for her all along."

Nolan pulled at his ear nervously. "But —"

"But what, Daddy?"

"I hate to think of you moving clear across this continent to live. You'd be so far away from us."

"I know it wouldn't be the same as if I was living here, but it's only three to four days by rail to the California coast. We would still see each other periodically. And I wouldn't be a recluse anymore."

Nolan rubbed the back of his neck. "Your mother and I understand about your pain and embarrassment, honey. We just figured with the passing of time and plenty of prayer, one day you'd wake up and say you could go back to church and society."

Adrienne's lips thinned into a bleak line as she looked at her husband, then said, "I think, dear, that as much as we wanted things to work out according to our own plan, it just may be the Lord has His mighty hand in this. We certainly wouldn't want to get in His way, and we both want what's best for Linda, no matter how it affects us."

Nolan's head moved in a slow nod. "You're right about that."

"And if this Blake Barrett is what he claims to be and is looking for a dedicated Christian wife as he says, it no doubt would work out well for Linda."

Nolan nodded again. "That is, of course, if

185

she found Barrett to be everything he seems to be, and she fell in love with him."

"Of course," Adrienne said. "But if God is in it, all those things will happen. And if He's not in it, He'll show her and us, I'm sure, even before she goes. But it makes sense. Getting out of Boston might be the best thing for her."

Linda praised the Lord in her heart for her parents' positive attitude.

Nolan closed his eyes for a few moments, then looked first at his daughter, then his wife. "Tell you what, ladies. As I see it, if the Lord has chosen Linda and Blake for each other, He's working out His plan to get them together. I know you would like to get out of here as fast as possible, Linda, but on the other hand, this is the rest of your life you're talking about. You don't want to hurry things and make a grave mistake. Right?"

Both women agreed.

"Okay, then, let's pray about this Blake Barrett mail order bride situation for a week. In the meantime, we'll have Pastor and Doris come to the house, and we'll discuss it with them. If, after a week's time, we feel the Lord is in this thing, Linda can send him a reply. Agreed?"

"Agreed," said Adrienne.

Both parents looked at their daughter.

Linda's hands were shaking.

"What is it, honey?" Nolan asked. "Have I said something to upset you?"

"No, Daddy. It's just that, well, if I wait too long to reply to the ad, Blake Barrett might choose someone else, and —"

"But Linda, look at it this way. If that happens, then Blake Barrett wasn't in God's plan for you, anyhow. If God has Barrett reserved for you and you reserved for Barrett, nothing's going to happen to change it. I just think we need to give it a few days of prayer. You sure don't want to marry the wrong man."

Linda suddenly relaxed. "You're right, Daddy. Let's pray about it for a week and talk to Pastor and Doris. If everything seems right then, I'll reply to the ad."

"Good!" said Adrienne. "I think we're going at it the right way."

Linda ran her gaze between them. "Mom, Daddy . . . it would be all right for me to go ahead and write the letter, wouldn't it? I mean, so I can have time to word it properly. And . . . and then I'll mail it when the week is up, if all seems right."

"Sounds like good thinking to me," said Nolan, and Adrienne nodded.

The next day, Linda sat down at her desk and prayerfully wrote her letter to Blake Barrett without dating it. She would do that just before she mailed it. She gave him her testimony of when she was saved and what brought it about. She also told him of her love for the Lord, and of her dedication to Him. Then she told him about herself.

Haman Warner smiled as he sat in the comfortable overstuffed chair in his apartment after eating supper. His plan that would ultimately send Blake Barrett to prison was almost perfected.

The bank had one of the most up-to-date vaults in California, which included a fairly new idea — safe-deposit boxes made of steel, wherein bank customers stored their valuables.

One of the bank's wealthiest customers — Horace Dodge — periodically stored large amounts of cash in his safe-deposit box. Dodge owned the Sacramento Stockyards Company and did a great deal of his business with cash, both in paying and receiving.

Dodge fully trusted Warner. In fact, Dodge liked Warner so much that he would always come to him first when he wanted access to his safe-deposit box. Only if Warner was occupied with a customer would another bank employee accompany Dodge into the vault.

There were two locks on each deposit box. It took a bank employee with a key to unlock one, and the customer with a key to unlock the other.

Warner had noted that the cash Dodge brought in was always in a small canvas bag marked *Sacramento Stockyards Company* on both sides. For several days now, while staying at the bank alone past working hours on the pretense of doing some necessary work, Warner had entered the vault and devised a way to pick the lock that fitted Dodge's key.

Pondering his plan as he sat in his easy chair, Warner said aloud, "All right, Haman, ol' pal, all you have to do now is wait till Dodge comes in the next time to put that bag of money in his box. When he does, you'll pick the lock and take the bag.

"It's good that muddle-brained Blake Barrett has moved into his dead papa's house. Since Bradley often had you over to do some drinking with him, you know the house well. All you have to do is plant the canvas bag in a place where Blake isn't likely to stumble onto it, but a thorough search by Sheriff Claude Perkins and his deputies will turn it up."

Some three weeks had passed since Blake Barrett had sent his ads to the eastern newspapers. He stopped by the post office on his way home from work on a rainy afternoon, and when the postal clerk handed him his mail, Blake quickly sorted through it so see if there might be a letter in response to one of the ads.

He was excited to find a letter from a Henrietta Malcolm in Washington, D.C., but decided to wait till he got home to read it.

Upon entering the large house through the back door, Blake removed his dripping hat and raincoat, hung them on wall pegs, and sat down at the kitchen table. He quickly opened the letter from Henrietta Malcolm and read it.

A frown crinkled his brow as his eyes ran line after line. Shaking his head in disappointment, he said, "No, Miss Malcolm. You and I aren't for each other." With that, he wadded up the letter and envelope and tossed them into the wastebasket by the cupboard.

During the next several days, more letters came in response to his ads. Some — like that of Henrietta Malcolm's — he threw away upon reading. Some he kept to read more carefully.

A few days went by with no more letters coming. Blake was down to two that he had kept, and was seeking the Lord's guidance as to which one he should answer first. Since he couldn't get peace in one direction or the other, he decided to answer both of them and see what developed.

The next day he stopped at the post office on his way home, dropped the two letters in the box, then went to the counter to pick up his mail.

"Only one piece of mail today, Mr. Barrett," said the postal clerk as he handed him an envelope.

"Thanks, Rob."

Blake paused to look at the letter in his hand. The penmanship was beautiful. It was from a Miss Linda Forrest in Boston, Massachusetts. *I wonder if the rest of her matches her handwriting,* he thought.

When he climbed into his carriage, the sun was slanting low in the west. *Why wait? Let's see about Miss Linda Forrest.*

Blake unfolded the letter and again was struck with the beauty of the handwriting. He was impressed with Linda Forrest's sweet way with words and her clear-cut testimony of salvation.

Something clicked in his mind.

He read it again, this time more slowly. A warm feeling came over him as he felt this young woman's love for the Lord, and he could tell she was fully dedicated to serving Him.

Blake had supper at the Borahs' café, then went home. His loneliness was magnified by the big house around him. He went to the library, fired a lamp, and sat down in his big overstuffed chair to read Linda Forrest's letter again.

And again.

"Lord," he said, "this sounds like a very sweet Christian young lady. She's a few years younger than I, but the age span isn't all that much. I feel I should write back to her. I'll give You time to put peace in my heart if I'm to do that."

The next evening, Blake had perfect peace about writing back to Linda. In his letter, he told her he had passed up several inquiries and had recently written to two young ladies. Linda's letter, however, impressed him most of all. He told her about his church and the avenues of service to the Lord it offered him. He told her a little more about his bank work, but still didn't mention that he was the wealthy owner of the Pacific Bank and Trust Company. He asked that she write back if she was still interested and tell him more about herself.

In the larger eastern cities in 1877, the United States mail was delivered to businesses and residences five days a week.

On a cool day in late September, Linda Forrest was applying a feather duster to the furniture while her mother visited new neighbors who had moved in down the street.

She was in the parlor when she heard foot-steps on the front porch. It was the time of day when the mail usually came, and she laid down the duster and tiptoed to the front window of the parlor. One peek through the lace curtains told her it was Mr. Gladstone, the postman.

The postman hummed a tune Linda didn't recognize as he stuffed mail into the box then went his way down the street. She waited till she knew he would be several doors down, then opened the door, grabbed the mail, and hurried back inside.

She began sifting through the envelopes, and her heart almost stopped when she saw one addressed to her. The name in the corner was Blake Barrett, and the address was 420 Vine Street in Sacramento.

She laid the other mail on a chair in the hallway and dashed to her room with Barrett's letter. Her pulse raced as she read his encouraging words. Hastily she took out paper and pen, prayed for help in making her reply, and dipped the pen in the inkwell.

Since Blake Barrett wanted to know more about her, she told of being a Sunday school teacher and of singing in the choir. She didn't feel she was being untruthful, for that's what she had been actively doing up until June 9, and would still be doing if Lewis had not jilted her. She also told him interesting things from her childhood and gave him information about her wonderful parents.

When Adrienne returned from her visit, Linda took Blake Barrett's letter to her and asked her to read it. Adrienne was impressed by the tone of the letter. When Nolan came home, he read it and remarked that Barrett seemed to be a levelheaded young man and a gentleman.

Linda let her parents read her reply, and though it was very possibly going to take her away from them, they felt she had done well in composing the letter and told her they were sure Mr. Barrett would like what he read.

That evening the Stanfords came by to check on Linda and were glad to see her looking happy as they stepped through the door.

The Forrests had asked them to come and talk to Linda shortly after she had read the ad by Blake Barrett in the *Boston Herald*. Both Stanfords had agreed at the time that Barrett sounded like a solid, well-grounded Christian.

When the Stanfords saw Linda's eyes, the pastor said, "What's happened, Linda? I can tell you're elated about something."

"I got a letter from Blake Barrett in Sacramento!"

"Oh? How does it sound?"

"Very promising," Nolan answered for her. "Linda, would you care if Pastor and Doris read Blake's letter?"

"Of course not. We're relying very much on their advice. I'll go get it."

When Linda returned with Blake's letter, she found the Stanfords seated in the parlor with her parents. She placed the envelope in the pastor's hand and said, "I want to know what you think. Both of you."

The Stanfords read the letter at the same time. When they had finished the pastor said, "There's no question that this young man knows the Lord and is sincere in seeking God's will for his life."

"I agree," Doris said.

Pastor Stanford turned to Linda and said, "You will recall that when we came at your parents' request and talked to you about this mail order bride idea and read Blake Barrett's ad, I told you then that I felt it would be all right for you to pursue it."

"Yes, sir."

"Doris and I have talked about this a lot. And we've prayed much about it. We've been very concerned about your reclusion as time has passed."

"Yes, Pastor."

"We understand your deep embarrassment, and though we'd like to see you overcome it and go on with your life right here in Boston, we also realize that the Lord may want to take you elsewhere so you can get on with your life. I like what I know about Blake Barrett. It appears that he wants a godly wife and is diligently seeking the Lord's help in finding her."

"One impressive thing in this letter," Doris said, "is that this young man isn't trying to hurry anything. He says that he wants to provide you an apartment in someone's home, or a room at a boardinghouse, to give both of you time to get acquainted. He states that if for any reason you want to call the whole thing off, he'll understand and pay your way back to Boston. The young man has his head on straight. God may just be in this."

Adrienne had long since given her blessing to Linda's pursuit of the mail order bride idea, but she still felt a strong sense of protection of her daughter that made her say, "Pastor, you have no doubt that the Lord would lead in this manner to bring two young people together and eventually have them marry? Should she even consider the possibility of marrying a man she's never met?"

Stanford smiled. "If God is in it, Adrienne, of course she should marry him, in spite of the fact that she's never met him before. And as for Linda and Blake not knowing each other before she goes to possibly become his bride, the same thing happened under God's leadership with Isaac and Rebekah in Genesis 24. They had never met, but when the man of God brought Rebekah to Isaac, he loved her and married her."

Adrienne and Nolan looked at each other and smiled.

"I hadn't thought of Isaac and Rebekah in the light of Linda's situation with Blake, Pastor," said Adrienne.

"We talked about it after we were here the other night," Doris said. "Isaac and Rebekah had not so much as exchanged letters. Yet the Lord had them picked out for each other, and when they met, they knew it."

"I will say one word of caution," said the pastor. "Linda must be very careful to make sure Blake is the man God has chosen for her. But if the Lord brings them together, then all will be well."

"Pastor," Linda said, "I've already written a reply to the letter you just read. Based on what all of you have just said, I'm going to mail it."

10

Less than two weeks after mailing her second letter to Blake Barrett, Linda Forrest was making herself a new dress in the sewing room when she heard her mother at the front door of the house, talking to someone.

A moment later, Adrienne came into the sewing room with an envelope in her hand.

Linda's eyes widened. "Is . . . is it from Blake?"

"It sure is, honey." Adrienne turned to leave. "I'll let you read it in private."

"It's all right, Mom," Linda said quickly. "Stay here."

Adrienne leaned against the door frame. "Okay. You go ahead and read it, and you can tell me what he says if you want."

Linda hastily opened the envelope, took out the four-page letter, and began to read.

After only a few lines, she giggled.

"What's so funny?"

"He's telling about some things he did as a boy. When he was ten years old, there was a girl who sat in the desk just ahead of him at school. She had carrot red hair that was always in long pigtails. She was older than him, and she continually gave him a bad time. One day, he'd had all he could take. He took the lid off the inkwell in his desk and dipped one of her pigtails in the ink. The girl ran up to the teacher and showed her the jet black tip of her pigtail. Blake got a whipping in front of the whole class, and the teacher sent a note home with him for his parents, telling them what he did. It was to be returned with both parents' signatures. He had no choice but to deliver it. When his parents learned what he'd done, he got a real whipping from his father!"

Adrienne was pleased to see her daughter laugh. Blake Barrett had already put some happiness back into her life.

Linda laughed even harder as she read more tales from the life of young Mr. Barrett and shared them with her mother, and Adrienne found herself laughing with her.

Linda read a few more lines out loud, then paused for a moment and said, "Blake's mother is dead, Mom. He says she was saved after she married his father, and she led Blake to the Lord when he was nine. His father is dead, too, but he died lost."

"Oh, I'm sorry to hear that."

Linda read on silently and stopped suddenly, saying, "Oh, bless his heart."

"What, honey?"

"Listen to this. 'Linda, forgive me if I'm wrong, but I detect that you are possibly going through some kind of heartache. Please tell me if I'm right. And if I am, would you share it with me?' "

Adrienne smiled. "You haven't written anything about Lewis, have you?"

"Nothing."

"Well, bless his heart, indeed. Honey, this is some young man. He's so perceptive that he senses the deep hurt you're carrying, just by reading between the lines of your letters. I like that in him. I'm sure your father will, too."

Linda read further and commented to her mother that Blake said he was glad to hear some of the interesting things that happened in her childhood, and that her parents sounded like wonderful people. He hoped one day to meet them.

That evening when Nolan arrived home, Linda gave him Blake's letter to read while she and her mother looked on. As Adrienne predicted, Nolan was impressed with Blake's keen discernment of Linda's heartache, though she had told him nothing about being jilted on her wedding day.

"So what do you think, Daddy? In my next letter, shall I tell Blake about what Lewis and Janet did?"

"Most definitely," Nolan said. "If the Lord leads you two together, Blake will have to be told about it. Why not tell him now?"

"Then I'll write him tonight and tell him the whole thing."

Again, in less than two weeks, a reply came from Blake. Linda excitedly opened the envelope at the kitchen table. Adrienne stood by the cupboard and watched while her daughter began to read.

When she had read the first paragraph, Linda looked up at her mother. "He says he's not surprised at the source of my heartache. He thought that's what it might have been. But he's surprised at the way it happened . . . on the very day of the wedding."

She read on, and her eyes filled with tears.

Adrienne's brow furrowed. "What's wrong, honey?"

"Nothing, Mom. It's just that Blake is so tender and kind. He says his heart goes out to me, and if the Lord should lead us together, he'll do everything he can to help heal my broken heart. Oh, Mom, he's so special. He has such a kind and tender way with words."

Again, she looked up and said, "He says he thinks it's time we exchange photographs. He asks if I will send one right away. He'll do the same. Mom, I don't have anything recent. I can't go out on the streets to a photographer;

201

I might meet someone I know. What should I do?"

Adrienne laid a hand on her shoulder. "I'm going shopping with Frances tomorrow. While we're downtown, I'll go to one of the photography studios and hire a photographer to come to the house."

Linda gave her mom a hug and went to her room with the letter in hand. She sat down in her overstuffed chair and read the letter again. Blake Barrett seemed to be everything a woman could want in a husband. However, she struggled against the deep scars in her heart left by Lewis Carter. Would she be able to trust Blake? Or any man, for that matter? If she married Blake, would she always live in fear that the day would come when he'd reject her for another woman?

She wrestled with it for a while, then told herself that just because Lewis had turned out to be a hypocrite didn't mean Blake would. She felt that she was moving in the right direction by corresponding with Blake, but she knew if things developed seriously between the two of them, she would enter the relationship with some fear. Her scars went deep, and she couldn't help the emotions they dredged up.

When two weeks had passed, another letter

came from Blake. He had received Linda's latest letter, along with her photograph. He commented that she was more beautiful than he had imagined, and added that her letters showed him she was just as beautiful on the inside. He explained that the photograph he'd sent was one taken when he graduated from college. Though a few years had passed since then, he assured her he still looked very much the same.

Linda waited for a few days before writing back, wanting to see his picture before doing so. When another week had passed, and the photograph had not yet arrived, she wrote to tell him so.

Blake's return letter said that the photograph must have gotten lost in the mail — something that wasn't uncommon. He would have another photograph taken as soon as he could and send it to her, but he knew he was ready to get serious. He strongly believed the Lord was leading them together. It was almost Christmas. Would Linda consider coming to California by mid-January in view of becoming his bride?

When Linda sat down with her parents and discussed Blake's letter, Nolan said, "Don't you want to see what Blake looks like, honey, before you commit yourself?"

Linda chuckled. "I don't need to see his

picture, Daddy. His letters have told me enough about him to know he's the kind of man who will make a good husband."

Nolan grinned mischievously. "But what if he's real ugly?"

This time Linda laughed. "I don't think he is, but even if I'm wrong, it's what's inside that counts."

"How do you picture him?" Adrienne asked.

"Oh, about six feet tall. Blond. Blue eyes. Handsome."

"Strange. That's how I've pictured him, too."

"It'll be interesting to see how close you girls come to that," Nolan said.

"I feel I should write him back and tell him I'm coming," Linda said. "We've gone as far as we can in letters."

"I believe you're right, honey," Nolan said. "As much as I hate the thought of you going so far away from us, it's time for you to commit yourself to the courtship. Don't you think so, Adrienne?"

Adrienne blinked at the tears welling up in her eyes. "Yes. I feel the Lord is in it. Linda needs to write Blake and tell him she'll come."

"By going in mid-January," Linda said, "I'll have a little time yet to get ready."

"It'll be here before you know it," Nolan replied as he put an arm around her. "We're going to miss you something awful. But the most important thing is for you to be happy. And that can only be when you're in the center of God's will. Let's look at the calendar and set a date."

The next day when Nolan came home from work, he had railroad tickets for Linda's journey. She would leave on Wednesday, January 16, change trains in Chicago, and arrive in Sacramento on Saturday the 19th.

That evening Linda wrote a letter to Blake, giving him her departure and arrival dates. She commented that if he was not able to get a picture taken and in her hands before time to leave, it was all right. She was sure she would know him at the depot.

Blake's return letter arrived on January 4, containing more than enough money to cover her tickets and travel expenses. He explained in the letter that he had posed for a photograph a few days ago and had hoped to have it to put in this letter. However, when he went to the photographer to pick it up, he was told apologetically that something was wrong with his camera. The picture had not turned out. The photographer had ordered another camera from San Francisco, but it would be several days before he'd receive it. By that time it would be too late to get a picture taken and get it to Linda before departure date. They would find out now if she really could pick him out of a crowd at the Sacramento depot.

As the days passed and time drew nearer for Linda to depart Boston for Sacramento, she realized just how deep the scars were from Lewis's betrayal. As excited as she was at the prospect of leaving Boston and finding the husband God had for her, she also felt a deadness inside and wondered if she would ever really be able to fall in love with Blake. She vowed in her heart that if the Lord put them together, she would be a good wife to him.

On Thursday, December 27, Haman Warner was at his desk at the Pacific Bank and Trust Company when he saw Horace Dodge enter the bank, carrying the canvas bag. Haman had begun to worry that Dodge had changed his routine. It had been several weeks since he'd come in to place cash in his safe-deposit box.

Warner sprang out of his chair as Dodge drew up. "Good morning, Mr. Dodge. Safe deposit?"

"That's right, Haman," said the older man. "I won't need it till Monday. I would've just left it in the safe at the office if it was only overnight, but I'll feel better with it in this vault over the weekend."

Haman chuckled. "Well, it's absolutely safe in here, sir."

"I have no doubt about that."

Moments later, as Horace Dodge left the bank, Haman sat down at his desk, smiling to himself. His plan was in motion.

On Friday afternoon at quitting time, the bank employees were leaving two and three at a time. Blake Barrett came out of his office to find Haman bent over a stack of papers. Moving up to Haman's desk, he said, "How about I buy you supper this evening?"

Haman looked up, ran splayed fingers through his coal black hair, and said, "I'll have to take you up on it another time, boss. I've got to finish these reports before I leave, and it's going to take me a couple of hours yet. They've got to be ready first thing Monday morning."

"Okay," Blake said with a smile. "Maybe one evening next week."

"Sure. I'll plan on it."

As they spoke, the last of the employees were going out the door. One of the tellers called back, "Mr. Barrett, should I lock the door?"

"Don't bother, Clarence," said Blake. "I'm right behind you."

Haman watched impatiently as Barrett passed through the bank's front door, then paused and looked back, saying, "See you Monday, Haman."

Haman waved. "See you Monday."

When the latch on the door clicked, Haman left his desk and rushed to the front of the bank. Inching up to one of the large windows, he peered past the edge, keeping out of sight. After a long moment, he saw Blake pull onto the street in his buggy and drive away.

Moving swiftly, Haman went back to his desk, took a companion key from a drawer, and went to the vault. It had already been locked by one of the other employees. He smoothly worked the combination and swung the door open. Lighting a small lantern, he carried it inside and went to work on the safe-deposit box belonging to Horace Dodge.

Using the companion key and a long needle, it took him only a few minutes to open the box. He smiled to himself when he took out the canvas bag lettered on both sides: *Sacramento Stockyards Company*. He closed the box and whispered gleefully, "What a surprise you're gonna have Monday morning, Horace ol' boy! Yeah! And what an even bigger surprise you're gonna have, Mr. Religious Fanatic Blake Barrett! Even God can't help you now!"

On Sunday night, when church services were in progress, Haman was in his apartment. He placed the canvas bag in the same valise he had used when carrying the stolen money home from the bank. "Twelve thousand dollars!" he muttered. "I'd sure like to pocket this money myself, but compared to what the result of this little caper will bring, the twelve thousand is less than peanuts!"

He broke into a laugh. "Haman, ol' pal, you will soon be the owner of the Pacific Bank and Trust Company! You'll be a multimillionaire almost overnight, and Blake Barrett will be a helpless jailbird!"

There was little traffic on the streets of Sacramento as Haman walked across town, doing his best to stay in the shadows. When he reached the block where Blake's large house was located, he headed down the alley, continually glancing around to make sure nobody saw him. The coast was clear as he went through the backyard gate.

He moved stealthily up to the back door and picked the lock. Once inside the house, he took a match and a candle from his pocket and struck the tip of the match with his thumbnail, then touched the flame to the candle. He placed the dead match back in his pocket and started through the house. He must find the perfect place to stash the money.

Haman knew the ground floor well. He went from room to room, opening cabinets and closet doors, but wasn't satisfied with any place he found.

He went upstairs and soon found Blake's bedroom. As he looked around, he decided anything stashed in there could well be stumbled upon by Blake. When he returned to the hall, a door caught his attention. It was a walk-in storage closet, and something familiar caught his eye.

An old trunk. This was Blake's trunk. Haman had seen it when visiting Blake's apartment. Blake had once told him the trunk contained mementos from his childhood — toys, clothing, school papers, and the like. He had commented that he usually went through the trunk on his birthday each year, reminiscing about his childhood.

Haman knew Blake's birthday was almost a month away. He wouldn't be disturbing the trunk until then.

On Monday morning, Haman sat at his desk keeping eye on the front door of the bank. Horace Dodge would come to pick up his twelve thousand dollars soon, and when he did, Haman would be too busy to take him inside the vault. He wanted to be at his desk when the theft was discovered.

It was near eleven o'clock when Dodge entered the bank. Haman's heart pounded savagely in his chest as Dodge headed straight toward him. Haman had planned to see that Sandy Benton took the man into the vault, but Sandy had customers at her desk. And Hortense Reed was inside Blake's office.

Haman picked up some papers off his desk and rose to his feet.

Dodge drew up at the small gate, smiled, and said, "Good morning, Haman. I need to get into my box."

"Oh . . . uh . . . sure, Mr. Dodge." He waved the papers in his hand. "I've got someplace to be at the moment, but . . . uh . . . I'll get someone to take you in."

As he spoke, the head bookkeeper came from the bookkeeping room. "Hal . . ." Haman called to him.

Hal Grainger stopped. "Yes, sir, Mr. Warner?"

"Mr. Dodge is here to get into his safe-deposit box. Would you mind taking him in?"

"Of course not," said the amiable Grainger. "Be glad to."

Haman loaned his companion key to Grainger.

As soon as the two men disappeared into

the vault, Haman sat down to wait. He felt a pulse thumping in his temples.

What was taking so long?

Suddenly Horace Dodge's angry voice came from inside the vault, and Grainger stammered something Haman couldn't make out.

Dodge stormed out of the vault, carrying the metal box the canvas bag had been placed in on Friday. It was empty, and Dodge was swearing at the top of his voice as he roared, "Where's Blake Barrett? I want to see Barrett!"

Grainger appeared right behind him, his face drained of all color.

Bank employees and customers turned to gape at the angry man.

Haman left his desk and approached Dodge. "What is it, Mr. Dodge? What's wrong?"

"Somebody broke into my safe-deposit box, Haman! My money's gone!"

The door to Blake Barrett's office swung open, and Barrett emerged with a wide-eyed Hortense on his heels.

When Dodge saw Barrett, he waved the empty metal box, bellowing, "Somebody broke into my safe-deposit box, Barrett! I put twelve thousand dollars in there on Thursday, and it's gone!"

Blake was stunned. "Mr. Dodge, I don't know how anyone could have done that. There's no way they could get into your box without your companion key!"

Dodge shook the box at Barrett. "Well, look for yourself! The money's gone! Haman can tell you, I put it in there on Thursday!"

"That's right, Mr. Barrett," Haman said. "I took him in myself. He put a canvas bag in there that had the name of his company on it."

Blake turned to the head bookkeeper. "Hal, would you go get Sheriff Perkins, please? If he's not available, bring one of the deputies."

Grainger nodded and ran for the door.

"Mr. Dodge, come into my office. We'll have the law here in a matter of minutes."

Haman stood beside Hortense as Blake ushered Dodge into his office and closed the door.

"How could this happen, Haman?" Hortense asked. "It takes two keys to get into those safe-deposit boxes."

"I have no idea," he said, shaking his head.

"With only one key, the other lock would have to be picked, wouldn't it?"

"Well, yes, but it takes a professional locksmith to do a thing like that. Or —"

"Or what?" Hortense said.

Haman wanted to plant a seed of doubt in

213

the secretary's mind. "Or a clever criminal who works right here at the bank, and nobody suspects him."

"Wha-a-at?"

"Think about it. It would have to be someone in the bank. It couldn't be a customer. Because no customer can go into the vault unless accompanied by a bank employee, or Mr. Barrett himself, of course."

Hortense was appalled at the thought. "Oh, Haman. I just can't believe there's a thief — a criminal — amongst us."

"Then tell me how Mr. Dodge's box was opened."

"I . . . I don't know."

"It had to be someone who works in this bank."

"But who?"

"I have no idea. But I'm sure Sheriff Perkins will find out."

Inside Blake Barrett's office, Horace Dodge was fit to be tied. He refused to sit down, instead pacing the floor while Blake stood by his desk.

"Barrett," Dodge breathed hotly, "will you tell me how this could happen? It takes two keys to open those boxes! I have one of the companion keys this bank issued to me, and my son has the other one. Neither one of us could have gotten into the vault without a bank employee going with us. We didn't steal that money! Someone employed by you did!"

Blake shook his head. "No, Mr. Dodge. None of my employees would do a thing like that."

Dodge moved up to him, put his nose close to Blake's, and said with challenge in his voice, "Then you tell me how it was done!"

While Blake was contemplating it, there was a tap on the door. "Mr. Barrett," came Hortense's voice, "Sheriff Perkins is here."

Blake opened the door. Sheriff Claude Perkins was a tall man in his late fifties. He had a heavy jaw, steel gray eyes, and a paunch that hung over his belt.

"Come in, Sheriff," Blake said. "Did Hal explain what happened?"

"Yes, he did. Hello, Horace."

Dodge moved close. "What are you gonna do about this, Sheriff?"

Perkins gave him a direct look. "I'm gonna catch the thief and get your money back," he said flatly. "Just like Hortense was saying to me before she knocked on that door, it has to be one of the employees of this bank."

Blake's features lost color. "Sheriff, I just can't believe there's someone on my payroll who went into that vault with the bank's companion key and picked the other lock."

"That's the way it has to be, Blake. Tell me of another way."

Blake felt sick all over, for he had no other answer. Wiping a palm across his face, he said, "How are you going to find the thief?"

"I'll start by questioning each employee one at a time. Sometimes I can trip 'em up. Sometimes I can detect guilt by their reactions to certain questions. You don't have any objections if I question 'em, do you?"

"Of course not. I want the guilty party caught and prosecuted. I also want Mr. Dodge's money returned to him."

"I'll do my dead-level best to make that happen."

"Sheriff," Blake said, "I simply can't believe I have an employee who's a thief. And for that matter, one who could pick a lock on a safe-deposit box. That would take some know-how."

"That it would," agreed Perkins. "If the guilty employee didn't pick the lock, then he — or she — was somehow able to duplicate Mr. Dodge's key."

Blake shook his head, totally baffled.

"Tell me this, Blake," said the sheriff. "Do all your employees have keys to the bank's doors?"

"Yes. We alternate on who locks up at the close of the business day. And sometimes different employees have to come to work extra early. They have keys so they can do that."

"Mmm-hmm," Perkins said, stroking his jaw. "And do all of the employees have the combination to the vault lock?"

"Yes, so they can get into the vault if they come to work early and there's something in there they need."

"And they all have access to the bank's companion keys that go to the safe-deposit boxes?"

"Yes. But only the depositors have the companion keys."

"Okay," said Perkins. "Take me into the vault and let me look at it. I especially want to see Horace's box."

Horace Dodge followed along as Blake led the sheriff into the vault. Haman pretended to be busy at his desk, but he watched them furtively as they walked past him. His mouth went dry, and his heart was still pounding.

Perkins carefully examined the locks on the safe deposit. To Barrett and Dodge he said, "I can't find any scratches or marks that would tell me this lock was picked."

"So what does that mean?" Dodge asked.

"One of three things. Number one, the thief somehow has a duplicate of your key. Being a bank employee, he would have easy access to the bank's companion key. Number two, the thief is so good at picking locks that he picked the companion lock without leaving one little shred of evidence. Or number three, someone with a duplicate of Horace's key is in cahoots with a bank employee, and they used their respective keys and stole the money in the safe-deposit box together."

Blake felt as if he were in a nightmare. He cleared his throat and said, "When do you want to question my employees?"

"I'll start right now. One at a time. In the privacy of your office, if that's all right."

"Of course. I have a desk outside the office, too."

"All right. You bring 'em to me."

"I have to get back to my office," Dodge said. "I'll return in a couple of hours. I want to talk to you, Sheriff, after you've questioned everybody."

"Sure enough, Horace. Don't you worry. I'll get to the bottom of this. You can count on it."

11

Haman Warner had managed to endure the sheriff's pointed questions without flinching a muscle and stayed busy with paperwork throughout the long hours of watching each employee enter Blake Barrett's office and come out again.

It was now midafternoon, and Sheriff Claude Perkins had questioned the last bank employee.

Blake sat at his outside desk with Horace Dodge seated facing him.

Haman watched from the corner of his eye when Perkins came out and said, "Well, Blake, that's all of them."

Dodge rose to his feet, his features like granite. "So which one is it, Sheriff?" he demanded. "Are you going to make an arrest?"

Perkins took a deep breath and let it out through his nostrils. "No arrest, Horace. Not at this point. I'm completely baffled."

Blake started to speak, but Horace beat him to it. "You mean all this questioning has netted you nothing?"

"Nothing."

"What about all this Don't-you-worry-I'll-get-to-the-bottom-of-this-you-can-count-on-it stuff?"

Flustered, Perkins snapped, "I will get to the bottom of it, Horace! It's gonna take me a little time! Just settle down!"

"Settle down? I'm missing twelve thousand dollars! What do you mean, settle down? What are you gonna do now?"

"I'm not sure just yet. I've got to think on it."

"Well, while you're thinking on it, the thief is gloating because he's got my money and he's gotten away with his crime!"

"I'm telling you, Horace, I'll catch that thief! Have a little patience, will you? I'm the sheriff this county elected to do a job, and I'll do it. Just give me a little time."

"Okay, okay," Dodge said. "You know where to find me when you've got something to tell me." With that, he bumped open one of the small gates and stomped out of the bank.

The next morning, Sheriff Perkins arrived at his office ahead of his deputies. He turned the key in the lock and opened the door. Before he stepped inside, something on the floor caught his eye.

He bent down and picked up a white sheet

of paper that had been folded and slipped under the door. The message was scrawled in large letters:

I saw Blake Barrett carrying a strange-looking package when he left the bank and climbed into his buggy last Friday afternoon.

I have placed a note identical to this one under the door of Carl Stokes, editor-in-chief of the *Sacramento Gazette*.

Perkins gritted his teeth as he stepped inside and closed the door. "This is preposterous!" he hissed. "Whoever wrote this is barking up the wrong tree! Blake Barrett wouldn't steal a drop of water from the Pacific Ocean!"

The bank had been open for only a few minutes when Haman looked up from his desk and saw the sheriff come in. He had been disgusted when Perkins hadn't put Blake through the questioning like everyone else. But now he knew the whole picture was about to change.

Perkins approached Sandy Benton, who smiled and said, "Good morning, Sheriff. Any clues yet?"

"Morning, Sandy. I'm working on it. Is Mr.

Barrett in his office?"

"Yes, he is."

"I need to see him. It's very important."

"I'll tell him you're here."

While he waited, Perkins glanced at the bank's vice president. "Morning, Haman."

"Good morning, Sheriff. How goes the investigation?"

"Can't comment at the moment, but I'm on it."

Haman smiled pleasantly. "I'm sure you are."

Sandy reappeared at Barrett's door. "You can come in, Sheriff."

Haman felt a thrill rush through his body. His scheme was working perfectly, and right on schedule.

As Perkins passed through the gate, Hortense Reed came from a side room and greeted him. He returned the greeting and stepped into Blake's office to find the bank president standing behind his desk.

Blake studied Perkins's solemn features. "You look upset, Sheriff."

"I am." He pulled a sheet of paper out of his shirt pocket. "Sit down, Blake."

Blake did as he was told and said, "What's wrong?"

The sheriff held the paper so Blake could see it but kept it folded. "Before I show you this note I found under my office door when I arrived this morning, I want to say something."

Perkins looked Barrett square in the eye. "Blake, you and I have known each other a long time. Since you were a kid and I was a greenhorn deputy sheriff."

"Yes, sir."

"I have absolute faith in your honesty and integrity. Not for a moment do I believe what this note implies. Got that?"

Thin lines penciled themselves across Blake's forehead, but he said nothing.

Perkins reached across the desk. "Here. Read it."

Blake's face blanched as he read the note. "Sheriff, this is a lie! I carried no package out of this building when I left at the close of the day on Friday. Haman could testify to that, and so could two of my tellers."

"I know it's a lie, Blake. That's why I told you how I feel about you before I let you read the note."

"Have you talked to Carl Stokes?"

"Yes, and he doesn't believe it, either. He told me to tell you so."

"That's good. We have the newspaper's checking accounts and Carl's personal accounts."

"He mentioned that."

223

"So, what now? The person who wrote this note is obviously the thief."

"Well, since the writer of the note involved Carl, I have to search your house. That will clear you should more accusations appear around town somewhere."

"Fine. I want you to search my house. Let's not give this underhanded culprit any leverage."

"All right. I'll let both of my deputies help me do the search. It'll go faster. How soon can you come to the house and let me in?"

"I'll give you a key, and you can go in right now."

Perkins lifted a palm toward him. "No keys. I'll want you with me when we do the search."

"Well, let's go right now and get it over with."

Deputies John Findlay and Vance Ohlman followed the sheriff into Blake Barrett's house after Blake opened the door and stepped aside to let them enter.

When they were all inside, Blake said, "Anything I can do, or any questions I can answer, you gentlemen feel free to holler."

"Thanks, Blake," Perkins said. "You boys take the upstairs, and I'll search on this floor with Mr. Barrett by my side."

The deputies went up the winding staircase, and Perkins said, "I'll start right here in the parlor and work my way toward the rear of the house."

"It's all yours, Sheriff."

Some twenty minutes passed, and Perkins and Barrett were in the library. The sheriff was taking books from the shelves, flipping the pages, and replacing them when Vance Ohlman's voice called, "Sheriff, we need you up here!"

Perkins looked at Blake and frowned as he said, "Come along."

They mounted the stairs two at a time.

Ohlman was waiting at the top of the stairs with a solemn look on his face.

"What is it?" Perkins asked.

The deputy pointed down the hall. "John will show you."

Blake eyed Findlay, who stood at the open door of the walk-in storage closet next to his bedroom. He glanced down and saw the open lid of his old trunk.

"We didn't touch it, Sheriff," Findlay said. "We thought it best if you took it out."

Blake was shocked to see his old mementos, toys, and clothing piled next to the trunk, and a canvas bag on the bottom of the trunk with lettering on its side that read *Sacramento Stockyards Company*.

"Sheriff," he said in a quavering voice, "I

have no idea how that got in there."

Perkins leaned over and picked up the bag. Pulling the snaps loose, he took out a thick wad of paper money and said, "We have to count it."

Blake stood in silence as the sheriff divided up the money between himself and the deputies.

After a few minutes, Findlay said, "Three thousand nine hundred and fifty, Sheriff."

A minute or so later, Ohlman reported four thousand three hundred, and Perkins's portion brought the total cash in the bag to exactly twelve thousand dollars.

Perkins sighed as he stuffed it all back in the bag.

"Sheriff," Blake said, "I'm telling you the truth. I didn't do this thing. Somebody got into that safe-deposit box, took the money, then somehow got into this house and put it in the trunk."

"Blake," Perkins said with a weary voice, "I know that. What I told you earlier still stands. But you must understand that the evidence makes it appear that you are the thief. At this point, I have no choice. My hands are tied. By law, the evidence against you is cold and hard. I must arrest you."

Blake stared at Perkins as if he were seeing him for the first time in his life. "Sheriff, I can't believe this. I'm innocent! I know how it looks, but I did not steal that money! I have a bank to run. You can't lock me up in jail!"

The sheriff's jaws clamped hard. "I have to, Blake. But you'll get a trial."

"A trial? But if you have to arrest me on the basis of what looks to be evidence of my guilt, a jury will convict me with the same evidence. It'll be a long prison term. Twelve thousand dollars makes it grand theft."

"Who's your attorney?"

"Dan Laymon. But neither he nor his partners are criminal lawyers. The best one I know in town is David Rice. He banks with us."

"Then he's your man. And a plenty good one, too. Rice will be swift to point out to a judge and jury that as owner of the bank, you are worth a substantial amount of money. Twelve thousand to you, I'm sure, is a very small amount. Why would you go to all the trouble of breaking into Horace Dodge's safe-deposit box for that measly amount? And why would you be so foolish as to hide it in your house in the Sacramento Stockyards Company bag so it could convict you?"

"You're right, Sheriff. I wouldn't. But like you said, the evidence is right here, cold and hard."

Horace Dodge was returning to his office

from the stock pens, the familiar sound of bawling cattle in his ears. As he came near the office building, he saw Sheriff Claude Perkins guide his horse off the road and trot toward him.

Dodge stopped at the small porch that fronted the office building and raised a hand of welcome to the sheriff.

Perkins nodded and called out, "Howdy, Horace!" He reined in and swung his leg over the horse's back. When both feet were on the ground, he said, "I've got something for you."

Dodge watched with interest as Perkins opened his saddlebag and pulled out the canvas bag.

"It's all here. Twelve thousand dollars."

Dodge took the bag and held it to his chest, saying, "Am I glad to get this back! Thank you, Sheriff. Come into the office and tell me where you found it, and who stole it."

When they were seated, Dodge said, "Let's hear it. Where'd you find it?"

"My deputies found the bag in a trunk in Blake Barrett's house."

Dodge sucked in a sharp breath and stared in open-mouthed astonishment. "Blake? Blake Barrett picked the lock of my safe-deposit box and stole the money?"

"I don't believe he's guilty, Horace. I believe he was framed. But I'm afraid I'm going to have a tough time proving it."

"Wait a minute! Your deputies found the money in his house, didn't they?"

"Yes, but —"

"Yes, but what? The man's guilty! I hope he rots in prison!"

"He's not guilty, Horace! I said he was framed. I've known Blake since he was still wet behind the ears. He hasn't got a dishonest bone in his body. Somebody set him up."

"Why would anybody do that? What's to be gained?"

"I don't know, but I'm going to work on it. Blake doesn't deserve to go to prison."

"Well, if he stole my money, he does!"

"The jury will have to decide that, Horace," Perkins said, rising from the chair. "In the meantime, I'm going to do everything I can to try to find the real thief. See you later."

Horace Dodge was counting his money before Perkins shut the door.

Blake was in a state of shock as he was ushered to a cell at the county jail. If only he could wake up from this nightmare!

Deputy Vance Ohlman turned the key in the lock, peered through the bars at him, and said, "Mr. Barrett, I want you to know that I'm in agreement with Sheriff Perkins. I don't believe you stole that money. You spoke of attorney David Rice. Would you like me to go to his office and ask him to come see you?"

"I'd appreciate that very much," Blake said. "And would you do a couple of other things for me?"

"Just name it, sir."

"You do your banking with us, don't you?"

"Sure do."

"You know my vice president, Haman Warner?"

"Yes, sir."

"Would you tell him what's happened and ask him to come and see me as soon as possible? He's going to have to run the bank till I get this thing straightened out."

"I'll take care of it, sir. And what else?"

"I need to see my pastor . . . Duane Clarke."

"Yes, of course. Pastor Clarke. I'll get him for you. Which man do you want to see first?"

"Start with my pastor. Then Dave Rice. And then Haman Warner."

"Be back as soon as I can," Ohlman said.

At the moment, there were no other prisoners in the jail. Blake sat down on the cot and put his face in his hands. "Oh, dear Lord in heaven," he prayed, "how can this be? Lord, You know I'm innocent. Please help me. My life is ruined if I go to prison. And . . . and there's Linda. Dear, sweet Linda! She's coming here to marry me. Please, dear God! You know who did this awful thing. Please bring him to justice and clear me!"

He began to pace the floor as he continued to pray.

Nearly a half hour had passed when Blake heard voices in the hallway leading to the sheriff's office. The door of the cell block swung open, and attorney David Rice and Sheriff Perkins approached his cell.

"Hello, Blake," Rice said. "I'm sorry about this. Sheriff Perkins told me the whole thing."

"Vance is looking for Pastor Clarke," Perkins said. "The pastor's out in the country, making some visits. And Haman will be here as soon as he can."

Blake nodded, then turned to Rice. "Will you take my case?"

"Of course. But I have to tell you, it doesn't look good. With the sheriff finding the stolen money in your house, the jury is going to take it as hard evidence."

"So I don't have a chance, is that what you're telling me?"

"I'm not saying that. The sheriff's trying to come up with some kind of evidence to clear you. In the meantime, my plan will be to plead your impeccable past before judge and jury, plus what you've done for the community. And I'll use the common sense leverage:

why would a man who's a millionaire go to the trouble to steal a mere twelve thousand dollars?"

"We're doing all we can," Perkins said. "Don't you give up."

More footsteps sounded in the hall.

"Blake, let me go to work on this," said Rice. "We'll talk fee and all that later. Right now, I want to concentrate on the case. I have no doubt you're innocent. Somehow, some way, the fact that you're not guilty has got to come out. I'll do my best in your defense."

The door opened and Pastor Clarke entered.

"I know you will, Dave. Thank you."

Clarke moved up to the bars. "Blake, I can't believe this is happening."

"Neither can I."

To the sheriff and the attorney, Clarke said, "Deputy Ohlman told me all about it. Certainly Blake is going to be cleared of these charges."

"I've been back in the vault," said Perkins. "And I've been back in Blake's house. I'm trying to find some shred of evidence that will throw the guilt where it belongs and remove it from Blake. I'll keep trying."

"And I'm going to build the strongest case I can on Blake's character and impeccable past," said Rice. "Of course the best thing would be for Sheriff Perkins to come up with some substantial evidence that will clear Blake. But we're going to go with what we have when the trial comes."

"And when will that be?" Clarke asked.

"I talked to Judge Blevins," said Perkins. "It'll be Tuesday."

The pastor's eyes widened in disbelief. "Four days! Not much time to prepare."

"We'll do our best," Rice said. "Well, I need to get back to my office and do just that — prepare."

"And I'll get back on my investigation," Perkins said.

When both men were gone, Blake said, "Thank you for coming, Pastor. As you can see, I'm in real trouble."

"Yes. Have you got any idea at all who could have done this thing, Blake?"

"No, sir. As I'm sure Deputy Ohlman told you, it has to be one of my employees. But I can't come up with any suspect. Nobody in the bank has ever given me the slightest reason to suspect them of dishonesty."

"Well, one thing is for sure: God knows who the guilty party is, and He is able to let the finger of guilt point to him. Right now, you've got to cling to Romans 8:28 and believe that all of this has a purpose."

Blake closed his eyes. " 'And we know that

all things work together for good to them that love God, to them who are the called according to his purpose.' " He opened his eyes and said, "I remember you preaching on that verse not too long ago, Pastor. You pointed out in the sermon that all things that come into a Christian's life are not necessarily good, but they work together for good."

"Right. And you must hang on to that, Blake. Do you remember that I also pointed out in that sermon the word *purpose?*"

"Yes, sir. You mean, I must trust the Lord to work this whole thing out for me because He's allowed it to happen for a purpose."

"Exactly. Let's just go to Him in prayer right now and thank Him for His mighty hand on your life and that we know this ordeal was allowed to fall on you for a purpose."

Blake thought of Linda Forrest, who would also be affected by the ordeal. He had told no one about her and decided it wasn't yet time to tell his pastor.

Clarke prayed and wept as he asked the Lord to deliver Blake from this fiery trial while letting His purpose be accomplished in the process. He had just finished praying when Haman Warner came through the door, escorted by Deputy Ohlman.

Clarke reached through the bars and gripped Blake's hand. "I'll be going now. I'm sure you need to talk to Haman. See you to-morrow."

"Thanks for coming, Pastor," Blake said.

Clarke gave him a reassuring smile and excused himself to Warner and Ohlman.

"I've explained to Mr. Warner what has happened, Mr. Barrett," said Ohlman. "Did Mr. Rice get here?"

"Yes, and thank you for your help."

"My pleasure. I'll leave you two alone now."

Both men watched him pass through the door to the outer office, then turned and looked at each other.

While in his heart Haman was happy to see Blake behind bars, outwardly he showed deep concern on his face as he said, "How could a thing like this happen, Blake?"

"I don't know. Somebody really went to a lot of effort to frame me."

"Deputy Ohlman says the sheriff believes it's an inside job. That it had to be somebody who works in the bank."

Blake nodded. "Can't hardly be anyone else. But who, Haman? Who?"

Haman shook his head. "I don't have the faintest idea. I'm at a loss to even make a suggestion."

"Haman, I need your help."

The traitor's cool gray eyes settled on him.

"You've got it. What can I do?"

"Time is against us on this. The trial has been set for next Tuesday. You'll have to work fast, but I want you to do a background check on every employee. Even the women. Maybe you'll come up with something we didn't know about. Some black mark that would give us a hint as to who the guilty party might be."

"I'll get on it right away. We've got to flush the thief out in a hurry."

"How are our employees taking this?"

"Real hard. Not a one believes you're guilty. They're all pulling for you."

Blake chuckled hollowly. "All except one."

Haman nodded. "Well, yes. All except one."

Blake looked at Haman affectionately. "I don't know what I'd do without you. The load of directing the bank has fallen on your shoulders, and now I've asked you to take on more work."

"Hey, it's all right. Don't worry about over-loading me. I'm here to help in every way I can. If I run into anything at the bank that I can't handle, I'll ask your advice. Otherwise, I won't bother you with it. And as for this background check, I'll be on it with a vengeance. I want you cleared and out of this place. We need you at the bank."

Haman moved a little closer to the bars. "Blake, I'm going to do everything I can to find the real thief and prove his or her guilt. You are not going to prison."

Blake wiped tears from his eyes and said in jest, "I guess I ought to suspect even you."

"What did you say?" It felt like a hot blade lanced through Haman.

When Blake laughed, Haman heaved an inward sigh of relief.

"You're the one to benefit if I go to prison. As Dad stated in the will, you would become owner of the bank."

Haman squeezed Blake's arm. "There's just one hitch in your reasoning, Blake. I'm your true friend. And no true friend would do a thing like that. You rest assured, I'll leave no stone unturned to find the culprit."

Blake smiled. "If every person in the world could have one friend like you, they would be very fortunate. I mean that."

"I know you mean it," Haman said, "and I'm honored you feel that way. We're in this together, Blake. What hurts you, hurts me. It's almost more than I can stand to see you behind those bars. If I could change places with you, I'd do it. But since I can't, I'm going to flush out the dirty snake-in-the-grass who did this to you and laugh when he or she is behind bars!"

Blake reached through the bars and playfully cuffed Haman on the shoulder. "Go get 'em!"

Haman smiled and headed toward the door. "See you later."

When he was gone, Blake sat down on the cot and let his mind trail once more to Linda Forrest. As soon as he was cleared and released, he would wire her and tell her how eager he was to have her in Sacramento.

12

Blake Barrett's case went to trial as scheduled, but Sheriff Perkins had been unable to come up with any evidence to proffer reasonable doubt that Barrett had stolen the twelve thousand dollars. The prosecuting attorney, who respected Blake, had to use the evidence found in his house by the sheriff and deputies.

Attorney David Rice was left with only one line of defense — Blake's impeccable past, what he had done for the community, what he had done for his church, and the thought-provoking question: why would a man who was a millionaire risk prison to steal a mere twelve thousand dollars and then be so foolish as to hide it in his own house?

Haman Warner sat on the second row behind Blake and his attorney. Outwardly, he appeared to be deeply concerned for Blake. Inwardly, he was gloating over his own brilliance. He could tell the men on the jury wished they had not accepted their task. Indeed, Blake Barrett was much admired in the town, and though the evidence presented made Blake look absolutely guilty, they hated to bear the responsibility of sending him to prison.

When Judge Blevins dismissed the jury to decide their verdict, Haman left his seat. With every eye in the courtroom on him, he stepped up behind Blake and laid a hand on his shoulder.

Blake looked up with grim eyes as Haman said, "You hang in there, my friend. Maybe your impeccable life and character will be enough to sway the jury to overlook the evidence and acquit you."

Blake glanced at David Rice, who sat next to him, then said to Haman, "Dave just said the same thing. I hope you're both right."

Almost an hour and a half later, the jury returned, looking bleak. When they were seated, Judge Blevins set his eyes on Blake and said, "Will the defendant please rise?"

He then turned toward the twelve men who sat to his left and said, "Gentlemen of the jury, have you reached a verdict?"

The foreman rose to his feet. "We have, your honor. We find the defendant, Blake Barrett, guilty of grand theft as charged."

Blake's heart kicked in his chest, and his knees went watery. Rice took hold of his arm to steady him as a collective moan swept through the crowd.

Haman put his hands to his face and shook his head as if he were shocked and upset.

Reluctantly, Judge Blevins said, "Mr. Barrett, you have been found guilty of grand theft, which carries a penalty of not more than twenty years, and not less than fifteen years in prison. By the authority invested in me, I hereby sentence you to fifteen years at the California prison facility at Ukiah."

The gavel banged the desk, and Blevins said, "This court is adjourned."

Rice gripped Blake's shoulders. Through clenched teeth he said, "Blake, I cannot believe the boundless inhumanity inflicted by some human beings upon others. Why would someone in your bank do a thing like this to you?"

"I have no idea," Blake said. "Maybe . . . maybe it's not someone in the bank, even though everything points that way. Maybe the guilty party was smart enough to make it look like that, but he's really an outsider."

"I don't know how," Rice said dejectedly.

Sheriff Perkins stepped up behind them. "Blake, it just so happens there are two federal marshals here on their way to Ukiah. They arrived in town last night. Knowing you would probably be convicted, I asked them to wait till the trial was over, so if you did get convicted, they could take you with them. I'm turning you over to them, and they need to leave right away."

Blake glanced at the two federal men, who stood within earshot, looking on. They nodded to him.

Pastor Clarke was directly behind Perkins. He moved up and said, "Sheriff, I'd like a few minutes alone with Blake."

"Sorry, Pastor, but these men have to be in Ukiah by nightfall. As you know, it's almost a hundred miles, and they're on horseback. They've got to leave now."

Tears filmed Pastor Clarke's eyes as he gripped Blake's hand. "A great injustice has been done here," he said. "But don't give up. Hang on to Romans 8:28 and remember that the church will be praying for you. God knows who the real thief is, and we'll be praying that God will bring him to light."

"Pastor, I hate to interrupt," said the sheriff, "but Blake has to go."

Haman crowded in. "Blake," he said, "this is so horrible! I'm so sorry this has happened. I'll take good care of the bank, and when you get out of prison in fifteen years, I'll give it back to you."

Blake nodded, feeling numb all over. "Haman, I'll need you to sell the house for me. Just put the proceeds in an account in my name, will you?"

"I have a better idea. How about I just live in the house till you get out of prison, then you'll still have it. All your belongings will still be here."

"I . . . I hadn't thought of that. You sure you want to do that?"

"Of course."

"I don't know how to thank you."

"Hey, what are friends for?"

"Let me hear from you now and then."

"I will. And I'll get up there to see you, too."

Blake thought of Linda. Turning to Perkins, he said, "Sheriff, before I go with the marshals, I need to send a wire to someone back east."

One of the marshals stepped up and said, "We can't wait for that, Mr. Barrett. We've got a horse out here for you to ride, and we've got to leave right now."

"Then can I send a wire from the prison, Marshal —"

"Adams. Roy Adams. My partner over there is Marshal Jack Plummer. And, no, they don't allow prisoners to send wires from the prison. You can't even send a letter from the prison till you've been there on good behavior for six months. But you can receive mail right away. C'mon. Let's go. We've got a long ride ahead of us."

Panic rose in Blake. He couldn't let Linda come to Sacramento and then find out he was in prison. She must be told before she climbed aboard that train. "Marshal Adams, I need a few minutes to talk to my friend here." He pointed to Haman with his jaw. "Please. I must send a wire to someone in the East. I'll have him do it for me."

"We have to get going," said Adams.

"Five minutes? Would you grant me five minutes?"

Adams looked to his partner.

Jack Plummer shrugged. "Sure. Let's give him five minutes."

"Thanks," said Blake.

"But only five," said Adams.

While the sheriff, the two federal men, and the pastor looked on, Blake and Haman moved into a corner out of earshot.

Keeping his voice low, Blake said, "Haman, I'm going to tell you about something I haven't even shared with my pastor."

Haman's curiosity rose. "What is it?" he said in a low tone.

Blake quickly explained to Haman about Linda Forrest coming from Boston to become his mail order bride.

"She's supposed to board the train in just a few days," Blake said. "I need you to wire her immediately and explain what has happened.

Tell her I'm innocent but I couldn't prove it."

Haman took a pencil from his shirt pocket and a small envelope from his suit coat pocket. "What's her address?"

Blake told him Linda's address and repeated it to make sure Haman had gotten it right, then said, "Tell her where the prison is, and ask her to write me. Explain that I won't be able to respond for six months, but I want to know how she's doing. Tell her I love her, Haman, with all my heart."

Haman wondered how Blake could say that when he hadn't even met her, but he said, "Will do, my friend."

"Time's up!" Roy Adams called. "Let's go, Barrett."

A crowd of people stood outside the courthouse and watched the two deputies escort Blake to a waiting horse. Pastor Clarke, Haman Warner, and Sheriff Perkins followed.

Blake was handcuffed before the marshals boosted him up into the saddle. As they rode away, he looked over his shoulder several times. The crowd called out to him, telling him they knew he was innocent. Tears filled Blake's eyes as Pastor Clarke and Haman waved to him.

Brokenhearted, but trying to cling to Romans 8:28, Blake straightened in the saddle as Sacramento's Main Street passed from view. When they reached the edge of town, the marshals put the horses to a gallop with Blake's horse between them.

A few stars were twinkling in the sky overhead as the three men rode up to the gate of Ukiah prison. Blake gazed at the deeply shadowed, somber walls and said in his heart, *Lord, how could a thing like this happen to me? What purpose could You have in letting me be locked up in this place for fifteen years? Help me, Lord. Help my faith not to waver.*

The U.S. Marshals ushered Blake inside the prison and turned him over to Daryl Watkins, who was the chief guard on the night shift. They handed Watkins the papers on Blake that had been given to them by Sheriff Perkins, then bid Watkins good night.

Watkins sat Blake down in a small office, made records from the papers, then provided him with prison clothing. Blake's stomach turned over at the thought of wearing the drab clothes marked *Ukiah State Prison.*

Watkins went over the prison rules and daily schedule with Blake and warned him to obey the rules at all times. He was told he would be put on a chain gang within a day or two, and it would be in his own best interest if he worked hard and gave the guards no trouble.

"Now, there's one more rule here, Barrett. That's the talking rule."

Blake waited for him to proceed.

"The cells have solid walls between them. You will not be able to see the inmates on either side of you. The only way to talk to them is through the bars on your cell door. But don't. There's no talking between inmates except the one who shares your cell. It so happens that right now you won't have a cell mate. Talking between inmates is allowed only at meals. When you go on the chain gang, you're not allowed to say a word to anyone but the guards. Do you understand?"

"You've made it plain enough," said Blake.

"All right, let's get you to your cell."

While they were walking through the cell blocks, Watkins said, "Sometime tomorrow, you'll be brought to Warden Hall's office. He always meets with each new inmate for a little discussion. He's a very gruff man, and tougher than harness leather. Just smile and call him sir, and you'll get through it all right."

The next morning, just after breakfast, Blake was escorted to the warden's office. Warden Clarence Hall was indeed as tough as Daryl Watkins had told him, if not tougher. He did not like convicts and was ready to discipline severely any man who got out of line. Blake remembered his "sirs" and did well with the warden, but he was glad when the discussion was over.

As the guard walked him back to his cell, Blake asked if he could have a Bible. They stopped off at a storeroom, and Blake carried his new Bible to the cell with him. He was told that he was now scheduled to go on the chain gang in four days.

For two days Blake spent most of his time praying and reading his Bible. In tears, he asked God why this horrible thing had to happen to him. He prayed for an increase in faith, asking the Lord to help him not to doubt His goodness or His Word. He also prayed for Linda, imploring God to take care of her and to guide her in the direction He would have her to go, now that Blake had been removed from her life.

On the afternoon of the third day, Blake was sitting on his cot reading his Bible when two guards appeared at the cell door with a prisoner between them.

"Got a cell mate for you, Barrett."

"There you go, Huffman," said one of the guards, giving him a gentle shove into the cell.

Before closing the door and locking it, the guard with the key said, "Barrett, you might try to get along with Huffman here. He's in

248

for murder. Gonna hang in exactly a week. You see, we don't have a death row in this prison, so we have to put the condemned men in with those who are just doing time. Don't irritate him. He might try to murder you, too."

The door slammed shut and the key turned in the lock.

Huffman stood at the bars, watching the guards walk down the corridor. When their footsteps had died out, he turned around to find his cell mate standing behind him. Blake put out his right hand and said with a smile, "I'm Blake Barrett."

"Larry Huffman," said the new inmate, meeting his grip. "How long you in for?"

"Fifteen years. I've only been here three days."

"What'd you do?"

Blake sighed. "Why don't we sit down?" He sat on his cot, and Larry eased onto his.

"I've been told," said Blake, "that there are few guilty men in prison — according to them. They were framed, or the arresting lawman had it in for them."

"Yeah. That's what I hear," said Huffman.

"Well, I really am innocent."

Huffman looked at him intently, then said, "I'd like to hear your story."

"Okay, but if you get bored at any spot, just

say so, and I'll shut up."

"Shoot."

When Blake had finished his story, Huffman said, "You know what, Blake? I believe you. There's a clean-cut look about you, and there's something in your eyes that tells me you didn't steal that money."

"Thanks. I wish the jury had been as kind as you."

There was a silent moment, then Huffman said, "I know you've got to be curious about who I murdered and why."

"Yes, but I really don't have to know anything about it, Larry."

"Might as well. You've got to live in this cell with me for a week. I'm not innocent, Blake. I planned very carefully to kill the man I murdered, and I did it as planned."

"I see." Blake's features paled a bit.

"The man's name was Melvin Packman. He was a burglar."

Blake nodded.

"What happened . . . Packman broke into my widowed mother's house one evening when she was visiting some neighbors down the street. He about had his bag full when she walked in and caught him in the act. When she tried to run, he grabbed her and strangled her to death."

Blake's features twisted. "Oh, how awful!"

"I won't go into the details of it," Huffman said, "but the law caught him. He was brought to trial. But —" Huffman choked up for a moment. "But he got off on a technicality. Because of some quirk in the circumstances of his arrest that came out in the trial, the judge declared a mistrial and set him free. That was more than I could take. I went after him to exact my own justice. And I did. I got my hands on him and strangled him to death, just like he did my poor mother."

Blake pondered Huffman's story and studied his face. "Are you glad now that you killed Packman?"

Larry scrubbed a palm across his mouth and said, "No. I didn't feel the satisfaction I thought I would. And on top of that, killing him didn't bring Mom back. And now they're gonna hang me."

"It wasn't worth getting your own justice, was it?"

"No. And I'm scared, Blake. I'm scared to die. I'm afraid of what lies out there beyond my last breath."

Forgetting his own heartaches and problems, Blake said, "Larry, do you believe this Book is the Word of God?" He picked up his Bible from a small table.

Larry had not noticed it before. He bit down on his lower lip and nodded. "Yes. I have no doubt about that. I know it says there's a burning hell out there for murderers like Melvin Packman and . . . and Larry Huffman."

"Yes, and for all other kinds of sinners who die in their sins. I can help you lose your fear of dying, Larry, if you'll let me."

An ecstatic Haman Warner walked out of the law offices of Laymon, Studdard, and Griswold. The briefcase in his hand held the papers that declared him owner of the Pacific Bank and Trust Company. He now had exactly what he had gone after. Blake Barrett was behind bars, and the will left by Bradley Barrett had made Haman Warner a millionaire.

The very same day, Haman moved into the Barrett house. He took over the master bedroom and closet, stuffing Blake's clothes in a closet in a bedroom down the hall. One day, when he had time, he would burn Blake's clothes.

He rearranged the furniture in the house to suit himself and went through cabinets, dressers, and chests of drawers to see if he could find anything of value. While he was pawing through a drawer that held some nice pieces of jewelry, he thought of Blake's personal bank account. He had taken a look at the account that morning and found it quite sizable. He was trying to figure a way to get that money in his own hands but couldn't come up with a surefire plan. He would think on it some more.

The next day after work, he went through more drawers in search of valuables he could sell for cash. "Funny," he told himself, "no matter how much money a man gets his hands on, he always wants more."

He decided to spend the rest of the evening in the library and lit a couple of lamps. He had never done a lot of reading, but the hundreds of books on the shelves suddenly seemed interesting. He was about to look for a book to read when his eyes fell on Blake's desk at one end of the room. More drawers to go through!

Setting a lamp on the desk, he pulled open the top drawer. There were letters under a metal clip addressed to Blake from Linda Forrest.

"Ah, yes!" he said aloud. "Linda Forrest. I really should get around to sending her that wire."

Haman took out the letters and began reading them. When he got to the envelope that contained the letter with her photograph, his eyes widened. "Oh, Linda!" he gasped. "You are so beautiful!"

He braced her picture in a standing position against a couple of thick books and gazed at it, captivated by her beauty.

"Oh, Linda," he said in a whisper, "I wish there was some way I could have you for myself."

He thought about the wire he'd promised Blake he would send. If only there were some way he could pose as Blake and make her his mail order bride. But how? If Blake had a picture of Linda, certainly Linda had a picture of Blake.

He read the letter that had contained the picture, then opened and read the next letter. He was surprised to find her saying that she'd never received his photograph. This stirred him to keep reading. He was able to pick up that Blake had Linda believing he was only a bank employee. He had not revealed to her that he was the owner of the bank. Probably wanted to surprise her in person that she was marrying a millionaire.

Linda's final letter caused Haman's heart to quicken pace when he read the date of her departure from Boston and the arrival date in Sacramento. She was due to arrive on Saturday, January 19 — only a little more than a week from now! He smiled when he read her words:

"Blake, if you're not able to get a picture taken and in my hands before my scheduled time to leave Boston for Sacramento, it's all right. Though you've never described yourself to me, I have you pictured in my mind. I'm sure I will know you when I step off the train at the depot."

Haman could hardly sleep that night for thinking of the beautiful woman in the photograph. How proud he would be to show her off as his wife!

He began working out a scheme to pose as Blake Barrett. The first obstacle was if Blake had been able to get a picture taken of himself and sent to Linda. If so, no scheming in the world could pull it off. If not, there had to be a way. But how could he know for sure? Send a wire and ask if she'd gotten it? But that would be to downplay her own romantic words about already picturing him in her mind.

No. She might catch on that something was wrong. Haman would simply go ahead and send the wire as Blake had asked him to. Tomorrow . . . or the day after that.

The next day, Haman stopped at the post office after work to pick up his mail. Since the postal people knew about Blake being in prison, they might let him have Blake's mail. He would try it. Who knew what he might find?

The postal people were cooperative, telling Haman how nice he was to look after Blake

Barrett's affairs. When Haman went through the mail, he was delighted to find another letter from Linda. He couldn't wait to get home to read it. He scurried to a corner of the post office and tore it open.

It was dated January 11, 1878:

> My dear Blake,
> This is the last letter I will write. Our next contact will be when we meet in person at the Sacramento depot on Saturday, January 19!
> And let me say again — it's all right that you were not able to get a photograph taken and sent to me. It's more exciting this way! I'm sure I will know you when I see you. I will just look for the handsomest twenty-seven-year-old man in the depot!
> With great expectancy,
> Linda

Haman could hardly contain himself. His idea was not impossible, after all! He could impersonate Blake, even to the point of talking and acting like a Christian. Blake had talked to him on numerous occasions about being saved, and Haman had been around other Christians enough to know their jargon. He was sure he could pull it off.

He read the brief letter again, then said to himself, "There's still one big problem, Haman, ol' boy. You can't impersonate Blake in Sacramento. You'll have to get clear out of California. Go somewhere else, somewhere you're not known."

He snapped his fingers. "Wait a minute! That bank in Wyoming!"

Haman had learned just the previous day that there was a bank for sale in Cheyenne City, Wyoming. The owner had died, and his widow had put it up for sale.

As he thought about it, Haman knew several bank owners in California who would love to purchase the successful Pacific Bank and Trust Company of Sacramento. He would sell it to the highest bidder.

The next morning, Haman told the bank employees that he would have to be away from the bank possibly all day, then he drove his buggy to the town of Stockton, where he was unknown. There he entered the Western Union office and wired the widow in Cheyenne City, using Blake Barrett's name, to see if the bank was still on the market, and to ask how much she wanted for it. The return wire came back in less than an hour, saying the bank was still for sale, and the widow named her price.

Haman was happy to learn that the price

was less than he would get out of the Pacific Bank and Trust Company. He wired the widow a firm offer for the price she was asking. Within another hour, the deal was agreed upon.

Haman then wired Linda — as Blake Barrett — telling her some changes were taking place in his career. He would be moving to Cheyenne City, Wyoming, to work in a bank there. He was sending the wire from Stockton because he was on an assignment from the Pacific Bank and Trust Company and needed to send it right away. She must wait in Boston until she heard from him in Wyoming, which would be a few weeks. He asked for her to send a return wire by the messenger who delivered the telegram to her door. He would wait in Stockton till he heard back that she had received it.

Linda Forrest was in her room, making final preparations for her trip in two days, when she heard a knock at the front door. She could hear her mother's footsteps and a male voice saying something Linda could not make out. Then came her mother's voice: "Linda! You have a telegram here from Blake!"

She rushed to the front door and saw a tall, skinny messenger in a Western Union uniform.

As she drew up, Adrienne said, "Honey, this man needs you to read the telegram right now, because he has a note from the telegrapher that an immediate reply is needed."

"All right." Linda's eyes were dancing as she took the paper and read it.

"So what is it, Linda?" Adrienne asked.

"Blake says he's changing jobs. He's leaving the bank in Sacramento and taking a job in a bank in Cheyenne City, Wyoming. He wants to know I've received this telegram, and I'm to wait a few weeks until I hear from him."

"He must be bettering himself by this job change."

"I'm sure he is," Linda said. "All right, sir. Please send this wire for me: 'Received your wire. Am excited for you. Will wait in Boston until I hear from you again.' "

13

Haman Warner drove away from the Western Union office in Stockton, happily shaking the telegram he held. "Yes! Things couldn't have worked out any better than this! Linda, honey, just wait'll you meet your darling 'Blake'!"

That evening, Haman sat at the desk in the Barrett library, reading Linda's letters over again and letting his eyes devour her beauty as he kept glancing at her photograph.

Grinning, he said, "I'll go along with this Christianity stuff for a while, to keep your favor, but in time I'll turn you from it. I'll keep you so busy doing fun things you won't want to go to church. I'll do it ever so slowly, but ever so surely. You wait and see. The day will come when you'll wonder why you ever embraced that 'Jesus Christ stuff' in the first place."

At the Ukiah State Prison, Blake Barrett found Larry Huffman in a state of confusion on spiritual matters. He dealt with him about salvation, hoping to lead him to the Lord so he would die on the gallows a saved man. Though Larry would say he believed the Bible was the Word of God, he still threw up a wall between himself and Blake, unwilling to listen to what Blake was trying to show him from the Word.

Each day when Blake returned to the cell, weary from working on the chain gang, he pressed the gospel to Larry's heart, but Larry would only listen a little while, then turn the subject to something else.

On the evening before Larry was to be executed, he sat on his cot, holding his head in his hands.

Blake's heart was heavy for him. He had prayed continuously that the Lord would convict Larry so powerfully that he would come to Jesus. Looking at him by the lantern light in the cell, Blake said, "Larry, you've listened to me these past six nights, but you really haven't listened. You're going into eternity tomorrow morning at sunrise. I've shown you in God's Word that unless you turn to Jesus in repentance of your sin and ask Him to save you, when you hit the bottom of that rope, you will keep on going right down — all the way to hell."

Larry looked at Blake through misty eyes and said, "I haven't been honest with you, Blake."

"What do you mean?"

"You asked me on the first night if I believed the Bible is the Word of God. I told you I had no doubt that it was. I should have said that I think it might be, but again, it might not be."

"Larry, you told me that you know the Bible says there's a burning hell out there for murderers like Melvin Packman and Larry Huffman. That's what you said, didn't you?"

"Yeah."

"And what was my response?"

Huffman thought on it a moment. "You said: 'Yes, and for all other kinds of sinners who die in their sins.' "

"Right. I said that because it sounded like you thought murderers ought to go to hell, but people guilty of lesser sins shouldn't have to. Is that what you meant?"

Larry's hands were trembling. "I . . . I guess so."

"You guess so?"

"Blake, I'm not sure about anything right now. I'm not sure there's a hell or a heaven."

Blake knew if he was going to reach the condemned man, it had to be tonight. He could pull no punches. "Larry, what you just said about not being sure of anything right now . . ."

"Yes?"

"That's not true. You're sure of one thing."

"What's that?"

"You're going to die tomorrow morning at sunrise."

Blake's words were like hammers, striking hard with reality. Larry bent his head low and rubbed the back of his neck.

"Well, aren't you?" Blake pressed.

Without looking up, the condemned murderer said, "Yes."

"So where are you going when you take that plunge?"

"I don't know if I'm going anywhere."

"Excuse me?"

Larry chewed on his lower lip for a moment. "I told you I haven't been honest with you."

"Okay. Be honest now."

"My parents taught me from the time I was a little boy that humans are only a higher form of animal. That when we die, like the lower forms, we simply go out of existence. They said there is no punishment for sins. There is no hell. There is no heaven. There is no afterlife, and there is no holy God to face in judgment."

"Wait a minute," Blake said, praying in his heart the Lord would help him say the right thing. "You said your parents taught you there is no punishment for sins."

"They did."

"You don't believe that."

Larry raised his eyebrows. "How can you be so sure?"

"What about Melvin Packman? He sinned when he murdered your mother, didn't he?"

"Absolutely."

"And didn't you tell me you went after him to exact your own justice because the law didn't punish him for what he did?"

Huffman looked at Blake, wide-eyed. "Uh . . . yes."

"So you really do believe there should be punishment for sin."

"I guess you'd say I do. I went after Packman and put punishment where it belonged."

"Then how about the righteous God of heaven who created us? What's so hard about believing that God punishes sin just like you did?"

"If there is a God."

"You know there is."

"What makes you think so?"

"Because God says you know He exists."

"Aw, c'mon."

"Romans 1:19 says of the whole human race, 'That which may be known of God is manifest in them; for God hath shewed it unto them.' God has shown every man that

He exists — even you. We're being honest here, right?"

"Yes."

"Then tell me you're an atheist. Tell me there is no God."

Huffman's shoulders slumped. "I can't tell you that. You're right. I know God exists."

"Of course you do. Now, again, are you afraid to die?"

The condemned man's countenance seemed to sag. "Yes."

"But why should you be if when you die you're simply going out of existence?"

Tears filled Larry's eyes. "I'm not going out of existence. I'm going to hell."

"Because you murdered Melvin Packman?"

"No. Because I've refused to let Jesus save me."

"Murderers and all other kinds of sinners can be forgiven for their sins if they will repent, turn to Jesus, and believe He will do all the saving all by Himself . . . and if they will call on Him. Remember? 'For whosoever shall call upon the name of the Lord shall be saved.' "

"Would . . . would you go over those verses you showed me last night?"

Blake turned to Romans 6:23. "Here, Larry, read it to me."

" 'For the wages of sin is death; but the gift of God is eternal life through Jesus Christ our Lord.' "

"Remember I pointed out that since eternal life is a gift, it can't be earned by good deeds and religious rites."

"Yes."

"And I also pointed out that you can't have eternal life unless you receive Jesus into your heart and your sins are washed away in His precious blood. John 1:12 says, 'As many as received him, to them gave he power to become the sons of God, even to them that believe on his name.'

"If you are going to go to heaven tomorrow morning, you must acknowledge to God that you are a hell-deserving sinner, then repent of your sin and believe that Jesus died for you on the cross and shed His blood for you . . . and that He raised Himself out of the grave so He could save you. Call on Him in faith, believing that He will save you by His grace, and He will do it."

As Larry Huffman's eyes filmed with tears, Blake could tell the Holy Spirit was doing His work on the condemned man.

Blake said, "You'll hang at sunrise in the morning, Larry. You have only a few hours to live. You will either receive Jesus tonight or reject Him. If you don't receive Him, you do reject Him. Reject Him, and you will die without Him."

Suddenly Larry broke into sobs and said, "I'm not going to reject Jesus any longer, Blake! He died for me so I could be saved from hell and the wrath of God. Will you help me? I want to be saved right now!"

With Blake's guidance, Larry Huffman wept his way to Jesus Christ and received Him in repentance of his sin. His relief was so great that he continued to weep for some time.

Guard Anthony Tubac appeared at the cell door. "What's the matter with Huffman, Barrett?"

"Nothing's the matter," Blake replied. "What just happened to him is the best thing that could ever happen to him."

Larry looked up at the guard and said unashamedly, "I just opened my heart to Jesus. He saved my soul and washed my sins away in His blood. He forgave me of all my sins — even the murder I committed. When they hang me in the morning, I'm going to heaven!"

Tubac laughed, and in a scoffing tone, said, "I've seen this before. Convicts do this sort of thing a lot when preachers come around. Just another case of jailhouse religion, looks to me. Even without a preacher."

Larry wiped tears and said, "I can't speak for the other men, Mr. Tubac, but you're wrong about me. I didn't get religion just now. I received salvation. Salvation is a person, not a religion. That person is the Lord Jesus Christ. I can die now without fear."

Tubac's features pinched with sudden emotion. He'd never seen a man who was condemned to hang with the kind of peace he saw on Larry Huffman's face.

"You really mean that, don't you?" said Tubac.

"Yes, I do. I don't even understand it, but I have no fear of death."

"You can't understand it, Larry," Blake said, "because it's the peace of God. God's own peace, that He gives His children when they need it."

"All I can tell you is that it's real," said Larry.

Anthony Tubac scratched his head and walked away, mumbling to himself.

Later that night, when the lights were out in the cell block, Blake sat beside Larry on his cot and whispered, "Do you think you can sleep?"

"I'm not sure. It's not because I'm afraid of dying in the morning, but still, I'm sort of tensed up."

"It's only natural. I'd like to pray with you."

Keeping his voice to a whisper, Blake put his arm around Larry's shoulders and asked the Lord to continue to give Larry peace. He thanked the Lord for the amazing maturity Larry was showing for having only been saved a couple of hours, and he thanked God for allowing him the privilege of leading Larry to Jesus.

Both men returned to their cots. In a little while, Blake heard Larry's soft, even breathing, which told him his cell mate was asleep.

Dawn was about to break on the eastern horizon when Blake heard a steel door open at one end of the cell block. He sat up and saw the glow of a lantern in the corridor. Footsteps echoed off the cold rock walls, and presently Anthony Tubac appeared, carrying a food tray in one hand and a lantern in the other. Blake met him at the bars and said softly, "He's sleeping."

Tubac shook his head in amazement. "I have his breakfast," he whispered. "He's supposed to get it if he wants it. Would you wake him for me?" As he spoke, Tubac set the lantern on the floor next to the barred door.

Blake gently shook Larry and told him Tubac was there with his breakfast.

Larry sat up, rubbed his eyes, then looked toward the guard. In a low tone, he said, "I really don't want any breakfast, Mr. Tubac."

"Most of 'em don't. I can imagine it would be pretty hard to eat, knowing you're about to face the noose."

"It's not that," said Huffman. "It's just that in a little while, I'll be having breakfast with my Lord Jesus at the heavenly table. Earthly food means nothing to me now."

Tubac nodded slowly. "All right. Now, ordinarily the prison chaplain accompanies the condemned man to the gallows, but Chaplain Worthington is home ill."

"That's all right," said Huffman. "I'll be fine."

"Mr. Tubac," Blake said, "I'd like to read some Scriptures to Larry before . . . before they come for him. Is it all right if I light our lantern in here? I know it's against the rules, but —"

"Not a problem. Go ahead and light it. I'm really at a loss for words, Huffman, but you amaze me. I've never seen a man so calm who was about to go to the gallows."

"It's Jesus in my heart, Mr. Tubac. You need to open your heart to Him, too."

Tubac gave him a weak smile and said, "I'll be back shortly."

Blake read several passages of Scripture to his new friend as dawn spread its gray glow on the eastern sky. When the sky turned orange, the steel door at the end of the cell block rattled, and footsteps were heard again. There was a rumble of low voices among the other inmates. They all knew this was Larry Huffman's day to die.

Anthony Tubac and another guard turned the key and swung open the cell door. "Okay, Huffman," Tubac said. "It's time."

Tears coursed down Larry's cheeks as he embraced Blake in manly fashion and said, "Thank you, my friend, for caring about my hellbound soul, and for leading me to the Lord. If you hadn't, I would now be on my way to hell."

"Larry, if Jesus hadn't saved me many years ago, I wouldn't have cared about your soul. The praise goes to Him."

"Blake . . . I'll meet you in heaven."

Blake swallowed the hot lump in his throat. "Yes, my brother, I'll meet you in heaven."

He pressed his face to the bars and watched as Larry and the two guards walked away. The other inmates looked on in silence while the condemned man was escorted out of the cell block. When the door clanked shut, Blake sat down on his cot and prayed.

"Thank You, Lord, for allowing me the privilege of leading Larry to You."

Suddenly the truth of the whole matter flashed into his mind: *If I hadn't been put in this prison, Larry would have died lost and gone to hell!*

More tears flooded his eyes as he said, "Oh, dear Lord! If for no other reason . . . seeing Larry saved is worth being convicted of a crime I didn't commit and being sent here as an innocent man! I thank You that Romans 8:28 always holds true, even when we mortal Christians can't see how it's going to prove itself in our lives."

Blake's mind then went to Linda. He was expecting to hear from her any day now. He whispered, "Lord, I don't know how Romans 8:28 is going to prove itself true in Linda's life over this unfair prison sentence of mine, but I know it will. I have no idea how she reacted when she received Haman's wire. Please help her. Help us both."

Some forty minutes after Larry Huffman had been taken away, the breakfast bell started ringing in the mess hall. Both steel doors at the ends of the cell block rattled, and several guards moved along the cells, unlocking doors, and saying, "Breakfast time! Step lively now!"

Blake rose to his feet as his door was unlocked. He was in the line when Anthony Tubac drew up and said to the other guards, "I need to talk to Barrett a minute. I'll bring him to the mess hall personally."

Tubac took Blake by the arm and guided him back to his cell. "Just wanted to tell you how the hanging went."

Blake waited, eyes fixed on Tubac's face.

"Huffman went to his death with a smile, Barrett. They always give the condemned man the choice whether or not to have a hood dropped over his face before the noose is placed around his neck. Well, your friend refused the hood. I'm telling you, his face was beaming. He had tranquillity on his face like I've never seen. He was looking heavenward when the lever was thrown, and the last thing I saw before he plunged down was a smile!"

"Praise the Lord!" Blake said.

By now, the last of the inmates had moved past the cell. Tubac glanced toward the line of men who filed out the door, then turned back and said, "Barrett, I have to go off duty after I take you to the mess hall. But I want you to show me how to be saved as soon as I can spend some time with you. Will you do that?"

"I sure will! You work it out. It will be my pleasure!"

"When I come back for my shift tonight, I'll find a reason to come and see you."

In less than two weeks after putting the Pacific Bank and Trust Company on the open market, Haman Warner had sold it.

His employees were quite surprised, but relieved, for Haman had not been his old jovial self since inheriting the bank. He had been difficult to please and was making their lives miserable. They were glad to see the bank sold to someone else.

Haman's only regret as he left the bank without telling anyone where he was going was not being able to clean out Blake Barrett's personal account. It was a substantial amount, but he wouldn't risk prison to steal it.

On the day before leaving for Cheyenne City, Haman packed what few belongings he was going to take with him. Among them was an old trunk that held some mementos from his childhood. From an attaché case, Haman took out clippings from the *Sacramento Gazette*, which told the whole story of Blake Barrett's arrest, conviction, and incarceration at Ukiah State Prison for a fifteen-year sentence.

Chuckling to himself, Haman stuffed the clippings into a large envelope and placed it in the trunk. "Can't let my most clever deed be forgotten," he said aloud. He dropped the worn old lid of the trunk, placed a heavy-duty padlock in the latch to secure it, and pocketed the key.

Before leaving for Wyoming, Haman made

a quick trip to Stockton and sent a wire to Linda, telling her it would only be a few days until he sent the wire for her to come west.

After two days of travel, Haman arrived in Cheyenne City to find a cold wind whipping across the Wyoming plains and some six inches of snow on the ground.

He closed the deal on the Great Plains Bank the next day and bought a house four days later. Having the house secured, he wired Linda and told her to come as soon as possible. He told her he was happy with his new job at the Great Plains Bank, and that he had purchased them a house. He was sure she would love it. The house came furnished but if she wanted to replace any of the furniture, or wanted any redecorating done, he would take care of it before they married.

Haman — assuming the name Blake Barrett — was warm and friendly to his employees, and everyone who worked for the bank was happy about their new owner and president.

Life was pleasant for Haman Warner. Because of his ingenuity, he was now a very rich man, and while the real Blake Barrett languished in prison, Warner would even have Blake's beautiful mail order bride.

On his third day in Cheyenne City, Haman

asked around town if there was a church that preached hellfire and brimstone, "ye must be born again," and the cross and blood of Jesus Christ. He was told of two churches. The next day was Sunday. He visited one church that morning and the other in the evening. From what he could tell, both churches were the kind Blake Barrett would belong to.

He decided he liked the pastor of the first church he'd visited, and on Monday went to his office. Pastor Ronald Frye remembered meeting "Blake Barrett" on Sunday morning. Haman used the jargon he had learned from being around Blake and other Christians, and convinced Frye he was born again. He then explained that Linda Forrest would be coming from Boston in view of becoming his mail order bride, and that she, too, was a Christian. Haman told the pastor that he and Linda would become members of the church, once she arrived and got settled. This delighted Frye, and he readily agreed to perform the wedding.

Linda was home alone when the telegram from Blake came. Her parents showed mixed emotions when they came home and she let them read it. They wanted her happiness, but they also dreaded putting her on the train.

With each passing day, Linda experienced a myriad of emotions herself. She was secure in her home with loving parents to take care of her, yet she still couldn't bear the thought of going among people who knew about her wedding tragedy. There was nothing left but to relocate and start a new life.

Without having met Blake Barrett, Linda found it a bit frightening to step out into unknown territory. She had misgivings about living in Wyoming, based on what she'd heard about the Indian troubles. California was much more settled and civilized, but on the other hand, maybe living in the Wild West would be good for her. She was always ready for a challenge, and this would certainly be new and different.

While she waited to hear again from Blake, Linda and her mother went shopping for her trousseau. They purchased several new outfits, along with some personal items. Linda had three large trunks, and each day she did some packing.

Adrienne valiantly tried to keep her sorrow from showing. She was going to miss this precious daughter very much. In the evenings — in the privacy of their bedroom — Adrienne wept in Nolan's arms. They spent much time in prayer, entrusting Linda into God's loving care.

It was a cold, sunny day in Boston — exactly a week from the day the telegram from Stockton had come — when Blake's final wire arrived, telling her to come to Cheyenne City as soon as possible.

That evening when Nolan came home, Linda and Adrienne informed him that the telegram had come. Nolan immediately headed for the railroad station to make reservations for Linda's trip west. Having received a refund for the previously unused tickets, he used the money to purchase new tickets. She would leave in two days and arrive in Cheyenne City two days after that.

The next day, Nolan went to the Western Union office in Boston and sent a wire to Blake Barrett, informing him of the day and time of Linda's arrival.

On that same day, Adrienne and Linda spent a lot of time talking, then right after lunch, Linda went to her room with a melancholy look on her face. She opened the trunk that held her wedding gown and the articles that made up her hope chest when she had planned to marry Lewis Carter. Once again she emptied the trunk, looking at each piece and reliving each memory. Somehow, with Blake now in her life, the hurt was dulled. Still, tears slipped silently down her cheeks as she remembered happy times with Lewis.

While she slowly placed the items back in the trunk, laying the wedding dress on top, she felt a presence behind her and turned to see her mother standing at the open door.

"I just had to look at them once more, Mom," Linda said, then turned back and firmly closed the lid on her past.

Adrienne gathered her daughter in her arms, and they wept together for a few moments.

"Mom, if you can find some girl in the church who could use these things — even the dress — give them to her. It would be a shame for them to go to waste. You understand why I don't want to take any of them with me."

"Of course. I'll do as you wish, honey. Now, it's time for me to start dinner. And I want to do it alone. This is your special farewell dinner."

"All right, Mom. I'll finish packing."

Adrienne had invited Pastor and Mrs. Stanford to dinner, and each person around the table did their best to make it a joyous occasion. After a tearful good-bye to the Stanfords, Linda helped her parents do the dishes and clean up the dining room and kitchen. As they worked together, they reminisced about Linda's childhood and growing up in this house.

Soon it was bedtime. Linda hugged and kissed both her parents, reminding them that it was only two days on the train to Cheyenne City, and she and Blake would undoubtedly come back to visit them, too.

When she walked into her room with the realization that this would be her last night to sleep in it, at least until she and Blake came back for a visit, she let her gaze roam lovingly over every corner and piece of furniture. She had spent many happy hours in this room. It held many girlhood memories and little secrets.

She forced herself to shake off the melancholia and prepare for bed. Everything was ready for her trip tomorrow. As she slid between the sheets, she told herself she must forget the past and look to the future.

Linda expected to lie awake all night but surprised herself when she awakened from a deep sleep as the morning sun came through the window and kissed her face.

She lay there for a few minutes, talking to the Lord and placing herself on this day of departure into His capable hands.

14

The conductor's voice carried through the Boston depot, calling, "All abo-o-oard! All abo-o-oard!" as Linda Forrest embraced and kissed her parents.

"I'll write as soon as I get there and give you the address of the apartment or boarding-house where Blake puts me. I love you both with all my heart."

Nolan and Adrienne clung to each other as they watched their daughter board the train and sit down next to a window. Still wiping tears, she gave them a forced smile.

The big engine hissed, the whistle blew, and the giant steel wheels began to turn.

As the train rolled out of the station, Linda watched her parents longingly as they stood among the crowd on the platform. Then she squared her shoulders and began drying her tears.

An elderly woman across the aisle leaned her way and said, "Anything I can do for you, honey?"

"No, ma'am. Thank you. I'm going west to get married. I just told my parents good-bye."

"I see," said the lady. "Well, I wish you all the happiness in the world."

Linda dabbed at her eyes and smiled at the woman.

The train was now rolling full speed down the tracks. While sitting quietly and listening to the steady rhythmic click of the wheels, Linda breathed a prayer for guidance as she took this big step in her life.

Soon a sweet peace flowed over her and a tiny smile tugged at the corners of her mouth. A feeling of anticipation replaced the fear in her heart. It was all going to work out, and she would find true happiness far removed from the devastating tragedy and embarrassing situation in Boston.

She put her mind on Blake and thought about her new life in Cheyenne City. He hadn't said anything in his telegrams about finding a good Bible-believing church, but by the way he had written in his letters about his church in Sacramento, she knew he must have found something similar by now.

Linda changed trains in Chicago and continued on across Iowa and the plains of Nebraska. Late in the afternoon on the second day of her journey, she heard a passenger behind her say it was only an hour until they arrived in Cheyenne City.

She wondered if she looked presentable. It

had been a long and tiring trip, sitting up in the hard coach seats, and she had gotten very little sleep.

Linda left her seat and walked through the swaying coach to the washroom. As she stood at the washbasin and looked in the mirror, she mumbled to her reflection, "What I wouldn't give for a nice hot bath and a change of clothes."

She gave her face a quick splash of cold water and combed her shiny auburn hair, securing it rather severely at the nape of her neck, then replaced her small-brimmed hat at a becoming angle on her head. With one final look in the wavy mirror, she straightened her shoulders and mentally prepared herself to meet Blake Barrett.

When she returned to her seat, Linda let her eyes roam over the great rolling plains, which were patched with snow. She could tell the wind was blowing stiffly as it plucked at the barren limbs of the few trees. So this was where she was going to live if everything worked out well with Blake. It was nothing like Massachusetts. The vast open spaces enthralled her. The whole world seemed bigger. Her eyes sparkled with excitement at such a great adventure.

Suddenly, doubts assaulted her mind. She was no longer under her parents' roof, nor within the safety and security of those walls. Maybe this wasn't such a good idea after all. She barely moved her lips as she said to herself, "I could just stay on the train. Not get off in Cheyenne City. Just go on to the next stop and catch a train back home."

She took a deep breath. "No," she whispered. "I would just be going back to all the old heartache and embarrassment. I certainly don't want that. I . . . I'm sorry, Lord. Please forgive my lack of faith. You've made it clear that I should come west to Blake and a new life. I'll go on to Cheyenne City and let You take care of me."

Linda thought of Psalm 138:8: "The LORD will perfect that which concerneth me."

Yes, she thought, *I must trust His leading.*

She whispered a prayer for God's guidance, and almost instantly a peace stole over her. She looked down at her hands, which were clinched tight, and relaxed them in her lap. She smiled to herself and looked out the window at the vast, windswept prairie.

Moments later the conductor came through the car, saying, "Cheyenne City, ten minutes! Ten minutes to Cheyenne City!"

Linda's heart thudded against her rib cage and her mouth went dry. The big moment was almost upon her.

Blake's letters had revealed his heart to her,

284

and she felt she knew it well. His letters had also caused her to form a physical picture of him in her mind. But would she really know him on sight?

The train chugged into the Cheyenne City railroad station to a waiting crowd. When the train ground to a halt, excited passengers grabbed their hand luggage and headed for the nearest door. Linda rose from her seat, took her overnight bag from the rack, and slowly followed.

Her heart was still pounding. When she reached the door and started down the steps, she whispered, "Please help me, Lord."

As she stepped onto the platform, her eyes roamed the crowd.

There was no tall, blond, blue-eyed man of twenty-seven in sight.

Haman Warner was tingling with excitement and a bit of nervousness as he watched the train roll to a halt.

Soon the passengers were alighting from the coaches. His eyes searched the doors of each coach, eager to catch sight of the young woman in the photograph he had memorized.

Suddenly there she was, standing on the platform, overnight bag in her hand, eyes scanning the crowd.

Haman couldn't believe his eyes. Linda

Forrest was even more beautiful than her picture. His nerves tensed as he watched her look around, trying to find Blake Barrett. He adjusted his hat, steeled his nerves, and threaded his way through the crowd toward her.

When Linda had taken a few steps from the coach, she stopped, letting her eyes sweep the crowd.

Abruptly, she saw a man who appeared to be about six feet in height moving toward her, smiling. He had coal black hair and steel gray eyes. He could be twenty-seven years of age, but his features were less handsome than she had pictured in her mind. Her heart thundered in her breast as she waited for him to speak.

He drew up, the smile still on his lips, and said, "Hello, Linda. I must say, your beauty is greater than the camera could capture."

"B-Blake?"

"Yes. I'm so happy you're here."

"Thank you," she said, trying to cover her surprise. Other than his height, he was nothing like she had pictured him.

"You have luggage on the train, I presume," he said.

"Ah . . . yes. There are three trunks in the baggage coach. They have name tags on them."

Haman looked toward the baggage coach and said, "I'll have them loaded in my carriage." He pointed toward the parking lot. "See that black one at the second hitching post? Gray gelding in the harness?"

Her eyes followed his pointing finger.

"Go on over there and climb in. I'll get a porter and have your trunks there in a few minutes."

Linda studied his back as he hurried away, then took a few steps. She paused and looked back to where she had last seen Blake a few seconds before. Something didn't click. She couldn't put her finger on it, but she immediately felt her guard go up.

She walked toward the carriage he had pointed out and thought about his letters. He had seemed to be such a gentleman, yet a real gentleman would not have pointed to the carriage and told her to go get in it. He would have walked her to it and helped her climb in.

When she reached the carriage, she laid her overnight bag on the backseat and struggled a bit with her long dress before settling on the front seat. She pondered her meeting with Blake and struggled with the inner feelings disturbing her.

"Linda," she said to herself in a low whisper, "you formed your own preconceived idea of what he would look like and how he would act toward you. You were wrong, that's all." She swallowed hard and told herself to give it time and to dwell on the positive.

The man posing as Blake Barrett arrived shortly, leading a porter who pushed a luggage cart. While the porter struggled to load the trunks in the rear of the carriage by himself, Haman stepped up to the side where Linda sat and said, "We'll be on our way in a couple of minutes."

"Fine," she said, attempting to seem relaxed.

Haman could tell that something was wrong. He feared that Blake may have given her a description of himself in one of his letters.

"Linda," he said, fixing her with a concerned look, "is something wrong?"

"Hmm?" His question threw her off balance.

"You seem a bit upset. Is something wrong?"

"Wrong? Oh, no. Of course not."

His gray eyes continued to question her.

She cleared her throat. "Blake, there is nothing wrong. I'm just a bit surprised."

"About what?"

"Well . . . you."

"Me?"

"Yes. It's strange how I had you pictured

differently, that's all."

"In what way?"

The porter stepped up and said, "The trunks are loaded in the carriage, Mr. Barrett."

"Fine. Thank you."

The man's face showed disappointment.

"Oh! Excuse me," said Haman, reaching in his pocket for a coin. He laid it in the porter's hand. "Thank you."

The porter nodded, then stared at the insignificant tip in his hand and pushed the cart away.

When the porter was out of earshot, Haman turned back to Linda and said, "We were talking about how you had me pictured differently. In what way?"

"Oh. Well, somehow I had you pictured a bit lighter complected, with blond hair and blue eyes. Don't ask me why. It was simply the mental image I had formed of you. Since you were never able to get a photograph of yourself to me . . ."

Her words trailed off, but Haman didn't notice as he inwardly rejoiced that Blake hadn't described himself to Linda.

"Are you disappointed?" he asked, frowning.

"Oh, no! Of course not! And I might say that at least I had you pictured tall like you are."

"Well, good!" He rounded the carriage, climbed up beside her, and snapped the reins.

As they rode through the streets of Cheyenne City, Linda glanced to the west. In the distance she saw the rugged outline of the Rocky Mountains against the sky.

She looked back at Haman and smiled, saying, "Magnificent, aren't they?"

"They sure are. You've never seen the Rockies before?"

"No. Don't you remember? I told you in one of my letters that I'd never been west of the Blue Ridge Mountains in Virginia."

"Oh, sure! I remember now. Well, anyway, you just wait till you get up close to those Rockies. They'll knock your eyes out!"

He swung the carriage onto Main Street. "I've made arrangements for you to stay in the town's best hotel. There it is, up there on the right, three blocks away. The Wyoming Hotel. See the sign?"

Linda gave him a puzzled look. "Hotel? In your letter you said you'd get me an apartment in someone's home or a room in a boardinghouse."

Haman's face flushed. "Oh. Well, yes, I did. But since it'll only be a week or so till we get married, I figured the hotel would work out better. Besides, it's nicer than any apartment or boardinghouse room in the whole town."

Linda's brow furrowed. "A week or so? Blake, I don't understand. In the same letter you said we would give ourselves plenty of time before we married to make sure it was the Lord's will . . . to make sure we were right for each other."

Haman chuckled to mask his jangled nerves and said, "Linda, my sweet, I'm so sure we are right for each other, I have no doubt we'll marry inside of two weeks."

She felt off balance again. "I'm sorry, Blake, but this just isn't the way you talked in your letters."

Realizing he was moving too fast, Haman said, "No, I'm the one who's sorry, Linda. You'll have to forgive me. It's just that . . . well, now that I've met you in person, I know I'm in love with you. I'm sorry if I sound pushy."

His words made Linda relax a bit, and she said, "I'm a little tired from the long train ride, Blake. I hope you understand."

"Sure." Haman admired her beauty from the corner of his eye. He had seen few women with such perfect features.

As they drew near the Wyoming Hotel, Linda expected Blake to pull up in front of it, but he kept the carriage moving.

"Aren't we going to the hotel?" she asked, glancing back at it.

"In a little while, but before we do, there's someplace I want to take you."

"Oh? Where?"

"Before I tell you, I . . . well, I have to say, Linda, that I've held something back from you."

Her heart began to hammer again.

"I didn't want you to know until you came to Cheyenne City that I'm not actually employed at the Great Plains Bank. Neither was I actually employed at the Pacific Bank and Trust Company in Sacramento."

Stunned at this news, Linda said, "Why did you lead me to believe that you're a banker? How do you make your living?"

Haman read the obvious confusion and disappointment in Linda's eyes. He guided the carriage over to the side of the street and pulled rein. "I didn't say I wasn't a banker. I said I'm not actually employed at the Great Plains Bank. You see, darling, I'm the owner and president of the Great Plains Bank, not an employee. I also owned the Pacific Bank and Trust Company in Sacramento."

Linda stared at him, speechless.

"I simply wanted you to come to me for myself, not for my money."

He waited for her reaction, but she was still unable to speak.

"I sold the bank in Sacramento and bought

the bank here so we could both get a fresh start in our lives together. The Great Plains Bank is Cheyenne City's largest, and it's doing well. When you marry me, Linda, all that I have will be yours. You will be a millionaire the instant you say 'I do.' "

Linda put a hand to her throat and blinked in amazement. "Oh, Blake, I don't know what to say. I had no idea."

Haman put his arm around her shoulders. "You're not angry with me for waiting till now to tell you?"

"Oh, no! Not at all! It's just such a shock."

Inside, Linda was relieved that Blake had held back good news. She had feared otherwise. And who could be upset at finding out she was going to marry a millionaire?

Haman was enjoying the feel of his arm around her, marveling at the fact that this beautiful woman would soon be his wife. "I told you I bought us a house, Linda . . ."

"Yes. I'm anxious to see it."

"I'll take you there in a little while, but first I want you to see the bank and meet my employees. I'd like to show you off to them."

Immediately she thought, *The Blake I imagined would have waited till tomorrow when I'm rested up and looking better.* But she wouldn't disappoint him by asking to put it off.

As they moved on down the street, Haman said, "I found us a good church. Tried two of them, which are both like the one I belonged to in Sacramento. I liked the pastor best at the first one. His name is Ronald Frye. Fine man. I told him about us, and he agreed to perform the wedding ceremony."

Linda smiled and said, "You've been a busy little bee, haven't you?"

"You might say that."

"So you've heard Pastor Frye preach?"

"Yes. Dynamic."

"Straight down the line doctrinally?"

"Oh, yes. He preaches Jesus Christ as the only way of salvation through His blood and by the grace of God. Preaches hellfire and damnation, too." Suddenly Haman was glad for the education in Bible terminology he'd received from being around Blake Barrett and other Christians.

"Good," Linda said. "I'll look forward to hearing him myself on Sunday."

Haman escorted Linda into the bank and introduced her to all his employees as his fiancée. They were warm toward her and welcomed her to Cheyenne City.

Haman escorted her to his plush office last, then with the door closed, took her into his arms and said, "What a wonderful life we have ahead, darling!"

Linda couldn't bring herself to use an endearing term yet, but she warmed to his embrace and said, "The Lord has been so good to me, Blake."

"Well, I want you to see the house the Lord has provided for us. Let's go."

Linda's eyes popped at the section of luxurious homes on Cheyenne City's north side. Haman drove her along the hilly streets that divided the huge yards, and her amazement increased when he swung into a long, curved driveway and headed for a huge house at the top of a tall, grassy mound surrounded with bare-branched cottonwood trees. She imagined how lovely they would look when they were loaded with leaves.

The two-story house was constructed of light-colored red brick with sturdy white pillars that held up the wide wraparound porch. It was beautiful but a little ostentatious for Linda's taste. But she figured the town would expect the bank's owner to live in something this grand.

The house had white window frames with glossy black shutters. There was snow on the big porch at the moment, and the flower pots that decorated the wide railings were bare. She pictured the colorful flowers she would put in them in the spring and the white furniture that would adorn the porch. It would be a good place to relax and cool off on summer evenings. She also pictured herself spending many happy hours tending the flowers that would bloom in the flower gardens surrounding the house.

"Oh, Blake," she gasped, "it's beautiful! And you're already living in it?"

"Sure am. Already have a housekeeper."

A housekeeper! Linda had never dreamed she would live in such luxury.

"Now, remember," Haman said as he drew the carriage to a halt at the front porch, "anything in here you want changed, you just say so."

Suddenly the front door opened and a short, squat little woman stepped out on the porch, smiling for all she was worth.

Haman alighted from the carriage and said, "Linda, meet Sadie Brown."

"Hello, Sadie," Linda said.

"I'm so glad to meet you, ma'am," Sadie replied.

Haman was busy doing something with the horse's bridle, so Linda lifted her skirt a little and climbed out of the carriage by herself, thinking that Blake Barrett needed to improve in the area of being a gentleman.

As Linda mounted the steps, Sadie said, "Mr. Barrett, she's even more beautiful than her picture!"

Haman rushed up the steps. "That's what I told her, Sadie."

The housekeeper was almost as round as she was tall, and had a pixie face wreathed in an almost permanent smile. Sadie had gained much wisdom and experience in her fifty-five years, and she detected the sorrow that shadowed Linda's sky blue eyes. When she began to talk to Linda about the Lord, the two of them hit it off immediately.

Haman hadn't realized it when he hired Sadie, but she belonged to the church where Ronald Frye was pastor. She talked a lot about the Lord, and when she learned that her pastor was slated to perform the wedding ceremony for the young couple, she assumed Mr. Barrett was a Christian.

Haman told himself he would find a way to get rid of Sadie when he began drawing Linda away from the church and that boring lifestyle. Now he took her by the arm and said, "Let's take my bride-to-be on a tour of the house, Sadie."

With Haman on one side and the housekeeper on the other, Linda was escorted from room to room, downstairs and up. The huge house was furnished with large, dark wood furniture covered in brocade. A profusion of flowered patterns greeted the eye upon entering each room.

Linda's first thought was to soften the decor. Given some time, she was sure she could give it just the right touch to retain its beauty yet tame it down somewhat. As they went from room to room, she made mental notes as to what it would take to improve it.

"So what do you think?" Haman asked her when she had seen the entire house.

"It's a very beautiful home," Linda replied, smiling, "but there are some things I would like to do to make it 'our' home. If I understood you correctly, the furniture was left here by the previous owners."

"Yes."

"So it would be all right if I wanted to replace some of the furniture with that of my own choosing, and have some redecorating done?"

Haman put an arm around her. "Of course, my sweet. Anything you want. This will be your home, and I want you to be happy in it." In his mind, he was thinking that he really didn't care what she did to it as long as it was grand and inviting to the many guests he planned on entertaining there.

Sadie looked at the couple and smiled. In the short time she had worked for Mr. Barrett, she had developed some misgivings about him but hoped she would overcome them.

As she studied Linda, she sensed the young woman was a strong Christian and had known some deep sorrow in her life. Sadie vowed to help clear that sad look from her eyes. She wasn't quite sure about the mister, but she would enjoy working for the missus.

"Well, darling," Haman said, "I'm sure you would like to go to the hotel so you can unpack and get some rest."

"Yes, I would," Linda said with a sigh.

Sadie hugged her good-bye and said, "See you later, ma'am."

"I'll look forward to it," Linda said, smiling.

15

During the next couple of days, Linda left the confines of the hotel room in the afternoon and walked Main Street to get to know Cheyenne City. As she entered stores, shops, and other places of business, she enjoyed being able to move among people again. Already her life was taking on a new sense of purpose.

The people were quite friendly to her. In some of the businesses, she was called upon to introduce herself and tell why she had come to Cheyenne City. Many people treated her like royalty when they learned she was to marry wealthy Blake Barrett, who now owned the town's most successful bank.

On the first evening, when Haman and Linda ate together at a restaurant, he started to eat without offering thanks, then caught himself in time. He wasn't at a loss for words as he prayed before the meal, for he had often eaten with Blake Barrett in restaurants and cafés. Even though he found it embarrassing to pray in public, he would do whatever was necessary to draw Linda to himself. Whatever it took, having beautiful Linda as his wife would be worth it.

The next day was Sunday.

An inwardly nervous Haman Warner took Linda to church. He had used some forethought and bought himself a Bible, even roughing it up a bit to give it a well-used look.

He could tell that Linda loved every minute of the service and he renewed his vow to wean her from such fanatical foolishness. This religious stuff had to go. Once they were married, he told himself, he would go to work on her. Little by little, he would change her.

When the offering plate was passed, Haman grudgingly dropped in a wad of bills to impress Linda.

Haman's discomfort became almost unbearable when the pastor went to the pulpit, opened his Bible, and began preaching. Haman tried to find the Scripture passages to which the pastor referred, but eventually kept his Bible closed to avoid letting Linda see his unfamiliarity with Scripture. His fumbling had not escaped her eye.

After the service, the people welcomed him and Linda, as did Pastor and Mrs. Frye. Linda felt an instant kinship with Carla Frye, who was also from New England.

Sadie Brown joined the crowd around Linda and gave her a hug, whispering in her ear that she was on her way to the Barrett house to cook Sunday dinner for Linda and Blake, and to come with a big appetite.

As Haman drove the carriage out of the church parking lot, Linda said, "You picked the right church, Blake. I love it. Pastor Frye is a tremendous preacher, and his wife and I have so much in common. I can't wait to go back tonight!"

Wasn't Sunday morning enough? Haman thought.

On Monday morning, Linda walked to Blake's house from the hotel to begin making some changes in decor. She enlisted the help of Sadie, who was more than happy to assist the beautiful young lady with the sad eyes. Sadie suggested that first they sit down in the kitchen and have some aromatic tea and some of her delicious sweets.

Linda enjoyed Sadie's company in the bright, cheery kitchen, which at this point was her favorite room in the house. They shared some favorite Scriptures together and talked about the Lord and His blessings to them. When their tea was finished, they got down to business on the decor.

Linda followed the same routine for the next two mornings, which included buggy rides to Main Street to make purchases for the needed improvements. Haman had given Linda money for that purpose.

On Wednesday evening, Sadie was feeding Linda and Haman supper, when suddenly Linda looked at the clock and said, "Oh! We're going to have to hurry, or we'll be late to prayer meeting!"

"I know you have to go your hotel room, Miss Linda," Sadie said. "You two go on. My friend Bertha, who always picks me up, will bring me to church. I'll see you there."

Haman's stomach tightened, but he couldn't reveal his true feelings yet. He rushed Linda to her hotel so she could change clothes and pick up her Bible.

Again Linda noticed Blake's discomfort at church but let it go without saying anything.

By Thursday evening, she was unable to dismiss her negative thoughts about Blake Barrett. More incidents of ungentlemanly conduct had taken place, and it puzzled her deeply. It seemed that he had changed personalities between the time he'd sent his letters and the time she'd arrived in Cheyenne City. Blake definitely did things to please her, but where was the kind and tender gentleman she'd come to expect?

On Friday night, Haman and Linda were sitting in a restaurant when he looked across the table at her and said, "Well, darling, you've been here a week now. What do you think about us getting married?"

Linda was thinking about her parents and the fact that she hadn't yet written to them. The reason was that she was still unsure of Blake and didn't want to write till she had something positive to tell them. She'd held off writing to Joline for the same reason.

When Haman's words penetrated her thoughts, Linda jumped slightly and said, "Hmm? I'm sorry. My mind was occupied."

A slight frown etched his brow. "I said you've been here a week now. What do you think about us getting married?"

Linda took a sip of coffee, then said, "I won't beat around the bush with you, Blake. In many ways, you've been kind to me. You've generously allowed me to redecorate the house, and you've let me order several hundred dollars' worth of new furniture. I appreciate this, but I have some questions I must ask you."

"Of course," Haman said.

She dabbed at her lips with a napkin, then said, "You seem on edge when we're at church. Don't you like it there after all?"

"Sure I do. It's just that — well, I haven't been myself since I came here to Cheyenne City. The move and all . . . and the load of getting adjusted to the new bank. Everything is so different here in the banking business than in California."

"You're not happy here?"

"Oh, it's not that. It's simply the huge adjustment. I love Wyoming. Everything's going to be fine. Especially since you're here."

Haman felt cold sweat bead his brow. He thought he'd covered his feelings well at church. He must be more careful.

Holding his gaze, Linda said, "Maybe what you just told me answers the other question I have."

"What's that?" Haman's insides were churning. What else had he done to make her question him?

"Blake, you're quite different in person than in your letters."

"In what way?"

"I . . . I don't want to hurt your feelings, but I have to be honest with you."

"I want you to be honest, Linda."

"In your letters, you . . . well, you seemed so tender and gentlemanly. I don't see those traits in person. You're a little blunt in your speech now and then, and you have yet to help me in or out of your carriage. Only once have you hurried ahead of me to open a door. If I'm walking beside you as we approach a door, it's usually me who has to open it . . ."

Haman's face flushed. "Linda, I'm so

ashamed of myself. You were right when you said a moment ago that what I told you about my conduct at church answers your second question. I just haven't been myself. Please forgive me. From this moment on, you'll begin to see the old Blake Barrett."

"All right, Blake," Linda said, smiling. "I can accept what you've said about the adjustment. I'm sure it hasn't been easy for you."

Haman reached across the table and took her hand. "I'm falling deeper in love with you every day, darling," he said.

Linda squeezed his hand in return, then said, "I need a little more time, Blake. How about another week?"

"Oh, that'll be fine," he said, relief flooding him. "One week from today?"

"How about we get married on Saturday, a week from tomorrow?"

"Of course. Saturday. Let's see . . . that's February 2. Good. We'll talk to the pastor about it on Sunday."

The next day, Linda happily sat down and wrote her parents a letter, telling them the news that Blake was owner and president of the Great Plains Bank in Cheyenne City, and that he was quite wealthy. The house he had bought was the next thing to a mansion, and it was in the nicest part of town. She was glad to tell them they had found an excellent church, and capped off the letter by informing them she and Blake would be getting married on February 2.

She also wrote a letter to Joline, giving her the same information.

On Sunday morning after the service, she and Blake talked to Pastor Frye about having the wedding on the following Saturday at the church, and Frye readily agreed. The bride and groom wanted a simple ceremony with only two others in the wedding party — Carla Frye and Sadie Brown as witnesses. They had already asked Sadie, and Carla readily accepted.

Pastor Frye announced the wedding in the Sunday evening service, and afterward the church people offered their congratulations.

During the week, Linda and Sadie went shopping to pick out the wedding dress, and Sadie bought herself a new dress for the wedding. The two of them also worked hard at the house, making more changes. On Thursday the new furniture arrived, and when Haman came home from his day at the bank, he was very pleased with what Linda had done to make the house take on her personality.

The wedding took place on Saturday afternoon at 2:00 P.M. It was attended by all of

Haman's employees, many of the business-men who did their banking at Great Plains Bank, and most of the members of the church.

Haman stood tall in a black suit with a paisley vest and black cravat. As he thought of the fact that he was standing where Blake Barrett had wanted to stand, his eyes took on an evil glint and a smirk curved his lips. He caught himself and blinked a couple of times, reminding himself to smile pleasantly.

Linda was exquisitely clad in a light blue dress of watered silk. It fit her perfectly and flattered her graceful figure. The high neck was edged in delicate lace, and the puffed sleeves tapered down at her wrists with a double row of lace. She wore a small blue hat the same shade as her dress and adorned in simplicity with small white flowers.

In her hands, covered with white lace gloves, she carried a small nosegay of white roses tied with blue satin ribbons. The whole effect made a lovely picture as she stood beside Haman in the muted glow of sunlight coming through the windows.

Pastor Frye began the ceremony with words of welcome to the guests, then read from Genesis chapter two about the wedding of Adam and Eve, which was performed by God Himself.

Though she struggled against it, Linda's mind kept flashing back to the wedding that almost took place in Boston. *This is not at all what I had pictured for my wedding when I was growing up,* she thought. *No bridesmaids, no maid of honor, no ring bearer and flower girl.* She felt tears prick at the back of her eyelids and blinked rapidly to dispel them.

Lost in her own thoughts, she was unaware of what the pastor was saying. Suddenly she became aware that Pastor Frye was looking at her strangely, and there was dead silence. They must be waiting for her reply, but she had no idea what the question was.

She blinked in confusion and said, "I . . . I'm sorry, Pastor. Would you mind repeating those words?"

Haman frowned at her, then looked back at Frye.

Frye smiled nervously and said, "Linda Forrest, do you take this man to be your lawfully wedded husband, to live together with him in the bonds of holy matrimony, and do you promise to keep yourself only unto him so long as you both shall live?"

"I . . . do," she replied.

From that moment, Linda made a concentrated effort to keep her mind on the rest of the ceremony.

It was over shortly, and before she knew it,

the pastor was giving his permission to kiss the bride. Then Pastor Frye introduced them as Mr. and Mrs. Blake Barrett, and they hurriedly walked up the aisle with Linda's hand tucked firmly in the crook of Haman's arm.

Haman had arranged for a large reception at the dining room of the Wyoming Hotel. He would have liked to serve liquor to perk up the occasion, but knew he dared not.

Linda enjoyed visiting with the friends she had made at church, some of whom were also employees at the Great Plains Bank.

Haman stood there, talking first to one person, then another, and smugly told himself he had pulled off his deception without a hitch. He always got what he wanted. He laughed inside as he thought of the real Blake Barrett, rotting in prison.

Linda valiantly turned her thoughts from Lewis and what might have been and determined in her heart to be a loving and submissive wife to Blake.

There was no time for a honeymoon. Haman told Linda it was too early yet to be away from the bank for any length of time.

As time passed, Linda and Sadie worked together around the house a good part of each day. Linda was still making little changes here and there, using some decorating schemes she had learned from her mother and from Aunt Beth. When Sadie wasn't helping Linda, she was doing her regular duties.

One day, as they were having tea together, Linda said, "Sadie, you've started to talk about your childhood on several occasions, but it seems there's always an interruption. How about telling me about it right now?"

"Oh. Well, all right," said the pudgy little woman. "I was six years old when I came to America from England with my parents. We settled in New York City, but my father began to hear things about the wild and woolly West. Soon he got the 'itch' to go west so bad that he packed us up, took us to Missouri, and joined a wagon train at Independence. We crossed the wide Missouri River and headed across the Nebraska plains."

Sadie went on for some time, telling tale after tale of the journey westward in the wagon train. Pretty soon she said, "That's all for now, honey. It's time for this housekeeper to get back to her work. I don't want the mister to fire me!"

Linda's eyes twinkled as she said, "If the mister fired you, the missus would just hire you right back!"

The two women had a good laugh together and went back to their separate tasks.

★ ★ ★

Some two weeks after she had written to her parents, Linda received a letter from her mother, which also had a note from her father tucked in the envelope. They were rejoicing that things were going so well for their daughter, and both reminded her how very much they loved her and missed her.

Linda was sitting in the library, weeping, as she held the letters in her hand, when Sadie stepped in and said, "What's wrong, honey?"

Linda looked at her through her tears and said, "Nothing's wrong, really, Sadie. I received a letter from my parents. I just miss them so much."

"Aw, honey, I know it's got to be hard."

She wrapped her ample arms around Linda and cuddled her as a mother would her small child. Linda wept some more, then finally gained control.

"I know I can't take your mother's place, honey," Sadie said, "but when you need to talk, I've got big ears."

Linda kissed the woman's plump cheek. "Thank you, Sadie. You are truly a blessing."

A few days later, Linda received a letter from Joline, which helped her a great deal. She had sent off another letter to her parents, and now took the time to immediately respond to Joline's.

Each day as they spent time together, Sadie told Linda more stories about her wagon train journey to Wyoming. Many of the incidents were humorous, but Sadie took note that even though Linda smiled, the smile never reached her pretty eyes.

One day in mid-March, a snowstorm was blowing outside. Linda and Sadie sat down in the kitchen and began polishing the silverware.

With cups of steaming hot tea before them, Sadie looked at the young woman with the sad eyes and said, "Linda, dear, you've never told me about your life in Boston. I'd like to hear about it."

"Well, I . . . I don't want to bore you."

"It won't bore me," Sadie assured her. "You've come to mean a lot to me. I'm very much interested in your past."

"Where shall I start?"

"Best place I know of is the beginning."

"You mean from the time I was born?"

"Yes."

Linda's lips curved in a sly grin. "All right. I clearly remember the day I was born. There was this sudden flash of light, the temperature took a sudden drop, and someone slapped me real hard on my posterior. Then I remember being dried off, and —"

Sadie shook with laughter. "You little

313

scamp! Now, get serious!"

It felt so good to Linda to be able to laugh and have a good time. She told Sadie of her happy childhood and growing up years. She told her some things about Janet that were actually pleasant in her memory, then told her of the day she opened her heart to Jesus, and how He had saved her and made Himself so real to her.

As she described her teen years she came to the point in time when she met Lewis Carter and slowly fell in love with him. Sadie listened quietly, wondering if she was about to learn why Linda carried the sadness in her eyes.

Linda stammered a bit as she told of her engagement to Lewis, the happiness she knew as the day of their wedding drew nigh; then she broke down and wept as she told of being left at the church on the day of the wedding as Lewis and Janet ran off together.

"Honey," Sadie said, "since I first laid eyes on you, I've known you hurt deep inside. It showed in your eyes. I'm so sorry for what you've gone through. I hope the sadness in your eyes will go away in time, as you go on in your life with the mister."

"Me, too," sniffed Linda. "But —"

Sadie looked her square in the eye. "But what, child?"

"Oh, nothing."

"C'mon, now. You can tell me. I'm your friend."

Linda shook her head. "No, Sadie. I really shouldn't."

"Is it about the mister?"

Linda cleared her throat nervously. "Y-yes."

"He's your husband, and you don't want to say anything about him to someone else."

"That's right."

"Let me guess. You're wondering about his relationship with the Lord."

Linda's eyes widened. "Why . . . yes. How did you know?"

"Because I've wondered too, dear. There's no witness of the Spirit between the mister and me when we're together. You know, like there is between you and me and other Christians."

"You've hit the nail on the head," Linda said. "Maybe all this change in his life has gotten him away from a close walk with the Lord, and his heart has turned cold."

Before Linda arrived in Cheyenne City, Sadie had actually seen a cruel side of the man she knew as Blake Barrett, but she would not divulge this to Linda. Instead, she took Linda's hands in hers and said, "Let's pray for the mister right now, honey. Let's ask God to work in his heart and bring him out of his backslidden state, if that's what it is."

"Oh, thank you, Sadie. Yes! Let's do that."

Sadie led in prayer, asking the Lord to do His work in Blake's heart and life. She then asked the Lord to help Linda stand by her husband and love him as a Christian wife should, and to bring Linda perfect happiness.

When both women had dried their eyes, Linda said, "I've got some work to do, Sadie."

"Me, too," said the plump woman.

"Maybe you can suggest what I should do with the two chairs from the sewing room I replaced with new ones. I can't throw them out, but they're taking up valuable space where I stacked them on the back porch."

"How about the attic?" Sadie asked. "There's quite a bit of room up there."

"The attic! That's one place in the house I haven't been. What's up there?"

"Just some old pieces of furniture the previous owners left up there. Some old paintings, among other things. And the mister's trunk that he brought from California."

"But there's still room for the sewing chairs?"

"Oh my, yes. Would you like me to help you carry them up there?"

"That won't be necessary, Sadie. You go on with your chores. I'll take them up."

The door leading to the attic was next to the hall closet on the second floor. Linda carried both straight-backed wooden chairs to the second floor and left one in the hall while she carried the other up the narrow passage and steep stairs. The air was close and had a musty smell. There was a layer of dust on most everything except the old trunk that sat near one of two small windows. Linda glanced at it curiously as she placed the chair in the opposite corner beside a dust-covered sewing machine laden with cobwebs. In another corner were some overstuffed chairs, a couple of small tables, and dusty, cobwebbed coal oil lamps. Behind them, leaning against an ancient potbellied stove, were several old paintings.

Moments later she returned with the other chair and set it beside the first. Glancing around, she decided it had been a long time since anyone had cleaned the attic. She'd attend to it soon. But the wind was howling outside, and snow was beating against the windows. It was cold up here, too. She'd worry about cleaning the attic some other time.

As she headed back toward the steep, narrow stairs, she glanced at Blake's trunk again, noting its large padlock.

As time passed, Haman Warner treated

Linda like a queen, often buying her gifts and making an effort to improve his gentlemanly virtues. He was so happy to have such a lovely creature as his wife.

Linda appreciated the kindness and attention he gave her, but he definitely wasn't the devoted Christian he'd led her to believe in his letters.

One evening, a couple in the church named Alex and Dorothy Helms had the Barretts to their home for supper. Haman was quite nervous but did his best to mask it.

After supper, the foursome was sitting in the parlor talking, and some discussion came up about certain Scripture passages in the Bible. Haman sat in absolute silence, for the passages were totally foreign to him. Both Linda and the Helmses wondered that Blake stayed out of the conversation. Certainly anyone familiar with the Bible would want to join in the discussion.

The conversation soon turned to what had brought Alex and Dorothy to the Lord. They gave their testimonies about when they had been saved, and the circumstances that led up to it.

Linda then told about when she was saved as a child in Boston under the preaching of her pastor. When she finished, all eyes went to Haman.

Cold sweat beaded his brow. He nonchalantly brushed it away as he said, "Well, ol' Blake here got saved when he was attending a revival meeting in San Jose, California, some ten or eleven years ago."

A red flag went up in Linda's mind. In one of his letters, Blake had told her how he got saved, and it didn't match what he'd just said.

As Haman drove the carriage on their way home, Linda sat close to him under the buffalo hide blanket, her arm entwined in his, and said casually, "Blake, I remember that in one of your letters you told me your mother had led you to the Lord when you were nine years old. You didn't say anything at all about being saved at a revival meeting when you were a teenager."

Haman felt a sharp ache of tension settle behind his eyes. "Oh, I guess I didn't tell it quite right, heh-heh. Of course, Mom led me to the Lord when I was nine. I . . . uh . . . I rededicated my life at the revival meeting in Santa Rosa."

"I thought you said it was in San Jose."

"Oh! What did I just say?"

"Santa Rosa."

"Mmm. Sorry. I meant San Jose."

Linda said no more. In her heart, she asked the Lord to help her make the best of a very disappointing situation.

A couple of evenings later, Linda had allowed Sadie to go to a widows' meeting at church that included supper. Linda had prepared a very special meal for Blake, recalling that in one of his letters he said he loved meatloaf.

When they sat down at the table, Haman began loading his plate with vegetables.

"Blake . . . ?"

"Mm-hmm?"

"Aren't you going to eat the meatloaf?"

"I really appreciate you fixing supper for me tonight, honey," he said in a soft tone, "but I really don't care for meatloaf."

Linda watched him carefully as she said, "You told me in one of your letters that you love meatloaf. When did your taste buds change?"

Haman suddenly burst out laughing and said, "Just a little joke, darling! I was simply having a little fun. Of course I love meatloaf! It's one of my favorite meals." As he spoke, he picked up the meatloaf platter and slid a couple of slices onto his plate.

Linda played along by giggling and said, "Blake Barrett, you ornery scoundrel!"

They laughed together, and Haman ate the meatloaf in spite of his dislike for it.

While the meal progressed, Linda decided to bait him. She got him on the subject of his childhood. In one of Blake's letters, he'd told her that his mother never spanked him as a child. When he was bad, she merely told his father when he came home from work, and Bradley Barrett had whipped him accordingly.

After Haman had told about some childhood incident, Linda asked casually, "Blake, how often did your mother have to whip you when you were a boy?"

Haman laughed. "At least three times a week, until I got big enough to outrun her. But boy . . . when she whipped me as a little guy, she used a leather belt and whipped me with the buckle end!"

Linda filed this latest inconsistency in her mind.

Over the past several days, she had looked through Blake's desk in the library, and all of his drawers and belongings in their bedroom, but had found nothing that would shed any light on the real man she had married. Deep in her heart was a growing concern that she'd made a big mistake in marrying Blake, yet in her mind she kept trying to find ways to give a reason for his inconsistencies. He was her husband, and she'd promised to love, honor, and obey him.

The next day, while Sadie was marketing, Linda thought of Blake's trunk in the attic.

Maybe its contents would reveal some clues to his strange behavior. She remembered the heavy-duty padlock, but by this time she was so upset that breaking the lock was something she'd just have to do.

She took a hammer from the kitchen cupboard and headed for the attic. As she climbed the stairs to the second floor, her only thought was that she wanted to find a way to restore Blake to his former self. She didn't know how the trunk might help do that, but she couldn't let things go on as they were.

Linda knelt beside the trunk and hit the latch several times until it broke and the padlock fell off. With trembling fingers and a prayer in her heart, she slowly lifted the lid and let her gaze drop to the contents of the trunk. Her eyes fell first on some homemade toys from Blake's childhood, along with some articles of outdated little boy's clothing, which lay on top of a beautiful old quilt. She ran her hands over the quilt, marveling at the workmanship that had gone into it. When she lifted it out of the trunk, a large brown envelope caught her attention. Unlike the other articles in the trunk, it was obviously quite new. Her heart beat faster, and her hands shook so badly she had to clasp them together for a moment to still them.

Closing her eyes, she said in a whisper,

"Lord, please give me strength for whatever I may find." She then untied the string that held the flap down and eased into a sitting position, emptying the contents of the envelope in her lap. It was a wad of newspaper clippings. They were from the *Sacramento Gazette* of recent date. She gasped when a headline seemed to leap at her:

BANKER BLAKE BARRETT CONVICTED OF GRAND THEFT

Her stomach fluttered as she unfolded the page and saw the photograph of Blake Barrett. He was blond, fair, and very handsome!

She lifted a shaky hand to her mouth as she read the story of Blake's arrest and conviction in court, and his fifteen-year sentence to the state prison at Ukiah, California. The same edition told of Haman Warner, the Pacific Bank and Trust Company's vice president, becoming owner and president of the bank due to instructions left in the late Bradley Barrett's will should circumstances ever render his son Blake unable to properly direct the bank.

A photograph of Haman Warner on the same page made her light-headed.

She felt ill as she read the other clippings, which told of the arrest and pending trial.

Two more photographs showed her the real Blake Barrett, who looked almost exactly as she had pictured him in her mind.

As she gazed at Blake's face in the newspaper clipping, she began to weep and say over and over, "Oh, my poor darling! How horrible! How horrible!"

16

Prison guard Glenn Domire waited while Blake Barrett shuffled into his cell after the evening meal and sagged onto his cot. Blake's ankles were chafed and aching from the chains he wore each day while working in the chain gang.

"Blake," Domire said, "I'm sorry about your ankles. In fact, I'm sorry you have to be in this place at all."

"Me, too," said guard Anthony Tubac, drawing up beside Domire. "But think what would've happened to us, Glenn, if he hadn't been put in here."

"We'd have gone to hell, that's what," said Domire. "We both know this man is innocent, but I'm sure glad he was sent here. I never would have heard the gospel if Blake hadn't been here and cared for my soul."

The sound of cell doors clanging shut echoed throughout the building as the inmates were locked in their cells for the night.

"I can't say I like it here, guys," Blake said, "but seeing Larry Huffman saved before he was hanged . . . and seeing you two and Charlie Jacobs and Hal Keeney saved is worth it all."

"I'll bring you some salve for those ankles, Blake," Tubac said. "It'll be about half an hour before I can get back."

"I appreciate it, Anthony."

Domire swung the door shut and both guards looked through the bars at Blake for a few seconds, then moved on.

Blake removed his shoes and socks and began rubbing his right ankle, which hurt the worst. His mind went to Linda as it did a hundred times a day. Why hadn't he heard from her? He knew by her letters that Linda was a sweet and compassionate person. Certainly she would write to him at least once after she received the wire from Haman.

Haman. Maybe somehow he had neglected to send the wire! Maybe Linda came to Sacramento as scheduled, learned of his imprisonment, and went back to Boston. If that was the case, she probably hated him by now.

No! Not Linda. She was such a sweet Christian, and so full of love for the Lord. If she knew he'd been sent to prison she would make some kind of contact. Wouldn't she?

A little more than thirty minutes had passed when Anthony Tubac appeared at Blake's cell door with a small jar in his hand. Blake started to get up.

"Just stay there," Tubac said, unlocking the door. "I know your feet hurt."

The guard stepped inside and handed Blake the jar. "This salve will not only heal the chafing, it'll ease the burning sensation, too."

"Good. Maybe I'll sleep better tonight than I did last night. Thank you."

"Anything else I can do for you?" Tubac asked, eyeing Blake's sore ankles.

"I was about to ask for a big favor."

"Name it."

"Have you got a few minutes?"

"Sure. I'll have to lock the door and talk to you through the bars. We aren't supposed to fraternize with the inmates."

Blake nodded.

The cell door clanked shut, and Anthony pressed his face to the bars. "What can I do for you, Blake?"

"You've heard of advertising in newspapers and magazines back East for mail order brides, haven't you?"

"Sure."

"Well, let me tell you my story."

"You sent for a mail order bride?" Anthony said, looking surprised.

"Yes, I did."

Blake told Anthony Tubac the whole story about meeting Linda Forrest by mail,

327

and of their plans for her to come to Sacramento to become his mail order bride. He explained that he had asked Haman Warner to send a wire to Linda and tell her what had happened and to ask her to write him at the prison.

"So you see, Anthony, I've heard nothing from Linda, and nothing from Haman. I don't know what's going on."

"That would be enough to drive a fella out of his mind," Tubac said. "Too bad the warden has this rule about no wires or letters going out from inmates till they've been here six months. What can I do for you?"

"I was hoping that possibly you might try to persuade Warden Hall to bend the rules a little bit because of my situation, and let me send a wire to Haman. I've got to know what's happened with Linda."

"I'll talk to him," said Tubac. "I can't guarantee anything, but I'll give it my best. See you tomorrow afternoon."

When Blake returned to his cell after another day of work in shackles, he pulled off his shoes and applied more salve to his ankles. He was just finishing when Anthony Tubac stepped up to the barred door and said, "Good news, my friend. Warden Hall has granted one wire, but only one."

"Great!" said Blake, rising to his feet. "Can I send it now?"

"You can't send it," said Anthony. "I have to send it for you."

"Oh. Well, all right. Can you do it now?"

"It's ten minutes after four. Will Haman Warner still be at the bank?"

"Oh, sure. Even though banks close at three, the work goes on until five. He'll be there. He's the owner and president of Pacific Bank and Trust Company in Sacramento."

"Okay. I'll send the wire and wait for his reply. See you in a little while."

While he waited, Blake sat on the cot and prayed, asking the Lord to make things all right for sweet Linda, and to let him somehow make contact with her. She had to hear it from him that he was innocent.

Almost an hour had passed when Anthony finally returned. "The news isn't good, Blake. The return wire was from a Chester Hamilton, who is now the owner and president of the bank. He said Warner sold the bank to him several weeks ago. He left Sacramento almost immediately, and nobody in town knows where he went."

Blake's heart seemed to stop. *Why would Haman sell the bank?* he asked himself. *And why hasn't he been in touch with me in all this time?* His mind was awhirl with questions.

What was going on? Had Haman wired Linda as he promised? Or did she come to Sacramento and learn that the man she was to marry had been convicted of grand theft and been sent to prison for fifteen years?

"Blake, I'm sorry."

"No fault of yours," Blake said. "Would . . . would you try to talk the warden into letting you send one more wire for me?"

"He wouldn't do it, believe me. But I can send a wire from me anywhere I want. Who should I contact?"

Blake's features brightened. "Send it to Linda's father, Nolan Forrest. I'll write the address down for you."

Blake went to the cell's small table, picked up a stub of a pencil, and wrote the Forrests' address on a scrap of paper. He handed it to Anthony through the bars and said, "Explain in your wire that you're a friend of mine, and ask the whereabouts of Linda. If she's there, ask if she knows about me and will write to me and let me know how she is."

"Will do," said Anthony. "Be back as soon as I can. Since they're three hours ahead of us in time, I may not hear back till tomorrow. You'll probably have to go to supper before I get back, but I'll let you know as soon as possible what I find out."

Blake thanked him and sat back down on

the cot. Linda's face came to his mind's eye. If only he could make contact with her! Somehow, though he had not met her in person, he had fallen in love with her. His heart yearned for her, and he knew he wouldn't have peace until she could hear it from him that he was innocent . . . that he loved her and was sorry for what had happened to destroy their plans for a life together.

Blake was in the mess hall eating supper when he saw Anthony Tubac come in the door and scan the room. The other inmates at the table looked quizzically at the guard as he came to their table and leaned close to Blake and said, "I'll see you at the cell later."

Tubac's countenance told Blake that something else was wrong. He lost his appetite and shoved his plate away.

He had been back in the cell about ten minutes when Tubac appeared at the bars.

Blake leaped off the cot. "What is it, Anthony?"

Tubac shook his head. "I couldn't get the wire to go through from our telegraph key in the office, so I went into town to the Western Union office. They told me the Midwest is getting all kinds of blizzards. Telegraph lines are down over a stretch of over five hundred miles. It'll be months before service can be restored."

Blake nodded solemnly. "Well, thanks for trying, Anthony."

"I don't know near as much as you do about the Bible, Blake, but from what I've been reading, it appears that the Lord allows difficult and unpleasant things to come into our lives so we'll draw closer to Him and trust Him more. Right?"

"That He does," Blake said.

"Well, what you're going through is sure difficult and unpleasant, but from what I can put together, the Lord says if you stay close to Him, pray a lot, and trust Him, it'll turn out all right."

Blake had to smile. "You've learned a lot in your short time as a child of God. I'm proud of you."

When Anthony was gone, Blake sat down on his cot, took off his shoes and socks, and began applying salve to his ankles, which were looking better. "Lord," he said, "I have to admit my faith has grown a bit weak lately. But Anthony's right. I'm going to stay close to You, pray a lot, and trust You to make all this turn out right. You are the God of the impossible. You can bring it about no matter what the circumstances are."

Linda rose from the floor beside Haman Warner's trunk and stuffed the clippings back in the brown envelope. She wrapped the string around it and carefully descended the steep stairway from the attic, then hurried toward the bedroom. She heard Sadie come in downstairs from her marketing.

As she stood at the dresser mirror and looked at herself, she hardly recognized the face that looked back at her with its huge, almost opaque eyes gazing out of a pale face.

She gave herself a mental shake and tidied the strands of hair that had loosened around her temples, then picked up the brown envelope. As she descended the stairs she heard Sadie singing a hymn as she put away foodstuffs in the pantry.

Linda wished she could slip out without saying anything to Sadie, but that would worry the dear woman. She went toward the sound of Sadie's singing and stepped into the kitchen. The portly woman's back was toward her at the pantry door.

"Sadie, dear," Linda said softly to avoid startling her.

Sadie turned to greet Linda, then frowned at what she saw. "Honey, what's wrong? You're so pale! Are you sick?"

Linda shook her head. "No, I'm all right. I —"

"You don't look all right. Come to the table and sit down."

"Sadie, I can't. I have a very important errand to run. I'll be back after a while."

Suspicion dawned in Sadie's eyes. "Have you found out something about the mister? You have, haven't you?"

As much as Linda loved and trusted her dear friend, she couldn't bring herself to tell Sadie what she'd found. The important thing was to get to the sheriff's office. "I . . . I can't tell you anything right now, Sadie. I must go. I love you."

With that, Linda disappeared into the hall.

Sadie blinked, shook her head, then turned back to her work.

Linda walked fast toward Cheyenne City's business district. The wind was cold, causing her to pull up the collar of her coat around her ears.

She thought of the damning evidence she carried in the brown envelope and found herself getting angrier at Haman Warner with every step. She deliberately slowed her pace and forced herself to breathe deeply. *That lying hypocrite!* she thought. *No wonder he kept fouling himself up! Nobody can be a perfect liar!*

She turned the corner onto Main Street. The Laramie County sheriff's office was on a corner three blocks away. With every step she had to fight her burning anger toward Haman Warner. But when she reached the door of the sheriff's office, she felt surprisingly calm.

Pausing for a moment, she looked up and down the street on both sides, making sure Haman was nowhere in sight. She glanced at the Great Plains Bank sign two blocks farther down the street, and her mind went to Blake Barrett languishing in that California prison as an innocent man.

She took a deep breath, twisted the doorknob, and entered the sheriff's office.

Sheriff Bob Coffield was in his late forties, a tall, rugged individual with abundant salt-and-pepper hair. His heavy mustache was almost totally gray. He was sitting at his desk in the inner office when there was a knock at the door.

"Yes, Darren?" he called. His booming voice carried easily to the next room.

The door swung open, and Deputy Darren McGivens said, "Sheriff, there's a pretty auburn-haired lady out here who would like to see you. She says it's very important."

Coffield rose to his feet. "Send her in."

The sheriff mentally agreed with the deputy when Linda came through the door. Indeed, she was pretty.

"Yes, ma'am," he said. "I'm Sheriff Coffield. Please sit down."

Deputy McGivens retreated to the outer office, closing the door behind him.

"I don't believe I've had the pleasure, ma'am . . ."

"I'm Linda Barrett —" Linda stopped abruptly when she realized her name was actually Linda Warner. The thought made her stomach lurch. "I'm Linda Barrett, Sheriff. I —"

"Oh, yes! Blake Barrett's wife. My wife and I have our checking account at your husband's bank. He seems to be a fine man. I heard that his fiancée had come from back East somewhere, and that the wedding had taken place after a couple of weeks. What can I do for you?"

Linda brought the brown envelope into view. Keeping a steadiness in her voice that she didn't feel inside, she said, "Sheriff, what I'm about to show you involves my husband, and it's not good. He came here from Sacramento, California. But he's not Blake Barrett. His name is Haman Warner. I only found that out about an hour ago." As she spoke, she opened the envelope and dumped its contents on the desk.

The sheriff frowned, then put his attention on the newspaper clippings.

"You will note the photographs with their

names under them, Sheriff. Do you see the one that says Haman Warner?"

"Yes," Coffield replied, blinking in amazement. "That's the man who recently purchased the Great Plains Bank."

"Correct. And on the same page is a picture of the real Blake Barrett, who now sits in the Ukiah State Prison in northern California for something he didn't do. There are two other pictures of Blake Barrett in there."

Linda waited quietly while Bob Coffield carefully read each and every clipping. When he read them again, he said, "Mrs. — Oh, I see now why you paused when you introduced yourself. You really aren't Mrs. Barrett. You're Mrs. Warner."

"Yes, and sick at heart to learn it," Linda said levelly.

Coffield nodded, thought on the situation a moment, then said, "There's definitely been some skullduggery by Mr. Warner. It looks to me like he stole the twelve thousand dollars himself and framed Blake Barrett so he could legally take over the Pacific Bank and Trust Company."

"Exactly," said Linda. "That's the way it looks to me."

"First thing to do is wire Sheriff Claude Perkins in Sacramento," said Coffield. "I'll tell him what Warner has done. I might get a

337

reply right away, and on the other hand, it could be a while. Would you like to wait, or should I come to your house when I get a return message?"

"I'll stay here as long as it takes, Sheriff. I'm sure not going home without you as an escort."

Coffield tugged at his mustache. "I see your point. You wait right here. I'll be back as soon as I can."

Linda sat alone in the sheriff's private office and prayed. "Lord," she said, "I realize You knew about this whole thing. Thank You for answering prayer and letting me find out about that vile man I'm married to. Poor Blake! What a terrible thing to be unjustly accused of a crime and to have everything taken away from him, even his freedom. Then Haman, that low-down skunk, took Blake's place with me. Oh, ughh-h-h! Lord, please let this thing be handled swiftly, so it's Warner behind bars and Blake Barrett breathing free air! Please let justice be done!"

Barely an hour had passed when Sheriff Coffield returned to the office. He tossed his wide-brimmed hat on a clothes tree in the corner and hung his sheepskin coat next to the hat, then sat down behind the desk. "I got through real quick, ma'am, and got a reply back from Sheriff Perkins."

"Good! What did he say?"

"Perkins says the information I gave him has him convinced that Warner stole the twelve thousand dollars from the safe-deposit box and planted it at Blake Barrett's house to frame him. Perkins says Warner was in the position to do so and has benefited exactly as Barrett's father had stated in the will should Blake become unable to properly run the bank. A man sure can't run a bank from behind prison walls. Those are Perkins's words."

"I'm glad he sees it like you and I do. So what now?"

"Well, Sheriff Perkins pointed out in his wire that since Warner purchased the Great Plains Bank under false pretenses, using Blake Barrett's name, he committed a felony. Even if he wasn't guilty of the theft and the frame, he would face a long prison term."

"That's where he belongs . . . behind bars."

Coffield nodded, his face grim. "And for what he did to you — marrying you under false pretenses — he deserves more than a long prison term. He oughtta be horse-whipped, and I'd love to be the guy to do it."

"And I'd like to help you," Linda said, letting a slight grin curve her lips. "But I guess that would be against the law, wouldn't it, Sheriff?"

"I s'pose so, 'cause I'd cripple him while I was at it. I guess we'll just have to let it be the prison term. Anyway, Sheriff Perkins told me to arrest Warner on suspicion of grand theft and impersonating another man, to purchase the bank under false pretenses. Perkins is having a deputy U.S. Marshal sent here from Denver to extradite Warner back to Sacramento. His actions are enough to reopen the grand theft case involving Blake Barrett."

Linda nodded, feeling a measure of satisfaction.

The sheriff rose from his chair and said, "I'll take a couple of my deputies with me and arrest Warner right now. I heard my men come in a moment ago." He glanced at the clock on the wall. "It's two-thirty. The bank closes at three. I'd rather arrest him with no customers in the bank, but this thing can't wait. You're welcome to stay here till we have him in a cell. Then it'll be safe to go home."

Linda stood up, her graceful jaw set in a stern line. "If it's all right with you, Sheriff, I'd like to go with you and maybe have a little part in the arrest."

Coffield raised his eyebrows. "What do you mean?"

"I'll explain it on the way to the bank."

The sheriff shrugged. "Well, okay."

Coffield waited for Linda to pass through

the door ahead of him, then walked toward Deputy McGivens, who was talking to two other men wearing badges. "Deputies Ted Larkin and Jay Bounds, I'd like for you to meet Mrs. Barrett. Well, actually Mrs. — Oh, that's good enough for now. Mrs. Barrett."

All three deputies looked at their boss skeptically.

"Let me explain it," he said with a sigh. "You have to know anyway."

At the Great Plains Bank, Haman Warner was seated at his desk behind a railing much like the one at the Pacific Bank and Trust in Sacramento. A beefy man in a business suit sat before him.

While Haman looked at the financial statement that lay before him, he said, "I'll have to meet with my officers, Mr. Trumbull, but I can tell you right now, this statement looks plenty good to warrant a thirty-thousand-dollar loan. We like to help new merchants establish themselves in Cheyenne City."

Trumbull smiled. "Good, Mr. Barrett. How soon will you have an answer for me?"

Haman's attention was drawn to the front door of the bank as Linda came in. Apparently Sheriff Bob Coffield had preceded her, for he was holding the door open for her to enter.

Haman returned his gaze to Trumbull, trying to recall what he had just said, then glanced at Linda again, who was walking his direction beside Coffield.

Haman always felt a little jumpy when he saw an officer of the law, but he assured himself there was nothing wrong. After all, the sheriff and his wife were customers of the bank. As Linda drew nearer, Haman expected to see Coffield veer off toward the tellers' cages, but he didn't.

". . . have an answer for me?" said Albert Trumbull.

Haman blinked and set his gaze on the beefy man. "What was that, sir?"

Trumbull chuckled hollowly. "Well, for the third time, how soon will you have an answer for me about the loan?"

Linda and Sheriff Coffield stopped at the small gate in the railing, waiting for him to finish his business.

Haman shook his head. "I'm sorry, Mr. Trumbull," he said. "My beautiful wife just came in, and she always takes my breath away."

Trumbull twisted his portly frame around, glanced at the lady who stood beside the sheriff, and turned back, smiling. "This lady right here, Mr. Barrett?"

"Uh . . . yes."

"She is indeed very beautiful."

"Thank you," said Haman, feeling a little tense. Neither Linda nor Coffield was smiling.

Trumbull hoisted his huge body out of the chair and extended his hand. Haman stood up and gripped it.

"You haven't told me yet when I'll have an answer about the loan, Mr. Barrett," said Trumbull.

"Well, let's see . . . how about tomorrow morning at ten o'clock. We have our loan meetings before opening time every morning."

"Fine," Trumbull said, letting go of Haman's hand. "I'll be in at ten in the morning."

Sheriff Coffield opened the gate for the big man and gave him a tight smile. Trumbull thanked him, nodded to Linda, and headed toward the front door.

"Hello, darling," Haman said. Then he nodded to Coffield. "Good afternoon, Sheriff." He didn't like the strange look in Linda's eyes, nor the grim lines on Coffield's face.

Haman's pulse quickened as he noticed Deputies Ted Larkin and Jay Bounds standing just inside the front door. When they saw him glance their way, they started moving toward him.

As two secretaries and Haman's vice president — who sat at the desk next to Haman's — looked on, Linda squared herself across the desk from her husband and firmly set her jaw. Haman let his eyes flick to Coffield, then the approaching deputies, then back at Linda.

The scorn in her eyes was something he had never seen there. His palms went moist and a cold ball settled in his stomach as she said, "The ruse is over, Haman."

17

Haman Warner felt like he'd been hit by a thunderbolt, and all strength drained from his body.

How did she find out?

The moment seemed to go on forever, as if time had stopped.

Finally the spell was broken when Linda brought the large brown envelope into view, opened it, and placed the stack of clippings on the desk before him. On top was the page from the *Sacramento Gazette* with the headlines:

BANKER BLAKE BARRETT
CONVICTED OF GRAND THEFT

Two faces stared at him from the page — his own and that of the real Blake Barrett.

Suddenly Haman's blood went hot. Through clenched teeth he said, "How dare you break into my trunk and paw through my private property!"

Linda's voice was crisp and emotionless as she said, "You'll be exchanging places with

Blake at the Ukiah State Prison, Haman Warner."

For a brief moment it looked like Haman might try to make a break for it as he stiffened and shoved back his chair. Deputies Larkin and Bounds had come through the gate and were flanking the sheriff. When their guns came out of their holsters in the blink of an eye and the deadly black muzzles lined on him, Haman eased back in the chair, licking his lips.

Sheriff Coffield took a step closer and said, "Haman Warner, you are under arrest for suspicion of grand theft in Sacramento, California, and for purchasing this bank under false pretenses, using the name of Blake Barrett. You're going to be extradited to Sacramento by a deputy U.S. Marshal, and there will be a new investigation of the twelve-thousand-dollar theft from a safe-deposit box."

The cold ball in Haman's stomach grew even colder.

"Cuff him," the sheriff said to Ted Larkin.

Haman's employees and customers were aghast as Deputy Larkin holstered his gun and took a pair of handcuffs from his belt. He jerked Haman to his feet and cuffed his hands behind his back.

Haman's legs felt weak as Larkin gripped

his arm and said, "Okay, Warner, let's go."

Linda picked up the clippings and stuffed them back into the envelope. Her scornful gaze met Haman's for an instant. He started to say something, but Larkin yanked him away and ushered him unceremoniously through the gate. Deputy Jay Bounds returned his gun to its holster and hurried ahead of them to open the door.

When the deputies and their prisoner were gone, Sheriff Coffield looked around at the bank employees and customers and said, "As you folks no doubt picked up, the man you thought was Blake Barrett is actually Haman Warner, who apparently framed the real Blake Barrett of Sacramento, California, for a crime he committed."

Their shock was complete, and no one said a word.

Coffield turned to the bank's vice president and said, "Mr. Stillman, take over here until further notice from me. Business will go on as usual. Understand?"

Stillman nodded. "Yes, Sheriff. I'll handle it."

The sheriff then turned to Linda, who was suddenly feeling empty and shaken. "Would you like me to escort you home, ma'am?" he asked.

She drew a deep breath. "Thank you, Sheriff, but that won't be necessary. I'll be fine."

"You look a little peaked. Are you sure?"

"I . . . I'll be all right. Thank you."

Under the wide-eyed gaze of the bank employees and customers, the sheriff and the auburn-haired woman crossed the lobby and moved outside.

When they were on the street, Coffield said, "As things develop, I'll be in touch with you, ma'am."

Linda nodded and turned toward home. Coffield headed the opposite direction to his office.

As Linda walked slowly along the street, she found all anger drained from her. In its place was a strange sense of peace, even though she felt a hollowness in her heart. "Thank You, Lord," she whispered. "At least this part is over."

Her legs were shaky as she climbed the steps of her porch and entered the front door. She removed her coat, draping it on a chair in the vestibule, moved past the parlor, and headed for the kitchen where she could hear Sadie humming a tune.

Sadie looked up from the bread she was kneading as Linda entered the kitchen. She threw up her flour-covered hands and rushed to the young woman's side.

"Oh, honey!" she exclaimed. "You look

like you've been through the Civil War! What's going on? Will you tell me now?"

Linda nodded. "Yes. I want to sit down though."

Sadie quickly wiped off her hands and pulled out a chair for Linda, who sat down and laid the brown envelope on the tabletop. Now that she was safely home and with her dear friend, she let go, bursting into sobs.

The portly woman folded Linda in her arms, pressing her head against her ample bosom. "Go ahead, honey," she said. "Cry it out. Then we'll talk about it."

Linda wept for several minutes, just letting out her pent-up emotions. When she grew quiet, Sadie sat down across the table from her and said, "Honey, you've become like my own daughter. I love you, and I want to help you any way I can."

The touch of Sadie's hand, the soothing words, and the sweet concern in her voice stemmed the flow of Linda's tears. She took a shuddering breath and reached into her dress pocket for a hanky, then looked into her friend's kind, troubled eyes and said, "I love you, Sadie Brown."

Sadie's face brightened. "Want to tell me about it now?"

Linda nodded and opened the envelope. "I found these newspaper clippings in my husband's trunk up in the attic. They tell their own story."

Sadie read the newspaper articles and looked at the photographs of Haman Warner and the real Blake Barrett. It was her turn to feel numb all over, and she finally said, "So your important errand was to take these clippings to Sheriff Coffield, I presume."

"Yes. He wired Sheriff Claude Perkins in Sacramento, and Perkins wired back for Sheriff Coffield to arrest Bla— I mean, Haman, immediately. You should have seen Haman's face when we walked into the bank. He looked like he was going to faint when I moved up to his desk, called him Haman, and laid these clippings in front of him. The bank employees and the customers were in total shock to see the man they thought was Blake Barrett arrested and put in handcuffs."

"Must've been a sight to see," commented Sadie.

"Yes. Haman is in jail now and will be extradited to Sacramento to face charges of grand theft. He will also be charged with purchasing the bank here illegally."

Linda put her hands to her face and sighed. Relief flooded her entire being as the dreadful secret was shared with someone who cared.

Sadie left her chair and patted Linda's shoulder. "I'll make some tea, honey."

While Sadie put the teakettle on and took cups and saucers from the cupboard, she revealed to Linda her own thoughts about the impostor and told her some of the cruel things he had done and said to her before Linda arrived from Boston. She had refrained from saying anything before now because Haman Warner was paying her a salary, and she felt she could not speak against him to anyone.

Linda expressed her sorrow that Sadie had been subjected to Haman's cruelty.

Sadie passed it off and said, "So now what?"

"In the morning I'll go see Pastor and Carla and tell them all about it. They need to hear it from me."

"Yes."

"I must stay here until I know the real Blake Barrett is out of prison. Once I know he's free, I'll return to Boston. But don't you worry. I'll see that you're taken care of financially until you can find other employment."

The teakettle began to whistle, and Sadie poured tea into a pot to let it steep for a bit before pouring cups for both of them. They sat quietly for some time, sipping the hot, soothing liquid, each lost in her own thoughts.

That evening, Linda and Sadie were sitting in front of the fireplace in the parlor when there was a knock at the front door. Linda started to get up, but Sadie beat her to it. "You just stay there and rest, honey. You've been through a lot today. I'll see who it is."

Moments later, Sadie returned and said, "Pastor and Carla are here to see you. They learned of the incident at the bank from the town's grapevine."

Linda rose from her chair. "Of course. Bring them in."

When the Fryes entered the room, Carla rushed to Linda and embraced her, saying, "I'm so sorry for what's happened."

"Me, too," said the preacher, standing close by.

Linda nodded. "I was planning to come and see you in the morning. Right now I still feel numb. But since you're here," she said softly, "if you'd like to sit down, I'll tell you the whole story."

The Fryes listened intently as Linda told them of how she was jilted by Lewis Carter, who ran off with her sister on the very day of her wedding. She then told of her mail contact with Blake Barrett, and the subsequent trip to Cheyenne City to possibly become Blake's bride. She filled them in on the newspaper clippings and Haman's arrest.

"The rest of the story you already know," said Linda.

Carla moved to her and put her arms around her. "You poor dear. You've been through more heartache and mental anguish than the average person suffers in a lifetime. I'm so glad you haven't let it embitter you toward life, and even more, toward the Lord."

When Carla had returned to sit beside her husband, Linda said, "I won't say that I understand why the Lord allowed all of this to fall on me, but I can't be bitter toward Him. The Lord Jesus went to the cross for me and saved me. He's never failed me, and I know He never will."

"You've stayed close to the Lord through all of this, Linda, and kept your faith in Him," the pastor said. "He's going to reward you for it. Well, we need to be going, but first we'd like to pray with you, Linda."

"Of course," she said, giving him a weary smile.

After the prayer, the Fryes offered to help Linda in any way they could. She thanked them, saying she would let them know if there was anything they could do.

That night, Linda chose to sleep in one of the guest bedrooms. She couldn't bear the thought of sleeping in the bed she'd shared with Haman.

Sleep escaped her, and as she lay awake in

the darkness, her thoughts turned to Blake Barrett and the sweet relationship that had developed between them through their letters. What a kind and loving Christian gentleman! So vastly different than Haman!

"Linda," she whispered, "you have to admit it. Now that you've seen the real Blake's photographs and you know he looks almost exactly like you pictured him, there's a flame in your heart for him. You never met him in person, and in spite of the scarred heart Lewis left you, you had actually fallen in love with the man whose letters drew you westward."

Tears welled up in her eyes, and her lower lip trembled as she said, "Linda, you've been soiled by Haman Warner, and you're his wife, no matter how much you hate it. What might have been with Blake is gone forever. But somehow, you've got to work up the courage to go to that prison and meet him face to face. He deserves to hear the whole story from you."

How long will Blake be kept there? she wondered. Certainly he wouldn't be released until Haman was convicted of the crime for which Blake had gone to prison. That could take weeks, maybe months. She must go as soon as possible!

While Linda lay awake, making plans to go

to California, Haman wrestled with his conscience in a jail cell. The only light came from the partially open door leading to the sheriff's office where Deputy Ted Larkin was doing some paperwork for the sheriff.

Haman was the only prisoner in the cell block that night. The silence surrounding him was suffocating. Or was it guilt pressing down on him like a shroud?

He flipped and flopped on the cot, trying to go to sleep, but it was no use. After a while, he sat up, holding the blanket around him.

"Haman, what have you done to yourself?" he said quietly. "You should have burned those clippings. Or better yet, there shouldn't have been any clippings! There shouldn't have been a prison sentence for Blake. You let your greed ruin you, that's what you did!"

His mind flashed back to a sermon Pastor Frye had preached a couple of weeks ago. Somewhere in the Old Testament . . . Numbers, was it? Or Leviticus? No. Numbers. "Behold, ye have sinned against the LORD: and be sure your sin will find you out."

Those last six words seemed to taunt him, over and over again: *Your sin will find you out! Your sin will find you out! Your sin will find you out!*

Haman buried his face in his hands. Hot tears surfaced as he regretted his evil deeds.

Why? Why had he been so greedy? Bradley Barrett had left him in a comfortable situation. He had an excellent salary, which Blake would have raised every year, and he had 5 percent of the net income of the bank.

"That should have been enough for you, Haman," he whispered. "But no, you had to have more! Your sin has tracked you down like the wild beasts Pastor Frye told about in that sermon. With what the authorities know, you'll be convicted and given Blake's fifteen years behind bars. But it will be more than fifteen years, Haman! You falsified yourself in every way to buy the Great Plains Bank! They'll probably add twenty years to the sentence! You'll be an old man when you get out. Thirty-five or forty years in prison — that's not life, that's only existence!"

He stood up and began pacing the cell. Tears coursed down his cheeks. His entire body trembled, but it wasn't from the cold air in the jail. It was from the horror rising up within him.

No! his thoughts screamed. *I couldn't stand being locked up in that prison! I couldn't stand it! No! No! No!*

He moved to the barred door and shouted, "Deputy Larkin!"

He heard the scrape of a chair on the wooden floor, then footsteps walking the narrow hallway between office and cell block. Yellow-orange light flooded the room as Larkin's long, tall silhouette stopped at the door, which he had shoved all the way open.

"You want something, Warner?" said the deputy.

"I need a pencil and a piece of paper."

"At this time of night? Go to sleep."

The deputy slammed the door and stomped back to the office.

"No!" cried Warner. "Come back! Please! I need pencil and paper!"

When there was no response, he shook the cell door hard, making it rattle. "Larkin!" he shouted. "Come on! I need pencil and paper!"

Rapid footsteps thundered in the hallway, and the door burst open. Larkin charged in and stopped inches from the bars, his face heavy with anger. "It's late, Warner! Why can't you wait till morning? What are you gonna write tonight?"

"I . . . I want to write a note to my wife. She won't come here to see me. That deputy U.S. Marshal could show up here in the morning, couldn't he? Denver's only a hundred miles away."

Larkin thought on it. "Yeah. He could show up in the morning."

"Then have a heart for my wife. At least let

me leave a note for her. There are some things I've got to say to her. I did her wrong. Let me tell her I'm sorry."

Larkin shrugged. "All right. One sheet of paper."

"That'll be enough."

Less than a minute had passed when the deputy returned with pencil and paper. Haman reached through the bars to take them. "Is it all right if I light my lantern so I can see what I'm writing?"

"Sure. Go ahead. But don't stay up all night writing it. I'm going home now. I'll get the note from you in the morning."

"Fine. Thank you."

Larkin halted at the door, letting the light from the office flow into the cell so Haman could get his lantern lit.

"Thanks," Haman said.

Larkin nodded and closed the door.

Haman sat down on the wooden chair by the desk and picked up the pencil. He paused to think, running splayed fingers through his thick black hair.

His conscience struck him with the impact of a sledgehammer. "Blake," he said, with a quiver in his voice, "you were nothing but good to me. You thought I was your friend. If you hadn't believed that, you would no doubt have figured out who framed you. And you were such a good and true friend to me. There's no way I could ever face you."

He heard the outside door of the office close. Deputy Ted Larkin was gone.

More tears spilled down his cheeks as he said with a choked voice, "And then there's Linda. Beautiful, sweet, innocent Linda. She tried to make a go of it, even when she was disappointed in the man she thought had written all those letters. Oh, Linda! I was angry at first that you had broken into my trunk. But I can't blame you. You were seeing through me more all the time, yet trying to be a good wife. I understand why you had to find out what was wrong.

"Linda, I can't blame you at all for the anger you feel toward me. I may very well have ruined your life. Blake sure won't want you, now that you've been married to me."

Linda couldn't sleep. After a while she left the bed, put on her wool robe and slid her feet into slippers, then went to an overstuffed chair by the window and sat down.

She hugged herself and looked out at the cold night sky, alive with a sliver of moon and millions of stars. She was still numb from all that had happened in the past twelve or thirteen hours. Sitting there, looking through the window at the dark night, she thought of the time she had stood at her bedroom window in Boston on that fateful night that was supposed to have been her wedding night. Again, the shimmering stars seemed aloof . . . distant.

Twice now Linda Forrest had been shaken to the very foundation of her being. As she looked through the window toward heaven, she said, "Lord, what is wrong with me? Am I not taking enough time to listen to You, and to know Your will? You said in Your Word, 'They that wait upon the LORD shall renew their strength; they shall mount up with wings as eagles; they shall run, and not be weary; and they shall walk, and not faint.'

"Please help me to wait upon You, and please renew my strength and lead me in the right paths. I want Your will in my life. And I want peace. You said You would give me perfect peace if I stayed my mind on You. Right now, I very much need that perfect peace."

She sat in the chair and fixed her mind on the Man who had gone to Calvary's cross, bore her sins, died for her, and rose from the grave. Soon God's perfect peace warmed her heart and soul. She finally rose from the chair and slid back under the covers. Smiling in the darkness, she said, "Thank You, Lord. My heart is still scarred from all it has endured, but Your blessed peace is indeed my balm in Gilead!"

Before she dropped off to sleep, Linda thought of her parents, and how all of this was going to affect them. They were under the impression that her marriage was wonderful, and that she was happily married to the man whose letters had so captivated her.

"Lord," she prayed, "they have to know. Please prepare their hearts so it won't hurt them too much when they find out."

She would write to them after she went to California and visited Blake. They would want to know the whole story.

She thought of the handsome man whose picture was in the *Sacramento Gazette*. What a horrible nightmare this had been for him.

"Lord," she whispered, "let Blake be freed real soon. What a terrible thing to be locked up when you know you're innocent! Put his life back together for him, Lord, as only You can do."

She fell asleep praying for Blake Barrett.

The next morning, Deputy Jay Bounds carried a breakfast tray down the narrow hallway toward the cell block. Deputy Larkin walked ahead of him, telling Bounds about Haman Warner's request for pencil and paper late last night.

"Well, after what he did to that poor woman," said Bounds, "I don't know if a letter will be apology enough."

"That's for sure," said Larkin, stopping at the door and turning the knob. He shoved the door open and stepped into the cell block, saying, "That pretty lady deserves a whole lot better than him, any—"

The breakfast tray bumped Larkin's back as he froze in his tracks, staring at Warner's cell.

"What's the matter, Ted? What're you stopping for —" Jay Bounds's mouth fell open at the sight before him.

Larkin said something low and indistinguishable as they beheld the lifeless form of Haman Warner. He had wound his sheet tight and formed a noose and rope with it, then tied it to one of the rafters in the cell.

The chair that came with the small desk lay on its side beneath his dangling feet.

A wan and weary Linda finished dressing her hair in front of the mirror, then left the guest bedroom. She was thinking of her first task — going to the railroad station — as she descended the stairs. The tantalizing aroma of ham and eggs, biscuits, and coffee met her nostrils. Not until then had she realized just how hungry she was.

She found Sadie at the stove, scooping scrambled eggs from a skillet onto a plate.

"Good morning," Sadie said, catching sight of Linda from the corner of her eye.

"And a good morning to you, Sadie dear," Linda replied. "Sure smells good in here." She went to the stout little woman and gave her a hug. "I love you, Sadie."

"I love you, too, sweetie," Sadie replied. "How'd you sleep?"

"All right once I got there. Took a while. Lots on my mind."

The two women sat down at the shiny clean table, and Sadie offered thanks to the Lord for the food.

As they ate, Linda told Sadie about the Lord giving her peace before she went to sleep last night. When she was on her second cup of coffee, Linda said, "Sadie, there's something I have to do."

"What's that, honey?"

"I must go to the Ukiah prison and see Blake. It may be a while before he gets out, since they have to convict Haman of the crime before Blake can be released. I know Blake may not be terribly thrilled to see me, but I feel I have to meet him face to face and tell him the whole story."

"I agree, honey, but what makes you think he won't be thrilled to see you?"

There was a long pause, then Linda said, "What he and I could have had is gone, Sadie. He had his heart set on my being his mail order bride. Now I'm just what's left of what might have been."

There was a loud knock at the front door.

Linda jumped up. "This time I'll do the running," she said. "You finish your breakfast."

She opened the door to the familiar face of Sheriff Bob Coffield, accompanied by a man she didn't know.

"Good morning, gentlemen," she said, hearing Sadie's short steps in the hall behind her.

"Good morning, Mrs. B— ah . . . Mrs. Warner," said Coffield. "This is Edgar White, a prominent attorney here in town. He worked with Haman in handling the legal details of the sale of the bank."

Linda smiled. "Good morning, Mr. White."

"We need to talk to you, ma'am," said Coffield. "It's very important. May we come in?"

"Certainly." Linda stepped back to allow them inside.

Sadie drew up, curiosity on her plump face, and Linda introduced her to Edgar White, explaining that he was Haman's attorney, and that he and the sheriff needed to talk to her.

When Sadie realized it was private business, she excused herself.

Linda took them to the parlor, and when they were seated, the sheriff said, "Mrs. Warner —"

"Sheriff, you can call me Linda," she interrupted. "I really don't like being called Mrs. Warner. You understand."

"Of course. Linda, I have something to tell you, and then, because of my news, Mr. White has some things to explain to you."

"All right."

"Linda, when my deputies went into the cell block to take Haman his breakfast this morning, they found him dead."

"Dead! What happened?"

"He made a rope out of his sheet and hanged himself from a rafter in the cell."

It took a few seconds for Linda to recover from this stunning news. "He didn't seem like the type to commit suicide . . ." she said, her voice trailing off.

"I don't know if there is a type, ma'am. Most people who do that surprise everybody who knows them."

Linda thought of the time when the police officer in Boston thought she was about to end it all in the harbor.

Coffield reached into his coat pocket and

took out a folded sheet of paper. "Haman left a suicide note, ma'am. It's addressed to you."

Linda's hand trembled as she took the paper from the sheriff.

"I can't say I feel sorry for him, Linda," he said. "He was a pretty bad man. While we were driving over here in Mr. White's carriage, I commented to him that there was a wicked man in the Bible named Haman. In the book of Esther, I believe."

"Yes," Linda said.

"Well, this wicked Haman who framed Blake Barrett and tricked you into marrying him ended up the same way as Haman in the Bible, with his neck in a noose. I call that poetic justice in both cases."

18

Linda unfolded the piece of paper and read its hastily scribbled message:

> Dearest Linda,
>
> What I did to you and Blake is more than I can live with. Neither can I stand the thought of spending years in prison. So, I'm taking the coward's way out.
>
> Please forgive me for ruining your life and for so wickedly deceiving you.
>
> Sheriff Coffield will see this note before you do. I am confessing here and now that it was me who picked the lock in Horace Dodge's safe-deposit box. I planted the $12,000 in Blake's house to frame him. I wanted the bank and all its wealth, and was willing to let him go to prison so I could have it. I want Blake's name cleared. He is innocent. Please tell Blake that I beg his forgiveness.
>
> Haman Warner

Tears welled up in Linda's eyes and began spilling down her cheeks. She realized that last night, even as she was asking God for guidance in her life and for Blake's freedom, He had already answered. Haman could have hanged himself without leaving his signed confession. Now that the authorities had it, Blake would no doubt be freed quite soon.

"Pardon me, ma'am," said the sheriff, "are you actually weeping for that low-down skunk?"

"No," she replied. "I'm weeping because the Lord has answered my prayers for Blake Barrett. Now that you have the confession of Haman's guilt in your hands, Blake can go free, can't he?"

"Of course. The investigation in Sacramento will come to a halt when I wire the news to Sheriff Perkins. However, I'll have to send him the note with an affidavit signed by me that it, in fact, was written and signed by Haman Warner."

"Tell you what," she said, wiping tears from her cheeks, "I can deliver it to Sheriff Perkins for you. As soon as I can purchase railroad tickets, I'm going to California to see Blake. I'm pretty sure I'll have to change trains in Sacramento to go to Ukiah. I'll see Sheriff Perkins and give him the papers."

"All right. I'll make up the affidavit right away. Now, Mr. White has something to discuss with you."

Linda put her attention on the lawyer as he said, "I'll have to address you correctly, ma'am. Legally you are Mrs. Warner. I came along because I felt it was important that you know your financial status now that you're Haman's widow."

Linda blinked in confusion. "Yes, sir?"

"Ordinarily, in a case like this, if there hadn't been a will you would have ended up with your husband's estate, but not until it had gone through the courts with a whole lot of fees going to a whole lot of people, including me. Were you aware that just after you married the man who called himself Blake Barrett that he came to me and made out his will?"

"No."

"I didn't think so. Well, he left his entire estate to you. Even though he was operating under an assumed name, it won't make any difference. You now own the Great Plains Bank, this house, and the money your husband carried in his personal account. Of course, the money you have in the joint account is yours. You're a very wealthy woman, ma'am."

It took a moment for Linda to absorb the news. Finally, she said, "Mr. White, this is all so sudden. You're saying the bank, the money in the accounts, and this house are mine as of this minute?"

"Yes, ma'am."

"I know we've kept about twenty thousand dollars in our joint account. Do you know how much is in Haman's personal account?"

"About a quarter of a million. Probably more."

Linda paused, letting the figure sink in. "So if I should decide to sell the bank, I can do it."

"You sure can. And I know what you're thinking. You'll want to sell it and give the money to the real Blake Barrett because, in essence, his bank was stolen from him."

"Exactly."

"Well, when you get ready to sell it, please let me know. I'll handle the legal procedures for you."

"I will, Mr. White. Thank you."

"Linda," said the sheriff, "when you get your train ticket and know the time of your arrival in Sacramento, please let me know. I'll wait till then to send the wire to Sheriff Perkins. That way he can meet you at the depot."

"I'll let you know today," she assured him.

Linda stood at the window and watched the two men climb into White's buggy and drive away.

"Oh, Lord," she said aloud, "thank You! Blake's life can at least be partly put back together. He'll have enough money to buy a bank somewhere, or even set up a new one.

370

He can go on with his life and put all his pain and sorrow behind him."

Two days later, a hired carriage pulled up in front of the house. As the driver stepped to the ground, Sadie opened the door and said, "The missus is almost ready, sir. She'll be right with you."

"Yes, ma'am."

"Her overnight bag is here, if you'd like to put it in the carriage."

"Sure," said the driver, dashing up to the porch.

Linda descended the staircase dressed in a dark blue travel suit with a crisp white blouse and a perky hat that matched the blue in her suit. In her handbag was Haman Warner's suicide note and the affidavit from Laramie County Sheriff Robert Coffield, confirming that the note was genuine.

She paused at the door to embrace Sadie and said, "When I come back, I'll put the house up for sale. As I told you last night, you'll be welcome to stay on until I actually leave Cheyenne City. But you'll get a year's salary to give you plenty of time to find another job."

Tears tumbled down Sadie's round cheeks. "I hate the thought of you leaving, sweetie, but you have to do what you believe the Lord wants you to do. I don't know how to thank you for being so generous to me."

"You don't have to thank me," Linda said, planting a kiss on Sadie's cheek. "All you have to do is promise to write me once a week after I'm gone."

"You've got that promise already."

"See you in a few days, Sadie."

"All right. Tell Blake I'm glad things turned out so well for him."

"I will."

As the westbound train rolled toward the majestic Rocky Mountains, Linda eased back on the seat and looked out the window. She let her gaze stray across the rolling hills of Wyoming. There were large patches of snow, with brown grass showing in between. Green pine trees dotted the hills amid leafless clumps of wild brush.

Linda smiled as she saw a mother black bear and two cubs moving alongside a half-frozen creek. Her attention was suddenly drawn to a huge bald eagle riding the wind currents high above the hills.

Though she was physically and emotionally tired, she felt a sense of joy and expectancy in her heart. "Lord," she whispered, "I want to thank You again that You're in control of my life. 'All things work together for good to them that love God,' You said. I don't know what You have ahead for me, but I know it will be all right. Thank You for letting things in Blake's life work out for good, too. Help him not to be bitter toward me for anything. I want us to at least be friends."

She scooted a little farther down on the seat and closed her eyes. Soon she was lulled to sleep by the steady rocking of the coach and the perfect rhythm of the clicking wheels beneath her.

Night was falling by the time the train pulled out of Salt Lake City. Linda made her way to the dining car and enjoyed a well-cooked meal, then returned to her seat and read her Bible for a while.

Soon she grew sleepy again and eased back on the seat. There was a baby crying somewhere behind her. Maybe someday the Lord would let her be a mother. Of course, first she had to have a husband. *Somewhere,* she thought, *the Lord has someone who will be willing to marry a widow.*

She thought again of the pain and shame she had suffered from the despicable deed of Lewis and Janet. But after everything else she had been through, it was only a dim regret now. She had thanked the Lord many times that He'd spared her from marrying Lewis, who was weak and irresponsible. Sooner or later he would have hurt her, anyhow.

Because the pain of Lewis and Janet's betrayal had receded, there was room to love again. She had never felt anything like love in her heart for Haman Warner, even though she had thought he was Blake Barrett.

Blake. She hadn't thought of it until this moment, but with Haman dead, this could put a new light on the situation if Blake still felt anything for her. But even if he did, would he want her?

Once again she recalled Joline's words of comfort and encouragement: "You will have your time to love. The Lord has the man, the time, and the place. Let Him work it out."

She was looking out the window at the stars that twinkled like diamonds against a black velvet sky. "Lord," she said in a low voice, "could it be that Blake is the man you have for me, after all? I mean, if You worked in his heart, You could fix it so he would want me in spite of my having been married to Haman. You are God. You can do anything. Anything but fail, that is.

"Lord, You know how I feel about Blake, even though I've never met him in person. Why do I feel this way unless You put it in my heart?"

She listened to the sound of clicking wheels

374

beneath her and realized that with each turn of the wheel she was drawing closer to California and to the man she loved. She thought of Psalm 138:8.

"Please, Lord," she said softly, "let Blake love me as I love him, and perfect that which concerns us."

It was a bright, sunny morning in Sacramento as Linda alighted from the train and saw a big man with a sheriff's badge on his vest. He was standing in an obvious spot, waiting for her to approach him.

With handbag in one hand and her overnight bag in the other, she moved up to the man and said, "Sheriff Perkins?"

"Yes, ma'am," he said, smiling. "And you're Mrs. Warner."

"Yes, sir."

"Here, let me take that bag."

"Thank you."

"My pleasure, ma'am. I've got a buggy in the parking lot."

They started walking, then Sheriff Perkins said, "Do you have the suicide note and Sheriff Coffield's affidavit with you?"

"Yes, sir. Right here in my handbag."

"Good. I'll take you to the hotel where you'll be staying and let you freshen up; then we'll talk business in my office. The hotel is just across the street from my office."

"Sheriff Coffield said you would make the hotel reservation for me. I appreciate that."

"My pleasure, ma'am. And the bill will be paid by the county."

"There's no need for that, Sheriff. I can afford to pay for the room."

"That's not the point, Mrs. Warner. We're just so happy to get this mess cleaned up, and to see Blake cleared of the charges. We're mighty glad to pay your hotel bill."

Perkins helped Linda into the buggy, then climbed in beside her. As he put the horse in motion, he said, "You and I have an appointment with Governor Hammond at three o'clock this afternoon."

"The governor?"

"Yes."

"Of California?"

"Yes, of course."

"Why do we need an appointment with him?"

"He's the man with the authority to set Blake free. He must see the suicide note and affidavit from Sheriff Coffield in order to proceed with Blake's release."

"Oh, I see."

"The governor is a personal friend of mine," said Perkins. "I got us the appointment today because of our friendship. Otherwise we'd have waited three or four days to see him."

Linda smiled. "It always pays to know the right people, doesn't it?"

"Sure doesn't hurt," Perkins said with a chuckle. "I was sort of surprised when the wire informed me you were supposed to have been Blake's mail order bride. He and I are friends, but I didn't know he had advertised for one."

"He was going to wait till I got here to let his friends know about me," she said.

"Well, little lady, let me say that he sure picked a good-looking one."

Linda blushed. "Why, thank you, Sheriff."

"So you're going to Ukiah to see him?"

"Yes."

"And you two have never seen each other?"

"That's right. Only photographs."

"And Blake doesn't know you're coming?"

"No. He doesn't even know what's happened with Haman, or anything. As far as he knows, I'm still in Boston."

Perkins chuckled. "Boy I'd sure like to be a fly on the wall when you walk into that prison and meet Blake!"

Linda's stomach knotted slightly. Indeed, that was going to be some moment.

An hour later, Linda left the hotel, walked

377

across the street, and entered the sheriff's office. She was introduced to deputies John Findlay and Vance Ohlman, then Perkins sat her down beside his desk.

Linda took an envelope from her handbag and laid it in front of him, saying, "Here's the suicide note and the affidavit, Sheriff."

Perkins removed them from the envelope and looked them over. "This will do it. Now, since we have some time, I'd like to hear how Haman made this marriage scheme work."

Linda told Perkins the whole story, starting with being left at the church in Boston on her wedding day. From there, she explained why she had responded to Blake's ad in the newspaper, then told him about receiving the wires from Haman — as Blake — telling her of his move to Cheyenne City. She explained about the marriage to Haman, her disappointment in thinking he was Blake, and the subsequent end to it all when she found the clippings.

Perkins shook his head in amazement. "Little lady, you truly have suffered heartaches that would have done most women in."

"They just about did, Sheriff," she said, "but the Lord gave me the strength to get through it."

Perkins smiled as he inserted the papers back into the envelope. "When the governor sees these, ma'am, Blake will be a free man real quick."

At five minutes before three that afternoon, Sheriff Claude Perkins ushered Linda into the capitol building and down the long hall to the office of Governor Will Hammond.

"Hello, Matilda," Perkins said at the receptionist's desk.

Matilda smiled and rose from her desk. "Good afternoon, Sheriff. And this is Mrs. Warner?"

"Yes. Linda Warner, meet Matilda Jones."

"Welcome to California, Mrs. Warner," Matilda said.

The name "Mrs. Warner" made Linda feel sick, but she masked it.

"Thank you, Mrs. Jones," she said, having noticed Matilda's wedding ring.

"The governor is ready for you . . . please come this way."

Matilda escorted them to the governor's office and introduced Linda.

Will Hammond was a tall man of sixty with a thick shock of silver hair and bushy eyebrows to match. He welcomed Linda and his old friend Claude Perkins, bidding them sit down in the chairs facing his desk.

"I want to tell you this young woman's story, Governor," said Perkins. "It will make you appreciate her very much, I guarantee you."

"I've allowed plenty of time for this meeting," said the silver-haired man. "Go right ahead."

Hammond listened intently as Perkins told Linda's story, up to the point of her agreeing to come to Sacramento in view of becoming Blake Barrett's mail order bride.

Perkins shifted on the hard chair and said, "Now, Will — I mean, Governor —"

"Forget the formalities, Claude," Hammond said. "I'm sure Mrs. Warner won't tell anybody we called each other by our first names."

"I promise," Linda said with a smile.

Hammond looked at Perkins. "You were saying . . . ?"

"You're aware of the situation with Blake Barrett — his arrest and conviction?"

"Of course. Blake's doing time at Ukiah."

"That's right. For a crime be didn't commit."

Hammond's bushy eyebrows arched. "Tell me more."

"That's why we're here. Let me finish the story."

It took Perkins another ten minutes to tell of Haman Warner's inheriting the bank because of the stipulation in Bradley Barrett's will, and of his underhanded purchase of the bank in Cheyenne City and wicked deception to marry Linda. He then explained how Linda had found the condemning clippings and taken them to Sheriff Bob Coffield, and of Warner's arrest and suicide.

Hammond's face showed the impact the story was having on him.

Sheriff Perkins slipped some papers out of an envelope and handed them to Hammond, saying, "Here's the proof you need that Blake Barrett is an innocent man."

Hammond read the suicide note and Coffield's affidavit, then laid them down and said, "I had a feeling Blake was innocent all along. But like everyone else, I had to accept the jury's verdict."

He smiled at Linda and said, "I'll send a wire to Warden Hall to release Blake immediately."

"Sir . . ." Linda said tentatively.

"Yes?"

"Could I ask a favor?"

"Of course."

"I agree that the warden should be wired immediately and that Blake should be released. But . . . but would you ask the warden not to tell Blake until I arrive? I'm catching the early northbound train in the morning. I'll arrive in Ukiah at ten-thirty. If someone from the prison could pick me up, I'd very much like to be there when Blake is told he's a free man."

Hammond nodded. "Yes, ma'am. I'll make it very plain in my wire. The warden will understand and comply."

Perkins rubbed his palms together. "Someone will have to pick us up, Will. I'm going with her. Blake's a good friend of mine. I'd like to be there to greet him when he walks out of that place. That is, if it's all right with you, ma'am."

"That's fine with me," Linda said. "You don't want to be a fly on the wall after all — is that it?"

Perkins laughed. "I'll just be me! We'll make that trip together!"

A dazzling smile lit up Linda's beautiful face, and her scarred heart beat double time.

Tomorrow, for the first time, she would see the man she loved. And she would watch him go free!

Early the next morning at the Ukiah State Prison, Blake Barrett prepared himself for another day on the chain gang. Breakfast was over, and he had ten minutes in his cell before he and his new cell mate would be taken outside, put in chains, and carried in a wagon somewhere away from the prison for the day's labor.

Jason Pugh, the new cell mate, watched Blake remove his shoes and rub salve on his ankles. Pugh had only been on the chain gang for two days.

He looked at Blake's red, chafed ankles and said, "Is that what mine are gonna look like in a few more days?"

"Yes. But you should have seen these ankles before Anthony gave me this salve. I'll let you use it when you want."

Pugh closed his eyes, dreading what was coming.

Blake had just finished tying his shoes when doors began to rattle along the corridor and guards assembled inmates for the chain gang.

Anthony Tubac appeared at the cell door and unlocked it. Both men stood up from their cots and moved forward as Tubac opened the door.

Smiling, Tubac said, "Not you, Blake. Jason, c'mon out."

Blake's brow furrowed. "Not me?"

"Nope. You're staying here today. No chain gang for you."

"I'm not complaining, Anthony, but why?"

Tubac grinned. "I can't tell you. Just enjoy the rest."

As Tubac closed and locked the barred door behind Pugh, Blake said, "You did this, didn't you? You used your influence with the warden to let me have a day of rest."

"Wish I could take the credit for it," Tubac replied, "but I can't. All I can tell you is that I had orders not to send you out on the chain gang today."

Blake watched the men filing out of the cell block for the day's hard labor, and said, "Thank You, Lord. I don't know what brought this about, but I sure can use the rest."

Blake had read three chapters in the Gospel of Mark that morning, and it was nearly eleven o'clock as he lay on his cot in the cell, thinking about Linda Forrest and praying that the Lord would let him hear from her. It wasn't like the sweet girl he had met through correspondence to just ignore him. And it wasn't like his friend Haman to ignore him, either. Something was wrong, but there was nothing he could do about it until they had the telegraph lines in the Midwest back in service. Then he would have Anthony try again to make contact with Linda or her parents in Boston.

Blake could not give up on Linda. She had captured his heart by her letters, and he had to believe that there was something keeping her from writing to him.

"But what is it, Lord?" he asked. "You

know what it is. Please let me hear from her."

Footsteps sounded in the corridor. Seconds later, they stopped at Blake's cell. He looked up to see Anthony standing there.

"Let's go, Blake."

Blake rose to his feet. "Go? Go where?"

"Warden Hall wants to see you."

"What's he want —"

"You'll see. C'mon."

Warden Clarence Hall was seated at his desk when Anthony ushered Blake through the door. He stood up and offered his hand across the desk. "Good to see you, Blake."

Blake shook his hand, puzzled at the warden's demeanor. Hall was usually a gruff man.

"Nice to see you, too, sir," Blake said.

"Sit down, Blake," said Hall, gesturing toward the chair positioned in front of his desk.

Blake eased onto the chair, glancing at Anthony, who stood behind him, and wondering why he was still there.

The warden leaned forward, putting his elbows on top of the desk. "I have some very good news for you."

"I could use some, sir."

"Well, this is the best news I could possibly give you. In a few minutes you're going to walk out of this prison a free man."

Suddenly it all seemed like a dream. Blake shook his head as if to clear it. "Pardon me, sir?"

"Your time in this prison is over. You're leaving to begin a new life as of today. You have been cleared of the crime for which you were sentenced here. Anthony tells me you've said all along that you were innocent, and now we know that to be a fact."

Tears flooded Blake's eyes. As he wiped them away, he thanked the Lord in his heart for this miracle.

"We knew this would be quite a shock to you, Blake," said the warden, "albeit a pleasant one. As soon as you can change into your regular clothes, you're free to go."

Overwhelmed, Blake said, "But what happened, Warden? How did my innocence come to light? Who was the person who framed me?"

Hall smiled. "Someone has come to the prison with your friend Sheriff Claude Perkins. That person and Sheriff Perkins will answer all your questions for you and take you back to Sacramento with them."

" 'That person?' Is it Haman Warner? Has Haman come with the sheriff?"

Hall ignored the questions and rose to his feet. "Anthony will take you now so you can shed that prison garb and get into your own clothes. When you're ready, he'll take you to the person who wants to see you before you see Sheriff Perkins."

As the two men walked down the hall to the room where Blake's clothes had been kept since he'd come to the prison, Blake said, "C'mon, ol' pal, tell me. Who's the person who came with Sheriff Perkins to see me? Is it Haman?"

"I can't tell you," Tubac said with a smile.

"Do you know who it is?"

"Yes."

"Why can't you tell me?"

"I'm sworn to secrecy."

"Really?"

"Yep."

"Why is it so secretive? If it's not Haman, it's my pastor. That's who it is! It's Pastor Duane Clarke!"

Tubac remained mum but couldn't stop the slight curve to his lips.

Ten minutes later, Blake was led back to the warden's office. Hall shook hands with him and said, "I'm sorry you had to put in time here, Blake, but I'll say you sure have been a model prisoner."

"I try to behave, sir," Blake said with a grin. He still felt as if he were walking in a dream.

"You take care, Blake," said the warden as

they stepped out into the corridor.

"You too, sir. Good-bye."

The two men moved down the corridor to a heavy steel door with no window. Anthony said, "The person who came to see you is just on the other side of this door." Then sudden tears filmed his eyes as he said, "Thank you for leading me to Jesus. The other guards you led to Him are all out with the chain gang, but I know they'd want me to thank you for them, too."

"The pleasure was mine, Anthony," said Blake, giving him a pat on the back.

"You have a happy life, my friend and brother, and I'll meet you and Larry Huffman in heaven."

"You sure will," Blake said with conviction.

Anthony took a deep breath. "When you and your friend inside this room are ready to go, you'll find Sheriff Perkins outside. He rented a buggy in town and will take both of you to the depot. The outside door of the room isn't locked."

"All right. And thanks for everything."

Anthony unlocked the door. "There you go."

Blake stepped through the door and started as it clanked shut behind him. He paused, and as his vision cleared, he saw he was in some kind of conference room. His head swung toward a shadow by a curtainless window.

And then he saw her.

19

Linda's sleep had been restless, fraught with ugly dreams of Lewis and Janet and Haman. When she awakened for the third time from a bad dream, she lay there, unable to go back to sleep. Finally, she prayed that God would give her sleep, and she fell into quiet, restful slumber.

Rising from bed early, she was excited yet nervous about meeting Blake for the first time that very day.

She fussed with her hair, first pulling it on top of her head in an upsweep. Then, thinking it looked too severe, she let it all hang down her back.

Shaking her head at herself in the small mirror, she said, "No, Linda, that's too casual for this occasion."

At last she pulled it back, forming a soft chignon at the nape of her neck with tendrils curling around her face and forehead.

"There, now," she said to herself, "that looks more like the real you — the Linda that Blake saw in the photograph."

She had chosen a delicate pink dress of fine

lawn cotton with a small white stripe in it. It had a round neckline and a delicate lace collar. The back was tied in a large bow, and it hugged her slender waist. She placed a white straw bonnet trimmed in pink on her head and tied the long pink satin ribbon in a becoming bow beneath her left ear.

When she had fluffed the bow, she stepped back from the mirror and looked at her image with a critical eye. She turned from side to side, standing on tiptoe to see as much as she could of herself.

I look a bit pale, she thought, and pinched her cheeks to bring a blush to them.

Breathing a fervent prayer for God's grace in what lay ahead, she left the hotel room to join Sheriff Claude Perkins for their train ride to Ukiah.

A pulse throbbed in Linda's temple as she stood near the curtainless window in the prison conference room. The California sunshine filtered brightly through the glass.

She had clasped her hands to keep them from trembling, and her mouth was a bit dry as she set her eyes on the man she loved.

Blake's jaw slackened as he beheld the beauteous vision in pink and white. The lovely young lady he had dreamed about and prayed for was now standing in front of him.

He closed his eyes, fearing that she would disappear when he opened them again.

But open them he did, and she was still there in all her loveliness.

Blake could only gasp, "Linda!"

It was a moment of magic.

Both were so elated at finally seeing one another, they rushed into each other's arms, tears flowing freely.

Their embrace was long and tender. As Blake held her, he said, "Linda, I love you! Oh, I've wanted to see you and tell you that for so long!"

She had to catch her breath to speak, then said shyly, "I love you, too, Blake. I'm here because I love you."

They clung to each other for what seemed like an endless time, then Blake took her hands in his and said, "You are even more beautiful than your picture. Warden Hall said the person who was waiting in here would tell me the whole story. I have no idea what's happened in your life, or with my friend Haman Warner, who was supposed to wire you and tell you about my being sent here. I asked him to explain that I was innocent, and to tell you I needed to hear from you. They won't let me send any mail, or even a wire. I had one of the guards try to contact you or your parents in Boston by wire, but bad storms have the telegraph wires down. Oh, Linda, I'm so glad you're here!"

"Me, too," she said. "Let's sit down over here at the table, and all your questions will be answered, I'm sure, as I tell you the story."

Blake looked toward the outside door and said, "Sheriff Perkins is out there, isn't he? I was told he came along with my mysterious visitor to take me to Sacramento."

"Yes, he's there."

"How soon does the train leave?"

"Late this afternoon."

"So we have time for you to tell me what's happened before we go?"

"Yes. Sheriff Perkins told me to take all the time we need."

As they sat down, Blake took hold of her hand and said, "You are so beautiful."

Linda blushed. "And you are so kind."

"Kindness has nothing to do with it," he said softly. "It's just the truth."

Smiling, she said, "This moment is a dream come true for me."

"For me, too," Blake said, squeezing her hand.

"I hope you'll still feel toward me as you do now when you've heard the story."

"Linda, nothing could change how I feel about you. Why, you came here today because you love me. That's what you said, didn't you?"

"Yes."

"Then that's all that matters. Now, tell me what has happened."

As the story unfolded, Blake was stunned to learn that his trusted friend had turned out to be his heartless enemy.

Linda explained in detail how Haman had sold the bank in Sacramento and bought the bank in Cheyenne City, and how he had impersonated Blake, both to the people of Cheyenne City and to her.

When she came to the part of the story about her marriage to Haman, she broke down and sobbed. Blake took her in his arms and told her she couldn't be blamed.

When she was able to go on, Linda said, "Blake, I know the biggest question you have is how it came about that you were found to be innocent by the law and are now free."

"It is," he said, "but I'll wait for that part of the story."

"Well, that part begins right now."

He eyed her dreamily and said, "You are the most beautiful lady in all the world. Inside and out. The Lord has so blessed me."

This is the Blake Barrett who wrote those precious letters to me, she thought.

Taking a deep breath, Linda went on. She

told him how she was having questions about the "Blake" she was married to and had even told him in person that he wasn't the same man as he was in his letters. She gave Blake examples of the times Haman had tripped himself up, and how she'd even baited him. She was sorely disappointed in "Blake," and her marriage to him had become miserable.

She went on to say that her misery and her nagging doubts about the man she'd married drove her to search among his belongings for answers. When she found nothing in drawers or closets, she finally broke the lock on his trunk and found an envelope containing clippings from the *Sacramento Gazette* about the real Blake Barrett's arrest, conviction, and prison sentence.

Blake shook his head in amazement at what he was hearing. Suddenly Linda reached into her handbag and pulled out the brown envelope. Removing the clippings from the envelope, she said, "Here they are. Take a look."

Blake spread the clippings before him, his eye catching the big page with the glaring headlines and pictures of both Haman and himself. "Well, I guess you figured it out real quick when you saw these pictures," he said.

"That's for sure. And let me tell you right here, that even though I had not seen a picture of you, I had a mental image. The day

Haman met me at the Cheyenne City depot, I was terribly disappointed. I just knew that you were tall, blond, blue-eyed, and handsome."

"Well, you had the first three right, anyway," he said, chuckling.

"I got all four right," she countered.

Getting serious again, Blake said, "So you took the clippings to the law, I suppose."

"Yes. Sheriff Bob Coffield in Cheyenne City wired Sheriff Perkins to advise him of what I had found, and that Haman was living in Cheyenne City as Blake Barrett. Sheriff Coffield and his deputies arrested Haman and jailed him. Sheriff Perkins wired for a deputy U.S. Marshal out of Denver to take Haman back to Sacramento so he could face grand theft charges."

Blake looked down soberly and said, "I never would have suspected Haman. So he's in Sacramento now?"

Linda let a few seconds pass, then said, "No. He's dead."

Blake's scalp prickled. "Dead?"

"He hung himself in his cell at Cheyenne City."

Blake shook his head from side to side and said, "I tried so hard to win him to the Lord. He wanted nothing to do with Him."

"One of the things that made me suspicious of him was that he had no spirituality and knew nothing of the Bible. Yet he maintained that he was a Christian." As she spoke, Linda reached into her handbag again and produced another envelope. "He left a suicide note . . . he asked you to forgive him."

Blake read the note, folded it, and gave it back to Linda without comment.

She then handed Blake the affidavit signed by Sheriff Bob Coffield. "It was the note and this affidavit that freed you today."

"By the hand of the almighty God of heaven," he added.

"Yes, praise His name."

Blake drew a deep breath. "I trusted that man implicitly. He wasn't a Christian, but I really thought he was my friend. Shows me the truth of Psalm 118:8: 'It is better to trust in the LORD than to put confidence in man.' "

Linda began to tremble as she looked at Blake with an expression of inward pain and apprehension. Her eyes glittered with unshed tears, and her lips quivered.

Blake took hold of a hand again and leaned toward her. "Linda, what's wrong?"

She bowed her head as tears glided silently down her pale cheeks and dripped off her trembling chin.

"Linda, what is it?" Blake asked, concern riding his voice.

She tried to speak, but choked on the first

word. Swallowing hard, she raised her head and squeaked, "Now that you know I've been married to Haman, you don't want me, do you? I feel so . . . unclean."

"Aw, honey," he said, taking both of her trembling hands in his, "that's not so. You're not unclean . . . I do want you. I love you! What kind of man — what kind of Christian would I be to turn away from you now? You're innocent in all of this."

"Oh, Blake," she said in tearful elation, "thank you! I thought it would be all over for us when you learned that I was Haman Warner's widow."

Blake cupped her face in his hands and lovingly wiped away the tears, saying, "Dear, sweet Linda, you've had so many heartaches. I want to give you all the happiness I can. I've got some money in an account at the Pacific Bank and Trust. That is, unless somehow Haman stole that, too. Right now, I don't know where I am as far as material goods, but I want to ask you something . . ."

Linda looked deep into his eyes, and her silence told him she was waiting for his question.

"Will you marry me?" he asked.

"Do you mean it?"

"I mean it. If you'll say yes, we'll take care of it as soon as we get back to Sacramento."

"Oh, yes, my darling! Yes! I'll marry you!"

They embraced and held each other tight for a long moment, then Linda drew back so she could look into his face. "Blake, do you recall the opening verses in Ecclesiastes chapter three, where it starts out, 'To every thing there is a season, and a time to every purpose under the heaven'?"

"Mmm-hmm. Says there's a time to be born and a time to die, and goes on about all the different times in people's lives on earth."

"Yes, and in verse 8, it says there is a time to love."

"I remember."

"My pastor in Boston was going to use that passage in the wedding that never took place. And when my whole world fell down around me, I thought a time to love would never come for me. Then when I married Haman, thinking he was you, and it turned so sour . . . again, I thought I would never have my time to love.

"My best friend in Boston was a girl named Joline Jensen. She's married and lives in Pittsburgh, Pennsylvania, now. Joline came and saw me often, because I just couldn't go out in public with the shame Lewis Carter and my sister had put on me. Once when Joline was there, she said, 'Linda, believe me, you will have your time to love. The Lord has the man, the time, and the place. Let Him work it out.' Well, I now have the man at this time and this place. My Jesus, indeed, has worked it out."

"Let's thank Him right now for the way He's made all things work together for good to both of us," said Blake.

Tingles ran up and down Linda's spine as Blake prayed and gave thanks to the Lord for answered prayer and fulfillment of Scripture.

When the amen came they embraced again, then Linda said, "Before we go, darling, let me fill you in on one thing."

She told him about her conversation with attorney Edgar White concerning Haman's will, and that she now legally owned the Great Plains Bank of Cheyenne City. She assured Blake that even if he had not wanted to marry her, she would have given the bank to him. In view of what Haman did in stealing the Sacramento bank from him, the Cheyenne City bank was actually his. She also told him of the large account Haman left behind in the Great Plains Bank, and that when they married it would belong to both of them.

Blake was overwhelmed at the news and praised the Lord that he could go back into the business he knew and loved, and most of all, that he could build his new life with Linda at his side.

Hand in hand, the happy couple stepped outside. They saw Sheriff Claude Perkins some fifty yards away, standing beside a horse and buggy. Perkins waved.

Blake stopped walking and said, "Linda, let me just smell the air of freedom for a moment."

They stood together, holding hands, and took in the beauty of the cerulean sky and the golden sun shining down on their world.

Blake took a deep breath and said, "Thank You, Lord, for Your goodness. And thank You for our time to love."

The *Sacramento Gazette* carried a front-page story of Blake Barrett's release from prison, and a photograph of him and his bride to be at the depot when they arrived with Sheriff Claude Perkins. Beneath large headlines was the story of Haman Warner's underhanded deeds, his death at his own hand, and the suicide note clearing Blake of all guilt.

Blake found his house just as Haman had left it and moved back in. Linda was going to stay at one of Sacramento's hotels, but when the couple went to Pastor Duane Clarke to make arrangements for their wedding, the Clarkes invited her to stay with them until she and Blake were married.

Linda immediately wrote to her parents to

tell them all that had happened, giving God the praise for answered prayer. With joy she informed them that in a few days she and Blake would be married.

She also wrote to Joline to confirm that she was right. God had the man, the time, and the place all worked out.

Blake and Linda wanted nothing elaborate for their wedding — just a small private ceremony with a few of Blake's closest friends. As they took their vows, both bride and groom were glowing with such happiness and contentment that they, the pastor, and the guests could strongly feel the heavenly Father smiling down on this blessed union.

Two days after the wedding, the newlyweds were eating breakfast together in the kitchen of the Barrett house.

Blake talked about how good Linda's cooking was, then said, "Sweetheart, I've been doing a lot of thinking."

"Yes?"

"As you know, we've already got two different families who want to buy this house."

"Mm-hmm."

"When I was at the bank yesterday, I asked the new owner if he knew of any towns in California that needed a bank. He said Stockton is growing rapidly, but the town has no bank. The people there have to do their banking at Manteca or Concord. When he said that, I remembered that not long before Dad became ill, he'd mentioned that he was thinking of starting a new bank in Stockton. I never thought any more about it until yesterday."

"Where is Stockton, darling?"

"Fifty miles straight south of here."

"Mm-hmm. And you're thinking that we should also sell the house in Cheyenne City and the bank, and establish a new bank in Stockton."

"That's it. I know there's a good church in Stockton. Pastor Clarke and the pastor there are good friends. His name is Brandon North. Excellent preacher. I've heard him several times when he and Pastor have exchanged pulpits. So the church question is already settled."

"That's the most important thing."

"Right. I just think that with all we've been through, we should start our new life together where there are no unpleasant memories to haunt us."

"I agree, darling. Let's make it a matter of prayer and let the Lord guide us."

Two days later, with peace in their hearts, the newlyweds started early and drove to Stockton. They found a quaint hotel to stay in while they took care of three main items of business.

The first thing was to locate a choice piece of property in the business district where they would have the bank building erected. They found the perfect lot, right on a corner where businesses were springing up.

Blake's money at the Pacific Bank and Trust Company was still intact, for which he was thankful. With checkbook in hand, he struck a deal by early afternoon. Thrilled at the way God was working, they went to work on the second item, which was to hire a contractor to build the new bank. Because Stockton was booming, three San Francisco contractors were busy erecting buildings in the business section, and by noon the next day, Blake was able to hire one to start work on the new bank building within three weeks.

The third item was to find property where they could have a house built. They drove through town for a while, with Linda making notes of some of the vacant lots marked for sale.

Blake was commenting that he would hire the same contractor to build their house when Linda looked longingly toward the hills east of town.

Blake followed her line of sight and said, "See something out there you like?"

"Mm-hmm. Country property."

"Country property?"

"Yes. I've lived in town all my life. How about a piece of property with some open space around it?"

"I'm game," he said, turning the buggy east and putting the horse to a trot.

They drove down several country lanes, spotting farms and vineyards, as they looked for land marked for sale. Linda noted a few acreages, pointing out the ones she liked best, and Blake liked them all.

The sun was dropping beneath the western horizon when they took a different road and started back in the direction of town. A cool breeze wafted over them.

They were about two miles from Stockton when Linda made a small noise, and Blake looked at her to see what the problem was.

She was smiling from one ear to the other and looking southward off the road toward a lovely two-story, pale yellow frame house. A tree-lined lane ran from the road to the house in a sweeping curve. A wide porch stretched across the front of the house, and the property was surrounded by a white picket fence.

"That house down there," said Blake, "is that what you're gasping about?"

"Yes! Isn't it beautiful?"

Dusk was gathering, but there was enough

light for Blake to see that she was right. "Yes, it sure is."

"Oh, Blake, turn down the lane and drive up to it. I want to see it up close."

"Honey, the people who live there will think we're awfully nosy if we do that."

"They won't mind, I'm sure."

"Okay. Whatever pleases the queen of my heart."

As they drew near, Linda said, "We'll just tell the people we're going to buy property and have a house built, and we like the style of theirs. So we'd like to look at it."

Blake chuckled. "Mrs. Barrett, you're a case, you are!"

"Well, it certainly isn't going to hurt if we —" Linda's hand went to her mouth. "Blake, look!"

Blake saw the For Sale sign affixed to a corner post where the lane met the road.

"Well, whattaya know!" he said. "It's for sale!"

"Yes, and the Lord's going to let us buy it!"

"How do you know if you want it, Linda? You haven't really seen it up close, and you haven't even looked inside."

"I just know this is our house, Blake!"

He guided the buggy down the lane toward the house. Soft lamplight glowed in many of the windows, and more light glowed onto the front porch through the front door, which stood open as if to welcome them in.

Glistening white shutters adorned the windows upstairs and down, and Linda took note of the beautiful drapes of muted colors.

As Blake drew the buggy to a halt near the porch, Linda squeezed his arm. "This is it, darling! I'm sure of it! I know it in my heart!"

Blake grinned, then pointed with his chin at the elderly woman who stood at the door, smiling at them.

When the newlyweds returned to their hotel room, Linda said, "What a dear, sweet lady. Too bad she had to lose her husband to consumption."

"Well, one good thing," said Blake, "at least her children and grandchildren in San Diego will be glad to have her living with them."

"I'm sure they will."

"Let's talk to the Lord right now and ask Him to direct us about the house. If we have peace about it in the morning, we'll go back and make a deal."

"I already have peace about it, darling," said Linda, "but let's pray."

When the sun broke the eastern sky the next morning, Blake felt as positive about purchasing the house as Linda did. After breakfast, the excited couple climbed into the buggy and headed for their new home.

By the end of March, the Barretts were in their home and the bank building was under construction.

Sadie Brown had been hired as housekeeper by the people who bought the house in Cheyenne City. She and Linda had a difficult and tearful good-bye.

Linda wrote to her parents, telling them all that had happened, making sure they knew that she and Blake were very much in love, living in the center of God's will, and superbly happy. She told them they were in a good Bible-believing church, and that they had told their story over and over again, giving God the glory for the way He made Romans 8:28 work out perfectly in their lives — even when there were very dark hours for both of them.

She wrote the same news to Joline, who responded with a long letter, saying how happy she was for both Linda and Blake.

During the first week of July, the bank opened, and by the end of the summer, it was showing excellent profits.

During this time, Linda and her parents were writing back and forth frequently, and by invitation of both Blake and Linda, the Forrests traveled to Stockton, arriving on Thursday, September 12.

When they got off the train in early afternoon, Linda and Blake were there to greet them. Nolan and Adrienne took to their son-in-law immediately.

They wanted to see the Stockton Bank and Trust Company, and were taken directly to the bank, where Blake introduced them to his employees and gave them a tour of the place.

That evening after supper, the Barretts and the Forrests were sitting on the wide front porch, enjoying the warm evening and the soft breeze.

Nolan asked Blake about prison life, and Adrienne wanted to know about the moment Linda and Blake first met that day at the prison. When the Forrests had been told enough detail to feel satisfied, Linda asked them about Pastor and Doris Stanford, and all Linda's old friends at church.

When the conversation slowed some, Adrienne looked at her daughter by the light of the lamps glowing from the parlor windows and said cautiously, "I have something to tell you about your sister."

"What about Janet, Mom?"

Nolan Forrest sat quietly and watched, hoping the subject would not upset Linda. He and Adrienne had agreed that it probably wouldn't, since Linda was so happily married to Blake.

"Your sister was in Boston a few weeks ago and showed up one evening on our doorstep. She said she was visiting some friends and just couldn't leave without seeing us."

Linda's features were noncommittal. "So how is it going for her and Lewis?"

"Well . . . Janet said they're fighting a lot, but they're still together. Your daddy and I thought you should at least know that we saw her."

"I'm glad to know she's still alive," Linda said. "And I hope she and Lewis get over their fighting, stay together, and go on to be happy."

Nolan released an inward sigh of relief. "Janet asked about you, honey," he said.

"Oh?"

"We told her you were in Stockton, California, married to a very successful banker."

"What did she say to that?"

"Nothing. She went on to another subject."

Linda nodded. "If she should come by again, tell her I wish her the best."

Both parents smiled.

"And tell her the same from me," said Blake.

"I appreciate your attitude," Nolan said. "Both of you."

"And so do I," put in Adrienne. "The Lord has done a real work in your hearts, and we're thrilled with the way He has blessed you."

20

One morning in mid-February 1880, Linda Barrett awakened at first light. She turned quietly and watched the sleeping man beside her. Admiring his rugged masculine features, she whispered, "Thank You for my wonderful husband, Lord. He's everything I thought he would be, and more. And thank You for blessing him in his business."

She was so grateful that God, in His wisdom, had let Lewis run away with Janet. If she had married Lewis, she'd have missed being married to the most wonderful man in all the world.

Linda smiled to herself as she remembered the time, right after being jilted, when she thought she could never love a man the way she'd loved Lewis. How wrong she had been!

"Lord," she said in a low whisper, "You never take something from Your children without giving them something better in its place."

She loved every minute of being married to Blake and enjoyed making their home comfortable and happy for him. There was only one thing to mar her happiness. With all her heart she wanted to give Blake a child. She lowered her hand to her midsection and wondered if a new little life was forming in her womb. She'd thought she was pregnant three months ago.

Maybe this time . . .

Blake Barrett whistled a lively tune as he left the small barn. Business at the bank was thriving, and he'd put in a long, satisfying day of work.

Both of the family buggies stood side by side next to the corral, and the bay mares were inside the barn, munching hay Blake had just pitched into the feed trough from the hayloft.

He moved across the porch and opened the door to the kitchen to find Linda sobbing at the kitchen table, her head down, resting on her arms.

"Sweetheart, what's the matter? What are you crying about?"

Linda shoved back her chair and ran to Blake, clinging to him as he folded her in his embrace.

"I went to Dr. Martin today . . . I thought I was pregnant. I was so excited! I wanted to come home and tell you that we were going to have a baby. Why can't I conceive?"

Blake held her close and stroked her shiny auburn hair. "Linda, darlin', I don't know why. Did Dr. Martin say anything about it?"

"Yes. He said he would have to examine me, and if he doesn't find anything obvious, he would have to do some tests. He said it might be something to do with either one of us."

"Well, then, we'll go to his office tomorrow and find out if there's a problem. It's time you were having a little girl who looks just like you!"

She worked up a smile, and said, "How about a little boy who looks like you?"

Blake held her tighter. "Either way would be all right with me, darlin'. But Linda . . ."

"Yes?"

"If we learn we can't have children, let's look into adoption."

"Oh, Blake, I'm glad you feel the same as I do about having children in our home."

"I love children, honey," he said with a chuckle. "I used to go to school with them!"

Linda laughed outright.

"Sweetheart, I'm so glad I married you," Blake said, kissing the tip of her nose.

"You didn't marry me," she said with a giggle. "I married you!"

"Oh, you did, eh?"

"Mm-hmm. When you came through that

door into the conference room at the prison, I said to myself, 'That's for me.' From that moment on you didn't have a chance. When we went before the preacher, I married you!"

This time he kissed her soundly.

The next day, Linda and Blake visited Dr. Martin. He examined them separately and did some tests, explaining that he would not be able to give a conclusive answer until he studied the test results, which he would have in a couple of days.

Two days later the couple returned to Dr. Martin's office and were escorted by his nurse to a small conference room adjacent to the waiting area.

Less than a minute had passed when Dr. Martin entered, carrying a folder in his hand, and sat down facing them. "I wish I could tell you everything was all right, folks," he said.

Blake took Linda's hand as the doctor's dreadful words told of Linda's inability to conceive. He explained that nothing could be done. She would never be able to bear children.

Linda fought to hold back the tears but finally gave in. When Blake put his arms around her, she pressed her face to his shoulder and sobbed.

Dr. Martin rose to his feet. "I'll give you two some privacy," he said.

Blake silently prayed as he held Linda.

After a few minutes, she gained control and took some deep, shuddering breaths before saying, "Darling, Romans 8:28 still applies. The Lord has His mighty hand on our lives as much now as He did when you were in prison and I was married to Haman Warner. It's hard to accept that I can never give you children, but if we can look into adoption, it would help me a great deal. It . . . it won't bother you that I can't bear children?"

"Of course not. I love you with all my heart, Linda. Nothing could ever change that. And for that matter, the problem could have been with me. Would it have bothered you if that was the case?"

"Absolutely not! The most important thing is that I have you as my life's mate. I love you more than words could ever express. You're the very essence of my life, and nothing could ever change that."

Her face was shiny with tears as she looked into his eyes.

"Well, then," he said, wiping the tears from her face, "we'll just go on loving each other and see about adoption."

Linda caressed his cheek and said, "With the Lord's help and yours, I'll be able to live with the fact that I can't give you our own natural children."

Blake pulled a clean handkerchief from his pocket and tenderly blotted the rest of her tears.

When he finished, Linda looked up at this man she loved so dearly and whispered, "God in His infinite wisdom has allowed this for a reason."

There was a tap on the door. "Okay if I come back in?" asked Dr. Martin.

As he sat down to face them, Martin said, "Sometimes my job isn't so pleasant — like having to give you the bad news a little while ago."

"That can't be an easy task, Doctor," said Linda. "I don't envy you."

"Dr. Martin," Blake said, "we'd like you to tell us about adoption procedures."

"All right. Basically, I just keep a list of people who want to adopt a baby. When a baby comes available, I notify people in the order in which they are listed. Sometimes a couple will specify a boy or a girl, and often they'll put a limit on how old a baby is.

"I learn of babies in need of adoption in many different ways. As far as older children — let's say three and above — I keep no list. To adopt an older child, you simply have to hear of parents who have died, leaving orphans behind, or of some other situation where a child has no home."

"Well, put us on your list," said Blake. "And we don't care whether it's a boy or a girl."

"And we'll take any age on your list," Linda said.

"Fine — your name will go on the list today. I'd also suggest you contact doctors in towns all over this area to get on their lists, too. That will raise your chances of adopting a baby as soon as possible."

"Thank you, Doctor," said Blake as he rose from the settee.

Blake and Linda paused in the outer office long enough to pay for the doctor's services, then climbed in the buggy and headed home.

As they drove along Stockton's streets, Blake said, "We'll make the rounds of the doctors in a twenty-mile radius on the next few Saturdays, honey. In the meantime, we'll keep our eyes open in case an older child becomes available and pray earnestly that the Lord will give us the child He wants us to have."

"All right, darling," Linda said, gripping his arm. "I just know that somewhere there's a precious little boy or girl for us to love and care for. God will show us in His perfect time."

"That's right, sweetheart. God's Word says, 'Be careful for nothing; but in everything by prayer and supplication with thanksgiving let your requests be made known unto God.'"

"That's one of my favorite Scriptures, Blake, and my experience has proven it to be true time and again."

Both were quiet for the rest of the way home. When they arrived, they worked in companionable silence to put away the horse and buggy, then went to the house. As they stepped inside, they surprised each other by simultaneously saying, "'Trust in the LORD with all thine heart; and lean not —'"

They broke off speaking, then finished in unison: "'. . . unto thine own understanding. In all thy ways acknowledge him, and he shall direct thy paths.'"

Blake and Linda laughed as they embraced and kissed. Then Blake said, "Let's pray about it right now."

They went to the parlor and got down on their knees in front of the couch and gave their burden to their precious heavenly Father.

Blake prayed first, then Linda. When they were finished, they lifted tear-stained faces and looked deeply into one another's eyes, seeing and feeling the peace only God can give.

★ ★ ★

One morning about a week later, Linda kissed Blake and sent him off to work as usual. She cleaned up the kitchen from breakfast and washed the kitchen windows inside and out. This was housecleaning day.

True to February weather in northern California, the temperature stayed cool, but the sun shone through the sparkling windows Linda had just washed.

A white apron covered her blue cotton dress, and she wore a flowered kerchief over her sun-streaked auburn hair. She had just finished mopping the kitchen floor when she thought she heard a knock at the front door.

As she stepped into the hall, the rather timid knock was repeated.

Linda whipped the kerchief from her head and glanced in the hall mirror, patting down some stray locks. As she hurried toward the door, she smoothed the front of her apron. She pressed a smile on her lips for the unknown visitor and swung open the door.

Her smile immediately drained away. She closed her eyes and opened them again to see if she were imagining the person standing before her. Finally, she said in a shaky voice, "H-Hello, Janet."

Linda's older sister dipped her head, not quite meeting Linda's gaze, and said in a low

419

tone, "Hello, Linda. I . . . I'm sure you're surprised to see me. If you don't want to talk to me, I completely understand. Just say so, and I'll turn around and go back where I came from."

Linda stared in disbelief. This was absolutely the last person she ever expected to find standing on her doorstep.

Janet was quite obviously expecting a baby, though she was dressed in her usual cheap way. Her eyes were painted up like a saloon girl's, and her face was excessively powdered and rouged.

As the shock began to wear off, Linda stepped back and made a gesture for her sister to enter, then guided her into the parlor and said, "Have a seat here on the sofa."

Linda picked up a straight-backed wooden chair and placed it in front of the sofa, then sat down on the edge. She immediately jumped back up and said, "Can I get you something?"

"I could use some water."

"Be right back."

Only a minute had passed when Linda returned with a glass of water and placed it in her sister's trembling hand. Her mind was in a whirl, and she prayed for strength and wisdom as Janet slowly drank the contents of the glass.

Linda could see that Janet was quite pale

beneath the rouge and powder.

"Thank you," Janet said, setting the glass on the small table next to the sofa.

"Of course," Linda replied. "Now, why don't you tell me why you're here."

Tears welled up in Janet's eyes and spilled over, making black streams down her cheeks. As she swiped at them with the back of her hand, Linda reached in her dress pocket and drew out a clean hankie, handing it to her.

Janet wept for a few seconds, then wiped her cheeks, smearing the black eye makeup even more. "Linda . . . I . . . well, it was wrong of me to take my own happiness at your expense. I'm sorry for all the hurt and heartache I've caused you. I've left Lewis. Living with him was a horrible nightmare."

At this point, she broke down and sobbed heavily, mopping tears with the wet hankie.

Linda let her cry but didn't try to comfort her.

"My marriage to Lewis was doomed from the start," Janet said, sniffing. "And that's because of what we did to you. I'm glad it wasn't you who got him, Linda. He's a beast . . . a terrible, inhuman beast! He beat me up time after time when he came home drunk and . . . and . . . abused me mentally, too. Oh, it was awful! He made my life a horrible nightmare, I tell you!"

421

"I'm sorry for that, Janet," Linda said quietly, still maintaining her distance.

Janet's hands trembled and her head jerked nervously as she said, "Please, little sister, can you find it in your heart to forgive me?"

Partly because she was so happy and content with Blake, and because she knew what Scripture said about forgiveness, Linda slowly nodded her head and said, "I forgive you."

When Janet broke into loud sobs, Linda rose from her chair and put her arms around her, holding her until she stopped weeping.

As Linda returned to the straight-backed chair, she said, "When is your baby due?"

"In about three months. The end of May."

"So you've left Lewis for good?"

"Yes."

"No chance you'll go back and try to make your marriage work?"

"No chance. Like I said, our marriage was doomed from the beginning."

Linda's lovely brow puckered. "So what brought you here?"

"I know Mom and Dad came here to see you . . ."

"Yes?"

"I visited them back in August. I was pregnant then but didn't know it."

"I see."

"They told me you lived in Stockton and

were married to a very successful banker named Blake Barrett."

Linda nodded.

"I'm terribly afraid of Lewis, Linda. He once told me if I ever left him he would hunt me down and kill me. I'm carrying this baby, but it wouldn't make any difference. He'd kill us both if he found me. I know Mom and Dad would never tell Lewis where you live, so I felt I'd be safe if I came here to Stockton."

"Do Mom and Daddy know you're here?"

"No. I thought it best not to tell them."

"So they don't know you're pregnant?"

"No. They've had enough to burden them. I don't want to put any more on them. I . . . I was just so terrified of Lewis that I took what money was in the house and got on the first train west from New York. In Cheyenne City, Wyoming, I got on a train that was going to Sacramento, then took a stagecoach from Sacramento to Stockton. The stage driver was kind enough to drive me right to the Western Hotel. I took a room there and had my luggage brought in. The man at the desk told me where your house was."

"And you walked out here from town?"

"Yes. Walking is good for expectant mothers, you know. By the way, are you expecting yet?"

"No . . . not yet." Linda would not divulge

her problem to her sister. At least, not at the moment. "But being in your sixth month, you shouldn't have walked that far."

"I'm fine. The most important thing is that I'm safe from Lewis. And if I can find a place to live in Stockton, I'll be close to you."

"Do you have enough money to stay till you have the baby?"

Janet shrugged. "I think so."

"Well, are you hungry?"

"A little."

"It'll be lunchtime in an hour or so. We'll just hurry it up a bit."

Janet stood up when Linda did.

Linda looked at her tenderly and said, "You can just sit here and rest while I make lunch."

Janet made a little pout with her lips. "Couldn't I sit in the kitchen so we can talk while you fix lunch?"

Linda smiled and wrapped her arms around her sister, saying, "It is good to see you again, Janet."

"You too, honey," Janet said, hugging her tight.

As they moved together down the hall, Linda said, "Does anybody know you've come here to Stockton?"

"No one."

"Then you're in no danger from Lewis."

"No. And I'm so thankful to be away from that cruel monster!"

When the sisters had finished lunch, Linda rose from her chair and said, "While I clean up and do the dishes, I want you to lie down and take a nap."

She had noticed that Janet looked weary, and Linda needed some time alone to think. This unexpected visit had been quite an upset.

"I'll help you," Janet said.

"No, you won't. I've traveled some myself," Linda said evenly. "I know how tiring it is, and it has to be worse when you're six months pregnant. Come with me; I'll take you upstairs."

Linda led her sister to a cozy guest room and said, "Take your shoes off. I'll be right back."

She returned carrying a pitcher of warm water and a towel. She poured the water in a basin on a small table by the window and said, "Here, Janet. Come freshen up, then you can lie down and take a nap. Come on downstairs when you feel like it."

Linda left her sister at the washbasin and went back to the kitchen to clean up the remains of lunch. Then she sat down at the kitchen table with a cup of hot tea.

Her nerves felt a little jangled. She bowed her head and sought guidance from the Lord Jesus.

Linda had prayed for Janet's salvation for years and had talked to her many times, trying to bring her to the Lord. Now would be a perfect time to witness to her again if Janet stayed with them. She'd need a place to stay till after the baby was born, and she'd be much more comfortable in the Barrett home than in a hotel . . . and they certainly had room for her. After the baby's birth, she would probably want to find a place of her own.

Linda thought of Blake. Knowing his tender and generous heart, she knew he would agree. They couldn't turn Janet away, even if she was Linda's rebellious sister.

That evening when Blake came in the back door, he stopped short at the sight of the cheap-looking woman sitting at the kitchen table. Janet had made up her face again and once more looked as if she belonged in a saloon.

The aroma of hot food filled the air as Janet stood up and said, "Blake, I'm your sister-in-law, Janet Carter."

Stunned, Blake had not yet found his voice.

"Linda's upstairs," Janet said. "She'll be down shortly."

"Shortly is now," came Linda's voice. She made a beeline for her husband and said, "Hello, darling. I see you've met my sister." With that, she planted a kiss on his cheek.

Linda's presence loosened his tongue, and he finally said, "We've met."

Blake found it hard to warm up to this woman who had treated Linda so ruthlessly, but he relaxed some when Linda explained why Janet had come there.

When Linda saw that Blake's tension had eased, she brought up Janet's need for a place to stay until the baby was born, explaining that Janet had taken a room at the Western Hotel. She went on to say that she'd offered to let Janet stay with them.

Although he was dubious at the news, Blake didn't show it. He would abide by Linda's decision. He was about to say so when a nervous Janet said, "Blake, if you'd rather I didn't stay here, I —"

"Of course I want you to stay," he said, forcing a smile. "You're Linda's sister, and you're in need of help."

"It will only be till I have the baby," Janet said. "I'll get a job just as soon as I can after the baby is born, and I'll get my own place. And I won't expect Linda to look after the baby while I work, either. I'll find someone to do that."

Blake felt better. "That's fine, Janet. Welcome to our home."

"Thank you," Janet said humbly. "You'll never know how much this means to me."

"It's our pleasure to help you," Blake assured her. "Right after supper, I'll drive into town and get your luggage from the hotel."

That night, Linda walked Janet to the guest room and said, "I'm so thankful Lewis didn't hurt you seriously, Janet. He never seemed like the type to brutalize a female."

"Well, you can't always tell a book by its cover, they say."

Linda kissed her sister's cheek and told her good night.

When the bedroom door closed, Janet chuckled to herself and sat down at the dresser to brush her hair. She wiped off her makeup and chuckled some more.

Later, she doused the lantern and climbed into the comfortable bed. Lying there in the dark, she said aloud, "Linda, ol' girl, you always were a sucker for a sob story! Lewis, kill me? That milquetoast wouldn't swat a fly! Drunk? Hah! I couldn't get him to drink enough at one time, even at one of my parties, to get drunk on!

"And beat me? The little sap wouldn't dare! I'd have had one of my bartender

428

friends beat *him* to a pulp!"

She interlaced her fingers and put her hands behind her head as she relived the developments in her marriage.

Lewis's conscience had eaten at him for months because of what he'd done to Linda. Janet recalled the day when Lewis came home and told her everything was changing in his life. It was in early August, before she knew she was pregnant.

Lewis had gone to a Bible-believing pastor in Manhattan for help. As the preacher dealt with him about his overwhelming sense of guilt, he had told Lewis that all would be forgiven by the Lord if he would repent and open his heart to Jesus for salvation.

It was then that Lewis told him of making a profession of faith in Christ as a teenager, but he hadn't meant business with God. There had been no repentance of sin. The pastor then led him to the Lord.

As Lewis told Janet the story, he began quoting Scripture, saying they were going to get into church and start serving the Lord.

Lewis's words made Janet fly into a rage. She cursed him and said she wasn't going to live with a Bible-spouting fanatic. She'd had enough of that stuff before leaving her parents' house to live on her own. And what's more, she wasn't going to change her lifestyle.

She liked the night spots and all that went with them.

Lewis was disappointed in her attitude and asked her to think it over.

She played along until the next day. When he was at work, she packed her belongings and hired a carriage to take her to the railroad station. Just before she got on the train, Lewis showed up. He'd gone home, worried that something like this might happen, and a neighbor told him Janet had left in a carriage.

They had a hot argument in front of the crowd at the depot, and Janet had threatened to call the railroad authorities if Lewis didn't leave her alone. He had walked away quietly.

When she arrived in Boston, Janet moved in with Sally Mansfield, an old girlfriend. While living there, Janet decided to visit her parents. She lied to them, telling them that she and Lewis were having marital trouble but were still together. She even asked about Linda.

It was then her parents told her they were going to California to see Linda, and gave her the details on who Linda had married and where she was living.

Janet chuckled to herself. Her gullible parents had believed that she cared for Linda. Hah! She was just curious, that's all. She couldn't care less about her religious fanatic of a sister, but asking about her had made Janet look good in her parents' eyes.

When Sally caught Janet making a play for her steady beau, she threw her out. Janet had no place to go, so she decided to look up her rich sister in Stockton, California.

Janet was sure that when Linda heard the sob story, she would let her move in with them. Hey, free food and lodging! Who could beat that?

Janet dreaded the church stuff she would have to put up with, living in a Christian household. But she would put on a good show for free food and lodging. She couldn't wait to get back to her wild life.

21

In the weeks that followed, Blake and Linda used their Saturdays to drive from town to town in a twenty-mile radius and put their names on doctors' lists as potential adoptive parents. They didn't let on to Janet what they were doing for fear she would feel self-conscious.

Even though Linda was glad to help her sister, it was a strain to have her as a "guest" in their home. She tried to focus on the coming baby and busied herself making a layette and sewing many loving stitches into each tiny garment she made.

There were tender moments when tears she couldn't contain dropped on the pieces she was sewing. Linda prayed for patience while she and Blake waited for an adoptive baby to become available, but sometimes the waiting felt unbearable.

Janet hated the Christian atmosphere of the Barrett home, barely tolerating prayer before each meal. It took every ounce of control to endure the church services on Sundays.

When approached by both Linda and Blake

about her salvation, Janet insisted that she was saved as a child, but told her sister and brother-in-law that salvation just didn't affect her as it did them. They saw through her explanation but couldn't get anywhere with her.

The Barretts took Janet to Dr. Martin and put her under his care for the rest of her pregnancy. They quickly learned that Janet was quite short of funds, and paid the doctor for her.

Wednesday, May 28, 1880, was a bright, sunny day in northern California. Janet was crankier than usual all day, and it was getting on Linda's nerves.

All day long, Janet had a nagging backache, and no matter where she sat or lay, she was unable to find a comfortable position. She was kneading her fists in the small of her back when Linda paused at the open door to her bedroom.

Moving into the room, Linda said, "The back pain's getting worse, isn't it?"

"Yes," Janet said through clenched teeth.

"Could I rub it for you?"

"Sure."

While Linda rubbed the aching spot, she said, "I think your baby's going to put in an appearance shortly."

"I hope so," said Janet. "I can't stand much more of this."

Linda smiled. "It'll be worth it all when you hold the little darling in your arms."

Janet said nothing.

When Blake came home that evening, Linda told him Janet would deliver soon. She'd made a good dinner of beef stew and biscuits, and when it was ready, Blake went up to Janet's room and walked her down the stairs so she could eat.

Janet ate very little, and after a few minutes she ran her gaze to both Barretts and said, "I'll have to ask you to excuse me. I just can't eat any more. I'm going back up to my room."

She plodded slowly and laboriously up the stairs, assisted by Blake, and made straight for her bed. When Blake was gone, she let her eyes roam the room.

Because of what Linda and Blake had done, all was ready for the baby. They had purchased a beautiful cradle, which sat nearby, and all the clothes and blankets so lovingly sewn by Linda were laundered and waiting in neat stacks in dresser drawers.

I'll be glad when the kid is born and this ordeal is over, Janet thought. *I hate being fat and ungainly. I want to get on with my life, and this kid has no part in it.*

After lying there a while, Janet carefully rolled off the bed, undressed herself, and slipped into a comfortable nightgown. Her feet and ankles were somewhat swollen, and it felt good to remove her shoes and stockings and wiggle her toes.

Back on the bed, she plumped up the pillows against the headboard and tried to settle herself comfortably against them. She picked up the book she'd been reading and opened it to a dog-eared page that marked the spot where she'd left off.

Soon there was a tap on her door, and Linda's voice said, "Okay if I come in, Janet?"

"Sure," Janet called. "Come on in."

"How is everything?"

"Quiet at the moment."

"Anything I can get you?"

"No. I'm fine."

"Okay. If you need me, give a holler."

Linda stepped into the hall, and Janet listened to her footsteps fading away.

After reading for a few minutes, her eyes grew heavy. She turned down the corner of a page and laid the book on the nightstand, then slid down under the covers. The lamp on the nightstand was still burning as she slipped into a light sleep.

Suddenly Janet sat bolt upright in bed, gasping. She grabbed her protruding midsection and emitted a low moan. The pain slowly subsided, and she lay back down.

All was well for a few minutes. She was about to drift back to sleep when the pain shot through her again. After a series of sharp pains, Janet gingerly worked her way to the side of the bed and swung her feet over the edge. Another pain hit her. She ejected a grunting sound and clutched her midsection. When the pain had passed, she struggled to push herself to a standing position.

When she was on her feet, she headed for the door, hanging on to pieces of furniture for support. Wrestling the door open, she braced herself on the door frame and weakly called, "Linda!"

The house was quiet, and the hall was dimly lit by a lamp on a small table near the stairs.

When there was no response, Janet groped her way along the wall in the direction of the master bedroom and called again, "Linda-a-a!"

Suddenly the door of the master bedroom came open, and Linda appeared, donning her robe. She rushed to Janet and put an arm around her. "Have you gone into labor?"

A pain hit as Janet nodded.

Blake's voice came from the open door. "Linda . . . anything I can do?"

"Yes!" she called over her shoulder. "Go get Dr. Martin! Come on, Janet, let's get you back in the bed."

Because of the pains, it was a slow process to get Janet to her bedroom. They heard Blake pound down the stairs just as Linda placed the pillows under her sister's head.

Another spasm shot through Janet, and Linda held her hand and brushed a wet lock of hair from her forehead as she let out a moan.

"Even though this is your first baby," Linda said softly, "your contractions are quite close together already. Maybe you'll have a quick delivery."

"I . . . hope . . . so," Janet said through her teeth. "I want . . . to . . . get this . . . over with."

Soon the pains were coming one right after the other. Linda was about to prepare herself to be a midwife when she heard male voices downstairs.

Dr. Martin hurried through the bedroom door and placed his black medical bag on the dresser. "How's it going, Mrs. Barrett?"

"There's hardly any time between pains," Linda replied. "I think she's about to deliver."

"Anything else I can do?" Blake asked.

"How about bringing up some hot water?" said Dr. Martin.

"Hot water coming up!"

"I'll get some towels, Doctor," Linda said, and hurried into the hall.

Janet was not a cooperative patient, but the kindly doctor did all he could to assure her that everything was fine.

Linda returned with the towels, and shortly thereafter, Blake came with the hot water. Once it was deposited on the dresser, he quickly disappeared.

Linda stayed with the doctor to help, and in just under two hours, a healthy, red-faced, beautiful little boy was delivered. Dr. Martin gave him a solid pop on the posterior, and he took in his first breath, followed by a high-pitched wail.

Linda announced to Janet that it was a boy, but the new mother didn't respond. Linda quickly cleaned Janet up and put her in a fresh gown while the doctor examined the baby from head to toe.

When the baby was all bundled up in a tiny blanket, Dr. Martin stood over Janet, smiling. "Here's your little son, Mrs. Carter. I know you want to hold him."

Shaking her head, Janet said, "Not right now, Doctor. I . . . I'm very tired. I need to go to sleep."

Dr. Martin turned his shocked face to Linda. He had never experienced a mother who wasn't eager to hold her newborn.

Linda shrugged, displayed open hands, and took the baby from the doctor. She moved about the room, baby in arms, and immediately lost her heart to the precious bundle of love. She caressed his fat little cheek and smiled as he reached up a tiny fist and tried to put it in his mouth, making a loud sucking sound.

"Well, goodness, little one," she said, tracing a fingertip across his brow, "are you hungry already? Auntie Linda will wake your mommy up if that's the case."

Dr. Martin let a grin curve his mouth. "I'd say he's probably more tired than hungry, Mrs. Barrett. It's pretty taxing on a little fella to come into the world."

"All right," Linda said. "Let's see if I can get him to sleep."

While the doctor checked the sleeping Janet one more time, and cleaned up his instruments and put them away, Linda gently rocked the baby in her arms and crooned to him. Soon he was asleep. She laid him in his cradle, covered him with another blanket, and stood looking down at him with tender eyes.

Blake appeared at the door. "Everything all right?" he asked.

"Just fine," said the doctor. "There's a new little boy in the world."

"A boy! So that will make him William Nolan Carter, if Janet sticks to what she said she'd name the baby if it was a boy."

"I think she will," said Linda, leaving the cradle to go to her husband. "Since I suggested he be named after his maternal grandfather."

Dr. Martin had been brought to the Barrett house by Blake. He closed his medical bag and said, "Well, if my ride is ready, I'll let you take me home, Mr. Barrett."

Blake glanced toward the cradle, then looked at Linda. "Can I take a look at him?"

"He's asleep, darling," she said. "You take Dr. Martin home first. The little guy will be awake after a while, then you can get a good look at him."

When Blake returned, Linda met him in the kitchen.

"Is he awake yet?" Blake asked.

"No, but let's go up so we'll be there when he does wake up. He'll be hungry, so you can get a look at him; then I'll wake Janet up to feed him."

Blake and Linda quietly entered Janet's room. The mother was still asleep. Linda took her husband's hand and led him to the cradle. At that moment, the baby began to fuss.

"See?" Linda said, reaching down to pick

him up. "I told you he'd be hungry."

A big smile lit up Blake's face as he got a close view of the wee one. "He's a dandy boy, isn't he?"

"That he is." Linda reached inside the blanket. "He . . . ah . . . he's wet. I'll have to change him."

Janet rolled her head on the pillows and moaned.

"I think she's waking up," said Linda.

"It's time for me to vacate the room," Blake whispered, heading for the door. "I'll see you later."

Linda smiled as she watched her husband leave the room, then laid the baby on the side of the bed. While she changed his diaper, he wiggled and thrashed his arms and legs about. His little gown was also wet. When she'd changed it and he was dry again, she rewrapped him in his blanket.

Suddenly the baby let out a lusty yell, and Janet moaned again as she opened one eye to see what was happening.

"I'm sorry to disturb you, Janet," Linda said, "but I think your son is hungry. You're the only one who can handle that."

Janet gave the baby a grudging look and said, "I guess you're right about that." She took the baby and pulled him close but didn't even look at him as she nursed. Instead she stared around the room and periodically closed her eyes.

In the quietness of the moment, Linda sat down on a chair next to the bed and said, "So, are you going to give him the name I suggested?"

Janet set dull eyes on her sister. "What was it?"

"You know, William Nolan, after Daddy."

"I don't care."

"He's your son, Janet," said Linda. "You ought to care!"

"Good enough."

"William Nolan Carter?"

"Yeah."

"Okay. Daddy will like that. So we'll call him Billy, okay?"

Janet nodded silently.

"Janet, you haven't even looked at little Billy. He's a beautiful boy."

"I'm tired," Janet said.

Linda couldn't believe the lack of enthusiasm her sister was showing toward the child she'd carried under her heart for nine months. Rising from the chair, she said, "I'll be back in a few minutes."

Some twenty minutes had passed when Linda returned to Janet's room. She was shocked to see Janet lying on her side with her back to the baby. She picked up a contented

Billy and said, "Do you want me to take him to our room?"

Janet shrugged. "Do as you like."

Linda had to bite her tongue to keep from lighting into her sister. She placed her little nephew in the cradle, picked it up, and headed for the door, pausing to say, "I'll have to wake you when he's hungry again."

Janet made a muffled grunt and rolled onto her other side.

When Linda reached the master bedroom, she gave the partially open door a shove with her foot, and it swung open.

Blake looked up from the book he was reading and laid it aside, hurrying to take the cradle from Linda's arms.

"I almost had to pry it out of her, Blake, but he's William Nolan Carter — Billy for short."

"What do you mean, 'pry it out of her'?"

"Just that. She doesn't care one bit for this precious baby. I asked her if she was going to take my suggestion for his name, and she couldn't even remember what it was. When I reminded her, she said she didn't care. Blake, I've never seen a mother so uncaring about her child. She wouldn't even look at him when she was nursing him. I don't know what's wrong with her."

"She's a strange one, I'll say that. Hard to believe she's your sister."

As he spoke, Blake leaned over the cradle and took a small fist loosely in his own large hand. The baby wiggled his fist out of Blake's palm and wrapped his tiny fingers around his thumb.

"Would you look at this, Linda? He's already got a strong grip."

"Of course he has," she said, picking the baby up. "He's Auntie Linda's big strong boy." She looked toward a small table in the corner. "Darling, would you hand me that towel over there by the washbowl?"

"Sure." As Blake picked up the towel, he said, "What are you doing?"

"I'm going to burp him. I'm sure Janet didn't bother to do it."

She raised Billy up to her shoulder and gently rubbed and patted his back until the required burp was forthcoming.

Blake chuckled. "He even belches like a he-man."

Linda giggled. She held the baby close to her breast and began rocking him in her arms while moving about the floor.

Blake eyed her with admiration, thinking, *She'd make a wonderful mother!*

As Linda continued to walk and rock Billy, Blake went back to his book. Soon the baby's blue eyes grew heavy and eventually closed.

Linda kissed his downy head and laid him in his cradle. Turning to Blake, she said, "Bedtime, Uncle Blake."

Soon the lamp was extinguished, and Linda released a long sigh as Blake crawled in beside her.

Blake took her in his arms in the darkness and said, "You want to talk about it?"

"About what?"

"That big sigh. What's behind it?"

She swallowed hard. "Oh, Blake . . . it's just that I don't understand why God would give Janet that precious baby when she doesn't even want him. And yet He's withheld a child from us, and we so desperately want one. Poor little Billy isn't going to be raised in the nurture and admonition of the Lord, but if he was our little boy he would. Why, Blake? I don't mean to be critical of the Lord. I just don't understand."

Blake kissed her ear in the dark and said, "Sweetheart, some questions just don't have answers this side of heaven. Our loving heavenly Father knows our hearts and how we would love to have our very own children. He also has a plan for our lives, and He knows what's best for us. In His holy wisdom, and in His own time, He will give us what's best."

"I know He will," she said in a whisper. "I don't mean to question His wisdom. I guess

445

the weak, human side of me takes over some-times." She was quiet for a moment, then said, "I'm already in love with that little boy, and I'm dreading the day Janet packs him up and takes him away. I have a strong notion she isn't going to stay in Stockton."

"Yeah, me too. The little guy has already crawled down into my heart. We'll just have to trust the Lord to give us strength when Janet takes him away from here."

Linda sniffed.

"Aw, honey," Blake said, pulling her closer, "you're crying."

"Blake, you know I love the Lord with all my heart . . . and I trust Him to do what's right and best for us."

"I know you do, darlin'. Let's talk to Him about it right now."

Blake led them in prayer, asking the Lord for grace, guidance, and encouragement.

When he finished, Linda kissed him and said, "You're the most wonderful man in this world, Blake Barrett."

"I fall a long way short of that, my love," he said, "but as long as you think so, what else matters?" Mr. and Mrs. Blake Barrett snug-gled close together, and the Lord of heaven gave them peace and sweet rest.

In the days that followed, Janet Carter

feigned illness so she wouldn't have to do more than feed her little son. Dr. Martin came to the house, and Janet convinced him she was weak and dizzy. He prescribed total bed rest for at least two weeks.

Linda waited on her sister hand and foot, while also taking care of her little nephew. One day, when Janet awakened after a long nap, Linda told her she'd written to their parents to let them know of Billy's birth, and of the name he'd been given.

Janet angrily told Linda she shouldn't have done that without asking her.

Shocked at Janet's reaction, Linda told her that Billy's grandparents had a right to know he was born.

Janet sulked for a day or so, but finally let it go.

When the two-week period was over, Janet still feigned weakness and dizzy spells. Dr. Martin was again consulted, and he told Janet she would have to rest for a couple of months before she could get a job.

Blake and Linda accepted the doctor's word, and because of their love for Billy and their desire to keep him under their roof as long as possible, they assured Janet she could stay until she felt up to getting a job and finding her own place.

Little Billy was a very good baby and seldom cried. His bright blue eyes were focusing better, and he stared with contentment at Blake and Linda when they held him, played with him, and talked to him.

He began to put on weight, and his fat little cheeks resembled rosy apples. He was the picture of health.

Linda kept encouraging Janet to hold Billy and care for him, but it was quite evident that apart from feeding her son, she wanted nothing to do with him.

Both Barretts lavished their love and attention on Billy, and once in a while an errant thought would push its way into Linda's mind. *I love him so much . . . why can't he be mine?* She would quickly ask the Lord to forgive her, and to help her wait on Him to provide their adoptive child. So far, there had been no word from any of the doctors.

One day when Blake was at work and Linda was outside doing yard work, Janet sat down in the master bedroom where the cradle was kept, to feed the baby.

Billy was crying as she picked him up. "That's enough of that bawling," Janet said curtly. "C'mon. Let's get you fed."

The baby had hardly started to nurse when he began to fuss.

"Cut out the bawling, kid!" Janet snapped. "Go on! Eat!"

Billy's normally happy little face turned red as he cried, and he repeatedly kicked and drew up his legs. His little hands were curled into fists as he thrashed them around.

Finally Janet had all she was going to take. She jumped up and stomped to the cradle, saying, "All right, young man, if you're gonna act like that, you can just go hungry!" and put him in the crib none too gently.

Billy wailed and cried at the top of his voice.

Outside, Linda could hear Billy. When he had been crying for nearly half an hour, she laid down her yard tools and went into the house. Inside, she could hear that Billy's crying had a different tone than usual, and she hurried up the stairs and practically ran down the hall to the master bedroom.

As she picked up the baby and held him close, she could feel his little legs drawing up and kicking. "What's the matter, honey?" she said. "Your tummy hurt? Where's your mother?"

"Janet!" she called as she went down the hall toward Janet's room. The door was closed.

"Yeah?" came a muffled reply.

Linda opened the door to find Janet sitting in her overstuffed chair, reading. Moving into the room, Linda blurted out, "Have you fed him?"

"I tried. All he did was bawl and fuss, so I put him back in his cradle."

"The way he's drawing up his legs, I think he's got a stomachache."

"No," Janet said, sneering. "He's just being naughty. He'll straighten up when he gets good and hungry."

"I don't think so. I think he has colic."

Janet shrugged and went back to her book.

Linda took the wailing baby back to her bedroom. Laying him on the bed, she tenderly cooed to him. "Oh, you're wet, honey. Auntie Linda will take care of that."

She noticed that Billy kept drawing up his legs while she changed his diaper. She sat down in the rocking chair and placed the distressed baby on his tummy across her knees, gently rubbing his back as she tried to ease his discomfort. Soon she realized it wasn't going to work. Something had to be done.

Janet looked up from her book in irritation when Linda came back into her bedroom, carrying the crying baby.

"I'm going to take him to Dr. Martin," Linda said in a controlled voice.

"Aw, let him bawl. He'll get over it."

Linda's whole countenance suffused with anger, and her words came out breathlessly. "Janet, you're unfit to be a mother! You ought to be ashamed of yourself!"

"Well, I never wanted to be a mother in the first place! The kid's only a nuisance, anyway. And besides, he looks like Lewis! And that makes me sick!"

"So you're not going to go with me to take Billy to the doctor?"

"Nah. You want to take him, have at it."

"You're a shameful excuse for a human being!" With that, Linda whirled toward the door and carried the crying baby from the room.

Dr. Martin's nurse was at the front desk and could hear the baby before Linda opened the door. She rose to her feet and said, "Hello, Mrs. Barrett. What's wrong?"

"It may be colic."

"Let's go back to the examining room. We don't have any patients at the moment, so Dr. Martin can see the baby right away."

Dr. Martin looked up from the cupboard where he was filling medicine bottles and moved toward Linda. "Little fella sounds like he's hurting. Let's take a look at him."

He lifted the baby from Linda's arms and laid him on the examining table, then unbuttoned the romper and pressed experienced fingers to Billy's little belly. "It's colic, all right. I'll be right back."

Linda tried to soothe the baby with touch and cooed to him until the doctor returned from the cupboard with a small bottle.

"These are peppermint drops, Mrs. Barrett. Let me show you how to administer them. You can take the bottle with you and give Billy some more if the first dose doesn't do it. I think it will, however."

Linda watched as the physician placed a few drops of peppermint liquid into a small cup with some warm water. He mixed it with a spoon, then pulled some of the mixture into a small dropper and placed it in Billy's mouth, squeezing the tube to release it. The crying baby made a gurgling sound, swallowed it, then coughed and started crying again.

The doctor gave Billy three more dropperfuls of the soothing liquid, and said, "It's okay to pick him up now, Mrs. Barrett. Hold him close, but don't jiggle him."

Linda gathered the crying child into her arms and pressed him close to her heart. She talked to him in a soothing tone, holding him tight, as the doctor looked on. Within five minutes, the wailing began to diminish, and in another three minutes or so, the baby stopped crying altogether.

Linda pulled him away from her chest so she could look into his face. Billy looked up at her through big tears that still clung to his eyelashes and gave her a tiny smile as if to say, "Thank you!"

Linda's heart swelled with love for the precious child.

Before they were out of town, Billy was fast asleep in the buggy seat next to Linda, totally exhausted from his ordeal.

When they arrived at the house, a postal delivery wagon was just ahead of them and turned into the lane. Linda followed and pulled rein as the wagon stopped in front of the house.

Janet was nowhere to be seen when Linda carried the sleeping baby and a package into the house. She mounted the stairs, moved past Janet's room, and tenderly placed Billy in his crib. She then opened the package and found clothing for the baby, with a letter from her parents saying how elated they were to be grandparents.

They hadn't seen hide nor hair of Lewis. They hoped someday soon they could come to Stockton to see their new grandson, or that Janet would bring him to Boston, and they offered to send the train fare if she would come.

Linda took the package and letter to Janet, but she showed no interest in seeing her parents in Boston, California, or anywhere else.

22

By the time little Billy Carter was six weeks old, Linda and Blake were strongly attached to him. They had bought a baby carriage, and one lovely day, Linda returned to the house after wheeling him up to the road and back. She parked the carriage at the front porch and carried Billy inside.

Janet was sitting in the parlor, reading a book. She gave Linda a quick glance as she came into the room, then went on reading.

"Janet, you need to get outside and breathe some fresh air. I'm going to put Billy's carriage in the buggy and go into town to the market. I'd like you to come along."

Janet didn't respond.

"Did you hear me?"

Janet slowly lifted her head and met Linda's gaze. "I don't feel like going into town. You and Billy go on."

"You'd feel better if you'd get some fresh air and exercise," Linda said. "Come on. You can hold Billy while I drive the buggy."

Janet's features turned to stone. "I said I don't feel like going into town. I had a dizzy spell this morning when I was brushing my hair. I'm doing better, but I'm not ready to venture out yet. I'll go with you next time."

"Is that a promise?"

"Yes."

"All right." Linda looked down at the baby in her arms and said, "Let's get your diaper changed, Billy, and head for town. Mommy will go with us next time."

Though Janet held the book in her hands and let her eyes rest on the pages, her mind wasn't on the story she'd been reading. She was eager for Linda to leave.

It seemed like an eternity before Linda returned from upstairs, carrying Billy, and said, "We'll be back in a couple of hours."

"Have fun," Janet said dully.

As soon as Linda was out the door, Janet hurried to a parlor window and peered around its edge, staying out of sight. She watched her sister put Billy in the baby carriage and wheel him around the corner of the house. Then Janet moved to a side window and watched until Linda and the carriage disappeared from sight.

Ten minutes later Linda drove the buggy past the house and up the long, curved lane toward the road.

When the buggy vanished from sight, Janet said aloud, "Tell you what, Auntie

Linda, you can have the brat!"

She rushed upstairs and down the hall to the master bedroom and made a beeline for the dresser. In the second drawer, underneath several of Linda's nightgowns, was an envelope bound with a piece of string. Janet had taken advantage of other times when she was in the house alone to search until she found money.

She grasped the envelope and pulled off the string, letting it drop to the floor, then took out the stack of fifty- and one-hundred-dollar bills. She chuckled as she stuffed the bills back in the envelope and ran down the hall to her room.

It only took a few minutes to stuff what belongings she planned to take in her overnight bag. She put the envelope of money in the bag and darted from the room, rushing down the stairs and out the back door.

Two hours later, Linda drove the buggy past the house and pulled up in front of the small barn. She lifted the baby carriage from the back of the buggy and set it down, then picked Billy up from the front seat and said to the horse, "Maisie, I'll come back and put you in the corral after I give Billy to his mother for feeding. Come on, Billy. I know you're hungry."

When she'd reached the back porch, she noticed the back door was ajar. "Funny," she murmured, "I know I closed that door tight."

She picked up Billy, who was beginning to fuss, and left the baby carriage at the steps. No one in the kitchen. She glanced inside the parlor to see if Janet was there, then carried Billy up the stairs.

"Janet! We're back! It's feeding time! Billy's hungry, and —"

She entered Janet's room and found it vacant.

"Janet! Where are you? Billy's hungry!"

She went to her own bedroom door. "Janet! Are you in h—"

It was then she saw the open dresser drawer and a familiar-looking piece of string on the floor. When she examined the bottom of the drawer and found the envelope of money missing, she knew Janet had gone. A quick stop in Janet's room and a look in the closet confirmed it. With the crying baby in her arms, she returned to the horse and buggy at the corral, placed Billy on the seat, and drove for town.

Blake Barrett had a customer at his desk when Linda entered the bank with Billy in her arms.

She paused at a secretary's desk and talked

to her, waiting for Blake's customer to depart.

As soon as the customer was gone, Linda drew up to Blake's desk and said in a low voice, "Honey, I need to talk to you."

Blake took Billy and tickled the baby under the chin as he led Linda to his inner office. "What is it, honey?" he asked as she sat down.

"Janet's gone."

"Gone? What do you mean?"

"Billy and I came to town a couple of hours ago. When we got back home, Billy was fussing because he was hungry. I looked for Janet but couldn't find her. The envelope of money we keep in the dresser drawer was gone, and when I checked her room, most of her clothes were gone. She left her trunk. But she's gone, Blake. She won't be coming back."

"You know, I'm not really surprised," he said. "She certainly cares nothing about her son. And all she did was use us."

Linda nodded. "I think she's been planning this since she came here. She must have snooped around when we weren't home until she found the money. Today I almost insisted that she come to town with Billy and me, but she refused, saying she would go next time. Looks like she was just waiting until she was alone in the house to take off."

"I think we should tell the sheriff so he can try to find her," said Blake. "There was over a thousand dollars in that envelope. We ought to at least get that back."

"I agree."

"What about Billy's meal? He's not acting hungry."

"I bought him a couple of bottles and some milk at the store. Fed him before coming over here."

"Well, good. You go on back home, honey, and I'll go to the sheriff's office right now. Maybe he can find Janet."

Linda had supper started that evening when Blake came home from work.

"Hello, Mrs. Barrett," he said as he came through the back door.

"And hello to you, Mr. Barrett." She stood on tiptoe and kissed him. "Any word on my sister?"

"Nothing. Sheriff Tyler checked with Wells Fargo. She definitely didn't take a stage out of here. He wired the railroad people at Sacramento, but they've had no passenger of Janet's description. It's as if she vanished into thin air."

"Exactly as she planned it, I'm sure," Linda said, shaking her head. "Good ol' Janet . . . still showing her true colors. She disgusts me, Blake, but I can't help being concerned about her, especially about her spiritual condition."

"I know, honey. I hate to see her go on and make a worse mess out of her life, but there's really nothing else we can do. If the sheriff can't find her, we sure can't."

"You get washed up, darling," Linda said. "I'll get supper on the table. Would you mind checking on Billy while you're upstairs? If he's awake, bring him down with you."

While the Barretts ate supper with Billy cooing contentedly in his cradle next to the table, Linda said, "Blake, do you see what I see in all of this?"

"Yes, ma'am. The Lord didn't make Janet run away from Lewis and come here, but He knew it was going to happen, even before we started praying for a child to adopt."

"And He's given us Billy," she said, blinking at the tears surfacing in her eyes. "What about adoption, Blake?"

"The law says we can't legally adopt Billy without the consent of at least one of the natural parents, unless they're confirmed dead. Since that's not the case, we'll give Billy a home, and he'll still be our little boy, even without adoption. And we won't try to find Lewis. He's certainly not a fit father."

Linda nodded. "And besides, he doesn't even know Billy exists."

"Honey," Blake said, "who would have imagined the Lord would answer our prayers for a child in this way?"

"Nobody," she said, smiling. "But knowing that God's wisdom is far above our own, I can accept His perfect will and thank Him with a grateful heart. We now have our own little son."

Blake left his chair, picked up the baby, and said, "Did you hear that, Billy? This lady over here isn't Auntie Linda anymore. She's your mommy! And I'm not Uncle Blake anymore. I'm your daddy!"

When Linda stood up, Blake put an arm around her, and together they praised the Lord for His goodness and for answered prayer.

As they sat down to finish their meal, Linda said, "I feel sorry for Janet. What a mess she's made of her life."

"I know, honey. All we can do is pray for her and commit her into God's hands."

They ate silently for a few minutes, then Linda said, "What will we do about Billy's name? Since we can't legally adopt him, his last name can't be Barrett. But it's going to be very awkward as he grows up."

Blake thought on it for a moment. "We can't use Carter for his name, Linda. It would just make things too difficult. He'll have our name, even though it's not official." He looked down at the happy baby in the cradle and said, "Hello, William Nolan Barrett. Welcome to your permanent home. Your permanent mommy and daddy love you with all their hearts."

It was almost as if little Billy understood, for his eyes sparkled and a smile curved his lips.

Linda sent a letter to Nolan and Adrienne Forrest, informing them of Janet's running away and leaving Billy with them.

The Forrests were disappointed that Janet hadn't changed, but they were glad that Blake and Linda were going to raise little Billy as if he were their own.

Time moved on.

On May 28, 1882, little William Nolan Barrett turned two years old. His parents gave him a party, and several families from the church came.

Billy laughed and giggled and had a great time.

Blake and Linda continuously praised the Lord for the way He had worked in their lives, primarily for giving them a son. He had also prospered the Stockton Bank and Trust Company. And they were superbly happy in their church.

Blake and Linda fell deeper in love every

day, and life was beautiful.

On the Saturday following Billy's second birthday, Blake was at the barn, greasing the wheels of the two family buggies, when movement caught his eye. He focused on the lane that led from the road and saw a man walking toward the house in the shade of the trees.

The man was too far away for Blake to identify. He put more grease on a wheel and waited for the man to draw nearer.

When the stranger disappeared past the corner of the house, Blake followed to see who he was and what he wanted.

Billy's bedroom was right next to the master bedroom. Linda laid him in his little bed and said, "All right, son. Time for your afternoon nap. Give Mommy a big kiss."

The child hugged her neck and planted a juicy kiss on her cheek. "Doo-night, Mommy."

"Good night, sweetheart," she said, smiling. For Billy, any time he was put in bed was "Doo-night."

Linda stroked his head tenderly for a moment and watched his eyes close. Within seconds, Billy was asleep.

Her lower lip quivered as she said in a whisper, "Thank You, Lord. Thank You for letting me be Billy's mommy."

She tiptoed from the room, went downstairs to the kitchen, and opened the pantry door. Just as she was taking a small sack of flour from a shelf, she heard a knock at the front door.

Linda hurried down the hall, humming one of her favorite hymns. She opened the door, then froze at the sight of a familiar face. Her face drained of color, and a shaky hand went to her throat as she gasped, "Lewis!"

Linda was vaguely aware of the back door opening and closing as Lewis Carter stood at the front door and removed his hat.

He looked at her nervously and said in soft voice, "Linda, I'm sorry to show up at your door like this, but I —"

"What's going on?" came Blake's steady voice as he drew up, noting Linda's pallor. "Who is this man, Linda?"

She was still trying to find her voice when the stranger said, "Mr. Barrett, I'm Lewis Carter."

Blake felt as if he'd been hit by lightning. There was a sudden dangerous look in his eyes as he jutted his jaw and said huskily, "What do you want?"

Linda glanced at Blake. A fearful look crossed her features, but Blake dispelled it with a gentle smile. He then looked at Lewis for the answer to his question.

"Mr. Barrett, I . . . I'm not here to cause

you or your wife a problem." Then he turned to Linda, "I'm looking for Janet."

"Why did you come here?" Linda asked, taking hold of Blake's hand.

His strong, comforting arm went around her waist.

"I've tried for nearly two years to find her. I . . . I went to your parents' home in Boston shortly after Janet left me, but your father wouldn't let me get a word in edgewise. He told me to leave or he would call the police."

"Can you blame him?" Linda asked, her voice edged with ice.

Lewis looked at her blankly, then scrubbed a hand across his mouth. "I suppose not."

"So what brought you here?" Blake said. "What makes you think we would know where Janet is?"

"Well, sir, just recently — a couple of weeks ago — I stumbled onto an old girlfriend of Janet in Boston, and she told me that Janet had gone to Stockton, California, a couple of years ago, to see her sister. I thought maybe you would know her whereabouts. I arrived here by stagecoach from Sacramento this morning, and someone in town was nice enough to tell me where you live."

"Janet was here two years ago, Mr. Carter," Blake said, "and stayed with us for a while. But one day she left quite suddenly without

465

notice, and we haven't seen her since. We have no idea where she went. That's all I can tell you."

As he spoke, Blake gently pulled Linda back, and started to close the door.

Lewis raised his palms and said, "Please, Mr. Barrett . . ."

Blake checked the swing of the door.

"I don't blame you for feeling hostile toward me, sir," Lewis said. "You know what I did to Linda. And it was a vile and wicked thing to do. Linda wouldn't have married you unless you were a Christian. May I ask you, as a Christian, sir, to allow me a few minutes to make my apology to her?"

Blake looked at Linda and said, "Whatever you say, honey."

When Linda turned back to Lewis, his eyes were filled with tears.

"All right, Lewis," she said. "Say what you want to say."

Lewis Carter's lips quivered and his hands shook. "Linda, first let me explain that I was a hypocrite when I courted you. I claimed to be a Christian, but I wasn't. I'm now a genuine child of God by the new birth through the blood of the Lord Jesus Christ."

This got their attention, and they listened as Lewis told of how his guilt over what he'd done to Linda had driven him to seek help from a pastor in Manhattan. The pastor had led him to Jesus. When Lewis went home and told Janet he wanted to found their home on the Word of God, she had flown into a rage and left him.

Lewis poured out his heart to Linda, admitting that what he'd done was horribly wrong, and with tears he asked her forgiveness.

Both Barretts were touched by Lewis's sincerity.

After a long moment, Linda said, "Lewis, I believe you're truly saved. You've asked for my forgiveness . . . and you have it."

Overwhelmed, Lewis wiped tears from his face and said, "Thank you, Linda. I only deserve your wrath and scorn. Thank you."

"Lewis, I only deserve God's wrath and scorn," she said. "He forgave me, so I can forgive you."

"Would you like to come inside, Lewis?" Blake asked.

Lewis's eyes widened. "Why, yes, sir. I would be honored."

When they were seated in the parlor, Linda said, "Lewis, I'm happy to know you're now a genuine Christian. When you ran off with my sister, I told myself no real Christian would have done such a thing."

"And you were right."

"So Janet left you because you got saved

and wanted to live for the Lord?" Blake asked.

"That's right. She said she liked the life she was living, and she wasn't going to change. It was then she got mad and left me."

Blake and Linda exchanged glances, recalling how Janet had told them of Lewis's beating her and abusing her mentally. His sincerity had convinced them it was Lewis who was telling the truth.

Lewis looked at Blake and said, "I appreciate you allowing me to make my apology to Linda, sir. Thank you."

Blake nodded. "I'm glad you were willing to apologize to her."

"And Linda . . . now that you've forgiven me, my big concern is for Janet. I really did come to love her, and I've got to try to find her. I want to lead her to the Lord, if possible."

Suddenly, a tiny voice came from upstairs. "Mommy! Mommy!"

Linda's blood ran cold. She looked at Blake and said, "Sounds like our son's nap is over. I'll go see about him."

"Oh, Linda," Lewis exclaimed, "you have a son! How old is he?"

"He had his second birthday a week ago," Blake said.

"And what's his name?"

"William Nolan Barrett . . . after Linda's dad."

"Oh, yes, of course. I'm sure that made your father very happy, Linda."

"Yes," she said, feeling like her nerves were strung so tight they would snap.

"I'd love to see your son before I go."

Linda glanced at Blake. His smile told her she should go ahead . . . what else could they do? Without another word, she left the room.

It was quiet for a moment in the parlor, then Lewis said, "Mr. Barrett, I'm sure I don't have to tell you what a wonderful person Linda is."

Blake nodded.

Lewis rubbed at his temple. "I never deserved her, anyhow. I'm glad the Lord gave her such a fine husband. The person who told me how to find your house explained that you own the Stockton Bank and Trust Company."

"Yes. And speaking of Linda, I'm the one who's blessed, Lewis. Linda is the most wonderful woman in the whole world."

Billy was standing up in his crib when Linda entered his room. "Mommy!" he cried.

Linda picked him up. "Hello, punkin! You didn't sleep very long."

Billy stroked her face.

"Mommy loves her big boy," Linda said,

kissing his warm little cheek. "Does Billy love Mommy?"

Billy smiled and said, "Wove oo."

Linda held him close, cuddling him in her arms. She wondered if Lewis would see the slight resemblance between himself and Billy. "Lord," she prayed, "please don't let anything happen that would take this baby boy from us."

When Linda walked into the parlor with Billy in her arms, he spotted his father and reached for him, crying, "Daddy! Daddy!"

As Blake left his chair to take the boy in his arms, Lewis smiled and said, "Look at that handsome boy!" He stood up and came closer, saying, "Do you call him Nolan, like your father, Linda?"

"No, we call him Billy."

"Hi, Billy!" Lewis said, tickling him under the chin. "What a big boy you are!"

Safe in his father's arms, Billy giggled and gave Lewis a winsome smile.

Linda held her breath, hoping Lewis wouldn't notice Billy's mouth and smile, which were very much like his own. The shape of his head was like Lewis's, too. At least his coloring was different.

"That's a mighty fine boy, folks," Lewis said. "Well, I'd better be going."

Just as Linda began to relax, Lewis said,

"Oh, before I go . . . since you're a banker, Mr. Barrett, would you happen to know of any jobs available in town? I do manual labor."

"Well, I can't say right off," Blake replied. "But I don't understand. You're wanting a job here in Stockton?"

"Yes. You see, I'm fresh out of funds. I'm going to continue to look for Janet, but I can't go any further until I have some money in my pockets. Even when I find a job, it'll take a while to save up enough to continue my search."

Blake felt Linda tense up.

"Look, Lewis," Blake said, "tell you what. Linda and I would really like for you to find Janet and do what you can to lead her to the Lord. How about if we give you a few hundred dollars . . . say, seven or eight hundred. That would take you a long way in your search, wouldn't it?"

Oh, bless him, Lord, Linda thought.

Lewis was shaking his head. "Oh, no, Mr. Barrett. I couldn't take your money. I just couldn't do that. I'll find a job and earn it. I sure thank you for the very kind offer, though."

"Really, it's no problem. We have plenty, and we're glad to share it."

"Thank you very much, sir, but I can't accept charity. I took a room at a boardinghouse over on Clayton Street. Twelve thirty-one is the address. If you should hear of a job opening, would you let me know? I'll start looking for work tomorrow."

Realizing that Lewis's mind was made up, Blake said, "Sure. If I hear of anything, I'll let you know."

Lewis told Billy good-bye, thanked Linda and Blake for their graciousness, and left.

When Blake closed the door and turned around with Billy in his arms, Linda was sheet white.

"Blake," she said with a quiver in her voice, "if he stays in Stockton very long and comes back to this house many more times, he's going to see that Billy has some of his features."

"Maybe not," Blake said. "And even it he does, that won't prove anything. No matter what, we must not let him know Billy is his son."

"Then no matter what," she said, "we won't."

"Here, Mommy, I'll give you your little boy now. I've got to get back to my grease job on the buggies."

As Linda took Billy from him, she said, "Blake —"

"Hmm?"

"Will you feel threatened by Lewis being

here in town, since he's the man I once planned to marry?"

"Threatened? Of course not." He put his arms around her, squeezing Billy between them, and looked deep into her eyes. "I feel no threat, darlin', because I know you love me."

She raised up on tiptoe and kissed his lips. "Sweetheart, you couldn't get rid of me if you tried."

Blake kissed the tip of her nose and said, "And I'm not going to try."

23

Lewis Carter landed a job at the local lumberyard. He also began attending the same church where the Barretts had their membership. Blake and Linda introduced him as a friend of theirs, and Lewis was treated well by the pastor and the people.

Soon, Lewis began dropping by the Barrett house about once a week to be sociable, and he always came on Saturdays or on the evenings when he knew Blake would be home. Each time, he eyed little Billy with admiration and spent time playing with him while Blake and Linda looked on with trepidation.

On his fourth visit, Lewis was at the door with a package under his arm. It was a Saturday morning. Blake smiled and said, "Come in, Lewis. A present for me?"

Lewis laughed. "Sorry, Blake. This is for my little pal, Billy."

Both men could hear Linda laughing in the parlor, and Billy giggling and squealing happily. When they walked in, Linda was running from Billy as he chased her around the room. She glanced at them, then swept up the giggling child in her arms. "Mommy's big boy sure can run fast!" she said as she kissed his little cheeks. "Look, Billy, Uncle Lewis is here! Can you say hello?"

Billy smiled and said, "Hi, Unca Woois!"

"Hi, little buddy." Lewis held out the package. "Uncle Lewis brought his little pal a present!"

Billy clapped his hands and giggled.

When Linda put Billy down, she flicked a glance at Blake and saw him hunch his shoulders.

Lewis dropped to his knees and set the package in front of Billy. "Okay, let's see if you can open it. Uncle Lewis will take off the string. Let's see if Billy can get the paper off."

While Billy began ripping the paper loose with Lewis's help, Linda moved next to Blake, wringing her hands. He put an arm around her shoulder and gave her a tight squeeze as if to say, "I'm afraid, too."

The gift was a miniature hay wagon, complete with a team of perfectly carved wooden horses. Billy clapped his hands excitedly, and Lewis showed him how to play with his new toy.

On the following Saturday, Lewis arrived in midafternoon when the Barretts were sitting on the front porch. Billy was playing in the yard with some neighbor children about his age.

"Come sit down, Lewis," Blake called as Lewis watched Billy.

Lewis flicked a glance at Blake and said, "After I get my hug!"

Billy turned from his friends long enough to run, arms outstretched, to Lewis, who held the boy for a moment, then put him down so he could return to his friends.

Linda leaned close to Blake and whispered, "Should we ask how long he thinks it will be till he takes up his search for Janet?"

"I'll do it, honey," Blake said.

"That's some boy you've got there," Lewis said as he climbed the porch steps and took a seat beside the Barretts.

"I sure would agree with that," Blake said. "He'll grow up to be a fine man someday."

Lewis nodded. "That he will." Noting that Linda had not spoken, he smiled at her and said, "How's Billy's mommy today?"

"I'm fine, Lewis," Linda responded, pressing a smile on her lips.

Lewis set his eyes on the children and quietly watched their happy activity.

Blake waited a few minutes, then said, "Lewis, when you take up your search for Janet, where are you going to start?"

"I have a hunch she's still in California.

476

And the first place I'm going to look is San Francisco."

"Why San Francisco?"

"Because it's known for its saloons and night spots. I've got a hunch those famous places on the Barbary Coast drew her like a magnet."

"So . . . ah . . . when do you think you'll have enough money to head for San Francisco?"

Lewis's eyes remained on Billy. "What say, Blake?"

"I was wondering when you figure you'll have enough money saved up to head for San Francisco."

"Oh. Well, I'm looking at about another month. Then I should have enough to take up the search again."

Linda's heart sank. "Lord," she said, silently moving her lips, "I need Your help. I can't take another month of this torture."

That night, as Lewis sat in his room at the boardinghouse, he relived the events of the day. He kept thinking of Billy as he played in the yard with his little friends. There was something about the boy's smile and the way he laughed.

In the middle of the night, Lewis jerked awake and sat up in bed. He had been dreaming about Billy and why his smile seemed so familiar.

It was Thursday evening when Lewis found himself in the Barrett home once more. He had studied Billy on Sunday while at church, and again during the midweek service on Wednesday. He had to see him again to be sure.

The Barretts and their guest were in the parlor, and Billy was on the floor, playing with his toy hay wagon. The adults were talking when suddenly Billy gave a shrill cry.

One of the wheels had come off the toy wagon, and Billy was in tears. Blake left his overstuffed chair and dropped to his knees beside the boy. Patting Billy's head, he said, "Don't cry, son. Let's look at the damage. Maybe Daddy can fix it."

A quick examination told Blake it could be easily repaired. All he needed was a screwdriver. He picked Billy up and said, "Daddy will fix it, son."

"Need my help?" Lewis asked.

Blake shook his head no. "Thanks, but it's quite simple. Billy and I will go out to the kitchen and fix it. We'll be right back." Blake picked up the toy and left the parlor with Billy still sniffling.

Lewis looked at Linda and said, "Billy's

such a fine boy. I hope he grows up to be a real asset to society — a preacher, a banker like Blake, or a doctor, lawyer, or merchant."

Linda pressed a smile on her lips. "I'm sure Billy will make his mark in the world."

Lewis nodded, waited a few seconds, then said, "Linda, there's something about Billy I need to ask you . . ."

Linda's heart froze. She'd observed Lewis studying Billy more and more on his visits. She had hoped against hope that this moment would never come, yet the resemblance between Billy and his real father was visible enough that Lewis was bound to see it. *Oh, Lord,* came her silent plea, *give me strength and wisdom.*

"What's the question, Lewis?" she asked as butterflies flitted in her stomach.

He held her gaze with steady eyes. "Was Janet pregnant when she showed up here two years ago?"

Linda's throat went dry.

Before she could come up with a reply, Lewis said, "Is Billy my son?"

The fear inside her took control, and she cried, "No, Lewis. Janet wasn't pregnant when she came here. Billy is our son!"

At that instant Linda became aware of Blake's presence as he carried Billy and the toy wagon into the room.

Blake had heard her words. He flicked a glance at her, then placed the boy on the floor with his wagon and said, "There you go, Billy. All fixed."

Lewis continued to stare at Linda as Blake went to her and took her hand.

She looked up with tears brimming in her eyes and said, "I . . . I'm sorry, Blake. I just couldn't —"

"Tell me the truth?" cut in Lewis.

Keeping a firm grip on Linda's hand, Blake looked at Lewis and said, "Billy is indeed your son. Janet gave birth to him three months after she arrived here. She told us you didn't know she was pregnant."

Linda began to breathe in gulps as she tried to keep from breaking down completely.

"Linda," Lewis said, "I'm sorry to upset you. But I had to know. I've been seeing little things about Billy that look like me. He even laughs like me. Please understand . . . I had to know."

Linda was so choked up she couldn't respond.

"We both understand," Blake said. "We knew you might see the resemblance. But please try to understand our situation. Janet was anything but a mother to Billy. Except for feeding him, she totally ignored him. It was Linda who took over the role as his mother."

Lewis looked pained.

"On top of that," Blake said, "Janet stole several hundred dollars from us and disappeared. She left Billy behind without a word. Linda has now become attached to Billy as if she were his natural mother. You can understand that, can't you?"

Lewis nodded solemnly. "Yes. I certainly can."

"And it's the same with me. I've become attached to this precious little boy as if I were his natural father. Linda and I love Billy with all our hearts, and we've given him a good home. As you can see, we clothe him well and we see to it that he eats well. Whatever he needs, we take care of it."

Lewis was biting his lower lip.

"And I think you can see that Billy adores us. And as far as he knows, we're his parents."

Without a word, Lewis left his chair and knelt down beside Billy as he played with his wagon. Extending his hands to him, he said, "Would Billy let Uncle Lewis hold him?"

Linda's heart was banging against her ribs. Lewis Carter had every right to take Billy from them.

Billy complied by holding his arms toward Lewis and saying, "Unca Woois ho'd Billy."

Lewis took him in his arms and rose to his feet, holding him close. There were tears in his eyes as he laid his head next to Billy's.

Blake and Linda looked on, heartsick.

As he set Billy on his feet, an openly emotional Lewis said, "I've got to think this situation over. I want to thank both of you for what you've done for my son. You've been wonderful to him. I'm sorry Janet turned out to be such a horrible mother. I . . . I'll be going now."

Linda stayed with Billy while Blake walked Lewis to the door.

Lewis stepped out on the porch and said, "Blake, I really mean it. I'm so grateful for what you and Linda have done for Billy. I'll never forget it." With that, he walked off the porch and headed up the lane toward the road.

When Blake returned to the parlor, Linda was on the sofa with Billy in her arms. Tears were streaming down her cheeks.

"Mommy cwy," said Billy. "Mommy cwy."

Blake sat down beside them and said, "Honey, only the Lord will be able to keep Lewis from taking Billy with him when he leaves here. Pray with me about it."

They both put their hands on Billy as they bowed their heads.

"Lord," said Blake, "You know our hearts, and You know what's going on in them right now. You also know what Lewis is feeling.

482

We both want what's right for Billy, Lord. And as far as Linda and I can see, this precious child would be far better off with us than with Lewis as things stand right now. Billy needs a mother. We would love to see Lewis find Janet, and we'd love to see her saved. But unless that happens, Janet isn't going to be a fit mother . . . ever.

"We can't wish Billy to be with her the way she is. And if Lewis is even able to find Janet, what about Billy during the time he's trying to get her saved? And if Janet never gets saved, then what? Lord Jesus, it isn't right that this little guy has to grow up without a mother's love and care. Please keep Your hand on Billy. We don't want to be selfish, but we do want what's best for him."

Suddenly, Linda burst into sobs. This startled Billy, and he began to cry. She quickly stifled the sobs, not wanting to frighten him.

He whimpered for a moment anyway, but soothing words from both Blake and Linda caused him to stop crying.

"Honey," Blake said, "we've got to trust the Lord in this. When I was in prison and you were married to Haman, it all looked pretty bad. But the God who put Romans 8:28 in the Bible got me out of prison and let us be together. We must trust Him in this crisis, too."

"I know, darling," she said, wrapping the little boy tighter in her arms. "I know."

That night, Linda lay awake after Blake had fallen asleep. Moving her lips soundlessly, she said, "Dear Lord, would You give us this precious child only to take him away from us? I don't think I can bear the pain of it."

Even as she prayed, Linda felt the physical pain that heartache brings.

The next day, Linda was doing some light yard work while Billy played on the lawn nearby. She heard the familiar rattle of the mail delivery wagon and watched it roll down the lane.

She walked to where the mailbox stood and smiled at the driver, who had only been her mail delivery man for a few weeks. "Hello, Mr. Forbes. How are you today?"

"Just fine, ma'am," said the elderly gentleman, tipping his hat. "And how's that husky boy of yours?"

"Billy's doing wonderfully."

"That's what I like to hear."

Forbes reached into a wooden box next to him and lifted up a small bundle of mail tied with a string. "Here you go, ma'am. Didn't you tell me you're originally from Boston, Massachusetts?"

"Yes, I did," Linda said, accepting the bundle.

"There's a letter in there from Boston, in case you'd like to start with it. You'll notice I put it right on top."

Linda glanced down at the return address. Looking back at Forbes, she said, "Thank you. The Forrests are my parents."

"Oh. Well, I'm sure you're eager to read the letter, so I'll be on my way. Good day to you."

"Same to you, Mr. Forbes."

The old gentleman waved at the little boy. "Bye, Billy! Take good care of your pretty mother!" With that, he snapped the reins and drove away.

Linda went to the porch, untied the string, and laid the rest of the mail down. She tore open the envelope and began reading her mother's handwriting:

July 14, 1882

Dearest Linda and Blake,

I hope this letter finds you and Billy well and happy.

I wish there weren't any bad news in the world, but then it would be heaven, wouldn't it?

Daddy and I just learned that Janet is

485

dead. She was working as a saloon girl in a place on the Barbary Coast in San Francisco. Two men were arguing over her, and a gun was drawn. There was a struggle, and the gun went off. The bullet hit your sister in the stomach.

She was taken to a hospital and lived long enough to give a nurse our name and address.

Daddy and I were so upset when the news came, but the Lord has eased our pain and given us peace in our hearts in spite of it, as I know He'll do the same for you.

Hope little Billy is doing well. Give him a big hug and kiss from Grandma and Grandpa.

Write soon.

Love,
Mom

Linda made her way to a chair on the porch, sat down, and wept. There was no question that Janet had died without Christ.

As she thought of her sister, her mind went to Lewis. Would knowledge of Janet's death cause Lewis to be drawn even more to Billy? If so, he might decide to take the boy with him when he left Stockton. She asked for the Lord's will to be done, then put her attention on Billy, who was now at the porch steps and starting to climb.

Blake stood in the kitchen that evening and read the letter. "Well, she's beyond our prayers now," he said, shaking his head.

"Janet had every chance to be saved, darling," Linda said. "She stubbornly chose to go the wrong way."

"Mm-hmmm. Like a multitude of other people in this world."

"What I fear now is that when we tell Lewis Janet is dead, he'll want all the more to take Billy with him."

Blake nodded. "Could be. But Janet was his wife, Linda. He has a right to know. It would be wrong to withhold it from him."

Linda closed her eyes and sighed. "You're right. We have to tell him. But let's pray hard about it before we do."

At bedtime — after little Billy was fast asleep — Blake and Linda knelt beside their bed.

"You go first, honey," he said.

With their arms about each other, they bowed their heads.

"Dear Lord," Linda prayed, "You have been pressing 1 Peter 5:7 to my heart ever since that letter came this morning. 'Casting all your care upon him; for he careth for you.'

Blake and I know You care for us, Lord Jesus. You went to the cross for us. You suffered, bled, and died for us. You allowed both of us to hear Your gospel, and because we believed and obeyed Your gospel, we're saved. Such love is beyond our understanding, but we praise You for it. Help us both to cast all our care upon You in this trial through which we're passing.

"Help us not to stand in the way of Your working it out for our good and for Your glory. Please do what is best for little Billy, who has come to mean so much to both of us."

At this point, Linda was weeping so hard she couldn't continue. Blake hugged her close to his side and took up the prayer. As with Linda, he asked for God's will to be done and for God to get the glory in whatever way He saw fit to handle the delicate situation concerning Billy and his real father.

When Blake said amen, he turned to Linda and saw a smile of perfect peace beaming from her face.

"Blake, darling," she said, "it's in God's capable hands. May His will be done."

The next day was Saturday. Blake was at the hayloft, forking hay into the feed trough for the horses, when he heard the animals nicker. He looked down to see Lewis come through the barn door.

Blake paused with the pitchfork in hand and looked over the edge of the loft.

"Hi, Blake," said Lewis. "The ol' pest is back."

"You're not a pest," Blake said amiably.

"I saw the barn door open and figured you'd be out here."

"I'll be done in just a minute, Lewis."

"Okay. I'll wait."

While Blake finished forking the hay down, Lewis said, "Billy all right?"

"Just fine."

Blake didn't know if Lewis had come to a decision about Billy, but one thing he was sure of, the news of Janet's death was going to hit him hard.

Moments later, the two men headed for the house.

"We got a letter from Linda's folks yesterday," Blake said.

"Everything all right back there?"

"Well . . . yes. Both of them are fine."

"I don't suppose they've heard from Janet."

"They didn't hear from Janet, but they did get word about her."

"Oh? What was that?"

"Linda's planning on letting you read the letter. She's doing some housecleaning upstairs. Let's go find her."

When they topped the stairs, Blake called out, "Sweetheart, Lewis is here! Where are you?"

"In Billy's room!" came her reply.

Before they reached the door to Billy's room, Linda stepped into the hall and headed for the master bedroom. "Hello, Lewis," she said. "I have something to show you."

"The letter from your folks?" he asked. "Or something in addition to that?"

Linda stopped abruptly and looked at Blake with wide eyes.

"I only mentioned the letter, honey. I thought it best that he read it for himself."

"Oh. All right," she said. "Blake, would you bring Billy, please? I think it would be best if we sit down in the parlor. I'll get the letter and meet you down there in a couple of minutes." She then disappeared into the master bedroom.

The men had just reached the parlor when they heard Linda's footsteps on the stairs. When she entered the room, Billy was in Lewis's arms. She handed the letter to Lewis and said, "I'll take Billy. It's best that you sit down."

Lewis gave her a quizzical look. To Blake he said, "Is this some kind of bad news?"

"I'm afraid so. Please sit down."

When Lewis was seated in an overstuffed chair facing the couch, Blake took his place beside Linda and Billy.

The Barretts watched with heavy hearts as Lewis removed the letter from the envelope. He glanced at them apprehensively, then began reading. All of a sudden his features turned white, then took on the hue of old stone. "Oh, no!" he cried. "She's dead! My Janet's dead!"

He bent over and buried his face in his hands and mumbled some words Blake and Linda couldn't understand, but they were able to distinguish the grief he felt.

Billy stared at his Uncle Lewis, wondering what was wrong with him.

Blake's firm hand was on Lewis's shoulder when Lewis brought his emotions under control. Sniffing, he looked up and said, "Thank you for the strength of that hand, Blake. Thank you."

"Nothing else I could do for you, my friend. Linda and I have prayed for you, I guarantee you that."

"I'm sure you have. And I appreciate your concern." Then to Linda he said, "You've got to be hurting, too. She was your sister, and I know that in spite of all she did, you still loved her."

Linda nodded. "I was deeply hurt when the

two of you ran off together, and I was very bitter toward both of you. I tried to hate you, but I couldn't. I never stopped loving Janet. And the thing that hurts the most is that she won't be in heaven. I'll never see her again."

Lewis sighed and put the letter back in the envelope, then stood up. Laying the envelope on the coffee table, he said, "I'd better be going. I've got a lot to think about."

"Will you be going back east, Lewis?" Linda asked.

"Probably . . . that's home. I've got to consider Billy in all of this."

Linda's pulse quickened, but she immediately told herself to calm down. She and Blake had placed Billy in God's hands, and she must leave him there.

During the next few days, Lewis went through his own private agony as he diligently sought God's will concerning Billy. He went by the Barrett home every evening to see Billy and spend time with him.

With each visit, tension mounted for Blake and Linda. Every night they prayed hard, asking God to do what was right for Billy, even if it meant giving him up. If the Lord would choose to let Lewis take Billy with him, they knew they would need the comfort and strength of the Holy Spirit in great measure.

Lewis's emotions were up and down as he prayed about Billy. Sometimes he became so upset that he actually felt ill.

By Friday night, after wrestling with the matter all week, he fell on his knees beside his bed. After some two hours of soul-searching prayer, he had the answer.

He rose to his feet and said, "All right, Lord. I've come to love little Billy so very much in these past weeks. It's going to be the hardest thing I've ever done, but he's my son, and what's best for him must come first. I'll do what You've told me to do."

24

The next day, a Saturday, Lewis Carter arrived at the Barrett house midmorning. When he came into the house, Blake and Linda could tell he was under a great deal of emotional strain.

Lewis asked if he could play with Billy on the lawn for a while, and the Barretts sat on the front porch, watching the two of them together.

When Lewis first started romping on the grass with his little son, he felt his resolve weakening. "Help me, Lord," he prayed in his heart. "I can do all things through You. This is the toughest chore I've ever faced in my life. This precious child is my own flesh and blood, but I know I can't give him the home and family the Barretts can. Lord, You helped me make this most difficult decision . . . please give me the grace and strength to see it through."

As Blake and Linda watched Lewis, Linda said, "Blake, do you suppose he's made up his mind?"

"I don't know, honey, but he looks like he

hasn't slept too well."

They had to smile when they saw Lewis down on all fours playing horsey, with Billy on his back giggling and squealing for joy.

After about an hour of romping with his two-year-old son, Lewis carried him up to the porch, puffing from exertion, and said, "Whew! This little bronco rider will wear a fella out in a hurry!"

Linda had brought some lemonade from the kitchen, and she handed Lewis a cool glass and said, "Maybe this will help."

He put Billy down and drank the lemonade in a few gulps.

Linda sat down and pulled Billy onto her lap.

While Billy drank lemonade from a small glass, Lewis said, "I've come to a decision."

He sat down in his usual front porch chair, facing them. "I've been thinking and praying a lot about Billy and what's best for him."

"We have too," said Blake.

Lewis ran his gaze between Linda and Blake, cleared his throat gently, and said, "What I've decided is that you dear people should keep Billy and raise him as your own son."

Linda felt a hot lump rise in her throat, and tears flooded her eyes.

Blake could hardly believe his ears.

Fighting his own tears he said, "If you're really sure . . ."

"Positive," Lewis cut in. "I could never give the boy the kind of home or the kind of life you and Linda have given him. You'll want to adopt him, won't you?"

"Why, yes, of course," said Blake, blinking against the tears that had gathered in his eyes.

"I knew you would, so I went by Judge Leonard Holman's house before coming here. I delivered some lumber to his house a couple of weeks ago and got to know him a little bit. I gave him the information he needed to have the adoption papers drawn up on Monday.

"I'm booked on the Sacramento stage Tuesday morning, which leaves at ten o'clock. Our appointment is set with Judge Holman an hour ahead of my departure. I'll sign Billy over to you, so you can adopt him legally. It'll all be done right there in the judge's chambers in the courthouse."

Linda's lips quivered as she said, "Oh, Lewis, thank you!"

"Yes, thank you!" Blake said. "You've made us the happiest people in the whole world!"

Weeping freely, Lewis said, "I'm thanking you. I can leave Stockton with peace in my heart, knowing that my son will have the best home and family possible. This is God's will for Billy."

Blake stood up and wiped tears from his cheeks, then stepped toward Lewis and wrapped his arms around him, trying to express his gratitude.

Lewis pounded him on the back and told him it was the hardest decision he'd ever had to make, but the Lord had given him the grace and strength to do what was right.

Linda placed Billy on Blake's chair, and when the two men let go of each other, she embraced Lewis and said, "I'm so glad you got saved, Lewis. And I'm so glad you were willing to listen to the Lord about Billy. Be assured, we will raise him according to the Word of God."

All the weeping had little Billy puzzled. As he sat in Blake's chair, he looked from one weeping adult to the other and screwed up his face to cry, although he wasn't sure why.

Immediately Linda picked him up and broke the tension. All three adults spoke to Billy, assuring him everything was all right. Then Linda pointed to some toys on the porch and told him to go play with them. When he was fully occupied, she turned back to the men, who were discussing the particulars of the adoption.

Lewis explained what the judge had told

him. All it entailed was the signing of papers. The whole thing wouldn't take more than a few minutes.

When they all sat down again, Lewis said, "Would it be all right if I write from time to time to see how Billy is doing?"

"Of course," Blake said. "We'll want to know how things are going for you, too. And we'll write you back each time."

"And Lewis," Linda said, "any time you can make a trip to California, you're welcome to come by and see Billy."

Lewis grinned. "I'll do it. He can just always know me as Uncle Lewis, okay?"

"Uncle Lewis it is," she said, smiling.

"We wouldn't have it any other way," Blake assured him.

Monday night had been a restless one for all three adults, and when they met at the courthouse under a flawless blue sky on Tuesday morning, they all looked a little tired.

Blake was carrying Billy. When he placed the child into Lewis's arms, he said, "Having any doubts?"

"None," Lewis replied. "I assure you, I haven't changed my mind. In fact, I feel more certain than ever about my decision. I have the peace of God in my heart."

498

Lewis Carter and the Barretts met with Judge Leonard Holman in his chambers. Lewis signed the necessary document to release William Nolan Carter so that Blake and Linda could legally adopt him. Within a few minutes the transaction was done, and Billy's legal name became William Nolan Barrett.

When they walked out of the courthouse, Lewis was carrying Billy. The sun was smiling in the vast blue sky, and the Barretts were thanking God in their hearts.

They strolled along the wide, dusty street toward the Wells Fargo office.

The stage was in and was being loaded when they drew up beside it on the boardwalk. Lewis had left his luggage there earlier, and it was already in the rack on top.

"So, Lewis," Blake said, "are you going back to New York or to Boston?"

"New York. That's been home for a while. I'm sure I can get my old job back on the docks. And I love the church in Manhattan. I'll get busy serving the Lord there."

"You know that Linda and I wish you the very best, Lewis."

"All passengers aboard!" came the stage driver's call. "Stage leaves in three minutes!"

Keeping Billy in one arm, Lewis hugged Linda, then Blake. His eyes filled with tears as he looked into Billy's eyes and said, "You are a special boy, Billy. I will always love you."

Billy put his chubby hand on Lewis's cheek and said, "Wove oo, Unca Woois."

The other passengers were boarding.

Tears streamed down Lewis's face as he handed the boy to Blake and said, "Here's your son, Blake. Handle him with prayer."

He then climbed inside the stage and settled at a front window, trying to smile as he looked at them.

"Tell Uncle Lewis good-bye, Billy," Blake said.

The driver hollered at the six-up team, and the stage began to roll.

"Doo-bye, Unca Woois," Billy said as Blake waved his little hand up and down.

In another moment the stage wheeled around the nearest corner and disappeared.

Linda moved up to her two men and put an arm around Blake and took Billy's hand. Both Mommy and Daddy wiped tears of joy from their cheeks and headed down the street, knowing that now, with Billy, they would have their very special time to love.

Mount Laurel Library
100 Walt Whitman Avenue
Mt. Laurel, NJ 08054-9539
(856) 234-7319

The employees of Thorndike Press hope you have enjoyed this Large Print book. All our Large Print titles are designed for easy reading, and all our books are made to last. Other Thorndike Press Large Print books are available at your library, through selected bookstores, or directly from the publishers.

For more information about titles, please call:

(800) 257-5157

To share your comments, please write:

Publisher
Thorndike Press
P.O. Box 159
Thorndike, Maine 04986